英語寫作思維重塑！

How To Speak And Write Correctly

約瑟夫・德夫林 Joseph Devlin 著
稅珍珍 譯

從基礎語法到進階修辭一網打盡，全方位提升表達力

從詞彙到結構，全面提升語言邏輯

從日常對話到專業寫作
逐字打磨、句句斟酌

破解英語寫作密碼、打造專屬英語風格
每一次表達都是自信的展現

目錄

簡介		009
第一章	對話的基礎：詞彙與必要條件	011
第二章	英語語法入門：構成與詞源解析	017
第三章	句子的藝術：句式結構與段落安排	045
第四章	修辭魅力：手法解析與應用技巧	065
第五章	標點符號指南：用法解析與規範	079
第六章	書信的技巧：格式與筆記要領	101
第七章	錯誤剖析：典型問題與糾正示例	129
第八章	避開陷阱：常見誤用與詞彙偏差	155
第九章	風格打造：措辭準確與規範表達	185
第十章	寫作與演說：技巧與內容指引	197

目錄

第十一章	俚語解析：起源與多元用法	205
第十二章	新聞寫作技巧：資格與對象選擇	219
第十三章	措辭的價值：簡潔與文化影響	227
第十四章	英語語言演變：起源與現狀探索	233
第十五章	文學巨匠與名作：偉大作家的遺產	241

INTRODUCTION 245

CHAPTER I
REQUIREMENTS OF SPEECH:
Vocabulary —— Parts of Speech ——
Requisites 247

CHAPTER II
ESSENTIALS OF ENGLISH GRAMMAR:
Divisions of Grammar —— Definitions ——
Etymology 253

CHAPTER III
THE SENTENCE:
Different Kinds —— Arrangement of Words ——
Paragraph 279

CHAPTER IV
FIGURATIVE LANGUAGE:
Figures of Speech —— Definitions and
Examples —— Use of Figures 295

目錄

CHAPTER V
PUNCTUATION:
Principal Points —— Illustrations ——
Capital Letters   305

CHAPTER VI
LETTER WRITING:
Principles of Letter-Writing ——
Forms —— Notes   319

CHAPTER VII
ERRORS:
Mistakes —— Slips of Authors ——
Examples and Corrections —— Errors   341

CHAPTER VIII
PITFALLS TO AVOID:
Common Stumbling Blocks —— Peculiar
Constructions —— Misused Forms   357

CHAPTER IX
STYLE:
Diction —— Purity ——
Propriety —— Precision　　　　377

CHAPTER X
SUGGESTIONS:
How to Write —— What to Write ——
Correct Speaking and Speakers　　　391

CHAPTER XI
SLANG:
Origin —— American Slang ——
Foreign Slang　　　　401

CHAPTER XII
WRITING FOR NEWSPAPERS:
Qualification —— Appropriate Subjects ——
Directions　　　　411

CHAPTER XIII
CHOICE OF WORDS:
Small Words —— Their Importance —— The Anglo-Saxon Element   421

CHAPTER XIV
ENGLISH LANGUAGE:
Beginning —— Different Sources —— The Present   429

CHAPTER XV
MASTERS AND MASTERPIECES OF LITERATURE:
Great Authors —— Classification —— The World's Best Books   435

簡介

在本書的準備過程中，作者一直持有以下的觀點，即讓本書幫助、服務它的目標讀者，也就是幫助那些既無時間也無機會、既無學習經歷也無學習意願的人看懂關於修辭、語法和寫作的複雜深奧的專著。對他們來說，這些作品就像鎖在寶箱裡的黃金一樣，他們無法打開，也無法觸碰。本書沒有任何狂妄自大之處，它既不是一本詳盡闡述風格定理的修辭手冊，也不是一本充斥著獨斷規則和特例的語法書。本書的目的僅僅是幫助日常生活中的普通人透過日常、普通的語言以合乎禮儀的方式表達自己。本書設下了一些大致的原則，能夠指導讀者在合適的範圍內使用口語和書面語。本書還介紹了許多俚語、習語等英語語言特有的詞彙和表達，除此之外還介紹了許多英語語言中常見的錯誤和陷阱。這樣一來，讀者就可以有效地辨識並避免它們。

作者感謝所有研究過該主題的人，在此不具體一一贅述。

這薄薄的一本書是語言學習道路上的指路牌，希望讀者能夠根據本書的指引實現正確的讀和寫。

簡介

第一章
對話的基礎：詞彙與必要條件

學習正確地說和寫非常簡單，因為涵蓋所有目的的日常對話和交流僅需要約 2,000 個詞彙量。掌握其中僅 200 個單字及使用方法，雖不能讓我們完全掌握英語這門語言，但足以正確地掌握英語的說和寫。與詞典的詞彙量相比，你可能覺得這個數量太少了！但從未有人用過詞典裡的所有單字，就算有人能活到瑪土撒拉（Methuselah）[01]那麼老也做不到這一點。除此之外，也不存在使用這麼多詞的需求。

新版大型詞典的詞彙量近 20 萬，但其中百分之一的詞彙量就能滿足你所有的需求。當然，你可能並不認同。你可能不滿足於使用最常見的詞彙，你想顯示出異於常人的優越，展現出你的學問。但實際上更可能表現出的是賣弄學問，甚至知識匱乏。比如，你不想稱「鏟子」為「鏟子」，你想叫它「剷平設備」，因為它能將土地磨平。然而，還是用這個你祖父稱呼的、熟悉而又簡單的名字比較好，這個名字經歷了時間的考驗，畢竟——老朋友總是好朋友。

在能實現同一目的的情況下，使用外來的、廣泛的詞替代熟悉的、準確的詞是一種愚昧無知的體現。偉大的學者、作家和禮貌的演講者們都會使用簡單的詞。

回到之前討論的囊括所有對話與寫作需求的詞彙量，也就是 2,000

---

[01] 瑪土撒拉，《聖經·舊約》裡提到的族長，活了 969 歲。—此書註腳均為譯者注

第一章
對話的基礎：詞彙與必要條件

個。我們發現，許多在社會上被認為是優雅的、久經世故的以及富有教養的人們使用的詞彙量更少，因為他們知道的也更少。當今世界上最偉大的學者所掌握的詞彙量不超過 4,000 個，然而常用的甚至不到一半。

莎士比亞，作為古往今來最偉大的天才，他作品中的詞彙量達到了龐大的 1.5 萬，然而其中將近 1 萬的詞在今天已經過時或失去意義。

所有聰明人都應該正確地使用母語。做到這一點僅需一點點努力、一點點關注、一點點學習，但是回報很豐厚。

讓我們來看看有教養的、彬彬有禮的人和教養不足的、粗俗無禮的人之間的區別。前者知道如何正確選擇和使用詞彙，而後者說話刺耳難聽、褻瀆人們的美好情感。後者常犯違背語法規則、使用荒唐畸形的用語等語法錯誤，這使得他令人不快，沒有人願意和他待在一起。

只需幾次課程，一個人就能掌握正確的英語的語法形式，這樣他能在上層社會的談話中表現不錯，或是得體地將他的思想付諸紙筆。

英語的簡單介紹

英語中的所有詞彙被分成九類，稱為詞類 (the Parts of Speech)。這些詞類分別是**冠詞** (Article)、**名詞** (Noun)、**形容詞** (Adjective)、**代詞** (Pronoun)、**動詞** (Verb)、**副詞** (Adverb)、**介詞** (Preposition)、**連詞** (Conjunction) 和**嘆詞** (Interjection)。在詞類中，名詞是最重要的，因為其他所有詞類都或多或少地依賴名詞。**名詞**表示人、事物、地點或抽象概念的名稱。名詞分為**專有名詞** (Proper Nouns) 和**普通名詞** (Common Nouns) 兩類。**普通名詞**表示一類人、事物、地點或抽象概念的名稱，比如 man（男人）、city（城市）。專有名詞表示人、事物、地點等的專有名稱，比如 John（約翰）、Philadelphia（費城）。在前面的例子中，man（男人）這個名詞屬於人類這一大類，而 city（城市）這個名詞也是所有人口聚集地的統稱；但 John（約翰）指的是人類中一個獨特的個體，而 Philadelphia（費城）指的是世界上所有城市中一個特定的城市。

名詞又可根據**人稱**（Person）、**數**（Number）、**性**（Gender）和**格**（Case）進行變化。無論是交談還是通訊，**人稱**是存在於說話者、聽眾以及談話內容之間的關係。有第一人稱（First Person）、第二人稱（Second Person）和第三人稱（Third Person）之分，他們分別代表了說話者、聽眾以及談話中提及的人或事。

數將大於一的和一區別開，分為單數（singular）、複數（plural）兩種。單數指一個，複數指兩個以上。複數最常見的形式就是在單數形式後面加 s 或 es。

性與名詞的關係和生理性別（sex）與個體的關係相同[02]。區別是生理性別只有兩個，而語言學中的性有四個，即陽性（masculine）、陰性（feminine）、無性（neuter）和共性（common）。陽性指所有雄性個體，陰性指所有雌性個體，無性指無生命的個體或所有沒有生命形式的存在，共性適用於目前無法確定生理性別的有生命個體，比如 fish（魚）、mouse（老鼠）、bird（鳥）等。有時透過擬人的修辭手法，我們認為的沒有生命的個體和嚴格來說無性的個體在語言中會被賦予陰陽性別。

例 1

我們提到太陽時會說：He is rising.（他在升起。）

提到月亮時會說：She is setting.（她在落下。）

---

[02] gender 指的是語言學中的性，sex 指的是生理性別，即個體無法選擇的、先天的性別。

第一章
對話的基礎：詞彙與必要條件

格是名詞與名詞、名詞與動詞、名詞與介詞的關係。格分為三類，**主格**(Nominative)、**所有格**(Possessive)和**賓格**(Objective)。主格是我們談論的對象，或是動詞動作的實施者；所有格表示所有關係；而賓格是被動詞動作影響的人或事。

冠詞是置於名詞前用來表示名詞是具體意義還是籠統意義的虛詞。冠詞分為兩類，不定冠詞 a 或 an 和定冠詞 the。

形容詞是修飾名詞的詞，用來表示名詞的特點、特徵。

定義

代詞是用來代替名詞、避免重複使用同一個名詞的詞。和名詞一樣，代詞也有格、數、性和人稱的分別。代詞分為人稱代詞(personal pronoun)、關係代詞(relative pronoun)和形容詞性代詞(adjective pronoun)三類。

動詞是用來表示動作或狀態的詞。動詞會根據時態(tense)、語態(mood)、數(number)和人稱(person)而變化，後兩者嚴格來說是屬於動詞的實施者。

副詞能修飾動詞和形容詞，有時也能修飾其他副詞。

介詞用來連接詞彙、表示各類詞所代表的對象之間的關係。

連詞能將單字、片語、分句和句子連接起來。

嘆詞用來表示驚訝或其他突發情感。

三個基本要素

英語的三個基本要素分別是：純粹（Purity）、清晰（Perspicuity）、準確（Precision）。

純粹要素指的是道地英語的應用。它排除了一切俚語、粗鄙之語、過時的說法、外地方言、模稜兩可的表達和各種不合語法的語言。除此之外，它還會排斥任何新興詞彙，直到它們被一流作家和演講者使用。

清晰要素要求用最明確的語言表達最清晰的思想，這樣的話，說話者和作者想傳達的思想或想法就不會產生誤解。所有模糊的、有歧義的和可能被誤解的詞是嚴格禁止的。清晰要素要求語言風格清楚、完全擺脫浮華學究和做作的表達和任何變形效應都要避免。

準確要素要求言簡意賅，沒有冗餘和同義重複，風格簡潔明瞭，能讓聽者或讀者立即理解說話者或作者的意思。它一方面禁止所有複雜的長句，另一方面又禁止太短而唐突的句子。它的目的是達到中庸之道，吸引聽者或讀者的注意力。

第一章
對話的基礎：詞彙與必要條件

第二章
英語語法入門：構成與詞源解析

想要正確地運用英語對話與寫作，就必須掌握基本的語法規則。無論我們怎樣拜讀大家之作、與大演說家交談、模仿他們，如果不知道正確的句式和詞彙關係的基本規則，我們在相當程度上就像鸚鵡一樣，僅僅是重複我們聽到的內容而沒有理解談話內容。當然，鸚鵡——作為自然存在的生物——無法理解說話內容，它只能重複學舌。從鸚鵡的嘴裡既能說出汙言穢語，也能說出優美讚揚之語。以此類推，在不了解一門語言的語法時，我們可能犯了極其嚴重的錯誤，還自以為說話非常準確。

語法構成

語法分為四個部分，即：拼寫學（Orthography）、詞源學（Etymology）、句法（Syntax）和韻律結構（Prosody）。

拼寫學是研究字母及其組合成單字的學科。

詞源學是研究詞的各個類別和詞義變化的學科。

句法研究的是句子裡單字的連接和排列。韻律結構研究的是說話和朗讀的方式以及詩歌的各個種類。其中前三個部分最受關注。

第二章
英語語法入門：構成與詞源解析

字母

字母（letter）是用來表示發音清晰的標記或符號。字母分為母音字母（vowels letters）和子音字母（consonants letters）。母音字母是指不受發音器官的阻礙發出的聲音，子音字母則需要和母音字母一起才能發出聲音。母音字母有 a、e、i、o、u，還有不在詞首或音節開頭時的半母音字母 w 和 y。

音節和單字

一個單字由一個或一系列音節構成。劃分音節的條件很多，但最好的方法是盡量根據語言器官的正確發音劃分。

詞類

冠詞

冠詞是放在名詞前面用來表示名詞是特指還是泛指的詞。

冠詞分兩種，*a/an* 以及 *the*。

A 或 *an* 被稱為不定冠詞（indefinite article），它不特指某個人或事物，而是指該名詞所代表的一類人或事物中的一個。因此，*a* man 指的是一個人種或種族裡的任何一個人（any man）。

The 被稱為定冠詞（definite article），它是指某個特定的人或事物。因此，*the* man 指的是某個特定的個體。

名詞

　　名詞是人、地點或事物的名稱，如 John（約翰）、London（倫敦）、book（圖書）。名詞分為專有名詞和普通名詞。

　　專有名詞指特指的人或地點的名稱。

　　普通名詞指一類人或事物的名稱。

　　名詞根據數、性和格進行變化。

　　名詞**數**的變化表明名詞是單個還是多個。

　　名詞**性**的變化表明名詞是男性、女性、無生命個體還是無性別差異個體的名稱。

　　名詞**格**的變化表明名詞所代表的人、地點或事物的狀態。這些名詞在句中的作用是作陳述或疑問的主語、談話中提及的事物的主人或擁有者、動作或關係的對象。

　　因此，在例句「John tore the leaves of Sarah's book.（約翰撕了莎拉的書頁。）」中，book（書）代表單個物體，leaves（書頁）代表兩個或以上的物體，這是名詞根據數的不同進行的變化；John（約翰）是男性，Sarah（沙拉）是女性，而 book（書）和 leaves（書頁）是無生命個體，沒有男性女性之分，這就是名詞根據性的不同進行的變化；John（約翰）是撕書的人，Sarah（莎拉）是書的主人，即該陳述句的主語，她仕由書被撕；而賓語 book（書）則與書頁相關聯，書頁合起來構成了書，這就是名詞根據格的不同進行的變化。

第二章
英語語法入門：構成與詞源解析

形容詞

形容詞修飾名詞，用來展示或指出該名詞的特點或特徵。

例 1　A black dog.（一隻黑色的狗。）

形容詞有三種形式，分別是原級（the positive）、比較級（the comparative）和最高級（the superlative）。

原級是指形容詞的簡單形態，沒有增加或減少該形容詞原本的程度。

例 2　nice（好的）

比較級增加或減少了該形容詞的程度。

例 3　Nicer（更好的）

最高級最大程度上增加或減少了該形容詞的程度。

例 4　nicest（最好的）

沒有比較時，形容詞用原級。

例 5　A *rich* man（一個富人）

兩個個體之間或一個個體與一個團體之間進行比較時，形容詞用比較級。

例 6

John is richer than James.（約翰比詹姆斯更富有。）

He is richer than all the men in Boston.（他比波士頓所有的人都更富有。）

一個個體與一個團體中的每個個體進行比較時，形容詞用最高級。

例 7 John is the richest man in Boston.（約翰是波士頓最富有的人。）

有的形容詞無法改變性質或狀態的程度，它們只能使用原級。

例 8

A *circular* road（一個環形島）

the *chief* end（首要目的）

an *extreme* measure（嚴厲措施）

形容詞的變形有兩種規則。一種是在原級後加 er 變為比較級，加 est 變為最高級；或者在原級前面加 more 變為比較級，加 most 變為最高級。

例 9

釋義	帥氣的	更帥氣的	最帥的
形容詞變形規則 1	handsome	handsomer	handsomest
形容詞變形規則 2	handsome	more handsome	most handsome

有兩個或以上音節的形容詞一般透過加字首 more 和 most 進行比較。很多形容詞的變形不規律，比如：bad-worse-worst；good-better-best。

代詞

代詞是用來代替名詞的詞。

例 10

John gave his pen to James and he lent it to Jane to write her copy with it.

（約翰把他的筆借給了詹姆斯，他又把筆借給了詹妮寫稿子。）

第二章
英語語法入門：構成與詞源解析

如果沒有代詞這句話就會變成：

John gave John's pen to James and James lent the pen to Jane to write Jane's copy with the pen.

（約翰把約翰的筆借給了詹姆斯，詹姆斯把筆借給了詹妮來寫詹妮的稿子。）

代詞分三種——**人稱代詞**（Personal Pronouns）、**關係代詞**（Relative Pronouns）和**形容詞代詞**[03]（Adjective Pronouns）。

人稱代詞，顧名思義，就是代替人、地點和事物名稱的代詞。人稱代詞有 I、Thou、He、She 和 It，以及它們的複數形式 We、Ye 或 You 和 They。

I 是第一人稱代詞，代表說話人。

Thou 是第二人稱代詞，代表聽者。

He、She 和 It 是第三人稱代詞，代表談話中提及的人或事物。

和名詞一樣，人稱代詞也根據數、性和格進行變化。第一人稱和第二人稱的性很簡單，就是它們所代表的說話人和聽者的性別。人稱代詞根據這些來進行變格：

第一人稱　男性或女性

	單數	複數
主格	I	We
所有格	Mine	Ours
賓格	Me	Us

---

[03] 現在多數通行的語法書中，只有「形容詞性物主代詞」這一說法，屬於形容詞代詞的範疇，後文會提到。

第二人稱　男性或女性

	單數	複數
主格	Thou	You
所有格	Thine	Yours
賓格	Thee	You

第三人稱男性

	單數	複數
主格	He	They
所有格	His	Theirs
賓格	Him	Them

第三人稱女性

	單數	複數
主格	She	They
所有格	Hers	Theirs
賓格	Her	Them

第三人稱中性

	單數	複數
主格	It	They
所有格	Its	Theirs
賓格	It	Them

第二章
英語語法入門：構成與詞源解析

注意：在口語和書面語中，除了朋友之間會使用 thou、thine 和 thee，其他時候很少出現。第二人稱主格和賓格的複數形式都是 you，所有格 thine 的複數形式則是 yours。

關係代詞之所以叫這個名字，是因為它們和已出現的詞或片語有關。

例 11

The boy *who* told the truth.（講出了真相的男孩。）

He has done well, *which* gives me great pleasure.（他做得不錯，這令我很開心。）

在這裡，who 和 which 不僅僅代表其他詞。who 指的是男生 (boy)，which 指的是他做得不錯 (he has done well) 這一狀態。

關係代詞指代的詞或分句被稱為先行詞 (Antecedent)。

關係代詞有 who、which、that 和 what。

who 僅指人。

例 12　The man *who* was here.（在那裡的那個人。）

which 指低階動物和無生命物體。

例 13

The horse *which* I sold.（那匹我賣掉的馬。）

The hat *which* I bought.（那頂我買的帽子。）

that 既指人又指物。

例 14

The friend *that* helps.（那位幫忙的朋友。）

The bird *that* sings.（那隻唱歌的小鳥。）

The knife *that* cuts.（那把切割的刀。）

what 是複合關係代詞（compound relative pronoun），包括先行詞和關係代詞，等同於 that which。

例 15

I did *what* he desired.（我做了他所期待的事。）

I did *that which* he desired.（我做了那件他期待的事。）

關係代詞的單複數同形。

who 可用於男性和女性；which 和 that 可用於男性、女性和中性；what 永遠用於中性。

that 和 what 沒有變形。who 和 whose 根據以下規律變形：

單數和複數		單數和複數	
主格	Who	主格	Which
所有格	Whose	所有格	Whose
賓格	Whom	賓格	Which

當 who、which 和 what 被用於問句中時，它們被稱為疑問代詞（Interrogative Pronouns）。

形容詞代詞擁有形容詞和代詞的性質，進一步分類如下：

指示形容詞代詞（Demonstrative Adjective Pronouns），直接指代人或

對象，分別為 this、that 以及它們的複數形式 these、those，還有 yon、same 和 selfsame。

分配形容詞代詞（Distributive Adjective Pronouns）指代單個的對象，分別為 each、every、either、neither。

非限定性形容詞代詞（Indefinite Adjective Pronouns）的使用或多或少不受限制。它們是 any、all、few、some、several、one、other、another、none。

形容詞性物主代詞（The Possessive Adjective Pronouns）指代物主關係。它們是 my、thy、his、her、its、our、your、their。

注意：形容詞性物主代詞和名詞性物主代詞的區別在於後者可以單獨存在而前者不行。比如：「Who owns that book?」（那本書是誰的？）「It is mine.」（它是我的。）不能說「it is my,」（它是我……），book 這個詞必須在這裡出現。

動詞

動詞是用來表示動作或動態的詞，或者說是用來陳述、命令、詢問的詞。

因此，John the table（約翰桌子）這個句子毫無主張，支離破碎。但一旦加入 strikes 這個詞，句子就有了主張（John strikes the table. 約翰撞上了桌子。），所以 strikes 作為動詞使句子完整且有意義。

沒有變形的簡單形式的動詞被稱為動詞原形（the root of the verb）。比如：love 是 To Love 的原形。

動詞分為**規則動詞**和**不規則動詞**、**及物動詞**和**不及物動詞**。

規則動詞指的是在動詞原形後面加 ed、在以 e 結尾的動詞後加 d 形成過去式的動詞；而不以 ed 結尾形成過去式的動詞則被稱為不規則動詞。

及物動詞指的是動作傳向或影響某個對象的動詞。

例 16　I struck the table.（我撞上了桌子。）

這裡，struck[04] 這一動作影響了 table 這個對象，因此 struck 是及物動詞。不及物動詞是指動作留在主語身上的動詞。比如：

例 17　Iwalk.（我走路。）　　I sit.（我坐下。）　　Irun.（我跑步。）

不過很多不及物動詞可以作及物動詞用。比如：

例 18　I walk the horse.（我遛遛馬。）

walk 在這裡是不及物動詞。

動詞因數、人稱、時態和語氣而變化。

動詞在數和人稱上的變化是根據主語來進行的。根據主語，動詞的變形表明了動作涉及的對象是一個還是多個；涉及的對象是說話人、聽者還是對話中談到的人或事。

時態

動詞因時間變化而擁有不同的時態，包括現在時（present tense）、過去時（past tense）和將來時（future tense），以及這幾種基本時態的變形，用來確切地表示動作發生的時間──是正在發生、已經發生，還是即將發生。

---

[04]　原文為 striking of action，為不影響中文讀者閱讀，故改為 struck。

第二章
英語語法入門：構成與詞源解析

語氣

語氣有四種──不定式（the Infinitive）、陳述語氣（the Indicative）、虛擬語氣（the Imperative）和祈使語氣（the Subjunctive）。

動詞的語氣表示了動詞使用的方式。如果動詞在使用中範圍廣泛模糊，沒有任何關於人稱、數、時間或地點的說明，那麼這就是不定式。

例 19　To run.（去跑步。）

該句中，我們不知道誰在跑步、什麼時候跑步、在哪裡跑步或其他任何關於跑步的資訊。

如果動詞被用來指示、宣告、詢問或做出直接的說明，那麼這就是陳述語氣。

例 20

The boy loves his book.（男生愛他的書。）

該句圍繞男孩做了一個直接的說明。

Have you a pin?（你有大頭釘嗎？）

這是一個簡單疑問句，目的在尋求答案。

如果動詞被用來表達命令或請求，那麼這就是祈使語氣。

例 21　Go away.（走開。）　　Give me a penny.（給我一個便士。）

如果動詞被用來表達疑問、推測、不確定，或當即將發生的動作決定於偶發事件時，這就是虛擬語氣。

例 22　If I come, he shall remain.（如果我來，他就留下。）

許多語法學家加入了第五種語氣──潛在語氣（the potential），來

028

表達能力、可能性、自由、必要性、意願或職責。它是透過 may、can、ought 和 must 一系列助動詞形成的。但整體而言，所有用法又可分別歸入陳述語氣和虛擬語氣。

例 23　I may write if I choose.（如果我想的話，我可以去寫作。）

句中的 may write 被一些語法學家歸入潛在語氣，但實際上片語 I may write 是陳述語氣；後半句 if I choose 表達的不是我有寫作自由的狀態，而是我實際的寫作這一狀態。

動詞有兩個分詞形態，現在時（the present）和未完成時（the imperfect）。有時現在時被稱為現在進行時，以 ing 結尾；過去時（the past）或完成時（the perfect）有時被稱為被動態（the passive），以 ed 或 d 結尾。

不定式將動詞以名詞形式呈現，將分詞以形容詞形式呈現。

例 24

To rise early is healthful.（早起很健康。）

An early rising man.（一個早起的人。）

The newly risen sun.（初升的太陽。）

分詞 ing 經常作名詞使用，常常等同於動詞不定式。

例 25

To rise early is healthful.（早起很健康。）

Rising early is healthful.（早起很健康。）

這兩個句子是一樣的。

動詞有現在時（the Present Indicative）、過去時（the Past Indicative）和過去分詞（the Past Participle），比如：

第二章
英語語法入門：構成與詞源解析

| Love | Loved | Loved |

有些動詞沒有過去分詞甚至是過去時，這些動詞被稱為不完全變化的動詞 (defective)。

現在時	過去時	過去分詞
Can	Could	（缺失）
May	Might	（缺失）
Shall	Should	（缺失）
Will	Would	（缺失）
Ought	Ought	（缺失）

動詞又分為主要動詞 (principal) 和助動詞 (auxiliary)。主要動詞是句子中不可或缺的成分，沒有它，句子或分句就毫無主張。助動詞的功能是和主要動詞的原形或分詞一起表達時間和方式。與簡單形態的時態和語氣相比，它們能更加準確地進行表達。

例 26 I am writing an exercise; when I shall have finished it I shall read it to the class.

（我在寫一份習題，寫完後就可以讀給全班聽。）

如果沒有主要動詞 writing、finished 和 read，這個句子就沒有意義。而有了助動詞 am、have 和 shall，該句的意思——尤其在時間方面——有了更加明確的表達。

助動詞有九個，即，be、have、do、shall、will、may、can、ought 和 must。它們被稱為助動詞是因為它們幫助動詞構成了複合時態 (the compound tenses)。

TO BE

to be 是助動詞裡最重要的一個。它有 11 個形態，即，am、art、is、are、was、wast、were、wert、be、being 和 been。

語態

主動語態（active voice）是指主語是動詞動作的使動方，而非受動方。

例 27

The cat catches mice.（貓抓老鼠。）

Charity covers a multitude of sins.（慈善團體掩蓋了大量罪行。）

被動語態（passive voice）：用來表示動作的及物動詞反過來指向實施者。也就是說，動詞主語指向動作的接受者，這時動詞的狀態被稱為被動語態。

例 28　John was loved by his neighbors.（約翰受到鄰居的喜愛。）

在這句裡，John 是主語，也是 loved[05] 的接受對象。動詞的動作反過來指向他，因此動詞的變形 loved 處於被動語態中。將任何及物動詞的完成時分詞和 to be 的 11 個形態中的任何一個放在一起，就形成了被動語態。

動詞變化形式

動詞變化形式（conjugation）指的是動詞按照語態（voices）、語氣（moods）、時態（tenses）、人稱（persons）和數（numbers）的順序排列。

---

[05]　原文為 loving，為方便讀者理解，故改為 loved。

第二章
英語語法入門：構成與詞源解析

以下是動詞 Love 主動語態的完全變化形式。

主要部分

現在時	過去時	過去分詞
Love	Loved	Loved

不定式

To love

陳述語氣

現在時

	單數	複數
第一人稱	I love	We love
第二人稱	You love	You love
第三人稱	He loves	They love

過去時

	單數	複數
第一人稱	I loved	We loved
第二人稱	You loved	You loved
第三人稱	He loved	They loved

將來時

	單數	複數
第一人稱	I shall love	We will love

	單數	複數
第二人稱	You will love	You will love
第三人稱	He will love	They shall love

現在完成時

	單數	複數
第一人稱	I have loved	We have loved
第二人稱	You have loved	You have loved
第三人稱	He has loved	They have loved

過去完成時

	單數	複數
第一人稱	I had loved	We had loved
第二人稱	You had loved	You had loved
第三人稱	He had loved	They had loved

將來完成時

	單數	複數
第一人稱	I shall have loved	We shall have loved
第二人稱	You will have loved	You will have loved
第三人稱	He will have loved	They will have loved

第二章
英語語法入門：構成與詞源解析

祈使語氣

（僅有現在時）

	單數	複數
第二人稱	Love(you)	Love(you)

虛擬語氣

現在時

	單數	複數
第一人稱	If I love	If we love
第二人稱	If you love	If you love
第三人稱	If he love	If they love

過去時

	單數	複數
第一人稱	If I loved	If we loved
第二人稱	If you loved	If you loved
第三人稱	If he loved	If they loved

現在完成時

	單數	複數
第一人稱	If I have loved	If we have loved
第二人稱	If you have loved	If you have loved
第三人稱	If he has loved	If they have loved

詞類

過去完成時

	單數	複數
第一人稱	If I had loved	If we had loved
第二人稱	If you had loved	If you had loved
第三人稱	If he had loved	If they had loved

動詞不定式

現在時	完成時
To love	To have loved

分詞

現在時	過去時	完成時
Loving	Loved	Having loved

To love 的變化形式

被動語態

陳述語氣

現在時

	單數	複數
第一人稱	I am loved	We are loved
第二人稱	You are loved	You are loved

第二章
英語語法入門：構成與詞源解析

	單數	複數
第三人稱	He is loved	They are loved

過去時

	單數	複數
第一人稱	I was loved	We were loved
第二人稱	You were loved	You were loved
第三人稱	He was loved	They were loved

將來時

	單數	複數
第一人稱	I shall be loved	We shall be loved
第二人稱	You will be loved	You will beloved
第三人稱	He will be loved	They will be loved

現在完成時

	單數	複數
第一人稱	I have been loved	We have been loved
第二人稱	You have been loved	You have been loved
第三人稱	He has been loved	They have been loved

過去完成時

	單數	複數
第一人稱	I had been loved	We had been loved
第二人稱	You had been loved	You had been loved

	單數	複數
第三人稱	He had been loved	They had been loved

將來完成時

	單數	複數
第一人稱	I shall have been loved	We shall have been loved
第二人稱	You will have been loved	You will have been loved
第三人稱	He will have been loved	They will have been loved

祈使語氣

（僅有現在時）

	單數	複數
第二人稱	Be(you)loved	Be(you)loved

虛擬語氣

現在時

	單數	複數
第一人稱	If I be loved	If we be loved
第二人稱	If you be loved	If you be loved
第三人稱	If he be loved	If they be loved

過去時

	單數	複數
第一人稱	If I were loved	If we were loved

第二章
英語語法入門：構成與詞源解析

	單數	複數
第二人稱	If you were loved	If you were loved
第三人稱	If he were loved	If they were loved

現在完成時

	單數	複數
第一人稱	If I have been loved	If we have been loved
第二人稱	If you have been loved	If you have been loved
第三人稱	If he has been loved	If they have been loved

過去完成時

	單數	複數
第一人稱	If I had been loved	If we had been loved
第二人稱	If you had been loved	If you had been loved
第三人稱	If he had been loved	If they had been loved

不定式

現在時	完成時
To be loved	To have been loved

分詞

現在時	過去時	完成時
Being loved	Been loved	Having been loved

（注意：人稱代詞 you 的複數形式自始至終用第二人稱單數。除了

038

To Be 的變形以外，從前使用的 thou 都被認為是過時了的。在第三人稱單數中，he 代表了 he、she 和 it 三個第三人稱代詞。）

副詞

副詞是修飾動詞、名詞或其他副詞的詞。

例 29　He writes well.（他寫作／字很好。）

在例句中，副詞表示了動詞動作完成的方式。

例 30

He is remarkably diligent.（他極其勤奮。）

He works very faithfully.（他工作忠心耿耿。）

在例句中，副詞修飾了形容詞 diligent（勤奮的）和另一個副詞 faithfully（忠實地），表示了勤奮和忠實的程度。

副詞主要的作用是用一個詞表達兩個或以上的詞表達的內容。比如：there 代表 in that place、whence 代表 from what place、usefully 代表 in a useful manner。

和形容詞一樣，有時副詞透過結尾的變化來表達比較和性質的不同程度。

一些副詞的比較級（the comparative）和最高級（the superlative）是透過加 er 和 est 實現的。比如：soon、sooner、soonest。以 ly 結尾的副詞則在前面加 more 和 most。比如：nobly、more nobly、most nobly。

少數副詞的比較級和最高級變化不規律。比如：well、better、best。

第二章
英語語法入門：構成與詞源解析

介詞

介詞將單字（words）、分句（clauses）和句子（sentences）連接起來，並展現它們的關係。

例 31 My hand is on the table.（我的手在桌子上。）

該例句展示了手和桌子的關係。介詞之所以叫介詞是因為它們一般被放置在需要連接或展示關係的單字前面。[06]

連詞

連詞將單字、分句和句子連接起來。

例 32

John *and* James.（約翰和詹姆斯。）

My father and mother have come, *but* I have not seen them.
（我父母來了，但我沒看到他們。）

最常見的連詞有 and、also；either、or；neither、nor；though、yet；but、however；for、that；because、since；therefore、wherefore、then；if、unless、lest。

嘆詞

嘆詞用來表達突如其來的情緒。

---

[06] 介詞英文為 preposition，該詞由 pre 和 position 組成，意思分別為「在⋯⋯前面」和「位置」。

例 33

Ah! There he comes; alas! What shall Ido?

（啊！他來了。唉！我該怎麼做？）

ah 表達驚訝，alas 表達苦惱。

當名詞、形容詞、動詞和副詞被喊出來時，它們都是嘆詞。

例 34

Nonsense!（胡說！）　　Strange!（奇怪了！）

Hail!（歡呼！）　　Away!（走開！）

我們在前面已經列舉了各項詞類，並且盡量簡潔地說明了它們各自的功能。雖然它們都屬於一個大家庭，但其中一些詞類間的關係比其他詞類更近。準確地指出兩個單字之間的關係和彼此依賴程度的分析叫做句法分析 (parsing)。為了更清楚地了解詞源的關係，本書在此給出一個上述詞類的簡略摘要：

名詞的含義被限定至一個。用不定冠詞修飾限定含義中的任何一個對象，而用定冠詞修飾特定的一個或幾個對象。

名詞的單數表示該類事物中的一個；其他的表示該類事物在數量上超過一個。它們是男性、女性或既不是男性也不是女性的事物的名稱，它們代表了陳述、命令或問題的主語──一件事物的主人或擁有者，或一個動作的對象，或介詞表達的關係。

形容詞表達了使一個人或事物與眾不同的性質。一種情況是，它們在沒有比較的情況下表示性質；另一種情況是，它們在兩者之間，或一方與另一個團體之間進行比較；第三種情況是，它們在一方與另一個團體中的每個個體之間分別進行比較。

第二章
英語語法入門：構成與詞源解析

代詞用來替代名詞。其中一類代詞僅用來作名稱的替代詞；另一類代詞特別用來指代在句子裡已經出現過的詞，這些代詞是替代詞；第三類代詞用來指代它們代表的人或事物。一些代詞被用在名稱和替代詞身上，少數代詞頻繁地被用於問句中。

陳述和命令透過**動詞**得以表達。動詞的不同變化形態可表示不同的數、人稱、時間和方式。在時間方面，陳述分為現在時、過去時和將來時；在方式方面，陳述分為肯定的、有條件的、無論條件是否滿足都不確定的、透過暗示表示條件不滿足的；動詞可以表達命令或請求，或者動詞的意義不透過陳述或命令進行表達。透過變形，動詞還能表達一個動作或狀態是 is（正在進行中）還是 was going on（過去正在進行中）。該變形有時被用作名詞，有時被用來修飾名詞。

陳述句裡的動詞由**副詞**修飾。其中，一些副詞能透過變形對動詞進行不同程度的修飾。

單字透過**連接詞**連繫起來。而一件事物與另一件事物的複雜關係透過**介詞**表現出來。突發情緒和呼喊則透過**嘆詞**表現。

根據含義，有些詞時而被歸入這個詞類，時而被歸入那個詞類。

例 35　After a storm comes a calm.（風暴過後是安寧。）

此時，calm 是名詞。

例 36　It is a calm evening.（這是個平靜的夜晚。）

此時，calm 是形容詞。

例 37　Calm your fears.（鎮靜下來，別恐懼。）

此時，calm 是動詞。

詞類

下面這句話包含所有詞類，讓我們從詞源學上進行句法分析：

例 38

I now see the old man coming, but, alas, he has walked with much difficulty.

（我看到那個老人正在走過來。但是，唉，他走得很艱難。）

I，人稱代詞，第一人稱單數，可能是男性，也可能是女性，主格，動詞 see 的主語。

now，時間副詞，用來修飾動詞 see。

see，不規則變形的及物動詞，陳述語氣，現在時，第一人稱單數，與主格（亦是主語）I 形態一致。

the，修飾名詞 man 的定冠詞。old，形容詞，原級，修飾名詞 man。

man，普通名詞，第三人稱單數，男性，由及物動詞 see 支配的賓格。

coming，動詞 to come 的現在時或未完成時，修飾名詞 man。

alas，嘆詞，表達遺憾或悲傷。

he，人稱代詞，第三人稱單數，男性，主格，動詞 has walked 的主語。

has walked，規則變形的不及物動詞，陳述語氣，完成時態，第三人稱單數，與主格（亦是主語）he 形態一致。

with，介詞，支配名詞 difficulty。

much，形容詞，原級，修飾名詞 difficulty。

difficulty，普通名詞，第三人稱單數，中性，由介詞 with 支配的賓格。

注意：much 一般作副詞。作形容詞時的變化規律為：

原級	比較級	最高級
much	more	most

第三章
句子的藝術：句式結構與段落安排

句子是單字按照一定規律排列的集合，它能傳達確切的意思。也就是說，句子能傳達完整的想法或看法。無論句子有多短，它都必須包含一個限定動詞（finit everb）和一個主語（subject）或實施者（agent），以引導動詞的動作。

例 1

  Birds fly.（鳥兒會飛。） Fish swim.（魚兒會游。）

  Men walk.（人會走路。）

這些都是句子。

一個句子總是包含兩個部分，主體和關於主體的陳述或說明。表示主體的詞彙被稱為主語（subject），表示陳述或說明主體的詞彙被稱為謂語（predicate）。

在以上例句中，birds、fish 和 men 是主語，而 fly、swim 和 walk 則是謂語。

英語中，句子可分為三種，**簡單句**（simple sentence）、**並列句**（compound sentence）和**複合句**（complex sentence）。

簡單句表達單一的想法，包含一個主語和一個謂語。

第三章
句子的藝術：句式結構與段落安排

例2 Man is mortal.（人終有一死。）

並列句包含兩個或以上的簡單句，它們在句中的地位相同，且簡單句中各個部分的意思都得到了傳達和理解。

例3

The men work in the fields and the women work in the household.

（田裡勞動的男人和家中勞動的女人。）

The men work in the fields and the women in the household.

（田裡勞動的男人和家中勞動的女人。）

The men and the women work in the fields and the household.

（田裡和家中勞動的男人和女人。）

複合句包含兩個或以上的簡單句，它們的連繫過於緊密，以致於它們需要互相結合才能完整地表達句意。

例4

When he returns, I shall go on my vacation.（他回來後，我就會去度假。）

其中「When he returns」需結合句子剩下的部分才有完整的意義。

分句（clasuse）是複合句中獨立的部分，比如上例中的「When he returns」。

短語（phrase）是一個包含兩個或以上單字、沒有限定動詞的片語。

沒有限定動詞，就不能陳述任何意義或傳達任何思想，因此也就沒有完整的句子。

動詞不定式（infinitives）和分詞（participles）是非限定動詞，不能作謂語。

例 5

I looking up the street（我看向街道……）

這不是一個句子，因為它沒有完整地表達一個動作。

A dog running along the street.（一條狗沿著街跑……）

在聽到這樣的表達時，我們會期待更多內容，更多關於狗的陳述——無論是它咬人還是喊叫，是倒地死去還是被車碾過。

因此每個句子裡必須有限定動詞，以修飾主語。當動詞是及物動詞，即動詞的動作有接收對象時，接收對象就是賓語。

例 6

Cain killed Abel.（該隱殺了亞伯。）

在該例句中，killed（殺人）的動作影響的對象是 Abel（亞伯）。

The cat has caught a mouse.（貓抓了一隻老鼠。）

在該例句中，mouse（老鼠）是 caught（抓）的賓語。

單字在句中的排列

在簡單句中，最自然的排列順序當然是主語——謂語動詞——賓語。很多情況下其他的排列形式沒有存在的可能。因此，例 7

The cat has caught a mouse.（貓抓了一隻老鼠。）

在例句中，我們不能將主語和謂語倒置，把它變成：

第三章
句子的藝術：句式結構與段落安排

The mouse has caught a cat.（老鼠抓了一隻貓。）

而不改變其意義。

而其他重新排列的結果，比如：

A mouse, the cat has caught.（一隻老鼠，貓抓了。）

雖然不影響我們對句意的理解，但這種陳述方式不夠通順，多少會讓人感到不協調。

然而，在長句中，除了主語、謂語動詞和賓語之外還有許多其他詞彙。此時，我們有更多的排列自由。我們可以將單字按照一定順序放置，以便最佳地表達句意。單字的排列順序是否合適取決於表意的清晰度和準確度。這兩點將給予句子結構一定的風格。

很多人都熟悉托馬斯・格雷的〈墓園輓歌〉[07]中的詩句——

例 8

The ploughman homeward plods his weary way.

（農夫朝著家的方向沉重緩慢又疲憊地走在路上。）

這句話可以透過排列組合形成 18 個不同的句子。以下是部分結果：

Homeward the ploughman plods his weary way.

The ploughman plods his weary way homeward.

Plods homeward the ploughman his weary way.

His weary way the ploughman homeward plods.

Homeward his weary way plods the ploughman.

Plods the ploughman his weary way homeward.

---

[07] 〈墓園輓歌〉，詩人托馬斯・格雷（Thomas Gray，西元 1716～1771 年）的代表作。

His weary way the ploughman plods homeward.

His weary way homeward the ploughman plods.

The ploughman plods homeward his weary way.

The ploughman his weary way plods homeward.

……

這句詩的其他任何一種排列組合都不太可能優於作者的原作。當然，作者這樣排列是為了押詩節的韻律 (rhythm) 和韻腳 (verse)。大部分排列組合的順序取決於我們希望放在不同詞前面來強調的內容。

如果要按照普通順序排列組合單字的話，我們不應忘記一個事實，那就是：句首和句尾分別是最能夠吸引讀者注意力的地方。這個位置的詞比其他地方更能得到強調。

格雷的詩句大意是：一個疲憊的農夫朝著家的方向沉重緩慢又疲憊地走在路上。但不同的排列組合表達的意義各有輕微的差異。有些排列讓我們更注重農夫，其他的則讓我們更注重沉重緩慢的步態，還有一些則讓我們更注重疲憊的身體狀態。

既然句首和句尾是最重要的位置，那麼次要的、無足輕重的詞就不應該出現在這些位置。句尾在兩個位置中更為重要，因此句尾應放置句中最為重要的詞。永遠不要以 and、but、since、because 和其他次要的詞作為句子的開頭，也永遠不要以介詞、次要的副詞或代詞作為句子的結尾。

句子中意義緊密相連的各個部分在排列上也應該緊密地連在一起。忽視這條原則寫出的句子，不是毫無意義，就是既滑稽又可笑。比如：

第三章
句子的藝術：句式結構與段落安排

例 9

Ten dollars reward is offered for information of any person injuring this property by order of the owner.

（按照財產擁有者的意願，將提供十美元獎金給提供破壞財產者資訊的人。）

This monument was erected to the memory of John Jones, who was shot by his affectionate brother.

（此碑是為紀念約翰・瓊斯而立，他被他慈愛的哥哥射殺。）

無論哪種句子結構，都必須遵守語法規則——語法一致原則，也就是某些詞在語法上的一致，必須得到遵守。

1. 動詞和主語保持人稱和數的一致。比如：I have、Thou hast（代詞 thou 在此用來說明動詞形式，儘管它幾乎過時了）、He has，它們展現了動詞為和主語保持一致而進行的形態變化。單數主語對應單數動詞，複數主語對應複數動詞。比如：

例 10 The boy writes.（男孩寫字。） The boys write.（男孩們寫字。）

動詞和主語的一致性遭到破壞，經常是因為混淆了：

(1) 集合名詞 (collective nouns) 和普通名詞 (common nouns)

(2) 外來名詞 (foreign nouns) 和英文名詞 (English nouns)

(3) 複合主語 (compound subjects) 和簡單主語 (simple subjects)

(4) 真實明顯的主語

集合名詞是指被當作整體的一群個體或事物。

例 11　class regiment（班集體）

強調一群個體或事物時，動詞用複數形式。

The class were distinguished forability.（這個班以能力優秀聞名。）

強調整體概念時，動詞用單數形式。

The regiment was in camp.（整個班都在營地裡。）

有時要區分外來名詞的單複數很難，所以在選擇動詞時更應謹慎。應查閱該詞，並根據查閱結果選擇動詞。

例 12

He was an alumnus of Harvard.（他是哈佛校友。）

They were alumni of Harvard.（他們是哈佛校友。）[08]

當句子中有兩個或以上指向不同對象，且由 and 連接起來的主語時，動詞用複數形式。

例 13　Snow and rain are disagreeable.（雨雪令人不快。）

當多個主語指向同一對象，且由 or 連接起來時，動詞用單數形式。

例 14　The man or the woman is to blame.（他或她，總有一個要受到責備。）

當同一動詞有一個以上擁有不同人稱和數的主語時，動詞的形態與意義最重要的主語一致。

例 15

He, and not you, is wrong.（是他，不是你，錯了。）

Whether he or I am to be blamed.（不是他，就是我受責備。）

---

[08]　alumnus—男校友，單數；alumni—校友，複數。

第三章
句子的藝術：句式結構與段落安排

2. 永遠不要在過去時的時態裡用過去分詞，反之亦然。這是個非常常見的錯誤。在生活中，我們時常聽到：

例 16

He done it.（他做的。）

而不是

He did it.（他做的。）

The jar was broke.（瓶子破了。）

而不是

The jar was broken.（瓶子破了。）

He would have went.（他本可以去的。）

而不是

He would have gone.（他本可以去的。）

……

3. 說到動詞 shall 和 will 的使用，那可是連大演說家都會觸礁的地方。人們總是胡亂替換這兩個詞。它們在意義上的變化取決於它們的主語是第一、第二還是第三人稱。在第一人稱中，shall 被直接用於表達一般將來時的動作。

例 17 I shall go to the city tomorrow.（我明天會去城市裡。）

在第二、第三人稱中，shall 被用於表達決定。

例 18

You shall go to the city tomorrow.（你明天要去城市裡。）

He shall go to the city tomorrow.（他明天要去城市裡。）

在第一人稱中，will 被直接用於表達決定。

例 19 I will go to the city tomorrow.（我明天要去城市裡。）

在第二、第三人稱中，will 被用於表達一般將來時的動作。

例 20

You will go to the city tomorrow.（你明天會去城市裡。）

He will go to the city tomorrow.（他明天會去城市裡。）

關於 shall 和 will 的用法，有一個古老的規則被寫進了韻文裡：

In the first person simply shall foretells.（第一人稱的 shall 僅僅是預告）

In will a threat or else a promise dwells.（而 will 則是威脅或許諾）

Shall in the second and third does threat.（第二、三人稱的 shall 是威脅）

Will simply then foretells the future feat.（Will 此時則預告未來）

4. 要特別注意區分主格和賓格。代詞是唯一保留了賓格獨特的結尾方式的詞類。記住，賓格跟在及物動詞和介詞後面。

例 21

不要說：

The boy who I sent to see you.（我送去見你的那個男生。）

而要說：The boy whom I sent to see you.（我送去見你的那個男生。）

在這句裡，whom 是及物動詞 sent 的賓語。

不要說：

第三章
句子的藝術：句式結構與段落安排

She bowed to him and I.（她向他和我鞠了躬。）

而要說：

She bowed to him and me.（她向他和我鞠了躬。）

因為我們要將 me 理解為接在介詞後面的賓格。

不過 Between you and I 又是一個非常常見的表達。本來應該是 Between you and me，因為 between 是後面要接賓語的介詞。

5. 使用關係代詞 who、which 和 that 時要注意：who 僅指人；which 僅指物。

例 22

The boy who was drowned.（那個被淹死的男孩。）

The umbrella which I lost.（我弄丟的那把傘。）

而 that 既指人又指物。

例 23

The man that I saw.（我看到的那個人。）

The hat that I bought.（我買的那頂帽子。）

6. 不要在該用比較級的時候使用最高級。

例 24

應該是：

He is the richer of the two.（他是兩人中更富有的那個。）

而不是：

He is the richest of the two.（他是兩人中最富有的那個。）

其他經常出現的錯誤有：

(1)使用雙重比較級、最高級。

例 25

These apples are much more preferable.（這些蘋果更好多了。）

The most universal motive to business is gain.（做生意最普遍的動機就是賺錢。）

(2)比較對象屬於不同的類別。

例 26　There is no nicer life than a teacher.（沒有比老師更好的生活。）

(3)將比較對象納入它不隸屬的類別。

例 27　The fairest of her daughters, Eve.（她女兒中最漂亮的，就是夏娃。）

(4)將比較對象從它隸屬的類別裡排除出去。

例 28

Caesar was braver than any ancient warrior.（凱薩比任何古代戰士都勇敢。）

7.不要用形容詞代替副詞，或用副詞代替形容詞。

例 29

不要說：

He acted nice towards me.（他對我很好。）

而要說：

He acted nicely toward me.（他對我很好。）

第三章
句子的藝術：句式結構與段落安排

不要說：

She looked beautifully.（她看起來很美。）

而要說：

She looked beautiful.（她看起來很美。）

8. 要將副詞盡可能放置在它修飾的詞附近。

例 30

不要說：

He walked to the door quickly.（他迅速地朝門走去。）

而要說：

He walked quickly to the door.（他朝門迅速地走去。）

9. 不僅要小心區分代詞的主格和賓格，還要避免使用過程中可能產生的歧義。

忽視代詞的指代作用所帶來的搞笑後果，已經由伯頓在下面的比利·迪·威廉姆斯（Billy Dee Williams）的故事裡做了很好的說明。比利·迪·威廉姆斯是一個喜劇演員，他敘述了他一次騎馬的經歷，這匹馬是經理漢布林的。

例 31

So down I goes to the stable with Tom Flynn, and told the man to put the saddle on him.

（我和湯姆·福林一起去馬廄，告訴他替他上鞍。）

On Tom Flynn?（替湯姆·福林上鞍？）

單字在句中的排列

No, on the horse. So after talking with Tom Flynn awhile I mounted him.

（不，替馬上鞍。和湯姆・福林聊了一陣後，我騎上了他。）

What! mounted Tom Flynn?（什麼！騎上了湯姆・福林？）

No, the horse; and then I shook hands with him and rode off.

（不，騎上了馬。然後我和他握手道別了。）

Shook hands with the horse, Billy?（和馬握手嗎，比利？）

No, with Tom Flynn; and then I rode off up the Bowery, and who should I meet but Tom Hamblin; so I got off and told the boy to hold him by the head.

（不，和湯姆・福林。接著我一路騎到包厘街，見到了湯姆・漢布林。於是我下來，告訴他牽住他的頭。）

What! hold Hamblin by the head?（什麼！牽住漢布林的頭？）

No, the horse; and then we went and had a drink together.

（不，牽住馬的頭。然後我們去喝了一杯。）

What! you and the horse?（什麼！你和馬嗎？）

No, me and Hamblin; and after that I mounted him again and went out of town.

（不，我和漢布林。在那之後，我又騎上了他出了鎮。）

What! mounted Hamblin again?（什麼！又騎上了漢布林？）

No, the horse; and when I got to Burnham, who should be there but Tom Flynn, —— he'd taken another horse and rode out ahead of me; so I told the hostler to tie him up.

第三章
句子的藝術：句式結構與段落安排

（不，騎上了馬。我到了伯納姆，在那裡見到了湯姆・福林。他騎了另一匹馬，比我先到。於是我讓馬伕把他牽走繫好。）

Tie Tom Flynn up?（把湯姆・福林牽走？）

No, the horse; and we had a drink there.

（不，把馬牽走。我們在那裡喝了一杯。）

What! you and the horse?（什麼！你和馬喝了一杯？）

No, me and Tom Flynn.（不，我和湯姆・福林。）

比利發現他的審計員哈哈大笑，於是他說，

Now, look here, —— every time I say horse, you say Hamblin, and every time I say Hamblin you say horse：I'll be hanged if I tell you any more about it.

（聽著，每次我在說馬，你就說是漢布林；每次我在說漢布林，你就說是馬。我再跟你聊下去就是見鬼了。）

句子分類

根據不同句型的構成原則，句子被分為兩類——**鬆散句**（loose sentence）和掉尾句（periodic sentence，又稱圓周句）。

鬆散句是指主要資訊放在前面，補充資訊放在後面的句子。丹尼爾・笛福（Daniel Defoe）正是因使用鬆散句寫作而出名。他寫作時先以主要資訊開頭，隨後補上一些相關資訊。比如，在《魯賓遜漂流記》的故事開篇他寫道：

句子分類

例 32

I was born in the year 1632 in the city of York, of a good family, though not of that country, my father being a foreigner of Bremen, who settled first at Hull; he got a good estate by merchandise, and leaving off his trade lived afterward at York, from whence he had married my mother, whose relations were named Robinson, a very good family in the country and from I was called Robinson Kreutznaer; but by the usual corruption of words in England, we are now called, nay, we call ourselves, and write our name Crusoe, and so my companions always called me.

（1632 年，我生在約克市一個上流社會的家庭。我們不是本地人。父親是德國布萊梅市人。他移居英國後，先住在赫爾市，經商發家後就收了生意，最後搬到約克市定居，並在那裡娶了我母親。母親娘家姓魯賓遜，是當地的一家名門望族，因而幫我取名叫魯賓遜‧克羅伊茨內。由於英國人一讀「克羅伊茨內」這個德國姓，發音就走樣，結果大家就叫我們「克羅梭」，以致連我們自己也這麼叫，這麼寫了。所以，我的朋友們都叫我克羅梭。）

掉尾句則是指主要資訊放在最後，相關介紹放在前面的句子。這類句子經常以 that、if、since、because 等詞開頭。

例 33

That through his own folly and lack of circumspection he should have been reduced to such circumstances as to be forced to become a beggar on the streets, soliciting alms from those who had formerly been the recipients of his bounty, was a sore humiliation（由於自己的愚蠢和不慎，他淪落到這麼個境地，以致於他不得不上街乞討，向那些曾經受他恩惠的人手裡懇求施捨，這簡直就是奇恥大辱。）

第三章
句子的藝術：句式結構與段落安排

顧名思義，很多人覺得鬆散句在寫作中是一種不受歡迎的句型。但這種想法過於理所當然。在很多情況下，鬆散句比掉尾句更合適。

一般對於講話（相對於寫作）而言，鬆散句更加合適。因為在談話中使用掉尾句時，聽者容易在談到最終主題之前忘記其他介紹資訊的分句。

這兩種句型在寫作中都得到了自由的運用。但在講話中，在開頭做出直接宣告的鬆散句占主導地位。

至於句子長度，相當程度上則取決於寫作的性質。然而，一般來說，短句比長句更受歡迎。現今，一流作家傾向於用短小、精悍、簡練的句子來吸引讀者的注意。他們遵循自己的座右銘 multum in parvo[09]，努力地在短小的行文空間裡塞下諸多內容。當然，極端簡略的寫作是人們極力避免的。句子可能由於太短、太碎片化、太簡略而無法接受評論的檢驗。長句在寫作中占有很重要的一席之地，它是辯論中不可或缺的部分、描述中必要的存在、介紹一般原則時具體闡述中必不可少的組成。運用長句時，經驗不足的作家不應全力追求厚重、乏味的句型。雖然詹森和卡萊爾[10]使用了這樣的長句，但切記，凡夫俗子是無法揮起偉人的巨錘的。幾乎沒有人能奢望達到強生和卡萊爾那樣顯赫的文學巨匠的地位。寫作新手千萬不要追求厚重的行文風格。英文中寫作風格最佳者為約瑟夫・艾迪生[11]。湯瑪士・麥考萊[12]說過：「如果你希望自己的行文風格博學而不迂腐、高雅而不浮誇、簡單且精緻的話，你一定要孜孜不倦地拜讀約瑟夫・艾迪生的作品。」艾迪生的作品除了優美，它的簡約

---

[09] 拉丁文：小中見大。
[10] 山繆・詹森（Samuel Johnson），英國作家、文學評論家和詩人；湯瑪斯・卡萊爾（Thomas Carlyle），蘇格蘭諷刺作家、評論家、哲學家等。
[11] 約瑟夫・艾迪生（Joseph Addison），英國散文家、詩人。
[12] 湯瑪士・麥考萊（Thomas Macaulay），英國歷史學家、政治家。

也讓我們重新想起那句有關文學的箴言——在能表達相同或類似意義的情況下，永遠使用簡單的而非複雜的詞。

麥考萊本身就是個值得效仿的、優雅的文體家。他就宛如被正午陽光親吻的潺潺溪流，溪流底下的河床裡，白色卵石清晰可數。戈德史密斯（Goldsmith）[13]也是一位有魅力的文風簡約的作家。

初學者應研究這些作家，把他們的作品當成學習手冊。這些作品經歷了時間的檢驗，到目前為止沒有，未來也不太可能出現超越它們的作品，因為它們已然是英文寫作裡接近完美的典範了。

除了語法結構外，句子的構成沒有任何固定的規律。最好的方法便是追隨一流作家的腳步，這些語言大師能把你順利地引上正途。

段落

段落（paragraph）是由一組連繫緊密、表達同一中心意思的句子構成的。段落不僅保留了文章劃分的順序，還替文章帶來了一種情趣，就好像往梅子布丁（plum pudding）裡加葡萄乾（raisins）一樣[14]。一頁滿滿的文字讓讀者反感，它加重了眼睛的負擔，並且如此乏味，讓人疲勞。但當文字被劃分成段落後，它就擺脫了厚重感，隨之而來的輕盈感給予了它無窮的魅力去吸引讀者。

段落就像淺淺河床裡的踏腳石，讓路人能依靠它一步步輕鬆地跨越河流。但如果踏腳石相隔的距離過於遙遠，路人很有可能因踩不中石頭而落入水面，不斷掙扎，直至再找到下一個踏腳處。書面寫作亦是如

---

[13] 奧利弗・戈德史密斯（Oliver Goldsmith），英國劇作家。
[14] plum pudding 雖然被稱為梅子布丁，但卻不含有梅子。在維多利亞時代之前，plum 指的是葡萄乾。

第三章
句子的藝術：句式結構與段落安排

此。透過段落，讀者可以輕易地從一處完整的思想向下一處轉移，並且保持對文章的興趣直到結尾。

段落中必須有一中心思想貫穿其間，該中心思想與文章談論的事情相關，也就是句意指向。比如，在一段文字中我們不能同時談論一幢著火的房子和一匹失控的馬，除非它們之間有某種連繫。在以下情況中，我們不能連續寫作：

例 34

The fire raged with fierce intensity, consuming the greater part of the large building in a short time.

（火勢猛烈地蔓延，短時間內就吞噬了這幢大樓的主要部分。）

The horse took fright and wildly dashed down the street scattering pedestrians in all directions.

（馬兒受到了驚嚇，凶猛地衝下街道，把行人們驅散到四面八方。）

這兩個句子毫無連繫，因此應該把它們分開放在不同的段落裡。

但當我們這麼說時，

例 35

The fire raged with fierce intensity consuming the greater part of the large building in a short time and the horse taking fright at the flames dashed wildly down the street scattering pedestrians in all directions.

（火勢猛烈地蔓延，短時間內就吞噬了這幢大樓的主要部分。馬兒受到了火焰的驚嚇，凶猛地衝下街道，把行人們驅散到四面八方。）

句子之間就有了自然的連繫，即馬兒受到驚嚇是火焰導致的，因此這兩個句子能夠結合起來，放在一個段落裡。

和句子一樣，段落裡最重要的位置是段首和段尾。所以因其結構和張力，第一句和最後一句能夠牢牢地吸引讀者的注意。一般來說，第一句最好是短句，最後一句可長可短，但一定要有張力。第一句的目的是清楚地陳述觀點，最後一句則應加強該觀點。

優秀的作家習慣將段落結尾用來重申觀點或與開頭相呼應。大多數情況下，段落可以被當作中心句的詳盡闡述。主要的想法或觀點就像是核心，圍繞它形成了段落裡的其他部分。任何人都可以就一個簡單的句子引申出上下文，方法是問幾個與該句相關的問題。

例 36

The foreman gave the order.（陪審團團長下了指令。）

一句話立刻可以引出好幾個問題：

What was the order?（指令是什麼？）

To whom did he give it?（指令是因為誰下的？）

Why did he give it?（為什麼下指令？）

What was the result?（結果怎樣？）

……

根據中心句，這些問題得到不同程度的回答。這些回答連同中心句形成了一個完整的段落。

如果我們去分析任何一個優秀的段落，就會發現它是由一系列內容組成的，每項內容都闡明、確認或加強了段落的主體思想或主要目的。同時，內容與內容之間的過渡簡單、自然而又明確，彷彿這些內容本來就存在於此。從另一個角度來說，假如我們發現段落裡一項或以上內容

063

第三章
句子的藝術：句式結構與段落安排

與其他內容之間沒有直接連繫，或者我們無法輕易地從一項內容移向下一項內容，或者（尤其是）我們在沒有完全了解各項內容的意義之前就調整它們的順序，那麼毫無疑問，這一段落的結構是有缺陷的。

段落結構的形成沒有特定的規律。最好的建議就是──近距離學習一流作家的段落結構。因為只有透過對最佳範本的模仿，無論是特意的還是無意的，才能讓我們掌握這門藝術。

英語語言裡，散文段落結構最佳的作家是麥考萊，演說文體的最佳模仿對象是埃德蒙・伯克[15]，而從描述和敘述的角度來說，段落寫得最好的則要數美國人戈德史密斯[16]和華盛頓・歐文[17]。

在印刷中，標記段落的是一行的縮排，即在左頁邊的段首空一格。

---

[15] 埃德蒙・伯克（Edmund Burke），愛爾蘭政治家、作家、演說家、政治理論家和哲學家。
[16] Goldsmith，資料不詳。
[17] 華盛頓・歐文（Washington Irving），19世紀美國最著名的作家，被譽為美國文學之父。

第四章
修辭魅力：手法解析與應用技巧

在修辭語言（Figurative Language）中，我們在用到詞彙的時候不會使用它們在日常對話中的通用意義，而是透過更生動、更令人印象深刻的方式來表達我們的意思。修辭提升了表達效果，就像鹽為食物帶來了美味和刺激，它們能美化、強調講話內容。除此之外，修辭還替表達帶來了能量和力度，牢牢地吸引聽者的注意力和興趣。修辭分四種，即：

1. **正字法**（Figures of Orthography），改變單字的拼寫；

2. **詞彙修辭格**（Figures of Etymology），改變詞彙的形式；

3. **句法辭格**（Figures of Syntax），改變句子的結構；

4. **修辭格**（Figures of Rhetoric），改變思維模式的、有效的說和寫的藝術。

我們應著重考慮第四種，因為它最為重要。修辭給予語言結構和風格，讓語言成為交流想法的合適媒介。

修辭格有豐富的分類，一些學者甚至將這個列表無限延長。實際上，任何能夠傳達想法的表達形式都能被劃分為修辭格的一種。

修辭格中最重要也最常用的有明喻（Simile）、暗喻（Metaphor）、**擬人**（Personification）、**寓言**（Allegory）、**借代**（Synecdoche，又稱提喻）、**借喻**（Metonymy，又稱轉喻）、**感嘆**（Exclamation）、**誇張**（Hyperbole）、

第四章
修辭魅力：手法解析與應用技巧

頓呼法（Apostrophe）、**想像**（Vision）、**對偶**（Antithesis）、**層進法**（Climax）、**警句**（Epigram）、**反問**（Interrogation）和諷刺（Ivory）。

前四種修辭格建立在相似性（resemblance）的基礎上，接下來的六種建立在連續性（contiguity）的基礎上，最後五種則建立在**對比**（contrast）的基礎上。

明喻（Simile，來自拉丁語 similis，即「像」）指的是兩個事物的相似性，是關於事物、行為或關係的相似性的陳述。

例 1

In his awful anger he was like the storm-driven waves dashing against the rock.

（他的憤怒彷彿風暴天拍打在岩石上的洶湧波濤。）

在這個句子裡，明喻讓主體更清晰，讓讀者留下更有力的印象。

例 2

His memory is like wax to receive impressions and like marble to retain them.

（他的記憶就像蠟上的印記、大理石上的刻痕一樣牢固。）

該句以一種有力的方式談論這個人的記憶。與簡單的陳述對比一下，

His memory is good.（他的記憶很好。）

有時，明喻也被用來形容不好的事物。比如，

例 3

His face was like a danger signal in a fog storm.

（他的臉就像大霧裡的危險訊號一樣。）

Her hair was like a furze-bush in bloom.

（她的頭髮就像盛放的金雀花叢一樣。）

He was to his lady love as a poodle to its mistress.

（他對另一半的愛就像捲毛狗對女主人的愛一樣。）

這樣的模仿是絕對不可以出現的。要記住，僅僅擁有相似性是無法構成明喻的。比如，把一座城市比作另一座城市不是明喻。要構成明喻這種修辭手法，比較的對象不能屬於同一類別。要避免諸如把英雄比作雄獅這種老掉牙的明喻，它們早就過時了。也不要追求牽強附會的明喻。不要說：

例 4

Her head was glowing as the glorious god of day when he sets in a flambeau of splendor behind the purple-tinted hills of the West.

（當他把華麗的燭臺放在西邊紫色調的山丘後面時，她的頭就像耀眼的天神一樣發著光。）

不用這個明喻，而只是簡單地說：

She had fiery red hair.（她有一頭火紅的頭髮。）要好得多。

暗喻（Metaphor，來自希臘語 metapherein，即「結轉或轉換」）則是暗示事物之間的相似性。與明喻用比喻詞來描述對象不同，暗喻直接拿其他詞替換掉對象的動作或行為。比如，如果我們這樣描述一個教徒：

例 5

He is as a great pillar upholding the church.（他就像支撐教堂的支柱一樣。）

這就是明喻。

第四章
修辭魅力：手法解析與應用技巧

但如果我們這樣描述他：

He is a great pillar upholding the church.（他是支撐教堂的支柱。）

這就是暗喻。

暗喻比明喻更大膽、更生動、更有畫面感。所以暗喻的使用被稱為「詞繪」[18]。它能夠賦予最抽象的想法以形態、顏色和生命。英語語言充滿暗喻，很多時候，我們無意地使用了很多暗喻。比如，當我們談到河床、山肩、山腳、指標、場景的關鍵時，都會使用暗喻。

不要混用暗喻，即在同一對象上使用不同的暗喻。

例 6

Since it was launched our project has met with much opposition, but while its flight has not reached the heights ambitioned, we are yet sanguine we shall drive it to success.

（自從專案下水後我們碰到了很多阻礙，雖然專案目前還沒有上升到應有的高度，但我們仍十分相信它能駛向成功。）

在該例句裡，「專案」最開始被比喻為一艘船，然後被比喻為一隻鳥，最後變成了一匹馬。

擬人（Personification，來自拉丁語 persona 和 facere，即「人」和「做」）指的是將無生命物體當作有生命物體一樣來描述。擬人可能是所有修辭格裡最生動有效的一個。

例 7

The mountains sing together, the hills rejoice and clap their hands.

---

[18] 原文 word-painting，即用詞語來描繪畫面。

（山巒齊聲合唱，丘陵歡欣鼓舞。）

Earth felt the wound; and Nature from her seat, Sighing, through all her works, gave signs of woe.

（大地感受到創傷；自然母親在原地嘆息著，完成所有使命後，露出了痛苦的神情。）

擬人相當程度上取決於生動的想像，它經常出現在詩歌寫作當中。擬人有兩種不同的形式：

1. 把人的特徵用在無生命物體上的擬人，比如前面提到的例子；

2. 把其他生命的特徵用在無生命物體上的擬人，比如 a raging storm（狂怒的風暴）、an angry sea（憤怒的海）、a whistling wind（呼嘯的風聲）等等。

寓言（Allegory，來自希臘語 allos 和 agoreuein，即「其他」和「說」）是一種具有象徵意義的表達形式。它和暗喻非常接近，實際上它就是暗喻的延伸。

寓言、暗喻和明喻有三個共同點：它們都以物體的相似性為基礎。

例 8

Ireland is like a thorn in the side of England.

（愛爾蘭在英格蘭旁邊像根荊棘一樣。）

這是明喻。

Ireland is a thorn in the side of England.

（愛爾蘭是英格蘭旁邊的一根荊棘。）

這是暗喻。

第四章
修辭魅力：手法解析與應用技巧

Once a great giant sprang up out of the sea and lived on an island all by himself. On looking around he discovered a little girl on another small island nearby. He thought the little girl could be useful to him in many ways so he determined to make her subservient to his will. He commanded her, but she refused to obey, then he resorted to very harsh measures with the little girl, but she still remained obstinate and obdurate. He continued to oppress her until finally she rebelled and became as a thorn in his side to prick him for his evil attitude towards her.

（從前，有一個巨人從海面上升起，獨自住在一個島上。他環顧四周，發現旁邊的小島上有一個小女孩。他覺得這個女孩對他很有用，於是決定讓她服從自己的意願。他命令她，但女孩拒絕服從。於是巨人改變了自己的態度，變得很嚴酷，但女孩仍然非常執拗頑固。巨人繼續壓迫她，最後女孩反抗成功，成了他旁邊的一根荊棘，不斷地提醒他自己惡劣的態度造成的後果。）

這就是寓言，其中巨人代表英格蘭，小女孩代表愛爾蘭。

雖然沒有明確指出，但兩個角色所代表的國家是顯而易見的。奇怪的是，英語語言中最完美的寓言是由一個幾近文盲而又無知的人在地牢裡寫就的。在《天路歷程》中，流浪鐵匠約翰‧班揚（John Bunyan）為我們奉獻了史上最優秀的寓言。而另一個非常優秀的寓言則是愛德蒙‧史賓賽（Edmund Spenser）的《仙后》。

借代（Synecdoche，來自希臘語 sun 和 ekdexesthai，即「和」和「接收」）是一種用區域性代表整體或用整體代表區域性的修辭手法。透過借代，我們給予描述對象一個稱呼。要麼稱呼是區域性，描述對象是整體；要麼稱呼是整體，描述對象是區域性。因此，我們在談論 a very limited number of the people（一小群人）的時候會用 world（世界）這個詞，因為 world（世界）是由一群群的人組成的。

例 9　The world treated him badly.（這個世界待他太不友善。）

　　這句話中，我們用整體代表區域性。不過這種修辭手法最常見的使用形式是以區域性代表整體。

例 10

　　I have twenty head of cattle.（我有 20 頭牛。）

　　One of his hands was assassinated.（他的一個手下被刺殺了。）

　　Twenty sail came into the harbor.（20 張帆離了港。）

　　sail 指的是 20 艘船。

　　This is a fine marble.（這座大理石挺不錯的。）

　　marble 指的是大理石雕像

　　借喻（Metonymy，來自希臘語 meta 和 onyma，即「變化」和「名字」）是一種用名稱來指代與之密切相關的事物的修辭手法。換句話說，用兩個密切相關的事物中的一個來指代另一個。在提到其中一個的名稱時，人們會自然而然地聯想到另一個。因此在我們談到酒鬼的時候，我們會說「He loves the bottle.（他喜歡酒瓶）」。這句話不是說他喜歡酒瓶這個玻璃容器，而是酒瓶裡裝的東西。一般來說，借喻分為三種：

　　1. 為了表達效果。

例 11

　　Gray hairs should be respected.（灰頭髮們應該得到尊重。）

　　「灰頭髮們」指的是年紀大。

第四章
修辭魅力：手法解析與應用技巧

He writes a fine hand.（他寫得一手好字。）

hand 指的是寫字。

2. 不指提及的對象，而是它所代表的事物。

例 12　The pen is mightier than the sword.（筆要比劍更有力。）

意思是文字的力量高於軍事力量。

3. 用容器指代容器裡的內容。

例 13　The house was called to order.（現在正式開庭。）

house 指的是房子裡的人。

感嘆（Exclamation，來自拉丁語 ex 和 clamare，即「出來」和「喊」）這種修辭手法指的是說話人不陳述事實，而是直接發出聲音以表達驚訝或其他情緒。

例 14

當人們聽到悲慘、不幸的故事時不說，It is a sad story.（這是個悲傷的故事。）而是感嘆一句，What a sad story!（這故事太悲傷啦！）

感嘆可以被定義為情感的聲音表達，儘管它也可以用在書面語中來表達情緒。因此，我們可以這樣用文字描述高聳的山：

例 15

Heavens, what a piece of Nature's handiwork! how majestic! how sublime! how awe-inspiring in its colossal impressiveness!

（天哪，這大自然的鬼斧神工！多麼奇絕！多麼壯觀！多麼雄偉壯麗，令人敬畏！）

這種修辭手法更多地被用於詩歌和激昂的演講詞，而非日常對話和寫作。

誇張（Hyperbole，來自希臘語 hyper 和 ballein，即「超過」和「扔」）指的是誇張的陳述，由比實際描述更宏大或更渺小、更好或更壞的表達組成。這種修辭手法的目標是透過誇大事實以加深讀者或聽者的印象。以下是一些例子：

例 16

He was so tall his head touched the clouds.（他高得彷彿頭都能碰到雲。）

He was as thin as a poker.（他瘦得和張紙一樣。）

He was so light that a breath might have blown him away.

（他輕得彷彿一口氣就能把他吹倒。）

大部分人可能都會過度使用這個修辭手法。我們在說話時，或多或少都帶有誇張的成分。有的人則更加過分，誇張成謊言。誇張的使用應該得到控制。在普通的演講和寫作中，我們應該在合理的範圍內、有限度地使用誇張這種修辭手法。

頓呼法（Apostrophe，來自希臘語 apo 和 strephein，即「來自」和「轉」）這種修辭手法，把缺失的當作存在的、把無生命的當作有生命的、把抽象的當作表面的。

例 17

O, illustrious Washington! Father of our Country! Could you visit us now!

（哦，赫赫有名的華盛頓！我們的國父！您現在來看看我們吧！）

My Country tis of thee,（我的祖國，）

第四章
修辭魅力：手法解析與應用技巧

Sweet land of liberty,（美麗的自由之鄉，）

Of thee I sing.（我為您歌唱。）

O! Grave, where is thy Victory, O! Death where is thy sting!

（死啊，你的毒鉤在哪裡？死啊，你得勝的權勢在哪裡？）

這種修辭手法和擬人非常相似。

想像（Vision，來自拉丁語 videre，即「看見」）把過去的或未來的當作現在的、把遙遠的當作附近的。它非常適合用來描述有生命的物體，因為能夠產生一種理想的存在的效果。

例 18

The old warrior looks down from the canvas and tells us to be men worthy of.

（老戰士從帆布上往下看，跟我們說要當真男人。）

這種修辭手法在《聖經》中得到了典型運用。《啟示錄》就是對未來的想像。使用這一修辭手法最多的作家是卡萊爾。

對偶（Antithesis，來自希臘語 anti 和 tithenai，即「反對」和「放置」）建立在對比的基礎上。它將兩個不同的事物放在對立的立場上。

例 19

Ring out the old, ring in the new,（辭舊迎新，）

Ring out the false, ring in the true.（去偽存真。）

Let us be friends in peace, but enemies in war.

（讓我們在和平時代做朋友，戰爭時代做對手。）

以下是一段對蒸汽機的描述，這是一個很好的對偶的例子。

例 20

It can engrave a seal and crush masses of obdurate metal before it; draw out, without breaking, a thread as fine as a gossamer; and lift up a ship of war like a bauble in the air; it can embroider muslin and forge anchors; cut steel into ribands, and impel loaded vessels against the fury of winds and waves.

（它可以刻出印章、壓碎堅固的金屬；劃出不會斷開的、細若遊絲般的線，把戰船像裝飾球一樣舉起來；它既能在棉布上刺繡，也能鍛造船錨；還能切割鋼鐵，迎著狂風巨浪驅動滿載的船舶。）

層進法（Climax，來自希臘語 klimax，意為「梯子」）指的是所有想法和觀念按照後一個比前一個更強烈、更深刻的順序排列直到結尾，最後反過來強調前面所有的想法和觀念。

例 21

He risked truth, he risked honor, he risked fame, he risked all that men hold dear, —— yea, he risked life itself, and for what? —— for a creature who was not worthy to tie his shoe-latchets when he was his better self.

（他賭上真相，賭上榮譽，賭上名聲，他賭上了人們注重的一切 —— 沒錯，他賭上了自己的人生。為了什麼？為了一個在他蒸蒸日上的時候不配幫他繫鞋帶的人。）

警句（Epigram，來自希臘語 epi 和 graphein，即「在……上面」和「寫」），原意是紀念碑上篆刻的銘文，所以後來它被用來表示深刻的表達。現在，警句指的是散文或詩歌中簡短的、帶有矛盾意義的句子。

第四章
修辭魅力：手法解析與應用技巧

例 22

Conspicuous for his absence.（他的缺席令人關注。）

Beauty when unadorned is most adorned.

（未經修飾的美就是對美最好的修飾。）

He was too foolish to commit folly.（他太笨了，連蠢事也做不出來。）

He was so wealthy that he could not spare the money.（他過於富有，以致於他沒有閒錢。）

反問（Interrogation，來自拉丁語 interrogatio，即「問題」）這種修辭手法藉疑問句來傳達確定資訊。

例 23

Does God not show justice to all?（上帝沒有對所有人展示公平嗎？）

Is he not doing right in his course?（在他的課程中他沒有做對嗎？）

What can a man do under the circumstances?

（一個人在這種情況下還能做什麼呢？）

諷刺（Irony，來自希臘語 eironcia，即「虛偽」）這一表達形式是指使用與原本表達意圖相反的詞。要想達到諷刺的效果，虛假、荒謬的程度要足夠明顯才行。

例 24

Benedict Arnold was an honorable man.

（班奈狄克‧阿諾德是個高尚的人。）

段落

A Judas Iscariot never betrays a friend.

（加略人猶大永遠不會背叛朋友。）

You can always depend upon the word of a liar.

（你總是可以相信騙子的話。）

諷刺（irony）是 ridicule、derision、mockery、satire 和 sarcasm[19] 的同父同母的兄弟。ridicule 暗示帶有蔑視的嘲笑；derision 指的是帶有敵意的嘲諷；mockery 是侮辱性的諷刺；satire 是機智詼諧的反諷；sarcaasm 是挖苦的諷刺；而 irony 則是偽裝的諷刺。

除此之外，還有許多其他的修辭手法。它們都為語言帶來了樂趣，讓語言傳達出不同於原本日常對話和寫作的意思。使用修辭手法的黃金準則就是讓它們與演講和寫作的特點和目的和諧共處。

---

[19] 這些都是諷刺的近義詞。

第四章
修辭魅力：手法解析與應用技巧

第五章
標點符號指南：用法解析與規範

　　林德利‧默里[20]和古德‧布朗[21]曾為標點符號立下了鐵則，但其中的大部分早已被打破，甚至被棄之不用。這些規則極其死板、嚴苛，過於關注細枝末節，對於日常寫作來說多少有些不實用。自那以後，措辭、文體和表達的方式發生了極大的變化。以前那些深奧複雜、意義隱晦的句子逐漸變得簡單明瞭，冗長拖遝的片語、模稜兩可的表達越來越少，寫作的目標向簡潔、短暫、清晰轉移。因此，標點符號得到了極大的簡化。在某種程度上，它和其他任何固定的規則一樣體現了作者的品味和判斷力。儘管如此，仍然有一些相關的使用規範不能取消，它們的原則必須得到嚴格的遵守。

　　標點符號的主要目的，是標記出寫作中按語法層面和意思層面劃分的意群，而不是標記出實際說話時的每個停頓。很多時候，一段話中使用的標點與一段文字中使用的標點不同。除此之外，一些標點符號的作用是替表達加上修辭效果。

　　主要的標點符號有：

逗號（The Comma）［,］

分號（The Semicolon）［;］

---

[20] 林德利‧默里（Lindley Murray），美國作家和語法學家。
[21] 古德‧布朗（Goold Brown），美國語法學家。

第五章
標點符號指南：用法解析與規範

冒號（The Colon）[:]

句號（The Period）[.]

問號（The Interrogation）[?]

感嘆號（The Exclamation）[!]

破折號（The Dash）[——]

括號（The Parenthesis）[()]

引號（The Quotation）[""]

還有一些表達其他關係的標點符號。但確切來說，以上標點符號被納入了模印體系中，其他一些就不知去向了。在以上標點中，前四個屬於語法標點，後五個屬於修辭標點。

逗號（The Comma）：逗號的作用是，在任何需要標點的地方將文字劃分開來，在不需要的地方則盡可能省略。它被用來標記句子能劃分的最小部分。

1. 下面是一系列單字或片語被逗號分隔開的例子。

例 1

Lying, trickery, chicanery, perjury, were natural to him.

（對他而言，撒謊、耍花招、哄騙、做偽證都再自然不過了。）

The brave, daring, faithful soldier died facing the foe.

（勇敢、無畏、忠誠的士兵面朝敵人死去了。）

如果單字或片語成對，則以一對為單位劃分。

例 2

Rich and poor, learned and unlearned, black and white, Christian and Jew, Mohammedan and Buddhist must pass through the same gate.

（無論富貴還是貧窮、接受了教育還是沒接受教育、黑人還是白人、基督徒還是猶太人、穆罕默德還是佛教徒，都要走過同一扇門。）

2. 短暫的引文前需使用逗號。

例 3

It was Patrick Henry who said, "Give me liberty or give me death."

（派翠克‧亨利說過：「要麼給我自由，要麼賜我死亡。」）

3. 當句子的主語是分句或很長的片語時，在其結尾處需使用逗號。

例 4

That he has no reverence for the God I love, proves his insincerity.

（他對我敬愛的上帝毫無崇敬之情，這證明了他沒有誠意。）

Simulated piety, with a black coat and a sanctimonious look, does not proclaim a Christian.

（穿上黑色大衣，做出聖潔的神情，模仿虔誠的行為也不能使你成為一名基督徒。）

4. 插入語的前後均需使用逗號。

例 5

The old man, as a general rule, takes a morning walk.

（老人，按照慣例，每天清晨會散步。）

5. 同位語的前後均需使用逗號。

第五章
標點符號指南：用法解析與規範

例 6

McKinley, the President, was assassinated.

（麥金利，那個美國總統，被暗殺了。）

6. 非限定性的關係從句需使用逗號。

例 7

The book, which is the simplest, is often the most profound.

（最簡單的書，往往最深刻。）

7. 在連續出現謂語動詞的並列句中，每個小句子結尾處需使用逗號。

例 8

Electricity lights our dwellings and streets, pulls cars, trains, drives the engines of our mills and factories.

（電點亮我們的房屋和街道，推動汽車和火車，驅動鋼鐵廠和工廠的引擎。）

8. 當動詞被省略，逗號代替動詞出現在句中。

例 9　Lincoln was a great statesman; Grant, a great soldier.

（林肯是一名偉大的政治家；而格蘭特，一名偉大的軍人。）

9. 稱呼的對象的後面需使用逗號。

例 10　John, you are a good man.（約翰，你是個好人。）

10. 在數字的書寫中，每逢三位數需用逗號隔開。

例 11

Mountains 25,000 feet high（25,000 英呎高的山）

1,000,000 dollars（1,000,000 美元）

與逗號相比，**分號**（The Semicolon）的劃分作用稍小。它常用作複合句的劃分，很多時候用於對比。

1. 分號用於劃分同一主語的不同分句。

例 12

Gladstone was great as a statesman; he was sublime as a man.

（作為一個政治家，格萊斯頓是偉大的；作為一個人，他是崇高的。）

2. 分號用於劃分第一部分的主語與第二部分的主語不同的複合句。

例 13

The power of England relies upon the wisdom of her statesmen; the power of America upon the strength of her army and navy.

（英格蘭的國力依靠於她的政治家的智慧；美國的國力則依靠於她的軍事力量。）

3. 分號用於 after、such as、namely、as、e.g.、vid.、i.e. 等詞後，介紹更多細節和進行說明的單字和縮略詞前。

例 14

He had three defects; namely, carelessness, lack of concentration and obstinacy in his ideas.

（他有三個缺點，即：粗心、注意力不集中，還有固執。）

第五章
標點符號指南：用法解析與規範

An island is a portion of land entirely surrounded by water; as Cuba.

（島嶼是指四面環水的一塊陸地，比如古巴。）

The names of cities should always commence with a capital letter; e.g., New York, Paris.

（城市的名稱應以大寫字母開頭，比如：New York、Paris。）

The boy was proficient in one branch; viz., Mathematics.

（男孩有一門科目非常擅長，那就是：數學。）

No man is perfect; i.e., free from all blemish.

（人無完人。也就是說，沒有人完美無瑕。）

除了常規用法外，冒號（The Colon）基本過時了。

1. 冒號一般用於提起引文的句子的末端。

例 15

The cheers having subsided, Mr. Bryan spoke as follows:

（歡呼聲逐漸平息，布賴恩先生進行了如下發言：）

2. 冒號被用於寫作對象的解釋說明前。

例 16　This is the meaning of the term:（這是該詞的釋義：）

3. 冒號被用於正式的引文前。

例 17

The great orator made this funny remark:

（這位大演說家做出了如下有趣的評價：）

4. 當書名的二級標題或副標題與一級標題或正標題同位，且連接詞 or 被省略時，常用冒號進行劃分。

例 18　Acoustics: the Science of Sound.（聲學：聲音的學科。）

5. 冒號用於信頭稱呼的後面。

例 19

Sir:（先生：）　　My dear Sir:（我親愛的先生：）

Gentlemen:（先生們：）　　Dear Mr. Jones:（親愛的瓊斯先生：）

……

在這種情況下，冒號後經常跟著破折號。

6. 有時冒號用於介紹一系列內容的細節。

例 20

The boy's excuses for being late were: firstly, he did not know the time, secondly, he was sent on an errand, thirdly, he tripped on a rock and fell by the wayside.

（這個男孩為遲到而找的藉口有：首先，他不知道時間；其次，他被派去做事；再次，他被石頭絆倒在路邊。）

句號 (The Period) 是標點符號中最簡明的。它被用於非疑問句和非驚嘆句的句尾。

1. 句號用於一個完整的句子的結尾。

例 21

Birds fly.（鳥兒會飛。）　　Man is mortal.（人不能永生。）

第五章
標點符號指南：用法解析與規範

Plants grow.（植物會長大。）

2. 句號用於縮略詞中。在每個縮略的單字的結尾處均需使用句號。

例 22

Rt. Rev. T. C. Alexander

D.D.

L.L.D

3. 在書的標題頁，句號分別用於書名、作者名、出版社名後。

例 23

American Trails.（美國田徑協會）

By Theodore Roosevelt.（狄奧多‧羅斯福著）

New York. Scribner Company.（紐約斯克里布納出版社）

問號（The Interrogation）用於問句。

1. 任何要求回答，甚至不要求回答的問題後面都應使用問號。

例 24 Who has not heard of Napoleon?（誰沒有聽說過拿破崙？）

2. 在一系列互相關聯的問題中，問號應用於系列問題的結尾處。

例 25

Where now are the playthings and friends of my boyhood; the laughing boys; the winsome girls; the fond neighbors whom I loved?

（我童年時期的玩伴和玩具如今在哪裡，那些愛笑的男孩、可愛的女孩，還有我喜歡的溫柔的鄰居？）

3. 問號常用作插入語，以表示疑問。

例 26

In 1893 (?) Gladstone became converted to Home Rule for Ireland.

〔在1893（？）年格拉斯頓提出要讓愛爾蘭自治。〕

應盡量少使用感嘆號（The Exclamation），尤其是在散文中。它的主要用途是表達某種情緒。

1. 感嘆號常與感嘆語以及用作感嘆語的分句一同出現：

例 27

Alas! I am forsaken.（唉！我被拋棄了。）

What a lovely landscape!（多美的景色啊！）

2. 強烈的情感表達需要使用感嘆號。

例 28

Charge, Chester, charge! On, Stanley, on!

（衝啊，查斯特，衝！上啊，史坦利，上！）

3. 當情感過於強烈時，可使用雙重感嘆號。

例 29

Assist him!! I would rather assist Satan!!（要我幫他！！那我寧願去幫撒旦！！）

破折號（The Dash）的使用範圍僅限於文章的突然中斷處。在所有標點符號中，破折號是被誤用最多的。

1. 破折號被用於突如其來的句式結構或情感的轉折處。

第五章
標點符號指南：用法解析與規範

例 30

The Heroes of the Civil War, —— how we cherish them.

（內戰英雄 —— 我們多麼珍視他們。）

He was a fine fellow —— in his own opinion.

（他是個不錯的人 —— 在他自己看來。）

2. 當一個單字或表達被重複以達到演說效果時，破折號用於它們的重複前。

例 31

Shakespeare was the greatest of all poets —— Shakespeare, the intellectual ocean whose waves washed the continents of all thought.

（莎士比亞是最偉大的詩人 —— 莎士比亞，他智慧的浪潮刷洗著全人類的思想。）

3. 破折號可用於暗示句子的結論。

例 32　He is an excellent man but ——　（他是個優秀的人，但 ——）

4. 破折號可用於暗示意料之外的發展或者不可預見的結果。

例 33

He delved deep into the bowels of the earth and found instead of the hidden treasure —— a button.

（他深入地球內臟，但卻沒有找到隱藏的寶藏，找到的是 —— 一顆鈕扣。）

5. 破折號可用來指省略的字母或數字。

例 34

J —— n J —— s 指的是 John Jones

1908 —— 9 指的是 1908 和 1909

Matthew VII: 5 —— 8 指的是 5、6、7 和 8

6. 當 namely, that is, to wit 等詞被省略時，此時可用破折號代替。

例 35

He excelled in three branches —— arithmetic, algebra, and geometry.

（他擅長三個分科 —— 算術、代數和幾何。）

7. 當作者不想寫某個詞的全拼時，可用破折號代替中間省略的部分。

例 36　He is somewhat of a r —— l（rascal）.（他有些卑鄙。）

碰到不文雅的詞就可以這樣處理。

8. 引文和引文作者間需用破折號隔開。

例 37

All the world's a stage. —— Shakespeare.（全世界是個舞臺。——莎士比亞）

9. 當問題和回答被放在同一段落時，應使用破折號將他們隔開。

例 38

Are you a good boy? Yes, Sir. —— Do you love study? I do.

（你是個好孩子嗎？是的，先生。—— 你喜歡學習嗎？我喜歡。）

括號（The Parenthesis）是用來將插入語與句子分隔開的。這類插入語解釋了句子成分，但與句子整體的連繫不大，去掉該插入語對句子整體

第五章
標點符號指南：用法解析與規範

並無影響。應盡量少使用括號，因為括號的使用表明句中有不屬於該句的成分。

1. 當一個句子被分隔開，造成分隔的單字應由括號標記出來。

例 39

We cannot believe a liar (and Jones is one), even when he speaks the truth.

我們無法相信一個騙子（瓊斯就是個騙子），就算他在說實話也不相信。

2. 在演講報告中，觀眾或贊同或反對的反應應當作插入語由括號標記出來。

例 40

The masses must not submit to the tyranny of the classes (hear, hear), we must show the trust magnates (groans), that they cannot ride rough-shod over our dearest rights (cheers).

人民大眾不能屈服於階級的暴政（沒錯，沒錯），我們必須讓權貴知道（呻吟）他們不能犧牲我們最重要的權利（歡呼）。

If the gentleman from Ohio (Mr. Brown), will not be our spokesman, we must select another. (A voice, —— Get Robinson).

如果這位來自俄亥俄的先生（布朗先生）不能當我們的發言人，那我們就必須另選他人。（一個聲音說道 —— 選羅賓遜）。

當括號的插入處沒有逗號時，括號前後不應使用其他任何標點。當插入處應有逗號時，如果括號裡的內容與整個句子有連繫，則應在括號前加上逗號；如果括號裡的內容僅與一個單字或一個短分句有連繫，括號前不應使用任何標點，但在括號結束後應加上逗號。

引號（The Quotation）的作用是表明引號內的內容是引用的。

1. 直接引用的內容，前後應加上引號。

例 41

Abraham Lincoln said, —— "I shall make this land too hot for the feet of slaves."（亞伯拉罕·林肯說過 ——「我要讓這片土地上不再有奴隸。」）

2. 當引用的內容裡包含了其他引用內容時，該引用內容需用單引號標出。

例 42

Franklin said, "Most men come to believe 'honesty is the best policy.'"

（富蘭克林說過：「大多數人開始相信『誠信是最好的方法』。」）

3. 當引用內容持續了多個段落時，每一段段首皆應使用引號。
4. 正式引用書、電影和報紙的標題時需使用引號。
5. 一般來說輪船的名字應用雙引號標註，雖然很少出現此種情況。

撇號（The Apostrophe）應歸入逗號，而不是引號或雙逗號。Apostrophe 一詞源於希臘語，意指轉移。省略或轉移的字母通常是 e。在詩歌和日常對話中，撇號指音節的省略。

例 43

I've = I have

thou'rt = thou art

第五章
標點符號指南：用法解析與規範

you'll = you will

……

有時有必要透過省略單字內的部分字母實現該詞的縮略形式。在這種情況下，撇號用來代替省略的字母。

例 44 cont'd = continued.

當年分在原文中被熟知或一系列年分數字不斷重複時，撇號還用於代替年分裡省略掉的數字，比如：

例 45 The Spirit of '76（76 年的精神）

I served in the army during the years 1895, '96, '97, '98 and '99.

（我在 1895、96、97、98 和 99 年服過兵役。）

撇號的主要作用是用來表示所有格。無論是不是專有名詞，所有名詞單數和不以 s 結尾的名詞複數，加上撇號和 s 就成了所有格。唯一的例外是，在詩歌中，為保證格律額外的 s 可能被省略掉，比如在《聖經》中有片語 for goodness' sake（我的天哪）、for conscience' sake（為了問心無愧）、for Jesus' sake（我的天哪）等等。人們習慣性省略 s，到現在這些片語已成為慣用語。所有以 s 結尾的名詞複數加上撇號就成了所有格，比如 boys'、horses'。人稱代詞的所有格則不可以使用撇號，比如 ours、yours、hers、theirs。

大寫字母

大寫字母（Capital letters）的作用是強調或把注意力吸引到一些詞上，以使讀者將它們和上下文區分開來。在手稿中，它們或小或大，且以下劃線標明。

兩條線指小號大寫字母（Small Capitals），三條線指大寫字母（Capitals）。

一些作家，尤其是卡萊爾，過度使用大寫字母導致其濫用。大寫字母的使用範圍僅限下面列出的情況。

1. 所有句子的第一個詞，實際上無論是何種寫作形式，第一個詞都應以大寫字母開頭。

例 46

Time flies.（時光飛逝。）　　My dear friend.（我親愛的朋友。）

2. 所有直接引用的內容都應以大寫字母開頭。

例 47

Dewey said, —— "Fire, when you're ready, Gridley!"

（杜威說：「準備好了就開火，格里德利！」）

3. 所有直接提出的問題都應以大寫字母開頭。

例 48　Let me ask you: "How old are you?"（讓我來問問你：「你多大了？」）

4. 詩歌的每一行都應以大寫字母開頭。

例 49

Breathes there a man with soul so dead.（有個人活著，但他的靈魂已經死了。）

5. 所有帶編號的從句都應以大寫字母開頭。

第五章
標點符號指南：用法解析與規範

例 50

The witness asserts:（目擊者斷言：）

(1)That he saw the man attacked;（他看到了受害者；）

(2)That he saw him fall;（他看到受害者摔倒；）

(3)That he saw his assailant flee.（他看到攻擊者逃逸。）

6. 短文和章節的標題應全部使用大寫字母。

例 51　CHAPTER VIII —— RULES FOR USE OF CAPITALS.

7. 書名中，名詞、代詞、形容詞和副詞都應以大寫字母開頭。

例 52　Johnson's Lives of the Poets（強生的《英國詩人傳》）

8. 羅馬數字均用大寫字母表示。

例 53　I II III V X L C D M —— 1，2，3，5，10，50，100，500，1,000。

9. 專有名詞以大寫字母開頭。

例 54

Jones（瓊斯）、Johnson（強生）、Caesar（凱薩）、Mark Antony（馬克·安東尼）、England（英格蘭）、Pacific（太平洋）、Christmas（聖誕節）。

諸如 river（河流）、sea（海洋）、mountain（山）一類的詞，在日常使用中不作專有名詞，因此無須以大寫字母開頭。但當這類名詞和形容詞或其他修飾成分一同代表特定的對象時，它們就變成了專有名詞。

例 55

Mississippi River（密西西比河）、North Sea（北海）、Alleghany Mountains（阿勒格尼山脈）等等。

大寫字母

　　同樣，對於四個重要的方向 north（北）、south（南）、east（東）和 west（西），當它們用來指代一個國家內的各個地區時，應該以大寫字母開頭。

例 56　The North fought against the South.（南方反抗北方。）

　　當專有名詞和其他詞形成複合詞時，如果該詞在專有名詞之前，則應以大寫字母開頭；如果該詞在專有名詞之後，則應在連字元後以小寫字母開頭。

例 57　Post-homeric（後荷馬時代）、Sunday-school（週日學校）。

　　10. 專有名詞的衍生詞應以大寫字母開頭。

例 58

　　American（美國的）、Irish（愛爾蘭的）、Christian（基督教的）、Americanize（使美國化）、Christianize（使基督化）。政治黨派、宗教教派和思想流派的名稱，首字母均應大寫。

例 59

　　Republican（共和黨人士）、Democrat（民主主義者）、Whig（輝格黨）、Catholic（天主教）、Presbyterian（長老會）、Rationalists（理性主義者）、Free Thinkers（自由思想者）。

　　11. 可敬的國家及政府職位的名稱應以大寫字母開頭。

例 60

　　President（總統）、Chairman（主席）、Governor（州長）、Alderman（高級市政官）。

　　12. 高等教育學校的學位名稱的縮寫均使用大寫字母。

第五章
標點符號指南：用法解析與規範

例 61

LL.D.（法學博士）、M.A.（文學碩士）、B.S.（理學學士）等等。同樣，授予高等教育學位的機構的名稱，首字母均應大寫。比如 Harvard University（哈佛大學）、Manhattan College（曼哈頓學院）……

13. 如果表關係的詞如 father（父親）、mother（母親）、brother（兄弟）、sister（姐妹）、uncle（叔叔）、aunt（嬸嬸）等在專有名詞前，那麼它們的首字母均應大寫。

例 62

Father Abraham（亞伯拉罕神父）、Mother Eddy（母親艾迪）、Brother John（兄弟約翰）、Sister Jane（姐妹珍妮）、Uncle Jacob（叔叔雅各）、Aunt Eliza（嬸嬸依萊扎）。

當 Father 被用來指早期基督徒作家時，應以大寫字母開頭。

例 63

Augustine was one of the learned Fathers of the Church.

（奧古斯丁是教堂裡最有學識的神父之一。）

14. 用來稱呼上帝的詞，首字母均應大寫。

例 64

God（上帝）、Lord（主）、Creator（造物主）、Providence（上蒼）、Almighty（全能的上帝）、The Deity（神）、Heavenly Father（天父）、Holy One（聖者）。

同樣，為表示尊敬，用來稱呼救世主的詞，首字母均應大寫。

比如 Jesus Christ（耶穌基督）、Son of God（上帝之子）、Man of Galilee（加利利人）、The Crucified（被釘在十字架上的人）、The Anointed One（受膏者），以及《聖經》角色的名稱，如 Lily of Israel（以色列的百合花）、Rose of Sharon（沙崙的玫瑰花）、Comfortress of the Afflicted（憂苦之慰）、Help of Christians（進教之佑）、Prince of the Apostles（使徒之王）、Star of the Sea（海洋之星）等。

上帝和耶穌的指代詞也應以大寫字母開頭。

比如 His work（上帝的造詣）、The work of Him（上帝的造詣）等。

15. 指代《聖經》或其中任何一部分的表達，首字母均應大寫。

例 65

Holy Writ（聖經）、The Sacred Book（神聖的書）、Holy Book（聖書）、God's Word（上帝的話語）、Old Testament（舊約）、New Testament（新約）、Gospel of St. Matthew（聖馬太福音）、Seven Penitential Psalms（七個悔罪詩篇）。

16. 《聖經》中衍生出來的或涉及《聖經》人物的表達，首字母均應大寫。

例 66

Water of Life（生命之水）、Hope of Men、Help of Christians（進教之佑）、Scourge of Nations（國家災難）。

17. 用來稱呼惡者的詞，首字母均應大寫。

例 67

Beelzebub（魔王）、Prince of Darkness（黑暗之子）、Satan（撒旦）、King of Hell（冥王）、Devil（魔鬼）、Incarnate Fiend（混世魔王）、

第五章
標點符號指南：用法解析與規範

Tempter of Men（誘惑者）、Father of Lies（謊言之父）、Hater of Good（憤世嫉俗者）。

18. 有著特殊意義的詞，尤其是那些著名歷史事件的名稱，首字母均應大寫。

例 68

The Revolution（革命）、The Civil War（內戰）、The Middle Ages（中世紀）、The Age of Iron（鐵器時代）等等。

19. 指代歷史上著名的民族事件的術語，首字母均應大寫。

例 69

The Flood（大洪水[22]）、Magna Charta（大憲章）、Declaration of Independence（獨立宣言）。

20. 一週中的日子、一年中的月分和季節的名稱應以大寫字母開頭。

例 70

Monday（週一）、March（三月）、Autumn（秋天）。

21. I 作代詞時和 O 作嘆詞時均需大寫。實際上，所有被喊出口的嘆詞均應以大寫字母開頭。

例 71

Alas! he is gone.（哎呀！他走了。）

Ah! I pitied him.（啊！我同情他。）

22. 所有 noms-de-guerre，即假名，以及榮譽稱號的首字母均應大寫。

---

[22] 《創世記》中的滅世洪水。

大寫字母

例 72

The Wizard of the North（北方大魔法師）[23]、Paul Pry（保羅·普瑞，打破砂鍋問到底的人）、The Northern Gael（北方蓋爾人）、Sandy Sanderson、Poor Robin（窮羅賓）[24]……

23. 擬人化時，也就是無生命的物體被賦予生命和動作時，擬人化的名詞或對象需以大寫字母開頭。

例 73

The starry Night shook the dews from her wings.

（繁星閃爍的夜晚搖去了她翅膀上的露珠。）

Mild-eyed Day appeared,（眼神溫和的白天降臨了，）

The Oak said to the Beech ── "I am stronger than you."

（橡木對山毛櫸木說道 ──「我比你強壯」。）

---

[23] 約翰·亨利·安德森（1814～1874），是蘇格蘭職業魔術師。安德森是將魔術藝術從街頭表演帶到劇院的開拓者，被譽為「北方大魔法師」。
[24] 《窮羅賓》(Poor Robin) 是 17 世紀和 18 世紀的英國諷刺年鑑系列圖書，從 1663 年開始作為《窮羅賓年鑑》(Poor Robin's Almanack) 出版。後來，以「窮羅賓」為筆名的其他類似著作在美國出版，並一直持續到 19 世紀。

第五章
標點符號指南:用法解析與規範

第六章
書信的技巧：格式與筆記要領

很多人認為書信（letter-writing）是一個非常簡單、容易掌握的寫作類型。但恰恰相反，書信是最難的寫作形式之一，需要很多耐心和練習來掌握其細節技巧。實際上，英語語言裡鮮有優秀的書信作家。書信構成了演講的直接形式，並且可被稱作遠距離談話。根據形形色色的主題、寫信人、寫信時的情緒、不同社會階層的收信人，書信的格式千變萬化。因此沒有固定規範來限制信的長度、風格和主題，僅在書信範圍和目的方面有大致的參考。除此之外，控告書的格式告訴了我們哪些習慣和先例應被准許。

所有對書面語有了解的人都應該知道寫書信的原則，因為幾乎每個人都會有需要聯絡遠方的朋友或熟人的時候。然而，相對來說很少人會選擇其他的寫作形式來實現這一目的。

在以前，如果一個文盲需要聯絡親朋好友，他（她）會找一名在學校工作的教師代筆。但這麼做有一個缺陷，那就是，所有的祕密都必須經他人之筆才能到達收信人手中，而祕密時常會遭到洩漏。

現今，很少有教育程度低到不會讀書寫字的人。無論他（她）的教育程度如何，自己寫信都比找人幫忙寫來得強。就算一封信寫成這樣：

第六章
書信的技巧：格式與筆記要領

例 1

deer fren, i lift up my pen to let ye no that i hove been sik for the past 3 weeks, hopping this will findye the same.

（親愛的朋友，我寫這封信是想告訴你，我已經生病三週了，希望你啟信安康。）

在了解寫信人的心意，以及他（她）盡自己最大努力不依靠他人親自動手的事實後，拼寫和結構上的錯誤也變得可以原諒了。

任何書信的種類、內容和口吻都取決於寫信的場合、寫信人和收信人的身分。隨意還是正式、樸實還是華麗、輕鬆還是嚴肅、開心還是沉重、宣洩情感還是就事論事，都取決於這三個條件。

寫信最首要、最重要的要求是自然和簡單。一封信不應帶給讀者緊張的閱讀感，而應是寫信人思想的自然傾瀉。我們不喜歡聊天時刻板呆滯的人，同樣，讀者也不喜歡刻板呆滯的信，如果一封信的口吻如聊天般輕鬆的話，那麼它立刻就能吸引讀者的注意力。

優秀的書信作者寫出的信也是優秀的，因為這樣的信自然地表達了作者的想法。他（她）無須思考措辭，詞彙和他（她）的想法一同噴湧而出。當你寫信給你的朋友約翰·布朗告訴他你的週日過得如何時，你不會去刻意搜尋字眼，或專門學習固定短語來討好或驚豔布朗。你只會說你如何度過那一天、在哪裡、和誰在一起以及當天發生了什麼，就像他在你面前聽你說話一樣。這樣一來，你的信就很自然，而正是這樣的信才符合書信往來的精神。

書信種類繁多，每種書信的稱呼和構成都不同。然而，無論哪種書信都需遵循「自然」這一原則，也就是說，寫信人絕不應在信中塑造虛偽的形象。一名受教育水準有限的普通街頭勞工將自己偽裝成博學多才

大寫字母

的大學教授是愚蠢且徒勞的行為。他可能有一顆聰明的腦袋，但絕不像大學教授那樣接受了良好的教育。除此之外，他也缺少社會帶給大學教授的光鮮外在。在寫信時，普通勞工需謹記的是，無論這封信是寫給誰的，人們對此的期望就是一封出自勞工的信。人們也不會試圖從信中尋找查斯特菲爾德勳爵[25]或格萊斯頓[26]的語法結構或遣詞造句的風格。寫信人還應時刻牢記的是這封信的寫作對象。如果這封信是寫給大主教或一些教堂高級聖職人員、國家高級官員的話，信中的用語顯然不應該和他寫給密友約翰·布朗的用語相同，就像他不能對大主教用「Dear John」這類表達一樣，他也不能用稱呼朋友和日常熟人的詞來稱呼大主教。不過，寫信給大主教也並不需要專門去鑽研，這與寫信給一個普通人沒有太大差別，所有的人需要知道的就是正確稱呼的格式以及如何最大限度地使用他們有限的詞彙量。以下是這樣一封信的範本：

例2

17 Second Avenue, New York City.

January 1st, 1910.

Most Rev. P. A. Jordan, Archbishop of New York.

Most Rev. and dear Sir:

While sweeping the crossing at Fifth Avenue and 50th street on last Wednesday morning, I found the enclosed Fifty Dollar Bill, which I am sending to you in the hope that it may be restored to the rightful owner.

I beg you will acknowledge receipt and should the owner be found I trust you will notify me, so that I may claim some reward for my honesty.

---

[25]　查斯特菲爾德勳爵（Chester field），英國著名政治家、外交家及哲學家。
[26]　威廉·尤爾特·格萊斯頓（William Ewart Gladstone），英國政治家。

第六章
書信的技巧：格式與筆記要領

I am, Most Rev. and dear Sir,

Very respectfully yours,

Thomas Jones.

請看這封信的簡潔程度。瓊斯並未向大主教建議如何尋找失主，因為他知道大主教會採取怎樣的措施，也就是在布道壇上宣布這件事。如果瓊斯能靠自己找到失主的話，他也就不會求助於大主教了。

這封信確實和他寫給布朗的信不一樣。儘管如此，這封信簡潔，沒有過於親暱，是一份樸實的宣告。並且，它和加上了修辭以及有著「充滿學識的、驚人的用詞」的信一樣，都能表達寫信人的想法和立場。

書信可以分為以下種類：友人和熟人之間的信件、商業關係的信函、公職人員的官方信、教師的教誨信以及那些講述每日要聞的信，即新聞簡報。

友人之間的信件（Letters of friendship）是最常見的信件種類，它們的風格和格式取決於寫信人和收信人之間的關係和親密程度。寫信給親朋好友時，人們在開頭和結尾可能都會用到對話中最常用的稱呼，無論這個稱呼是親暱的還是戲謔的。然而，人們還是應該保證自己的語言在得體和規範的領域內。信件和對話不同的是，說出的話語只會進入談話對象的耳朵，而寫下來的詞句則有可能被他人看到。因此，最好永遠不要寫任何他人看到會有損你形象的內容。你可以在信中用快樂的、玩笑般的、詼諧的語言傾訴你的感受，但千萬不要使用低階的語言，尤其不要使用任何有傷風化的。

從信件涉及的利益來考慮的話，商務信函（Business letters）無疑是最重要的。商業人士及企業的形象常常取決於他們與合作方的商務通訊。很多情況下，相比發展貿易和商業利益、爭取客戶，信函能讓人們自願地轉向對他人有利的情形。模稜兩可、敷衍了事的語言是成功路上的絆腳石。商務信函應該做到清晰簡潔、一語中的。除此之外，最重要的還是誠信，不要給對方錯誤的印象，或者讓對方寄希望於無法實現的獎勵。和商務活動一樣，在商務信函中誠信永遠是最好的原則。

官方信件（Official letters）幾乎都是正式的。它們應該做到清晰簡潔、語氣莊重，這樣能讓人們對國家法律和國家機構更尊重。

用來教導他人的信件（Letters designed to teach）和教誨信（didactic letters）屬於同一類書信。它們不過是以信件為載體的文學，一些大作家透過這種形式更好地強調他們的思想和觀念。這一寫作形式的最有名的例子就是查斯特菲爾德勳爵寫給兒子的禮節方面的書，這本書是以一系列書信的形式構成的。

新聞簡報（News letters）的作用是講述世界各地見聞、報導報社接收到的各類儀式和活動資訊。我們時代的一些大作家就是新聞工作者，他們的文筆流暢易讀、詼諧幽默，能讓讀者屏氣凝神，從頭讀到尾。

一封書信的主要部分為：

1. 信頭（the heading or introduction）；

2. 正文（the body or substance of the letter）；

3. 結尾（the subscription or closing expression）和署名（signature）；

4. 信封上的地址（the address or direction on the envelope）。

對於書信正文來說，沒有固定的格式或規範要遵守，因為這取決於書信的性質以及寫信人和收信人之間的關係。

其他三個部分則有按照習俗要遵守的特定的規範，所有人都應該熟悉並了解這些規範。

第六章
書信的技巧：格式與筆記要領

● 開頭

開頭（Heading）包含三部分，即地名、寫作日期和收信人（們）的稱呼。

例 3

73 New Street, Newark, N. J.,

February 1st, 1910.

Messrs Ginn and Co., New York

Gentlemen:

地名絕不能省略。如果地址在城市裡，那麼一定要寫上街道和號碼，除非城市非常大，地址又很顯眼，不會讓人把該地址和其他同名或名稱相似的地址弄混。再就是應該加上州名的縮寫，比如上例中的 Newark, N.J.（紐澤西州紐華克市），在俄亥俄州也有一個 Newark（紐華克市）。正是因為沒有遵守這一規範，很多書信不知去向。所有書信，尤其是商務信函中，必須寫上日期。在商務信函中日期絕不能寫在最下方，但是在寫給朋友的信裡是可以這麼做的。收信人（們）的稱呼根據通訊者間的關係而變化。根據不同的親密程度，寫給朋友的信可以以很多種方式展開。

例 4

My dear Wife:（親愛的妻子：）　　My dear Husband:（親愛的丈夫：）

My dear Friend:（親愛的朋友：）　My darling Mother:（親愛的媽媽：）

My dearest Love:（摯愛的愛人：）　Dear Aunt:（親愛的姑姑：）

Dear Uncle:（親愛的叔叔：）　　Dear George:（親愛的喬治：）

……

在不算親密的關係中，以下稱呼可能被用於信頭：

例 5

Dear Sir:（親愛的先生：）　　My dear Sir:（我親愛的先生：）

Dear Mr. Smith:（親愛的史密斯先生：）　　Dear Madam:（親愛的女士：）

……

對於有著神學博士學位的男性神職人員，應如下稱呼他們：

例 6

Rev. Alban Johnson, D. D.

My dear Sir: or Rev. and dear Sir: or more familiarly

Dear Dr. Johnson:

尊敬的神學博士奧爾本・強生：

我親愛的先生：或者尊敬的親愛的先生：或者更隨意點

親愛的強生博士：

羅馬的主教和英國聖公會（英國國教）的主教的尊稱為 Right Reverend（尊敬的）。

例 7

The Rt. Rev., the Bishop of Long Island. Or

The Rt. Rev. Frederick Burgess, Bishop of Long Island.

Rt. Rev. and dear Sir:

第六章
書信的技巧：格式與筆記要領

尊敬的長島主教或

尊敬的長島主教弗雷德里克・伯吉斯

尊敬的親愛的先生：

羅馬教會的大主教的尊稱為 Most Reverend（最尊敬的大主教大人），紅衣大主教的尊稱為 Eminence（最可敬的樞機）。

例 8

The Most Rev. Archbishop Katzer.

　　Most Rev. and dear Sir:

最尊敬的卡澤爾主教

　　最尊敬的親愛的先生：

His Eminence, James Cardinal Gibbons, Archbishop of Baltimore.

　　May it please your Eminence:

最可敬的樞機、巴德摩爾的紅衣大主教詹姆斯・吉本斯

　　最可敬的樞機，請允許我：

州長或地方行政長官以及美國總統的尊稱為 Excellency（閣下）。然而，更多時候人們用 Honorable（尊敬的）來稱呼州長或地方行政長官：

例 9

His Excellency, William Howard Taft,

　　President of the United States.

Sir:

威廉・霍華德・塔夫脫，閣下，

美國總統,

先生:

His Excellency, Charles Evans Hughes,

    Governor of the State of New York.

Sir:

查爾斯・伊萬斯・休斯,閣下,

    紐約州州長,

先生:

Honorable Franklin Fort,

    Governor of New Jersey.

Sir:

尊敬的富蘭克林・福特

    紐澤西州州長,

先生:

對於陸軍和海軍軍官,通常用 Sir(先生)來稱呼他們。他們的軍銜和駐紮地應在信頭標示清楚。

例 10

General Joseph Thompson,

    Commanding the Seventh Infantry.

Sir:

約瑟夫・湯普森將軍,

    第七步兵團統領,

第六章
書信的技巧：格式與筆記要領

先生：

Rear Admiral Robert Atkinson,

    Commanding the Atlantic Squadron.

Sir:

海軍少將羅伯特・阿特金森，

    大西洋海軍中隊統領，

先生：

公民政府的官員的尊稱為 Honorable（尊敬的），他們應被稱作 Sir（先生）。

例 11

    Hon. Nelson Duncan,

        Senator from Ohio.

    Sir:

尊敬的尼爾森・鄧肯，

    俄亥俄州參議員，

先生：

Hon. Norman Wingfield,

    Secretary of the Treasury.

Sir:

尊敬的諾曼・溫菲爾德，

    財政部大臣，

先生：

Hon. Rupert Gresham,
　　Mayor of New York.
Sir:

尊敬的魯伯特・格雷沙姆,
　　紐約市長,
先生:

大專院校的校長和教授通常被稱為 Sir（先生）或 Dear Sir（親愛的先生）。

例 12

Professor Ferguson Jenks,
　　President of ... University.
Sir: or Dear Sir:

弗格森・詹克斯,
　　……大學校長,
先生／親愛的先生:

社團、協會的會長和商業人士一樣被稱為 Sir（先生）或 Dear Sir（親愛的先生）。

例 13

Mr. Joseph Banks,
　　President of the Night Owls.
Sir: or Dear Sir:

第六章
書信的技巧：格式與筆記要領

約瑟夫‧班克斯先生，

夜貓子協會會長，

先生／親愛的先生：

醫學博士被稱為 Sir:（先生：）、My dear Sir:（我親愛的先生：）、Dear Sir:（親愛的先生：），如果關係較好的話，則稱呼其為 My dear Dr:（我親愛的醫生：）或 Dear Dr:（親愛的醫生：）。

例 14

Ryerson Pitkin, M. D.

Sir:

醫學博士瑞爾森‧皮特金，

先生：

Dear Sir:

親愛的先生：

My dear Dr:

我親愛的醫生：

沒有學位或頭銜的普通人被稱呼為 Mr.（先生）和 Mrs.（女士），尊稱則為 Dear Sir:（親愛的先生：）、Dear Madam:（親愛的女士）。任何年齡的未婚女性在信封上通通被稱作 Miss So-and-so（某某小姐），但在信頭被稱為，

例 15　Dear Madam:（親愛的女士：）

Mr. 的複數，比如稱呼一個企業時，是 Messrs（各位先生）。相對應的稱呼是 Dear Sirs:（親愛的先生們：）或 Gentlemen:（先生們：）。

在英國 Esq.（先生）被用來代替 Mr.，以顯示輕微的優越性。在英國有時會有人用到它，但基本上這個詞已經過時。使用該詞的習俗已經改變，且該詞也不受美國人歡迎。如果要使用這個詞的話，那麼只能用它來稱呼律師和太平紳士[27]。

結束語

結束語（Subscription），或者說信末（ending of a letter），包括表達尊敬非法刑罰及處理一些較簡單的法律程序的職銜。

或喜愛的謙稱以及署名。謙稱取決於寫信人和收信人之間的關係。朋友之間的信件結束語可以寫以下幾種：

例 16

Yours lovingly,（鍾愛你的，）　　Yours affectionately,（摯愛你的，）
Devotedly yours,（鍾愛你的，）　　Ever yours,（永遠都是你的，）
……

至於夫妻或者情侶之間，過分親暱的稱呼諸如 Your Own Darling（你的親愛的）、Your own Dovey（你的最親愛的）以及其他寵溺的稱呼應該盡量避免，因為它們顯得寫信人非常膚淺。愛無須這些無意義且無內涵的語言也可以得到強烈的表達。

正式的結束語有：

---

[27] justices of the peace，也譯作治安法官，是一種由英國政府委任民間人士擔任維持社區安寧、防止非法刑罰及處理一些較簡單的法律程序的職銜。

第六章
書信的技巧：格式與筆記要領

例 17

  Yours Sincerely,（你真誠的，）

  Yours truly,（你真摯的，）

  Respectfully yours,（你恭順的，）

  ……

這些稱呼根據寫信人設想的與收信人之間的關係而變化。

例 18

  Very sincerely yours,（你非常真誠的，）

  Very respectfully yours,（你非常恭順的，）

  With deep respect yours,（你帶有深深敬意的，）

  Yours very truly,（你非常真摯的，）

  ……

諸如下面這種詳盡的結束語被認為過於矯揉造作。

例 19

  In the meantime with the highest respect, I am yours to command,

  （同時，我帶著最高的敬意，隨時聽候您的差遣，）

  I have the honor to be, Sir, Your humble Servant,

  （先生，能成為您謙卑的僕人，實屬榮幸，）

  With great expression of esteem, I am Sincerely yours,

  （帶著崇高的敬意，我是您真誠的，）

  Believe me, my dear Sir, Ever faithfully yours,

（相信我，我親愛的先生，我永遠是您真誠的，）

正式信件的結束語最好不要使用這樣的修飾詞。如果你是寫信給瑞恩先生，告訴他你有一座房屋出售，介紹完房子、說明情況後，簽上你的姓名即可。

例 20

Your obedient Servant（您恭順的僕人）

Yours very truly,（你非常真摯的，）

Yours with respect,（尊敬您的，）

　　James Wilson.（詹姆斯·威爾遜）

不要說什麼不勝榮幸或者叫他一定要相信什麼之類的話，只要告訴他你是誠心出售房屋的，並把他當作潛在客戶來對待即可。

不要把結束語縮寫成 Y'rs Resp'fly（即 Yours Respectfully）。還有，署名時不要縮寫，以確保對方清楚你的性別。

例 21

直接寫

Yours truly,

John Field

你真摯的，

約翰·菲爾德

而不是 J. Field（J. 菲爾德），這樣對方才不會將你誤認為 Jane Field（女士名）。

名字寫全稱永遠是最好的。已婚女性應在姓名前加上 Mrs.（女士）。

第六章
書信的技巧：格式與筆記要領

例 22

Very sincerely yours,

Mrs. Theodore Watson.

你非常真誠的，

西奧多‧沃森女士

如果你是寫一封感謝信的話，結束語可以寫 Yours gratefully（你的感激的）或 Yours very gratefully（你的不勝感激的），以表達自己的謝意。

按照習俗來說，不要在署名後加學位或頭銜的縮寫字母，除非你是僅以頭銜為人所知的勳爵、伯爵或公爵。但在美國沒有這類頭銜，所以這種寫法完全無須計入考慮。不要把自己的署名寫成：

例 23

Sincerely yours,

　　Obadiah Jackson, M.A. or L.L.D.

你真誠的，

　　文學碩士、法學博士奧巴代亞‧傑克森

如果你是 M.A.（文學碩士）或者 L.L.D.（法學博士），通常無須自我介紹，一般來說人們都知道你的身分。很多人，尤其是神職人員喜歡在他們的署名後加上他們被授予的 honoris causa（名譽學位），即因名譽而獲得的學位，無須考試。這類學位不應寫在信末。

丈夫健在的已婚女性署名時應簽丈夫的名字，且在前面加上 Mrs.（夫人）。

例 24

Yours sincerely,

Mrs. William Southey.

你真誠的，

威廉・騷塞夫人

如果丈夫不在了，簽名應變成：

例 25

Yours sincerely,

Mrs. Sarah Southey.

你真誠的，

莎拉・騷塞夫人

這樣一來，人們在收到女士的來信時就可以知道她的丈夫是否健在。與丈夫分居但未離婚的女性也不應署丈夫的名字。

地址

地址（address）包含名字、頭銜和住所。

例 26

Mr. Hugh Black,

112 South gate Street,

Altoona,

Pa.

第六章
書信的技巧：格式與筆記要領

休‧布萊克先生，

南門街 112 號，

阿爾圖納，

賓州

關係好的朋友之間通常有親密的稱呼，比如愛稱、暱稱等等。人們常常在交流中隨意使用這些稱呼。但在任何情況下，這些稱呼都不能寫在信封上。信封上的內容一定要正確、得體，就像寫信給陌生人一樣。信封內容上唯一不好寫的就是頭銜。男士頭銜均為 Mr.（先生），女士均為 Mrs.（女士），其中未婚女性頭銜為 Miss（小姐）。連男孩都有頭銜，Master。當稱呼多位收信人時，男士的頭銜變為 Messrs.（各位先生），有時女士頭銜則變為 Mesdames（各位女士）。如果稱呼的對象已有頭銜，禮節上來說應該使用這些頭銜。但是，頭銜絕對不能重複。

例 27

我們可以寫

Robert Stitt, M. D.（醫學博士羅伯特‧斯蒂特）

但絕不能寫

Dr. Robert Stitt, M. D.（醫學博士羅伯特‧斯蒂特博士）

或者

Mr. Robert Stitt, M. D.（醫學博士羅伯特‧斯蒂特先生）

寫信給醫生時，最好將他的職業縮寫成 M. D.，以與 D. D.（神學博士）區分開來。相比於 Dr. Robert Stitt，最好寫成 Robert Stitt, M. D.。

在稱呼神職人員時，就算有其他頭銜，也要保留字首 Rev.。

例 28　Rev. Tracy Tooke, LL. D.（尊敬的法學博士特蕾西·圖克）

如果收信人有多個頭銜，按照習俗來說，只需寫最重要的那個。

例 29

不應寫

Rev. Samuel MacComb, B. A., M. A., B. Sc., Ph. D., LL. D., D. D.（尊敬的文學學士、文學碩士、理學學士、哲學博士、法學博士、醫學博士，塞繆爾·馬科姆）

正式格式應為

Rev. Samuel MacComb, LL. D.（尊敬的法學博士塞繆爾·馬科姆）

頭銜選擇了 LL. D.（法學博士）而不是 D. D.（神學博士），原因是 Rev.（尊敬的）能暗示收信人是 D. D.（神學博士），而不能暗示收信人 LL. D.（法學博士）的身分。

稱呼達官顯貴如州長、法官、國會成員以及其他政府高官時，需加上字首 Hon.（尊敬的），此時無須再加上 Mr. 和 Esq.。比如，我們應該寫 Hon. Josiah Snifkins（尊敬的約書亞·斯尼夫金斯），而不是 Hon. Mr. Josiah Snifkins（尊敬的約書亞·斯尼夫金斯先生）或 Hon. Josiah Snifkins, Esq.（尊敬的約書亞·斯尼夫金斯先生），儘管 Hon（尊敬的）經常被用來稱呼州長，他們有專屬的尊稱 Excellency。

例 30

His Excellency,

Charles E. Hughes,

Albany,

N. Y.

第六章
書信的技巧：格式與筆記要領

尊敬的閣下，

查爾斯・E. 休斯，

奧爾巴尼

紐約州

如果是寫信給總統的話，信封上應題作：

To the President,

Executive Mansion,

Washington, D. C.

總統親啟，

行政大廈，

華盛頓特區

專業人員諸如醫生、律師，以及透過合法途徑獲得大學學位的人，在信封上應該透過他們的頭銜來稱呼他們。

例31

Jonathan Janeway, M. D.（醫學博士喬納森・詹韋）

Hubert Houston, B. L.（法學學士休伯特・休斯頓）

Matthew Marks, M. A.（文學學士馬修・馬克斯）

……

收信人的住址應該清晰完整地寫出來，包括街道號，且城市或城鎮名的書寫需清晰可辨認。如果州名的縮寫可能與其他州混淆，那麼應該寫上該州名字的全稱。在信封上寫地址時，和信頭全部寫進一行的規矩不一樣，地址的每一項應獨立成行。比如：

例 32

    Liberty,

    Sullivan County,

    New York.

    立博蒂,

    沙利文縣,

    紐約州

    215 Minna St.,

    San Francisco,

    California.

    明納街 215 號,

    舊金山,

    加利福尼亞

    信封的右上角應留有貼郵票的空間。收信人的名字和頭銜應占一行，位於信封的中間位置。名字應不偏不倚，正好在中間，離兩邊的距離相當。

    如果是寫信給知名的大型企業、公司，或者大眾、市政官員的話，按照習俗，一般不寫街道號碼。

例 33

    Messrs. Seigel, Cooper Co.,

    New York City,

    賽格爾先生們，庫伯公司,

    紐約市

第六章
書信的技巧：格式與筆記要領

Hon. William J. Gaynor,

New York City.

尊敬的威廉·J. 蓋納，

紐約市

便箋卡

便箋卡（Notes）可以被認作是小型信件，使用場景主要限於邀請函及接受函、致歉信和介紹信。在寫這類便箋卡時，現代禮節傾向於非正式寫作。實際上，卡片禮儀已經取代了隆重的書信，非正式的卡片成為主流。致歉信連同名片一起發回，上面直接寫 Regrets 即可。我們通常會在邀請函和邀請卡上發現 R.S.V.P. 的字樣，它是法語 repondezs' ilvousplait 的縮寫，意思是「請回覆」。但在邀請函上這個縮寫不是必需的，因為接受過良好教育的人都知道，按禮節來說是要回覆邀請函的。如果寫給一家人中的年輕女性便箋卡，應稱呼長女為 Miss，再加上姓，而無須加上其教名。假設湯普森家（Thompson family）有三個女兒：長女 Martha（瑪莎）、Susan（蘇珊）和 Jemina（傑米娜）。Martha（瑪莎）應被稱呼為 Miss Thompson（湯普森小姐），兩個小女兒則被分別稱呼為 Miss Susan Thompson（蘇珊·湯普森小姐）和 Miss Jemina Thompson（傑米娜·湯普森小姐）。

不要在便箋卡的信封上寫 addressed 這個詞。

不要把朋友送來的便箋卡密封。

不要在明信片上寫便箋。以下是一些常見的便箋卡格式：

便箋卡

例 34

正式邀請函

Mr. and Mrs. Henry Wagstaff request the honor of Mr. McAdoo's presence on Friday evening, June 15th, at 8 o'clock to meet the Governor of the Fort.

19 Woodbine Terrace
June 8th, 1910

亨利・瓦格斯塔夫先生和夫人恭候麥卡杜先生於六月十五日（週五）晚八點出席與堡壘地方行政長官的會面。

伍德拜恩露臺 19 號
1910 年 6 月 8 日

這是一個正式招待會的邀請函，要求賓客著晚禮服到場。以下是麥卡杜先生以第三人稱寫的回覆樣本：

Mr. McAdoo presents his compliments to Mr. and Mrs. Henry Wagstaff and accepts with great pleasure their invitation to meet the Governor of the Fort on the evening of June fifteenth.

215 Beacon Street,
June 10th, 1910.

麥卡杜先生向亨利・瓦格斯塔夫先生和夫人致以問候，並愉快地接受六月十五日晚會見堡壘行政長官的邀請。

培根街 215 號
1910 年 6 月 10 日

第六章
書信的技巧：格式與筆記要領

以下是麥卡杜先生拒絕邀請的回覆樣本：

Mr. McAdoo regrets that owing to a prior engagement he must forego the honor of paying his respects to Mr. and Mrs. Wagstaff and the Governor of the Fort on the evening of June fifteenth.

215 Beacon St.,
June10th, 1910.

麥卡杜先生遺憾地表示，由於有約在先，故無此殊榮在六月十五日晚向亨利‧瓦格斯塔夫先生和夫人以及堡壘行政長官表示敬意。

培根街 215 號
1910 年 6 月 10 日

以下是一封寫給耶萊米‧雷諾茲先生的信。

例 35

Mr. and Mrs. Oldham at home on Wednesday evening October ninth from seven to eleven.

215 Beacon Street,
June 10th, 1910.

奧德海姆先生和夫人於十月九日（週三）晚七點至十一點在家恭候您的光臨。

阿什蘭大道 21 號
10 月 5 日

雷諾茲先生的回覆：

Mr. Reynolds accepts with high appreciation the honor of Mr. and Mrs. Oldham's invitation for Wednesday evening October ninth.

Windsor Hotel

October 7th

雷諾茲先生非常感激並接受奧德海姆先生和夫人十月九日（週三）晚的邀請。

溫莎旅館

10 月 7 日

或者

Mr. Reynolds regrets that his duties render it impossible for him to accept Mr. and Mrs. Oldham's kind invitation for the evening of October ninth.

Windsor Hotel

October 7th

雷諾茲先生遺憾地表示，由於公務在身，故不得不拒絕奧德海姆先生和夫人十月九日晚的邀請。

溫莎旅館

10 月 7 日

有時不太正式的邀請函寫在特別設計的小卡片上，使用第一人稱而非第三人稱。

第六章
書信的技巧：格式與筆記要領

例 36

360 Pine St.,

Dec. 11th, 1910.

Dear Mr. Saintsbury:

Mr. Johnson and I should be much pleased to have you dine with us and a few friends next Thursday, the fifteenth, at half past seven.

Yours sincerely,

Emma Burnside.

派恩街 360 號

1910 年 12 月 11 日

親愛的森茨伯里先生：

如果您能於下週四（十五日）晚七點半前來與強生先生和我還有幾位好友共進晚餐，我們將不勝榮幸。

你真誠的，

艾瑪・伯恩塞德

森茨伯里先生的回覆：

57 Carlyle Strand

Dec. 13th, 1910.

Dear Mrs. Burnside:

Let me accept very appreciatively your invitation to dine with Mr. Burnside and you on next Thursday, the fifteenth, at half past seven.

Yours sincerely,

Henry Saintsbury.

卡萊爾街 57 號

1910 年 12 月 13 日

親愛的伯恩塞德夫人：

我心懷感激地接受與伯恩塞德先生和您在下週四（十五日）晚七點半共進晚餐的邀請。

你真誠的，

亨利·森茨伯里

介紹信

介紹信（Notes of introduction）應該是經過深思熟慮後寫出的，因為寫信者實際上在拿自己的名譽為他們介紹的人當作保證。以下是一封介紹信的樣本。

例 37

603 Lexington Ave.,

New York City,

June 15th, 1910.

Rev. Cyrus C. Wiley, D. D.,

Newark, N. J.

My dear Dr. Wiley:

第六章
書信的技巧：格式與筆記要領

I take the liberty of presenting to you my friend, Stacy Redfern, M. D., a young practitioner, who is anxious to locate in Newark. I have known him many years and can vouch for his integrity and professional standing. Any courtesy and kindness which you may show him will be very much appreciated by me.

Very sincerely yours,

Franklin Jewett.

列剋星敦大道 603 號

紐約市

1910 年 6 月 15 日

尊敬的神學博士賽勒斯·C. 威利，

紐澤西州紐華克市

我親愛的威利博士：

我自作主張，向您介紹我的朋友醫學博士斯特西·雷德芬，一名渴望在紐華克市工作的年輕醫師。我與他相識多年，並願為他的誠信和專業水準擔保。如他承蒙您的關照和抬愛，我將感激不盡。

你非常真誠的，

富蘭克林·朱厄特

第七章
錯誤剖析：典型問題與糾正示例

以下例句中，括號裡的單字或片語是多餘的，應被刪除。

例 1　Fill the glass (full).（把玻璃杯灌滿。）

例 2　They appeared to be talking (together) on private affairs.

　　（看來他們在聊私事。）

例 3　I saw the boy and his sister (both) in the garden.

　　（我看到男孩和他妹妹在花園。）

例 4　He went into the country last week and returned (back) yesterday.

　　（他上週去鄉下，昨天回來了。）

例 5　The subject (matter) of his discourse was excellent.

　　（他的演講主題棒極了。）

例 6　You need not wonder that the (subject) matter of his discourse was excellent; it was taken from the Bible.

　　（他的演講主題非常棒，你無須為此感到驚訝，因為這個主題來自《聖經》。）

例 7　They followed (after) him, but could not overtake him.

　　（他們跟隨他的腳步，但卻無法超越他。）

第七章
錯誤剖析：典型問題與糾正示例

例 8　The same sentiments may be found throughout (the whole of) the book.

（同樣的觀點在本書內隨處可見。）

例 9　I was very ill everyday (of my life) last week.

（上週我每天都病得很厲害。）

例 10　That was the (sum and) substance of his discourse.

（那就是他演講的內容。）

例 11　He took wine and water and mixed them (both) together.

（他拿了酒和水，並把它們混在了一起。）

例 12　He descended (down) the steps to the cellar.（他下樓去了酒窖。）

例 13　He fell (down) from the top of the house.（他從房頂上摔了下來。）

例 14　I hope you will return (again) soon.（希望你早日歸來。）

例 15　The thing she took away here stored (again).

（她帶走的東西在這裡又出現了。）

例 16　The thief who stole my watch was compelled to restore it (back again).

（偷我錶的賊被迫把錶物歸原主。）

例 17　It is equally (the same) to me whether I have it today or tomorrow.

（今天得到它還是明天得到它，對我來說沒有區別。）

例 18　She said, (says she) the report is false; and he replied, (says he) if it be not correct I have been misinformed.

（她說，這個報告是錯的；他回道，如果報告不正確，那就是我得到了錯誤的資訊。）

例 19　I took my place in the cars (for) to go to New York.

（我在去紐約的車裡占了座。）

例 20　They need not (to) call upon him.（他們不需要打電話給他。）

例 21　Nothing (else) but that would satisfy him.

（除了那個，沒有什麼能讓他滿意。）

例 22　Whenever I ride in the cars I (always) find it prejudicial to my health.

（每次我坐車都覺得它對我的健康不利。）

例 23　He was the first (of all) at the meeting.（他是開會第一個到場的。）

例 24　He was the tallest of (all) the brothers.（他在幾兄弟中是最高的。）

例 25　You are the tallest of (all) your family.（你是家裡最高的。）

例 26　Whenever I pass the house he is (always) at the door.

（無論何時我路過房子，他都在門口。）

例 27　The rain has penetrated (through) the roof.（雨水浸透了屋頂。）

例 28　Besides my uncle and aunt there was (also) my grandfather at the church.

（除了我的叔叔嬸嬸，我的外公也在教堂。）

例 29　It should (ever) be your constant endeavor to please your family.

（讓家人開心應該是你不斷的追求。）

例 30　If it is true as you have heard (then) his situation is indeed pitiful.

（如果你聽說的是事實的話，那他的處境很可憐。）

例 31　Either this (here) man or that (there) woman has (got) it.

（無論這個男人還是那個女人，都沒有它。）

第七章
錯誤剖析：典型問題與糾正示例

例 32　Where is the fire (at)?（火災在哪裡？）

例 33　Did you sleep in church? Not that I know (of).

（你在教堂裡睡過覺嗎？沒有。）

例 34　I never before (in my life) met (with) such a stupid man.

（我從沒遇到過這麼蠢的人。）

例 35　(For) why did he postpone it?（他為什麼要把它推遲？）

例 36　Because (why) he could not attend.（因為他沒法參加。）

例 37　What age is he? (Why) I don't know.（他多少歲了？我不知道。）

例 38　He called on me (for) to ask my opinion.

（他喊住我，問我的看法。）

例 39　I don't know where I am(at).（我不知道自己在哪裡。）

例 40　I looked in (at) the window.（我看向窗戶。）

例 41　I passed (by) the house.（我路過那幢房子。）

例 42　He (always) came every Sunday.（他每週日過來。）

例 43　Moreover, (also) we wish to say he was in error.

（還有，我們想說他錯了。）

例 44　It is not long (ago)since he was here.（不久前他還在這裡。）

例 45　Two men went into the wood (in order) to cut (down) trees.

（兩個人到森林裡砍樹。）

其他冗長的例子可以以此類推。在新聞寫作中，很多地方經常出現一些從意義上來說沒有必要存在的，或者不需要被用來解釋文章的單字還有片語。

權威作家們犯過的語法錯誤

有時，就算是最頂尖的演說家和作家也會犯錯。許多在我們的認知裡不可能犯錯的權威作家都多多少少觸犯過基本的語法原則，違背一個或多個詞類的使用規則。實際上，有的作家甚至不斷違反所有九個詞類的規則，但他們仍然坐在榮譽寶座上，接受眾人的崇敬。麥考萊就曾錯用過冠詞。他寫道，

例 46

That *a* historian should not record trifles is perfectly true.

（一個歷史學家不應記錄瑣事，這句話是完全正確的。）

他應該用 an。

狄更斯[28]也錯誤地使用過冠詞。他稱《魯賓遜漂流記》為

例 47　*an* universally popular book（一本廣受歡迎的書）

正確寫法應該是 a universally popular book。

名詞和代詞之間的關係一直都是演說家和作家面前的絆腳石。哈勒姆[29]在他的作品《歐洲文學》中寫道：

例 48

No one as yet had exhibited the structure of the human kidneys, Vesalius[30] having only examined them in dogs.

---

[28] 查爾斯·狄更斯（Charles Dickens），英國作家，代表作有《大衛·科波菲爾》、《孤雛淚》、《雙城記》等。
[29] 亨利·哈勒姆（Henry Hallam），英國歷史學家。
[30] 安德列亞斯·維薩留斯（Andreas Vesalius），著名醫生、解剖學家。

第七章
錯誤剖析：典型問題與糾正示例

（到目前為止，還沒有人成功地展示過人類的腎臟，維薩留斯僅僅檢測過狗的腎臟。）

這句話的正確寫法應該是，

No one had as yet exhibited the kidneys in human beings, Vesalius having examined such organs in dogs only.

（到目前為止，還沒有人成功地展示過人類的腎臟，維薩留斯僅僅檢測過狗的腎臟。）

亞瑟·哈里斯爵士[31]在寫到狄更斯時這麼說：

例 49

I knew a brother author of his who received such criticisms from him (Dickens) very lately and profited by *it*.

（我認識他的一個兄弟作家，就在不久前，他從他（狄更斯）那裡得到一些評價，受益匪淺。）

這裡不應該用it，而應該用them，才符合criticisms這個詞的形態（複數）。以下是一些著名作家犯的代詞方面的錯誤。

例 50

Sir Thomas Moore[32] in general so writes it, although not many others so late as *him*.

（湯瑪斯·摩爾爵士整體而言是這麼寫的，儘管沒有很多人像他一樣這麼晚。）

—— 特倫奇的《英語的過去與現在》

---

[31] 亞瑟·哈里斯爵士 (Sir Arthur Helps)，英國作家。
[32] 湯瑪斯·摩爾 (Thomas Moore，西元 1779～1852 年)，愛爾蘭詩人、歌手、詞作者、表演家。

這裡應該用 he。

例 51

What should we gain by it but that we should speedily become as poor as *them*.

（我們從中所得的，不過是快速地變貧窮，像他們一樣。）

—— 愛麗絲的《關於麥考萊的散文》

這裡應該用 they。

例 52

If the king gives us leave you or I may as lawfully preach, as *them* that do.

（如果國王准我們離去，你們也好，我也好，就可以像他們那樣合法宣講。）

—— 霍布斯的《內戰史》

這裡應該用 they 或 those，後者能讓人更容易理解句意。

例 53

The drift of all his sermons was, to prepare the Jews for the reception of a prophet, mightier than *him*, and whose shoes he was not worthy to bear.

（他所有布道的主旨，都是讓猶太人做好準備，接納一位比他更強大、不配忍受他的先知。）

—— 阿斯伯里的《布道》

這裡應該用 he。

第七章
錯誤剖析：典型問題與糾正示例

例 54

Phalaris, who was so much older than *her*.（法拉里斯比她年長得多。）

—— 本特利的《關於法拉里斯的書信的論文》[33]

這裡應該用 she。

例 55

King Charles, and more than *him*, the duke and the Popish faction were at liberty to form new schemes.

（查爾斯王，還有比他更重要的公爵以及天主教派人士可以自由地商議新計畫了。）

—— 博林布魯克的《關於黨派的論述》

這裡應該用 he。

例 56

We contributed a third more than the Dutch, who were obliged to the same proportion more than *us*.

（我們的貢獻比荷蘭人高三分之一，而荷蘭人原本的定額應比我們高三分之一。）

—— 強納森・史威夫特的《盟國行為》

這裡應該用 we。

在以上所有例句中的代詞本應該用主格，但都錯用成了賓格。

---

[33] 原文為 Dissertation on Phalaris，該書全名為 Dissertation on the Epistles of Phalaris。

例 57　Let thou and I the battle try.（讓你和我去戰鬥吧。）

—— 阿農

這裡 let 是使動動詞，後面要接賓格。所以，這裡不應該用 thou 和 I，而應該用 you（單數）和 me。

例 58

Forever in this humble cell, Let thee and I, my fair one, dwell.

—— 普萊爾

（讓我和你，我的佳人，永遠地住在這個簡陋的小屋裡。）

這裡 thee 和 I 應該用賓格的 you 和 me。關係代詞的使用難倒了絕大多數作家。

就算在《聖經》裡我們都能發現關係代詞的錯誤使用。

例 59

Whom do men say that I am?（人們說我是什麼樣的？）

—— 聖馬太

Whom think ye that I am?（你覺得我是什麼樣的？）

—— 《使徒行傳》

在這兩個例句中都應該用 who，因為該詞不是跟在 say 或 think 後面的賓格，而是動詞 am 的主格。

例 60

Who should I meet at the coffee house t'other night, but my old friend?

第七章
錯誤剖析：典型問題與糾正示例

（那天晚上我在咖啡館除了見我的老朋友還能見誰呢？）

—— 斯蒂爾

It is another pattern of this answerer's fair dealing, to give us hints that the author is dead, and yet lay the suspicion upon somebody, I know not who, in the country.

（這位回答者的另一種公正做法是，暗示我們作者已死，並且把嫌疑指向了這個國家的某個人，我不知道是誰。）

—— 強納森‧史威夫特的《老爺船的故事》

My son is going to be married to I don't know who.

（我的兒子將要和一個我不知道的人結婚。）

—— 戈德史密斯的《好心人》

以上例句中的主格 who 是錯誤的，應該用賓格 whom。

代詞 thou 的主格複數形式 ye 在使用中常常代替賓格 you 出現，比如：

例 61

His wrath which will one day destroy *ye* both.

（他的憤怒，總有一天會將你們二人毀滅。）

—— 米爾頓

The more shame for *ye*; holy men I thought ye.

（你們越發羞愧，我就越容易想到聖人。）

—— 莎士比亞

權威作家們犯過的語法錯誤

I feel the gales that from *ye* blow.（我感覺到你們吹來的大風。）

—— 格雷

Tyrants dread *ye*, lest your just decree Transfer the power and set the people free.

（暴虐的人哪，你們害怕公正的法令轉移權力，讓人民獲得自由。）

—— 普萊爾

許多大作家在使用形容詞時不假思索，胡亂選擇比較的程度。

例 62

Of two forms of the same word, use the *fittest*.

（在同一個單字的兩個格式中，使用最合適的。）

—— 莫雷爾

作者本想給出好的建議，卻做了個糟糕的示範。在這裡他應該用比較級 fitter。

本身擁有比較級或最高級含義的形容詞不需要再在詞前加 more、most 或在詞尾加 er、est，因此以下例句違背了這個規則。

例 63

Money is the most universal incitement of human misery.

（金錢是人類苦難最普遍的誘因。）

—— 吉本的《羅馬帝國衰亡史》[34]

---

[34] 原文為 Decline and Fall，該書全名為 The History of the Decline and Fall of the Roman Empire。

139

第七章
錯誤剖析：典型問題與糾正示例

The *chiefest* of which was known by the name of Archon among the Grecians.

（其中最重要的一位是希臘人中的執政官。）

—— 德萊頓的《普魯塔克的一生》

The *chiefest* and largest are removed to certain magazines they call libraries.

（最重要的和最大的被轉移到他們稱為《圖書館》的雜誌上。）

—— 強納森・史威夫特的《書的戰爭》

The two *chiefest* properties of air, its gravity and elastic force, have been discovered by mechanical experiments.

（空氣的兩個最主要的性質 —— 重力和彈力，是透過力學實驗發現的。）

—— 阿爾伯斯諾

From these various causes, which in greater or *lesser* degree, affected every individual in the colony, the indignation of the people became general.

（由於這些或多或少都影響到殖民地中每一個人的原因，人民的憤怒變得普遍起來。）

—— 羅伯遜的《美國歷史》

The *extremest* parts of the earth were meditating a submission.

（地球最遙遠的地方都在沉思著服從。）

—— 阿特伯里的布道

The last are indeed *more preferable* because they are founded on some new knowledge or improvement in the mind of man.

（最後一種方法的確更可取，因為它們是建立在人類大腦的新知或進步的基礎上的。）

—— 艾迪生《旁觀者》

This was in reality the *easiest* manner of the two.

（這實際上是兩種方式中最簡單的一種。）

—— 沙夫茨伯里對一名作家的建議

In every well formed mind this second desire seems to be the *strongest* of the two.

（在每個頭腦健全的人看來，第二種欲望似乎是兩者中最強烈的一種。）

—— 史密斯的《道德情感理論》

以上例句通通誤用了最高級。只有兩個比較對象的時候必須用比較級。

談及可能性的時候，是沒有對比程度的，然而還是出現了以下這些表達：

例 64

As it was impossible they should know the words, thoughts and secret actions of all men, so it was *more impossible* they should pass judgment on them according to these things.

第七章
錯誤剖析：典型問題與糾正示例

（因為他們不可能知道所有人的言語、思想和私人行為，所以更不可能透過這些事情來批判人們。）

—— 惠特比的《基督教的必要性》

很大一部分作家把形容詞作副詞用，於是我們發現了以下例句：

例 65

I shall endeavor to live here after *suitable* to a man in my station.

—— 艾迪生

（以後我會努力過我這種社會地位的人應有的生活。）

I can never think so very *mean* of him.

（我永遠也不會把他想像成很壞的樣子。）

—— 本特利的《關於法拉里斯的書信的論文》

His expectations run high and the fund to supply them is *extreme* scanty,

（他的期待水漲船高，然而資金卻極度短缺，）

—— 蘭卡斯特的《關於精緻的論述》

關於動詞的最常見的錯誤用法是無視動詞和主語之間的關係。這種錯誤頻繁出現在動詞和主語相隔甚遠的句子裡，尤其是當動詞跟在另一個不同數量的名詞的後面時。這種錯誤常發生在 either、or、neither、nor，和 much、more、many、everyone、each 這些詞後面。

以下是一些作家犯錯的例句。

例 66

The terms in which the sale of a patent *were* communicated to the public.

（向大眾傳達專利銷售的條款。）

—— 朱尼厄斯的信

The richness of her arms and apparel *were* conspicuous.

（她的手臂和衣服十分華麗，這是顯而易見的。）

—— 吉本的《羅馬帝國衰亡史》

Everyone of this grotesque family *were* the creatures of national genius.

（這個怪誕家族的每個人都是民族天才的產物。）

—— 伊斯拉里

He knows not what spleen, languor or listlessness *are*.

（他不知道什麼是憤怒，什麼是倦怠，什麼是無精打采。）

—— 布萊爾的布道

Each of these words *imply*, some pursuit or object relinquished.

（這其中的每一個詞都暗示著放棄某種追求或目標。）

—— 伊比德

Magnus, with four thousand of his supposed accomplices *were* put to death.

（馬格納斯和他所謂的 4,000 名同夥一同被處死。）

—— 吉本

第七章
錯誤剖析：典型問題與糾正示例

No nation gives greater encouragements to learning than we do; yet at the same time *none* are so injudicious in the application.

（沒有一個國家比我們更鼓勵學習；但同時，在實施過程中沒有誰比我們更不明智。）

—— 戈德史密斯

There's two or three of us have seen strange sights.

（我們中有兩三個人見過奇怪的景象。）

—— 莎士比亞

過去分詞不能用於過去時，然而學富五車的拜倫卻忽視了這一點。他在〈塔索：悲嘆與勝利〉中寫道：

例 67

And with my years my soul *begun* to pant With feelings of strange tumult and soft pain.

（隨著歲月的流逝，我的靈魂開始因奇怪的騷動和輕柔的痛苦而喘息。）

另一個例句來自塞維吉的《漫遊者》，一個句子裡出現了兩次這類錯誤。

例 68

From liberty each nobler science *sprung*, A Bacon brighten'd and a Spenser sung.

（從自由中誕生了每一種更高貴的科學。點亮了培根，唱響了史賓賽。）

其他和分詞相關的錯誤如下。

例 69

Every book ought to be read with the same spirit and in the same manner as it is *writ*.

（每本書都應該以與寫作相同的精神和方式閱讀。）

——菲爾丁的《湯姆‧瓊斯》

The Court of Augustus had not *wore* off the manners of the republic.

（奧古斯都的法院並沒有消除共和國的風氣。）

——休謨的散文

Moses tells us that the fountains of the earth were *broke* open or clove asunder.

（摩西告訴我們，地上的泉源破開了，或是裂開了。）

——伯內特

A free constitution when it has been *shook* by the iniquity of former administrations.

（一部自由的憲法，當它被前政府的罪惡所動搖。）

——博林布魯克

In this respect the seeds of future divisions were *sowed* abundantly.

（在這方面，未來分裂的種子被大量播種。）

——伊比德

第七章
錯誤剖析：典型問題與糾正示例

以下例句中，現在分詞被用於動詞不定式。

例 70

It is easy *distinguishing* the rude fragment of a rock from the splinter of a statue.

（把粗糙的岩石碎片和雕像碎區域分開來是很容易的。）

—— 吉爾菲倫的《文學肖像》

在這裡，應該用 distinguish 而不是 distinguishing。

以下例句違反了 shall 和 will 的使用規則。

例 71

If we look within the rough and awkward outside, we *will* be richly rewarded by its perusal.

（如果我們從粗糙和尷尬的外面向裡看，我們將因細讀得到豐厚回報。）

—— 吉爾菲倫的《文學肖像》

If I should declare them and speak of them, they *should* be more than I am able to express.

（如果我要宣告並談論他們，他們應該比我所能表達的還要多。）

—— 祈禱書，讚美詩 11 版

If I *would* declare them and speak of them, they are more than can be numbered.

（如果我要宣告並談論他們，他們的人數就太多了。）

—— 伊比德

Without having attended to this, we *will* be at a loss, in understanding several passages in the classics.

（如果不注意到這一點，我們就會在理解經典中的一些段落時不知所措。）

——布萊爾的演講

We know to what cause our past reverses have been owing and we *will* have ourselves to blame, if they are again incurred.

（我們知道我們過去的挫折是由於什麼原因造成的。如果它們再次發生，我們就得責怪自己了。）

——艾麗森的《歐洲史》

關於副詞的錯誤使用在名家之作中極其常見。rather 是一個頻繁被誤用的副詞。特倫奇大主教在他的作品《英語的過去和現在》裡寫道：「It *rather* modified the structure of our sentences than the elements of our vocabulary.」這句話的正確形式應該是「It modified the structure of our sentences rather than the elements of our vocabulary.」

「So far as his mode of teaching goes he is rather a disciple of Socrates than of St. Paul or Wesley.」

這是萊斯利‧史蒂芬筆下的《塞繆爾‧詹森》。他應該寫成「So far as his mode of teaching goes he is a disciple of Socrates rather than of St. Paul or Wesley.」。

介詞是一個常常被部分大作家誤用的詞類。一些名詞、形容詞和動詞後面要接特定的介詞。比如，different 後面總是接 from、prevail 後面接 upon、averse 後面接 to、accord 後面接 with 等等。

第七章
錯誤剖析：典型問題與糾正示例

以下例句中，括號裡的介詞是應該使用的。

He found the greatest difficulty of (in) writing.

（他發現了寫作中最大的困難。）

—— 休謨的《英格蘭史》

If policy can prevail upon (over) force.

（如果政策能夠勝過武力。）

—— 艾迪生

He made the discovery and communicated to (with) his friends.

（他發現了這件事並和他的朋友們進行了交流。）

—— 強納森‧史威夫特的《老爺船的故事》

Every office of command should be intrusted to persons on (in) whom the parliament shall confide.

（每一個指揮部都應委託給議會委託的人。）

—— 參考萊

少數幾位著名作家違反常規，把介詞放在句尾。比如卡萊爾在《關於彭斯的研究》中提及，「Our own contributions to it, we are aware, can be but scanty and feeble; but we offer them with good will, and trust they may meet with acceptance from those they are intended *for*.」（我們知道我們對它的貢獻只能是有限和微弱的；但我們對它們寄予美好的期望，並相信他們可能會得到他們想要的。）

他應該寫「for whom they are intended」。

Most writers have some one vein which they peculiarly and obviously excel in.

（大多數作家都有一種獨特而又明顯擅長的寫作風格。）

—— 威廉・明托

這句話應該寫成「Most writers have some one vein in which they peculiarly and obviously excel.」

許多作家使用多餘的詞重複地表達同樣的想法和念頭。這叫做贅述（tautology）。

Notwithstanding which (however) poor Polly embraced them all around.

（儘管如此，可憐的波莉還是接受了他們。）

—— 狄更斯

I judged that they would (mutually) find each other.

（我判斷他們會找到彼此。）

—— 克羅基特

…as having created a (joint) partnership between the two Powers in the Morocco question.

（……在摩洛哥問題上兩個大國建立了夥伴關係。）

—— 《泰晤士報》

The only sensible position (there seems to be) is to frankly acknowledge our ignorance of what lies beyond.

（唯一明智的立場是坦率地承認我們對未來的無知。）

—— 《每日電訊報》

第七章
錯誤剖析：典型問題與糾正示例

Lord Rosebery has not budged from his position —— splendid, no doubt, —— of (lonely) isolation.

（毫無疑問，羅伯里斯勳爵的地位是顯赫的，是孤獨的。）

—— 《泰晤士報》

Miss Fox was (often) in the habit of assuring Mrs. Chick.

（福克斯小姐習慣於向奇科夫人保證。）

—— 狄更斯

The deck (it) was their field of fame.（甲板是他們的成名場所。）

—— 康貝爾

He had come up one morning, as was now (frequently) his wont,

（有一天早上，他像往常一樣來，）

—— 特羅洛普

The counsellors of the Sultan (continue to) remain skeptical

（蘇丹的顧問們仍持懷疑態度）

—— 《泰晤士報》

Seriously, (and apart from jesting), this is no light matter.

（說真的，這不是件輕鬆的事。）

—— 白芝浩

To go back to your own country with (the consciousness that you go back with) the sense of duty well done.

（帶著責任感回到你自己的國家。）

——霍斯爾伯里大法官

The Peresviet lost both her fighting-tops and (in appearance) looked the most damaged of all the ships.

（Peresviet 號在戰鬥中失去了兩個戰鬥機，看起來是所有戰艦中受損最嚴重的。）

——《泰晤士報》

Counsel admitted that, that was a fair suggestion to make, but he submitted that it was borne out by the (surrounding) circumstances.

（律師承認，這是一個合理的建議，但他認為這是由環境帶來的。）

——伊比德

另一個使用並不必要的單字和片語的情況叫做迂迴（termed circumlocution），也就是拐彎抹角，繞來繞去不講重點。此時應精簡敘事以節省空間。

這種情況可以比作從三角形的一端到另一端，不走直線而走三角形的另兩條線。比如在以下引用中，「Pope professed to have learned his poetry from Dryden, whom, whenever an opportunity was presented, he praised through the whole period of his existence with unvaried liberality; and perhaps his character may receive some illustration, of a comparison he instituted between him and the man whose pupil he was.」（教皇聲稱從德萊頓那裡學習了詩歌，只要有機會，他就毫不留情地讚美德萊頓的一生一世。也許他的性格可以從他和他的老師的比

第七章
錯誤剖析：典型問題與糾正示例

較中得到一些說明。），大部分連篇累牘的詞句可以省略，因此句子凝練為：

「Pope professed himself the pupil of Dryden, whom he lost no opportunity of praising; and his character may be illustrated by a comparison with his master.」

（教皇自稱是德萊頓的學生，他從不吝嗇讚美德萊頓的機會；他的性格可以透過與他老師的相比較來說明。）

「His life was brought to a close in 1910 at an age not far from the one fixed by the sacred writer as the term of human existence.」

（他的生命在1910年結束，離這位神聖作家所定義的人類存在時代不遠了。）

這句話的簡潔版本為，「His life was brought to a close at the age of seventy.」（他的生命在70歲結束。）；或者更簡潔，「He died at the age of seventy.」（他70歲去世。）

「The day was intensely cold, so cold in fact that the thermometer crept down to the zero mark.」（那天非常冷，冷得溫度計都悄然降到零度。），可以表達為「The day was so cold the thermometer registered zero.」（那天冷得連溫度計都降到零度。）

許多作家連篇累牘，有時在碰到他們不太了解甚至一無所知的對象時用這一招，意在「鋪陳」（padding），也就是填補空白。年輕作家要避開這一點，學會盡可能使用通俗易懂的詞句簡潔地表達想法和觀念。

實際上，從名家之作中可以找到很多語法、措辭以及風格上的錯誤。事實證明，人無完人，就連最優秀的作家都有失手的時候。不過，這些錯誤多是由於粗心，或在倉促之中犯下的，而不是因為知識所限。

通常來說，在說話時鮮少出錯的資深學者在寫作中也有可能犯錯。實際上，很多人都是完美的演講大師，他們在談話中從不出錯；但他們對語法的基本規則知之甚少，以致於無法寫出一個正確的句子。這類人從嬰兒時期開始聽到的都是正確的口頭語，所以使用合適的詞彙和格式已經成了他們的第二天性。對於孩子來說，學對的和學錯的一樣容易。在易受影響的年齡形成的印象，無論對錯，都會一直停留在腦海裡。就連鸚鵡都能學會正確用語。對鸚鵡說「Two and two make four」，它絕對不會說成「two and two makes four」。

然而，寫作卻是完全不同的情況。在沒有基礎語法知識的情況下，我們可以透過和大演說家交談學會正確的口頭語；但在同樣的情況下，我們無法學會正確的寫作。要寫一封日常信件，我們必須知道信件的結構、詞彙之間的關係。因此，每個人都有必要了解最基礎、最重要的語法規則。

第七章
錯誤剖析：典型問題與糾正示例

第八章
避開陷阱：常見誤用與詞彙偏差

就近原則

很多時候，動詞和主語之間被一些詞隔開，此時動詞應與離它最近的主語形式一致。大名鼎鼎的作家時不時也會掉入這個陷阱。以下是一些例句：

例 1

The partition which the two ministers made of the powers of government *were* singularly happy.

（兩位部長對政府權力的劃分感到特別開心。）

—— 參考萊

這裡應該用 was，和主語 partition 保持一致。

例 2

One at least of the qualities which fit it for training ordinary men *unfit* it for training an extraordinary man.

第八章
避開陷阱：常見誤用與詞彙偏差

（這些品格中，至少有一條能夠培養出普通人才，但培養不出優秀人才。）

—— 白芝浩

這裡應該用 unfits，和主語 one 保持一致。

例 3

An immense amount of confusion and indifference *prevail* in these days.

（這些日子，無數的困惑和冷漠大行其道。）

—— 《每日電訊報》

這裡應該用 prevails，和主語 amount 保持一致。

● 省略

錯誤的省略主要發生在介詞上。

例 4

His objection and condoning of the boy's course, seemed to say the least, paradoxical.

（他對男孩行為的反對和容忍看起來非常矛盾。）

objection 後面應該有介詞 to。

例 5

Many men of brilliant parts are crushed by force of circumstances and their genius forever lost to the world.

（很多聰明絕頂的人被環境壓垮，從而永遠失去了他們的智慧。）

有些人認為 genius 後面缺的動詞是 are，但這樣是不符合語法規律的。在這種情況下，正確的動詞永遠應該是 is。比如：Their genius is forever lost to the world.（他們永遠失去了自己的智慧。）

拆開動詞不定式

就算是大演說家和大作家，都有在動詞不定式中間加其他詞的習慣。未來有可能這種用法會變成正確形式，但目前來說，拆開動詞不定式是絕對錯誤的。

例 6

He was scarcely able to even talk.（他甚至連說話都很難。）

She commenced to rapidly walk around the room.

（她開始繞著房間快速地踱步。）

To have really loved is better than not to have at all loved.

（真正愛過總比從未愛過要好。）

在以上例句中，最好不要拆開動詞不定式。在日常交流中，甚至連大演說家都會違背這個規則。

紐約有位地方執法官，他是「the 400」的成員，很是為自己的措辭能力感到自豪。他講了這樣一個故事：一名犯人，一個死氣沉沉、傷痕累累的人。在他的臉上還能依稀看到曾經的幸福生活留下的痕跡，而此刻他憔悴的臉上寫滿了精疲力竭，垂頭喪氣地站在法官面前。

157

第八章
避開陷阱：常見誤用與詞彙偏差

「Where are you from?（你是哪裡人？）」，執法官問道。

「From Boston.（波士頓人）」，被告回答。

「Indeed.（確實）」法官說，「indeed, yours is a sad case, and yet you don't seem to thoroughly realize how low you have sunk.（沒錯，你的案子非常可悲，但你似乎完全沒有意識到你已經淪落到了何等境地。）」

這名犯人目瞪口呆，「Your honor does me an injustice,（尊敬的法官大人，請給我公正吧，）」他恨聲道，「The disgrace of arrest for drunkenness, the mortification of being thrust into a noisome dungeon, the publicity and humiliation of trial in a crowded and dingy courtroom I can bear, but to be sentenced by a Police Magistrate who splits his infinitives —— that is indeed the last blow.（醉酒被捕的羞恥、被丟到惡臭的地牢裡的窘迫，還有在擁擠昏暗的審判室公開侮辱我，我都能忍受。但被一個把不定式拆開使用的執法官審判，這真是壓死駱駝的最後一根稻草。）」

ONE

當用形容詞不定代詞 one 來替代人稱的時候，很容易引起混淆。當在句子或表達的開頭使用無人稱的 one 時，之後所有指代主語的詞都必須用 one。比如：

例 7

One must mind one's own business if one wishes to succeed.

（如果一個人想要成功，那麼他一定不要管別人的閒事。）

可能看起來有些囉唆、奇怪。但無論如何，這是正確的格式。一定不能說：

One must mind his business if he wishes to succeed.

（如果一個人想要成功，那麼他一定不要管別人的閒事。）

因為主語是無人稱的，所以不能使用僅指男性的代詞。

對於 any one 來說則不一樣。可以說：

If any one sins he should acknowledge it; let him not try to hide it by another sin.

（如果一個人有罪，那他一定要承認罪行；千萬不要讓他掩蓋罪行，這樣就又多了一項罪行。）

ONLY

無論是否接受了教育，這個詞對大部分人來說都很容易用錯。only 可能是英語語言中被誤用最多的單字。把它放在句中不同的地方會產生不同的句意。比如：

例 8

I only struck him that time.（我那次只是打了他。）

這句話的意思是，我只是打了他，而不是踢他或者以其他方式虐待他。

但如果把 only 換個位置，這句話變成 I struck him only that time.（我只是那次打了他。）

句意就變成，我只是那次打了他，其他時候並沒有打他。

還有一種可能的變化，即

I struck only him that time.（那次我只打了他。）

第八章
避開陷阱：常見誤用與詞彙偏差

句意再次發生改變，重點變成我只打了他，而沒有打別人。

我們在說話時可以透過重音表達不同的意思。但在書面語中，我們無法依靠重音，只能透過排列單字達到這個目的。使用 only 的最佳規則是把它緊緊地放在它要修飾或限定的詞前面。

ALONE

這又是一個會產生歧義、改變句意的詞。如果我們把上例中的 only 換成這個詞，句意會根據排列的不同產生不同意義。比如：

例 9

I alone struck him at that time.（那次只有我打了他。）

指的是只有我打了他，沒有其他人打他。而

I struck him alone at that time.（那次我只打了他。）

這一句的意思則是只有他被打，沒有其他人被打。再變化一下，

I struck him at that time alone.（我只有那次打了他。）

則是指那次是我唯一一次打他。

only 的正確使用規則同樣適用於 alone。

OTHER 和 ANOTHER

這兩個詞會改變它們修飾對象的意思。比如，

例 10

I have nothing to do with that *other* rascal across the street.

（我和街對面的另一個無賴沒有關係。）

明確指出我也是個無賴。另一個例子：

I sent the despatch to my friend, but *another* villain intercepted it.

（我送一份文件給我的朋友，但另一個罪犯把它攔截了下來。）

則清楚地說明我的朋友是一個罪犯。

一個好的解決辦法是，在能不用這些詞的情況下就盡量避免使用它們，比如以上例句。但如果必須使用的話，一定要確保句意清楚明瞭。要達到這一目的，就要確保帶有 other 和 another 的句子或片語能夠不依靠上下文，獨立表意。

AND 和關係代詞

永遠不要這樣在 and 後面接關係代詞：例 11

That is the dog I meant *and which* I know is of pure breed.

（我說的就是這種狗，我知道牠是純血統的。）

這是一個非常常見的錯誤。當前面的句子或分句裡出現了平行的關係代詞時，是可以這麼使用 and 的。

比如：

There is the dog which I meant and which I know is of pure breed.

（我說的就是這種狗，我知道牠是純血統的。）

這樣是正確的。

第八章
避開陷阱：常見誤用與詞彙偏差

鬆散的分詞

分詞或分詞短語一般來說修飾的是離它最近的主格。如果句子裡只有一個主格，那麼除去不是句子基本結構裡的分詞，其他所有的分詞都是修飾該主格的。

例 12

John, working in the field all day and getting thirsty, drank from the running stream.

（約翰成天在田裡忙活，渴了就去溪流邊飲水。）

這個例句中，分詞 working 和 getting 明顯是在指 John。

例 13

Swept along by the mob I could not save him.

（被犯罪集團洗劫一空，我也沒法幫他。）

但在這個例句中，分詞鬆散地分布在句子中，可能指說話人，也可能指提及的對象。這句話可能是說我被犯罪集團洗劫一空，也有可能是說那個我本想去救的人被犯罪集團洗劫一空。

例 14 Going into the store the roof fell.（走進商店，屋頂掉了下來。）

這句話可以理解為屋頂在被搬進商店的時候掉了下來。當然這句話的正確理解應該是一個人或人們走進商店的時候屋頂掉了下來。

在使用所有帶有分詞的句式結構時，應該明確地杜絕所有可能出現的歧義。分詞在句中的位置應該清晰地指向它修飾的名詞。一般來說，建議使用表意明顯的分詞。

破碎的句式結構

有時，句首和句尾的語法結構不同。這一現象來源於事實，人們寫到句尾時已經忘記了句首的語法。這種情況在長句中頻繁出現。比如：

例 15

Honesty, integrity and square-dealing will bring anybody much better through life than the absence of either.

（誠信、正直和公平交易的精神能讓人好好地過完一生，缺了誰都不行。）

這句話的結構在 than 那裡被破壞了。either 的用法，僅指兩者中的一個，這個詞的使用表明作者忘記了進行比較的有三種品格而不是兩種。這句話可能表達了以下三個意思，即：其中一種品格的缺失、其中兩種品格的缺失以及三種品格全部缺失。either 指的是兩者當中的任何一個，不能用於兩者以上的情況。

當我們犯了以上例句這樣的結構性錯誤時，我們應該把句子拆分開來，重組成其他的語法結構。比如：

例 16

Honesty, integrity and square-dealing will bring a man much better through life than a lack of these qualities which are almost essential to success.

（誠信、正直和公平交易的精神能讓人很好地過完一生，這三種品格對於成功來說不可或缺。）

第八章
避開陷阱：常見誤用與詞彙偏差

雙重否定

一定要記住，在英語裡兩個否定詞互相抵消，等於肯定。比如，

例 17

I *don't* know *nothing* about it.（我對於情況一無所知。）

意在表達我對於情況一無所知。但這句話自相矛盾，因為 nothing 的使用表明我知道一些情況（something）。這句話應該寫作：

I don't know anything about it.（我對於情況一無所知。）

我們經常聽到此類表達，比如，

例 18

He was not asked to give no opinion.（他不被要求給出任何觀點。）

實際表達的意思和它的本意恰好相反。這句話的意思是他被要求給出自己的觀點。

因此，我們應該盡量避免使用雙重否定，因為很容易出錯。在評論家發現錯誤之前，作家常常意識不到它們的存在。

第一人稱代詞

在寫作中，應盡量避免使用第一人稱。不要在道歉的時候使用第一人稱，也絕對不要使用以下的表達：

例 19

In my opinion（在我看來）　　As far as I can see（就我的考慮來說）

It appears to me（對於我而言）　　I believe（我認為）

等等。

你寫出的所有內容都是你的觀點。既然你是作者，就沒有必要再強調或重複你自己。

除此之外，經常用 I 顯得非常自我！這一點要極力避免。在文章中唯一可以使用第一人稱的時候就是在陳述不常見的觀點，並且很可能遭到反對意見時。

時態的順序

當兩個動詞互相依賴時，它們之間一定有明確的時態關係。

例 20

I shall have much pleasure in accepting your kind invitation.

（接受你的邀請我將感到非常開心。）

這句話是錯的，除非你的意思是你剛才拒絕了這個邀請，儘管不久之後你改變主意，決定接受邀請；或者你的意思是你現在確實接受了邀請，儘管這麼做你並不感到開心，但希望不久之後能感到開心。

事實上，複合時態的順序讓經驗豐富的作家都頭大。最好的應對方法是回到句中描述的時態，使用你在「當時」會用的時態。

例 21

I should have liked to have gone to see the circus.（我本應該喜歡去看過馬戲團的。）

第八章
避開陷阱：常見誤用與詞彙偏差

在這個句子中，要想找出正確的時間順序，就要問自己這樣一個問題：

What is it I should have liked to do?（我本來想做的是什麼？）

答案就是：To go to see the circus.（去看馬戲團。）

我不能回答：To have gone to see the circus.（去看過馬戲團。）

因為這個答案暗示我在想做什麼事的時候已經去過馬戲團了，但實際上我並不想表達這個意思；我想表達的是在說話的時候我希望自己已經去過馬戲團。動詞短語 I should have liked 表示當時我還有機會去看馬戲團，去看馬戲團在當時是可以實現的。

這一段解釋可以變成一個簡單的問題：What should I have liked at that time?（我當時想做的是什麼？）

答案就是：To go to see the circus.（去看馬戲團。）

所以這就是正確的時態。這句話的正確表達應為：I should have liked to go to see the circus.（我本應該喜歡去看馬戲團的。）

如果我們想談論比過去時態指向的時間點更早發生的事情，那就必須用不定式的完成時態。比如：

例 22

He appeared to have seen better days.（看來他原來日子過得很好。）

我們應該說：I expected to meet him.（我期待與他見面。）

而不是：I expected to have met him.（我期待與他見過面。）

應該說：We intended to visit you.（我們有意拜訪你。）

而不是：We intended to have visited you.（我們有意拜訪過你。）

應該說：I hoped they would arrive.（我希望他們能到達。）

而不是：I hoped they would have arrived.（我希望他們能到達過。）

應該說：I thought I should catch the bird.（我想我應該抓住那隻鳥。）

而不是：I thought I should have caught the bird.（我想我應該抓住過那隻鳥。）

應該說：I had intended to go to the meeting.（我打算去參加會議。）

而不是：I had intended to have gone to the meeting.（我打算去參加過會議。）

BETWEEN —— AMONG

這兩個介詞經常被隨意地換用。between 只能用在兩者之間，among 用在兩個以上的事物之間。

例 23

The money was equally divided between them.（他們把錢平分了。）

如果只有兩個人的話，這句話就是對的；如果是兩個人以上的話，這句話應該寫作：

The money was equally divided among them.（他們把錢平分了。）

第八章
避開陷阱:常見誤用與詞彙偏差

LESS —— FEWER

less 不可數,fewer 可數。

例 24

No man has less virtues.(人無完人。)

這句話的正確形式應該是:No man has fewer virtues.(人無完人。)

The farmer had some oats and a fewer quantity of wheat.

(農夫有一些燕麥和少量小麥。)

這句話的正確形式應該是:The farmer had some oats and a less quantity of wheat.(農夫有一些燕麥和少量小麥。)

FURTHER —— FARTHER

further 常用於指數量,farther 常用於指距離。

例 25

I have walked farther than you.(我走得比你遠。)

I need no further supply.(我不需要更多的補給了。)

兩句話都是正確的。

EACH OTHER —— ONE ANOTHER

each other 指兩個,one another 指兩個以上。

例 26

Jones and Smith quarreled; they struck each other.

（瓊斯和史密斯吵架了，他們打了彼此。）

這句話是對的。

Jones, Smith and Brown quarreled; they struck one another.

（瓊斯、史密斯和布朗吵架了，他們打了對方。）

這句話也是正確的。

不要說：The two boys teach one another.（兩個男孩互相教對方。）

也不要說：The three girls love each other.（三個女孩互相愛對方。）

EACH、EVERY、EITHER、NEITHER

這些詞經常被誤用。each 指的是兩個或以上對象中的每一個獨立的個體。

every 指的是兩個或以上對象中的每一個分別的個體。either 指的是兩者中的任意一個，不能同時用來指兩個對象。neither 是 either 的否定形式，既不指這個，也不指那個，對象是互相獨立的兩個人或事物。

以下例句展示了這些詞的正確用法：

例 27

Each man of the crew received a reward.（劇組裡的每個人都得到了獎勵。）

Every man in the regiment displayed bravery.

（團裡每個人都展現出了勇敢的一面。）

第八章
避開陷阱：常見誤用與詞彙偏差

We can walk on *either* side of the street.（我們可以走街道的任何一邊。）

Neither of the two is to blame.（兩個人都不應該責怪。）

NEITHER-NOR

當兩個單數的對象由 neither、nor 連接起來時，動詞用單數形式。比如，

例 28

Neither John nor James was there.（無論是約翰還是詹姆斯，都不在。）

而不是：

Neither John nor James were there.（無論是約翰還是詹姆斯，都不在。）

NONE

習慣上來說，這個詞既可接單數動詞，也可接複數動詞。比如，

例 29

None is so blind as he who will not see.

（沒有人像他那樣眼盲，因為他看不見了。）

None are so blind as they who will not see.

（沒有人像他們那樣眼盲，因為他們看不見了。）

不過，考慮到它是 no one 的縮寫形式，最好還是用動詞的單數形式。

RISE-RAISE

這兩個動詞常常被混淆。rise 指以任何方式向上移動或前進，比如，

例 30　rise from bed（起床）

還指價值上升，或者地位或排名上升，比如，

例 31

stocks rise（股票上漲）

politicians rise（政治家崛起）

They have risen to honor.（他們站起來致敬）

raise 指舉起、提升或提高。比如，

例 32

I raise the table.（我抬起了桌子。）

He raised his servant.（他讓他的職員升遷了。）

The baker raised the price of bread.（麵包店提高了麵包的價格。）

LAY-LIE

及物動詞 lay 和中性動詞 lie 的過去式 lay 經常被混淆，雖然這兩個 lay 的意義相差甚遠。作中性動詞 lie 的過去式時，lay 的意思是躺下或休息，沒有介詞的話不能直接在後面接賓語。

例 33

我們可以說：He lies on the ground.（他躺在地上。）

第八章
避開陷阱：常見誤用與詞彙偏差

但不能說：He lies the ground.（他躺地上。）

因為它是中性不及物動詞，所以不可以接直接賓語。但是作及物動詞時的 lay 就不一樣了，它可以接直接賓語，比如：

例 34

I lay a wager.（我打了個賭。）　　I laid the carpet.（我鋪了地毯。）

等等。

如果主語是地毯或其他無生命物體，我們應該說：

例 35

It lies on the floor.（它躺在地上。）

A knife lies on the table.（一把刀在桌子上。）

而不是用 lays。

但如果主語是人，應該說：

例 36

He lays the knife on the table.（他把刀放在桌上。）

而不是：He lies the knife on the table.（他把刀放在桌上。）

lay 是 lie（down）的過去式，所以它的正確用法是

例 37　He lay on the bed.（他躺在床上。）

lain 是 lie 的過去分詞，所以它的正確用法是

例 38　He has lain on the bed.（他躺在床上。）

我們可以用：

例 39

I lay myself down.（我躺了下來。）

He laid himself down.（他躺了下來。）

等類似表達。

用這兩個詞時必須記住，to lay 指的是去做某事，to lie 指的是休息這一狀態。

SAYS I —— I SAID

「Says I」是不正規的說法，不要這麼說。「I said」才是正確的形式。

IN —— INTO

仔細分辨這兩個介詞意義上的區別，不要把它們搞混。

例 40

不要說：He went in the room.（他進了房間。）

也不要說：My brother is into the navy.（我哥哥進入了海軍。）

in 指的是某人或某物 —— 無論是靜態還是動態 —— 存在於某地的狀態。

into 指的是進入的動作，比如：

例 41

He went into the room.（他進了房間。）

My brother is in the navy.（我哥哥進入了海軍。）

這兩句話是正確的。

第八章
避開陷阱：常見誤用與詞彙偏差

EAT —— ATE

不要認錯這兩個詞，eat 是現在時，ate 是過去時。

例 42

I eat the bread.（我吃麵包。）

這句話的意思是我在持續吃這個動作。

I ate the bread.（我吃了麵包。）

這句話的意思是「吃」這個動作是過去發生的。

eaten 是完成時態，但很多時候用的是 eat。因為 eat (et) 和 ate 的發音相同，我們應該注意分辨過去時 I ate 和完成時態 I have eaten。

人稱的順序

請記住，第一人稱優先於第二人稱，第二人稱優先於第三人稱。當沃爾西紅衣主教說 Ego et Rex（I and the King）時，證明了他語法用得很好，但侍臣做得很差。

AM COME —— HAVE COME

例 43

I am come.（我到了。）

側重的是我到了這裡，而

I have come.（我到了。）

過去時─過去分詞

側重的是我剛剛到達這裡。

當主語不是人的時候，應該用 to be 而不是 to have。比如：

例 44

The box is come.（盒子到了。）

而不是：The box has come.（盒子到了。）

過去時 ── 過去分詞

不規則變化動詞（irregular verbs），或者說，所謂的強勢動詞（strong verbs）的過去式和過去分詞的混用可能是粗心大意的演講者和作家最常犯的錯誤了。要避免這類錯誤，必須知道這些動詞的完全變化形態。這個知識並不難獲得，因為這樣的動詞不過幾百個，而在這幾百個動詞中只有很小一部分屬於日常用詞。以下是一些最常見的錯誤：

例 45

I saw（我看到了）說成 I seen（我看到了）

I did it（我做到了）說成 I donc it（我做到了）

I drank（我喝了）說成 I drunk（我喝了）

I began（我開始了）說成 I begun（我開始了）

I rang（我按了鈴）說成 I rung（我按了鈴）

I ran（我跑了步）說成 I run（我跑了步）

I sang（我唱了歌）說成 I sung（我唱了歌）

I have chosen（我選擇了）說成 I have chose（我選擇了）

第八章
避開陷阱：常見誤用與詞彙偏差

I have driven（我開了）說成 I have drove（我開了）

I have worn（我穿了）說成 I have wore（我穿了）

I have trodden（我走了）說成 I have trod（我走了）

I have shaken（我搖了）說成 I have shook（我搖了）

I have fallen（我摔跤了）說成 I have fell（我摔跤了）

I have drunk（我喝了）說成 I have drank（我喝了）

I have begun（我開始了）說成 I have began（我開始了）

I have rung（我按了鈴）說成 I have rang（我按了鈴）

I have risen（我拿起了）說成 I have rose（我拿起了）

I have spoken（我說了）說成 I have spoke（我說了）

I have broken（我打壞了）說成 I have broke（我打壞了）

It has frozen（它凍住了）說成 It has froze（它凍住了）

It has blown（它吹走了）說成 It has blowed（它吹走了）

It has flown（指鳥）（它飛走了）說成 It has flowed（它飛走了）

注意 —— to hang 的過去式和過去分詞是 hanged 或 hung。

例 46

當你在談論絞刑架上被絞死的人時，應該說：

He was hanged.（他被吊死了。）

當你談論的是動物屍體時，應該說：

It was hung.（它被掛了起來。）

就像這句話一樣：The beef was hung dry.（牛肉被掛起來晾乾。）

另外，你的大衣 was hung on a hook.（掛在鉤子上。）

介詞和賓格

不要忘記介詞後面永遠要用賓格。

例 47

不要說：Between you and I（你我之間）

而要說：Between you and me（你我之間）

不要拿兩個介詞修飾一個賓語，除非它們之間有緊密的連繫。

例 48

不　要　說：He was refused admission to and forcibly ejected from the school.

（他被拒絕接收，並且被迫從學校開除了出去。）

而　要　說：He was refused admission to the school and forcibly ejected from it.

（他被學校拒絕並開除。）

SUMMON — SUMMONS

例 49

不要說：I shall summons him.（我將召喚他來。）

而要說：I shall summon him.（我將召喚他來。）

summon 是動詞，summons 是名詞。

可以說：I shall get a summons for him.（我將召喚他來。）

而不要用 summon。

第八章
避開陷阱：常見誤用與詞彙偏差

UNDENIABLE —— UNEXCEPTIONABLE

例 50

如果我想表達我的哥哥性格很好的話，那麼，

My brother has an undeniable character.（我哥哥有著無可爭辯的性格。）

這句話是錯的。應該說：

My brother has an unexceptionable character.（我哥哥有著無可指摘的性格。）

An undeniable character 指的是無可否認的性格，無論好壞。An unexceptionable character 指的是無可指摘、無可批評的性格。

代詞

代詞的使用常出現很多錯誤。

例 51

不應說：Let you and I go.（讓你和我走。）

而應說：Let you and me go.（讓你和我走。）

不應說：Let them and we go.（讓他們和我走。）

而應說：Let them and us go.（讓他們和我走。）

let 是及物動詞，所以後面應該接賓格。

例 52

Give me them flowers.（給我那些花。）的正確說法是：

Give me those flowers.（給我那些花。）

I mean them three.（我是說他們三個。）的正確說法是：

I mean those three.（我是說他們三個。）

them 是人稱代詞的賓格，不能被用作指示形容詞代詞。

例 53

I am as strong as he.（我和他一樣強壯。）的正確說法是：

I am as strong as him.（我和他一樣強壯。）

I am younger than she.（我比她年輕。）的正確說法是：

I am younger than her.（我比她年輕。）

He can write better than I.（他字寫得比我好。）的正確說法是：

He can write better than me.（他字寫得比我好。）

在以上例句中，賓格 him、her 和 me 被錯用為主格。在每個錯用的代詞後會預設接一個以該代詞為主語的動詞：

I am as strong as he (is).（我和他一樣強壯。）

I am younger than she (is).（我比她年輕。）

He can write better than I (can).（他字寫得比我好。）

例 54

不要說：It is me.（是我。）

而要說：It is I.（是我。）

動詞 to be 放在 it 後面時與在 it 前面時的格是一樣的。這個規則適用於所有的情況，包括代詞。

第八章
避開陷阱：常見誤用與詞彙偏差

動詞 to be 要求後面跟著的代詞和它使用同一個格，這和代詞在問句裡的用法一樣；主格 I 對應的代詞是主格 who，賓格 me、him、her、its、you 和 them 對應的代詞是賓格 whom。

例 55

Whom do you think I am?（你以為我是什麼人？）的正確形式是：

Who do you think I am?（你以為我是什麼人？）

Who do they suppose me to be?（他們認為我是怎樣的人？）的正確形式是：

Whom do they suppose me to be?（他們認為我是怎樣的人？）

人稱代詞的賓格後面應該接介詞。

例 56

Who do you take me for?（你把我當成了誰？）的正確形式是：

Whom do you take me for?（你把我當成了誰？）

Who did you give the apple to?（你把蘋果給了誰？）的正確形式是：

Whom did you give the apple to?（你把蘋果給了誰？）

但如之前提過的，介詞不能用在句尾。因此，更好的說法是：

To whom did you give the apple?（你把蘋果給了誰？）

在及物動詞後要用代詞的賓格。

例 57

不要說：He and they we have seen.（我們見過他和他們。）

而要說：Him and them we have seen.（我們見過他和他們。）

用 SO 不用 THAT

例 58

The hurt it was that painful it made him cry.（疼痛太嚴重，讓他淚流不止。）

這句話應該說成：The hurt it was so painful it made him cry.

（疼痛太嚴重，讓他淚流不止。）

THESE —— THOSE

不要說 these kind、those sort。kind 和 sort 都是單數，對應的代詞應是 this 和 that。談到這些指示形容詞代詞時，請記住 this 和 these 指的是離自己很近的東西，that 和 those 指的是遠一點的東西。比如，this book（離我近）、that book（在那邊）、these boys（離得近）、those boys（有一定距離）。

THIS MUCH —— THUS MUCH

例 59

This much is certain.（這麼多是確定的。）的正確說法是：

Thus much or so much is certain.（這麼多是確定的。）

FLEE —— FLY

這是兩個各自獨立、不可混用的動詞。flee 的完全變化形態為 flee、fled、fled；fly 的則是 fly、flew、flown。to flee 的意思是逃離危險，to fly 的意思則是像鳥一樣飛翔。

第八章
避開陷阱：常見誤用與詞彙偏差

例 60

這樣形容一個人是錯的：He has flown from the place.（他從這個地方飛走了。）

正確說法是：He has fled from the place.（他從這個地方逃走了。）

我們可以肯定地說：A bird has flown from the place.（一隻鳥從這裡飛走了。）

THROUGH —— THROUGHOUT

例 61

不要說：He is well known through the land.（這裡的人都知道他。）

而要說：He is well known throughout the land.（這裡的人都知道他。）

VOCATION AND AVOCATION

不要搞混這兩個看似相同的詞。vocation 指的是人們為了謀生所從事的工作、職業，或專業領域的事務。avocation 指的是人們在工作、職業或專業領域的事務之外的閒暇時間裡所追求的東西。比如：

例 62

His vocation was the law, his avocation, farming.

（他是法律界人士，愛好是務農。）

WAS — WERE

在虛擬語氣中，複數 were 應用於單數主語。比如，

例 63

應該是：If I were（如果我）

而不是：If I was（如果我）

記住，複數的人稱代詞 you 永遠和 were 在一起出現，儘管它可能指一個以上的東西。所以，

例 64

應該是：you were（你是）

而絕不是：you was（你是）

例 65

If I was him（如果我是他）是一個很常見的表達。

正確說法應該是：If I were he（如果我是他）

裡面的兩個錯誤——表明狀態的動詞，和形態為賓格的代詞。這是動詞 to be 的使用規則的又一個展示，即在它後面和前面的代詞的格和它是一樣的。were 是 to be 的一個形態，因此主格 I 放在它前面，主格 he 放在它後面。

A 或 AN

在母音或 h 前面，a 變成 an，且 h 不發音，這樣發音聽起來悅耳、舒服，比如：an apple、an orange、an heir、an honor 等等。

第八章
避開陷阱：常見誤用與詞彙偏差

第九章
風格打造：措辭準確與規範表達

將自己的思想盡可能以高效的形式展現給讀者、讓讀者產生好感，是每一位作家的目標。一個擁有高尚思想和觀念，但卻無法將它們以引人入勝的方式展現出來的人，也就無法完全施展他智慧的力量，或者說無法在他所在的時代留下自己的印記；然而，很多無甚天分的人卻能夠憑藉膚淺的筆墨吸引諸多目光，在歷史上占據一席之地，讓同代人羨慕不已。

在日常生活中，我們經常看到擁有偉大思想的人被置於一旁、無人理睬，而能力平庸，有時甚至是能力微弱的人被選中完成偉業。前者無法克服性格上的缺陷：他們擁有偉大的思想和觀念，但這些思想和觀念都被困在他們的大腦中，就像圍欄後的囚犯，掙扎著想要獲得自由。然而，能夠打開這扇門的語言鑰匙卻無處尋覓，所以它們只得一直被困。

許多人在世上走了一遭，卻無人知曉。沒有為世界帶來什麼價值，也沒有實現自己的價值。這一切僅僅是因為沒有順從自己的意願，展現內心的想法。努力發掘自己的價值，不僅是為自己好，也是為他人好。這是每個人的職責。擁有好的學識或者能力並不是完全必要的。在各自的職位上，體力勞動者和哲學家一樣有價值。同樣，擁有許多天賦也不是必要的。一種能被正當運用的天賦比十種被誤用的天賦要好得多。常常，擁有一種天賦的人比擁有十種天賦的同齡人做得更好；常常，手裡

第九章
風格打造：措辭準確與規範表達

有一美元的人比手裡有二十美元的人走得更遠；常常，窮人比百萬富翁活得更舒服。這一切都取決於個人意願。如果一個人正確運用造物主給予他的天分，按照神的意願和自然法則生存，那麼他就在履行造物主給予他的職責。換句話說，當一個人做到自己能做到的最好時，那麼他就擁有了一個有價值的人生。

要想做到最好，一個擁有常規智商和教育水準的人應該能夠透過說和寫正確地自我表達。也就是說，他應能以智慧的方式傳達自己的思想，讓頭腦簡單的人也可以明白。演說家和作家傳達自己思想的方式被稱為風格，換句話說，風格也可以被定義為一個人透過語言傳達自己思想時所使用的獨特方式。它取決於措辭以及詞彙的編排。極少會有兩個作家擁有相同的寫作風格——也就是使用相同的獨特的格式來表達他們的思想，就像世界上沒有兩個從一個模子裡刻出來的人一樣。

正如人們擁有不同的口音和音調，人們的語言結構也各不相同。

假設兩名記者被給予同一個任務，比如報導一場火災，他們的口頭敘述會有所差異。儘管從客觀上來說，在談到主要事實時兩個人的描述是相同的，但他們的敘述風格是有區別的。

如果要你來描述上次慈善舞會裡的那位紅髮女士的舞蹈，你可以說

例1

The ruby Circe, with the Titian locks glowing like the oriflamme which surrounds the golden god of day as he sinks to rest amid the crimson glory of the burnished West, gave a divine exhibition of the Terpsichorean art which thrilled the souls of the multitude.

（紅髮的賽絲，她一頭紅褐色的秀髮像圍繞金色日神的旗幟那樣閃亮，那場景如同她在散發著深紅色光芒的西邊日落一般，神聖地展示出了驚嘆眾人的舞蹈藝術。）

也可以簡短地介紹道，

The red-haired lady danced very well and pleased the audience.
（這位紅髮女士舞姿綽約，觀眾皆為之讚嘆。）

前者是極度華而不實、堆砌辭藻的風格的範例，它需要裝腔作勢，以冗長的敘述來達到效果；而後者則是簡單自然風格的範例。毋庸置疑，後者的風格更被我們所青睞，而前者則極需避免。它替作家貼上了膚淺、傲慢、缺乏經驗的標籤。這種風格在新聞寫作中被剔除了出去，就算是最低俗的新聞也不再在它的欄目裡使用這類風格。矯揉造作和賣弄學問的文風已經完全遭到拋棄。追求能夠吸引讀者的風格是每一個演說家和作家的職責，這樣的風格能引領他進入這一行業，否則會將他拒之門外。常常，人們對於主題是否感興趣不僅取決於主題本身，同樣也取決於主題的呈現方式。有一些作家的呈現方式引人入勝，而有一些則讓人反感。以歷史記載為例，在一位歷史學家的筆下，某一歷史事件讀起來可能像木乃伊一樣枯燥無味、令人厭惡；而在另一位歷史學家的鬼斧神工下可能被描繪得唯妙唯肖，不僅能激起讀者的興趣，更能使讀者為之深深著迷。

措辭

風格的第一必要條件就是詞彙的選擇，這屬於**措辭**（Diction）。措辭是風格的一個特質之一，它涉及談話和寫作中的單字和片語。無論立

第九章
風格打造：措辭準確與規範表達

場如何，文學技巧的祕訣在於在合適的地方使用合適的詞彙。要做到這一點，我們有必要知道我們使用的詞彙的意思，我指的是它們的字面意思。許多同義詞看似可以互換，好像一個意思可以適用於三四個同義詞，但把這些同義詞放在一起分析時，我們可以清楚地看到它們的意思有明確的差異。比如，grief 和 sorrow 看似一樣[35]，但實際上卻不一樣。grief 指的悲傷是主動的，而 sorrow 指的悲傷或多或少是被動的；grief 指的悲傷是由困難和不幸等外界因素引起的，而 sorrow 指的悲傷常常是我們自己行為帶來的後果；grief 指的悲傷通常是大聲的、強烈的，而 sorrow 指的悲傷經常是安靜的、孤獨的；grief 指的是會喊出聲的悲傷，而 sorrow 指的是仍保持冷靜的悲傷。

如果你不確定某個單字的準確定義，立刻去查詞典吧。有時，大學者都會在常見詞的意思、拼寫或發音方面犯錯。無論何時，只要看到奇怪的詞就做個筆記，直到你掌握它的意思和用法。閱讀你能找到的最好的書，也就是那些家喻戶曉的語言大師的作品，向他們學習詞彙的使用、在句子中的擺放，以及向讀者傳達了怎樣的資訊。打入上流社會，仔細聆聽優秀的說話者，模仿他們的表達方式。如果對一個詞的用法感到迷惑，要不恥下問，弄明白它的意思。

確實，沒有豐富的詞彙量你也可以照常生活，但擁有豐富的詞彙量是一個優勢。當你獨居時，小鍋子同樣能滿足你做飯的需求，並且小鍋子更方便、更好用。但如果你的朋友或鄰居要來你家吃飯的話，你就需要一個大得多的鍋。這時候家裡如果有大鍋子的話就再好不過了，你不至於因為缺少這樣的廚具而陷入尷尬的境地。

盡可能地擴充詞彙量。如果你現在不需要它們，就把它們先記在

---

[35] 兩個詞都有悲傷的意思。

腦子裡。這樣一來，當你需要它們的時候，你就可以把它們拿出來使用了。

隨身攜帶筆記本，一碰到你不懂或一知半解的詞就趕緊記下來，等到有空的時候去查詞典。

純粹

純粹（Purity）指的是寫作時要使用卓越的、普及的、流行的詞彙，也就是說，那些大作家信手拈來、通用（不限於一個變化形態）、時興的詞彙。

在詞彙的選擇上有兩條指導性原則：用途和品味。用途指的是這個詞的使用是否正確；品味指的是這個詞是否適合我們的寫作目的。

不要用過時的、新潮到還未普及的、適用範圍過於狹隘的詞彙。以下是英語風格的十誡：

1. 不要使用外來詞。

2. 能用短詞，就盡量不用長詞。比如 fire 比 conflagration 要好。

3. 不要用技術詞彙，或者那些只有專家才懂的行話，除非這本書是專門為這類人寫的。

4. 不要使用俚語。

5. 不要用使用範圍過於狹隘的表達方式，比如該用 I think 的地方用 I guess，該用 I know 的地方用 I reckon 等等。

6. 寫散文時，不要用詩歌性的或老舊的詞彙。比如 lore、e'er、morn、yea、nay、verily、peradventure。

第九章
風格打造：措辭準確與規範表達

7. 不要使用平庸、陳腐的詞彙和表達。比如 on the job、up and in、down and out。

8. 不要使用還未普及的新聞詞彙，比如 to bugle、to suicide 等。

9. 不要使用不合語法規則的詞彙和格式，比如「He showed me all about the house.」。

10. 陳腐的詞彙、老舊的明喻暗喻就應停留在過去的時光裡，諸如 Sweet sixteen、the Almighty dollar、Uncle Sam、On the fence、The Glorious Fourth、Young America、The lords of creation、The rising generation、The weaker sex、The weaker vessel、Sweetness long drawn out 和 chief cook and bottle washer 這類表達應該被塵封起來，因為它們的使用氾濫。

有些明喻已經不再實用，應該退休，比如 Sweet as sugar、Bold as a lion、Strong as an ox、Quick as a flash、Cold as ice、Stiff as a poker、White as snow、Busy as a bee、Pale as a ghost、Rich as Croesus、Cross as a bear，還有無數這樣的表達，在此就不贅述了。

盡可能採用原創的表達。不要墨守成規，要努力創新。這並不是說讓你去創立新的風格，做一些出格的、稀奇古怪的事，或者革新通用習俗。要做到原創，不一定要引進新穎的東西或者開創先河，且無論從教育水準還是天分上來說，你很有可能也不是做這件事的料。跟隨公認的引領者，你就能在語言中找到自己的原創風格，嘗試著從另一個角度去更好地解讀一個想法。

例2

如果你談論或描述舞蹈，不要用 tripping the light fantastic toe（單踩著輕盈的小腳指頭）這種表達。

距離米爾頓[36]在作品〈快樂的人〉中使用這個表達已經兩百多年了，而你也不是米爾頓。除此之外，已經有無數人引用過米爾頓的這句話，它已不再獨特。不要使用過時的詞，比如 whilom、yclept、wis 等。對於那些正在被淘汰的詞，即現在仍在使用、但使用頻率逐漸減少的詞，也要謹慎使用，比如 quoth、trow、betwixt、amongst、froward 等等。同時，對於新詞，態度要謹慎。在結構和編排上放手創新，但不要發明新詞，這種事留給語言大師去做吧。也不要做第一個吃螃蟹的人，等到人們在演講中將它們的用法和優缺點測試完全後再去使用它們。

昆提良[37]曾說過：「Prefer the oldest of the new and the newest of the old.」教皇把這句話改寫得符合韻律，它的意思仍然得到了完整的傳達：

In words, as fashions, the same rule will hold, Alike fantastic, if too new or old： Be not the first by whom the new are tried, Nor yet the last to lay the old aside.

規範

規範（Propriety）指的是以詞的正確意義去使用它。和純粹一樣，詞彙的正確使用是最重要的，許多詞在實際使用中的意思和它們被定義的意思完全不同。prevent 以前的意思是「在……之前去做」，這個意思由拉

---

[36]　米爾頓（John Milton），英國詩人，代表作有〈失樂園〉、〈復樂園〉、〈力士孫參〉等。
[37]　昆提良（Quintilian），古羅馬時期的著名律師、教育家和皇室委任的第一個修辭學教授。

第九章
風格打造：措辭準確與規範表達

丁語衍生而來，現在它的意思變為了阻止、妨礙。要使風格規範化，就有必要避免混淆來源相同的詞，比如 respectfully 和 respectively。用詞時需使用被人們廣泛接受的意思，或者大家都在生活中使用的意思。

簡潔

簡潔（Simplicity）指的是「選擇簡單的詞，表達簡單明瞭」的意思。在能夠表達相同的，或基本相同的意思的前提下，永遠優先使用簡單的詞，而非複雜的複合詞。英語語言中的盎格魯撒克遜成分構成了我們日常生活中表達會用到的簡單字，它們強大、簡練、有力，常常出現在爐火旁、街邊、市場上、農場內的對話裡。正是簡潔的風格成就了《聖經》以及其他許多經典著作，比如《天路歷程》、《魯賓遜漂流記》、《格列佛遊記》。

清晰

清晰（Clearness）應該成為寫作新手首要考慮的原則之一。新手寫作時，必須避免所有晦澀、含糊的表達。如果一個句子（或短語）除了本意之外可能會讓人有其他的解讀的話，那麼這個句子（或短語）應被重寫，直到不再讓人產生疑慮。語義上緊密相連的單字、短語或分句應該盡可能被放在一起，這樣的話，它們之間的關係能夠得到更清晰地呈現。如果刪掉某個單字會影響句子的完整性，則這個單字應被保留。

一致性

一致性（Unity）讓句子中的各個成分與中心思想緊密相連，並且邏輯上保持一致。一個句子既可以有緊湊的、展現思維統一性的句式，也可以有鬆散的、表意混亂含糊的句式。互相之間幾乎沒有連繫的想法應該各自獨立成句，而不是被塞進一個句子裡。

不要在句子中間使用括號。結束一句話時，不要試著加上補充性的分句以繼續闡述該句的想法或觀點。

力度

力度（Strength）帶給了語言動感、能量和張力，並且能夠持續吸引讀者的注意力。力度之於語言就如食物之於身體，沒有力度的語言軟弱無力，無法在讀者腦海中留下印記。想要有力度，語言必須凝練，也就是說，用簡潔的語句表達盡量多的內容，要一針見血，一語中的。用批判的眼光審視一遍你的作品，把每一個去掉後不會影響句子清晰程度和表達力度的單字、片語和分句剔除出去，以避免累贅、重複和迂迴。把最重要的詞放在句子裡最顯眼的位置，如之前所說的，也就是句子的開頭和結尾。

和諧

和諧（Harmony）帶給語句流暢感。這樣一來，當句子被讀出來的時候，詞與詞之間的連接聽起來就悅耳動聽，和諧的文字聽起來才順耳。

第九章
風格打造：措辭準確與規範表達

大多數人在寫作時沒有考慮這些文字組合讀出來是什麼感覺，所以我們常常遇到刺耳、不協調的文字組合。比如：

例3

Thou strengthenedst thy position and actedst arbitrarily and derogatorily to my interests.

（汝鞏固汝之地位，武斷、毀損地對待吾之利益。）

刺耳、不協調的動詞可能來自貴格會教徒的人稱代詞 thou。這種格式已經基本過時，現在該代詞的複數形式普遍使用 you。要想得到和諧的文字，應避免發音拗口的長詞和特定的字母組合。

作者的特色表達

風格是作者個人特色的表達，展現了作者的寫作能力和水準。從寫作結構上來說，風格展現了作者的寫作能力；從品質上來說，風格展現了作者的寫作水準。

風格的種類

風格的分類方法有很多種，但名稱的多樣性導致很難按類列舉。實際上，風格的種類和作家的數量一樣多，因為沒有哪兩個作家會用一種格式寫出相同的風格。然而，我們仍然可以在眾多作家的寫作風格中分出大致的種類，比如 1. 單調；2. 樸實；3. 簡潔；4. 優雅；5. 華麗；6. 華而不實。

單調的風格（the dry style）包含所有的細節，但卻不做任何能達成文字美感的修飾。該風格的目標僅僅是透過正確的語法結構表達觀點。它的代表人有柏克萊[38]。

樸實的風格（the plain style）也不追求文字的修飾，該風格追求的是清晰凝練，不帶過多解釋或潤色的表達。該風格的代表人有洛克[39]和惠特利[40]。

簡潔的風格（the neat style）則是少量地追求文字的修飾。該風格的目標是實現正確的修辭、純粹的措辭以及清晰和諧的句子。戈德史密斯和格雷是此類風格公認的領軍人物。

優雅的風格（the elegant style）使用任何能美化句子的修飾、避免任何降低格調的表達。在此類風格中，麥考萊和艾迪生得到了眾人的加冕，所有人都應向這兩位大家致敬。

華麗的風格（the florid style）追求多餘的、膚淺的修飾，力求刻劃色彩明豔的畫面。莪相[41]是該風格的代表人。

華而不實的風格（the bombastic style）的特點是過量的詞彙、修辭和修飾，導致文學作品變得荒唐可笑、令人厭惡，就像小丑穿一身金箔一樣。狄更斯在《匹克威克外傳》中巴茲法茨中士的演講裡給出了很好的例子。風格可以是口語的、簡潔的、凝練的、冗贅的、唐突的、流暢的、古韻的、雋語式的、辭藻華麗的、乾巴巴的、緊張兮兮的、強烈的、做作的，這些風格的特點已經透過它們的描述詞得到了充分的表現。

---

[38] 譯者注：喬治·貝克萊（George Berkeley），18世紀最著名的哲學家，近代經驗主義的重要代表之一，開創了主觀唯心主義。
[39] 約翰·洛克（John Locke），英國經驗主義代表人物。
[40] 理查·惠特利（Richard Whately），英國修辭學家、邏輯學家、經濟學家、學者以及神學家。
[41] 凱爾特神話中的古愛爾蘭著名的英雄人物，傳說他是一位優秀的詩人。

第九章
風格打造：措辭準確與規範表達

實際上，風格和人物一樣繁多，並且它表達了作家的獨特性。換句話說，正如法國作家布豐恰如其分的評價：「The style is the man him-self.」（文如其人）。

第十章
寫作與演說：技巧與內容指引

　　語法和修辭規則是非常有用的。人們必須遵守這些規則，才能透過令人愉悅的、易於接受的方式傳達準確的意思，正確地表達想法和觀念。然而，生硬簡短的規則無法造就作家，這是自然法則，無可更改。如果一個人生來就沒有把思想付諸文字的能力，那麼他就無法成為作家，因為他可能沒有值得記錄的想法。如果一個人沒有想法需要表達，那麼也沒有想法能得到表達，沒有辦法「無中生有」。作為一個作家，必須在獲得文字表達能力之前就有一些想法和觀念。這些能力與生俱來，並且透過學習得到加強和提高。有句古老的和詩相關的拉丁引文是這麼說的：「Poeta nascitur non fit」。翻譯過來就是 —— 詩是自己出現的，不是被人作出來的。相當程度上，作家也是這樣。有些人在看書學習方面是高手，但他們甚至不能用看得過去的文字表達自己的觀點。他們的知識就像藏在寶箱裡的金子一樣，無論是對他們自己還是對整個世界都沒有價值。

　　學習寫作最好的方法莫過於坐下來，開始動筆，正如學習騎車最好的方法莫過於坐在單車上，開始踩踏板。一開始，先寫一些常見的事物，那些你熟悉的事物。比如說，可以先寫一篇關於貓的文章，就貓發表一些自己獨特的觀點。不要寫什麼「她年輕的時候可活潑了，但老了之後就非常嚴肅」，這種說法已經出現過 50,000 多次了。寫一寫你家的

第十章
寫作與演說：技巧與內容指引

貓都做過些什麼，她在閣樓裡是怎樣抓老鼠的以及抓到老鼠後做了什麼。熟悉的主題對於新手作家來說是最好的。如果你從沒去過，也不了解澳洲，那就不要嘗試描述澳洲的景象。永遠不要去尋找主題，你身邊就有無數個現成的。描述一下你昨天的所見所聞——一場火災，一匹驚慌失措的馬，一場街邊鬥狗。注意要用自己特有的風格去描述。要模仿大作家的風格，但並非逐字逐句地模仿。離開那條千萬人踩過的路，開闢一條自己的新路吧。

知你所寫，寫你所知，這是一條必須遵守的金科玉律。要想博學多才，就要學習。世界是一本開放的書，所有人都可以自由閱讀。自然之書浩瀚無垠，對於農夫和貴族來說一樣平等。學習自然的語氣和時態，他們比語法要重要得多。透過讀書學習知識是最可取的。不過這畢竟是純理論，沒有實踐。英語中最偉大的寓言——實際上是所有語言中最偉大的寓言——是由一個無知的，或者說所謂的無知的白鐵匠約翰·班揚[42]寫就的。以當今的標準來評判，莎士比亞不是一個學者。但以前沒有人，未來也很難有人能夠在思想表達方面達到和他一樣的高度。他只是簡單地讀了自然之書，然後用他自己絕妙的才能將它闡述了出來。

不要認為大學教育對於成為一名作家來說是必要的經歷，這還差得遠呢。有一些接受了大學教育的人仍然頭腦僵硬、人云亦云，不僅對世界沒有價值，對自己也沒有價值。有的人是如此的無足輕重，從任何角度來看他都沒有任何價值。一般來說，無足輕重的東西能夠貢獻的價值也非常有限。有的人看似無所不知，但他其實一無所知，這聽起來可能很矛盾，但經驗證明這種現象的確存在。

如果你很窮，那這不是你的缺陷而是你的優勢。貧窮是你努力的動

---

[42] 約翰·班揚（John Bunyan），英國著名作家、布道家。

力，而不是缺點。帶著好腦子出生比含著金湯勺出生好得多。如果世界依靠所謂的命運的寵兒的話，那麼一切早就變樣了。

從貧困的鬥獸場裡、苦痛的舞臺上、飽受忽視的小破屋中、默默無聞的林中小屋中、遭受壓迫的偏僻小道邊，以及帶有無窮無盡的髒活累活的昏暗閣樓裡和地下室中，出現了創造歷史的人們，他們把世界變得更加明亮、美好、高級和神聖。他們把世界變成了一個值得好好生活、好好道別的地方，他們透過自己的存在、留下的印記，有時甚至是透過鮮血，使這個世界變成一個更神聖的地方。貧窮是一種賜福，不是厄運。如果以正確的態度傳承，貧窮是一種福氣。它不但不會阻礙你的腳步，反而會全年齡層地提升你的知識水準。荷馬[43]是個唱著詩歌片段乞求施捨的盲人乞丐；偉大的蘇格拉底[44]，智慧的權威，雖然教導了無數雅典青年，卻經常由於囊中羞澀而三飢兩飽；神聖的但丁[45]也曾和乞丐一樣落魄，居無定所，孑然一人，卻在漫遊義大利的途中創作了不朽的詩篇；米爾頓曾在失明的日子裡「見過天使也不敢僭越的雷池」，在創作他的代表作〈失樂園〉時處於極度貧窮的狀態；莎士比亞很樂意為白馬劇院的顧客看馬、飲馬，只為賺幾便士去買麵包；伯恩斯[46]在犁地的時候突然湧出靈感，寫下了永垂不朽的詩歌；可憐的海因里希·海涅[47]飽受忽視、生活貧困，他在巴黎度過了「床褥墓穴」般痛苦的生活，但期間卻為他的祖國增添了文學榮譽；美國的伊萊休·魯特[48]儘管做著鐵匠的工作，卻努力使自己精通20餘種語言，最後成為美國的文學巨匠。

---

[43] 古希臘盲詩人，著作《荷馬史詩》。
[44] 古希臘著名思想家、哲學家、教育家、公民陪審員。
[45] 但丁·阿利吉耶里，13世紀末義大利詩人，以長詩〈神曲〉聞名。
[46] 羅伯特·伯恩斯（Robert Burns），蘇格蘭農民詩人，代表作〈友誼萬歲〉、〈往昔時光〉、〈一朵紅紅的玫瑰〉。
[47] 海因里希·海涅（Heinrich Heine），德國著名抒情詩人和散文家，患癱瘓症，在巴黎度過晚年。
[48] 伊萊休·魯特（Elihu Burritt），美國外交官、慈善家和社會活動家，他還是高產的演說家、記者和作家。

第十章
寫作與演說：技巧與內容指引

在其他領域，貧窮成為行動的動力。拿破崙出生時默默無聞，父親是落後的科西嘉島上勉強能夠餬口的公證人；亞伯拉罕·林肯，美國的驕傲，這個解放了黑奴的偉人出生於俄亥俄州邊遠林區的小木屋裡；詹姆斯·加菲爾[49]也是如此。尤利西斯·格蘭特[50]來自一個製革廠，而他成為世界上最偉大的將軍；湯瑪斯·愛迪生的發明生涯是從鐵路上做報童開始的。

這些偉人的案例是激勵我們行動的良藥。貧窮並沒有阻礙他們前進，而是使他們鬥志昂揚。因此，如果你家境貧寒的話，請把它當作通往成功的橋梁。要有雄心，設立一個能夠實現的目標，並付出所有努力去實現它。有一個關於湯瑪斯·卡萊爾的故事是這樣的：

卡萊爾榮膺愛丁堡大學名譽校長的稱號——這是文學界所能授予的最高榮譽。在結束就職演說、穿過大廳的時候，他發現一個似乎沉迷學習的學生。這位智者用他那獨特、突兀且粗暴的方式審問年輕人：「你學習的是什麼專業知識？」

「我不知道。」年輕人回答。

「你不知道？」卡萊爾大聲說道，「年輕人，你很愚昧。」

接著，他繼續發表他激烈的言辭，「孩子，在你這個年紀的時候，我在埃克爾費亨的小村莊裡、在野外，飽受貧窮的折磨。在那裡，只有牧師和我能讀懂《聖經》。雖然我那時非常貧窮、默默無聞，但在我的心裡，我可以看到名人堂裡有把椅子在等著我。於是我孜孜不倦、日夜學習。直到如今，我坐上了那把椅子，成為愛丁堡大學的名譽校長。」

---

[49] 詹姆斯·加菲爾（James A. Garfield），出生於俄亥俄州，美國政治家、共和黨人。他是繼林肯之後第二位被暗殺的美國總統。
[50] 尤利西斯·格蘭特（Ulysses Grant），美國軍事家、政治家，美國第18任總統。

風格的種類

另一位蘇格蘭人，帕特·布坎南[51]，著名的小說家，離開格拉斯哥前往倫敦的時候口袋裡只有 2.5 先令。「我來了，」他說，「為了西敏寺[52]裡的一方墓碑。」他算不上大學者，但他的雄心讓他成為世界大都會最偉大的文豪之一。

亨利·史坦利[53]是貧民院裡的流浪兒，真名為約翰·羅蘭茲。他在貧民院長大，但他懷有雄心壯志。於是他成長為一名偉大的探險家、作家，成為國會成員，並被英國君主封為爵士。

有成功的雄心，那麼你就會成功。把「失敗」從你的詞典裡剔除出去，不要承認它的存在。記住：人生的戰場中，只有不斷前進、永不言敗的人能夠獲勝。

讓所有的障礙變為你成功路上的踏腳石。

如果你身處逆境，那麼就下決心改變它。《天路歷程》是班揚在貝德福德監獄的服刑期間在廢棄的包裝紙上寫出來的。當時，他只能吃麵包喝水，食不果腹。不幸的美國天才愛德加·愛倫·坡[54]，在紐約福坦莫裡的一個小屋裡寫下了〈烏鴉〉這首英語文學中最絕妙，也是藝術性最高的詩篇。在他短暫又輝煌的職業生涯中，坡的經濟狀況從未樂觀過。然而，這既是他的過錯，也是他的不幸。在這方面他不是個好的榜樣。

不要認為圖書館裡浩如煙海的知識對於成為一名作家來說是必要的。很多時候，眾多的書本知識令人困惑。掌握為數不多的好書，並且融會貫通裡面的知識，對於你來說這就夠了。一位偉大的作家曾說過：「當心鑽研一本書的人。」這句話的意思是鑽研一本書（或者說一件事）

---

[51] 帕特·布坎南（Robert Buchanan），蘇格蘭詩人、小說家、劇作家。
[52] 英國名人墓地。
[53] 亨利·史坦利（Henry Stanley），威爾士記者、探險家。
[54] 愛德加·愛倫·坡（Edgar Allan Poe），19 世紀美國詩人、小說家和文學評論家。

第十章
寫作與演說：技巧與內容指引

的人都是大師。據說對《聖經》透澈的研究能讓人成為文學大師。確實，《聖經》和莎士比亞創造了知識精華的典範。莎士比亞集合了前人所有的精華，為後來人播撒了知識的種子。他是知識海洋的化身，能夠波及所有的思想大陸。

現在買書很便宜，多虧了印刷機的出現，最偉大的思想也變得觸手可及。書讀得越多越好，前提是這些書值得花時間閱讀。有時候在不知情的情況下，你的知識體系可能「中毒」。和食物中毒一樣，知識中毒的影響很難徹底擺脫，因此選書的時候要謹慎。如果你沒有辦法配齊所有的書——正如前文所說，這也不是必要的做法——你可以選擇大師的經典作品，好好吸收、消化它們，以提高你的文學底蘊。在別處，這個數量的藏書可以提供世界經典大師作品任你選擇。

你的大腦是個寶庫，不要放無用的東西進去，占掉有用資訊的空間。僅僅留下那些有價值的、有用的、你能隨時取用的知識。

要成為一名作家，就要向最好的作家學習。同樣，想要擁有高雅的談吐，就要向最好的演說家學習。想要學習正確地說話，就一定要去模仿公開演講的大師。認真觀察談話大師，聽聽他們是如何進行表達的。去聽最熱門的講座、演講和課程，無須模仿演講技巧，這些演講技巧是練習過程中自然形成的，而非刻意營造。你該關注的不是演說家如何表達自己，而應該關注他所使用的語言和語言的使用方式。你是否聽過今日大師的演講？過去也有很多演講大師，但他們現在已化作塵土，人們只能透過文字來欣賞他們的雄辯口才。不過，你可以做的就是去聽聽當今的演講大師的演講。對於許多人來說，還是前人的影響更為深遠。當談到演講的精髓時，我們總是會去聽前人的聲音。也許你一直為比徹和塔爾梅奇的言談感到著迷，兩位的言談都發人深省，他們用自己的聲音

風格的種類

征服了千萬人的心。兩位都是語言大師，他們將修辭的鮮花撒在雄辯的聖殿裡，向聽眾丟擲鮮花。聽眾沉迷於這些鮮花，並將它們存放在記憶的殿堂中。兩位都是學者、哲學家，然而卻被斯珀吉翁[55]——一個從現代角度來看沒有接受，或者說僅僅接受了少量教育的普通人——遠遠地超越。僅僅靠著演講，斯珀吉翁就吸引了成百上千的人來到他的禮拜堂。新教教徒、天主教徒、土耳其人、猶太人和伊斯蘭教徒蜂擁而至，聆聽、沉浸於他的教誨。德懷特·萊曼·穆迪——世界上最偉大的福音傳道者——並不是飽讀詩書的人，他的職業生涯是從在加拿大做皮鞋業務員開始的，但沒有哪個銷售員像他那樣用絕妙的口才吸引了無數的聽眾。「那只不過是個人魅力罷了。」你會這麼說，但這是絕無僅有的。是這些人嘴裡說出的話語，是他們的說話方式、風格和力量吸引了無數雙耳朵去傾聽。個人魅力或個人形象不是他們成功的原因。確實，如果考慮到外表的話，他們中有部分是殘疾人。斯珀吉翁又矮又胖，穆迪看起來像個鄉村農夫，把自己罩在披風裡的塔爾梅奇則是個邋裡邋遢的人，只有比徹看起來還似乎過得去。很多人認為，外貌形象不是聽眾關注的重點。丹尼爾·歐康諾[56]是個相貌平平、笨拙、難以相處的愛爾蘭公民權利保護者，然而他的巧舌為他贏取了上百萬的支援，甚至包括對立面的英國國會。他擅長長篇大論，並且精準地知道該說些什麼以吸引聽眾的注意力。

基本上在所有場合裡說話都要注重的是措辭和表達順序。無論一個人在其他方面有多精緻，如果他用詞錯誤，或者沒有按照合適的語言結構來表達，他就不會讓你留下很好的印象。但是一個人如果能夠正確用

---

[55] 斯珀吉翁（Spurgeon），浸禮會牧師，被稱為「牧師王子」。
[56] 丹尼爾·歐康諾（Daniel O'Connell），愛爾蘭民族主義運動的主要代表，英國下院天主教解放運動的領袖。

第十章
寫作與演說：技巧與內容指引

詞，語言表達聽起來很舒服，談吐令人舒服的話，無論他的地位多麼卑微，他都有可能吸引並影響你。

優秀、得體的演講者總是能夠影響他人的意願，對沒有這種表達能力的人們緊閉的大門，總是能為他們敞開。能夠侃侃而談、一語中的的人，永遠不會碌碌無為。各行各業、人類努力鑽研的每個領域都需要這樣的人，他的每一次轉身都是新的機遇。僱主們永遠都在尋找健談的人，那些能夠透過語言的力量吸引大眾、征服他們大腦的人。一個接受了良好教育的、有能力的、高雅的人，縱使他性格無瑕，如果他缺乏表達能力、不能以組織良好的語言表達觀點的話，那麼和一個能力不如他，卻能夠用準備充分、有效的語句表達自己觀點的人相比，他會錯失更多的機會。

還是那句話，這些演講技巧是練習過程中自然形成的，而非刻意營造。很大程度上，這句話是對的。但正是演講技巧能幫助人們正確地說話，正確度帶來流利度。只要願意堅持，付出一點點努力、一點點關注，每個人都可以擁有正確表達的能力。

為避免重複，在此強調以下建議：仔細傾聽優秀的演說家，並記錄下讓你印象深刻的字句。隨身攜帶筆記本，記錄下那些不同尋常的單字、片語和句子。如果你聽到一個不懂的詞，去查詞典。有許多詞是同義詞，意思相似，但是細分的話，它們各自表達同一意思的不同程度。有時，它們的意思甚至完全不同。要特別注意這些詞，找到它們的準確含義，並了解它們的使用範圍。

對批評持開放態度。不要怨恨批判，而要歡迎它。把它們看作能夠指出你缺陷的朋友，這樣你就能夠得到改進。

第十一章
俚語解析：起源與多元用法

在當今世界，俚語（slang）或多或少存在於社會的各個階層、各個行業，俚語中的單字和表達已經滲透到我們日常使用的語言中。它們於無形中滲透，以致於大多數人都沒有注意到它們的存在。現在它們已經與標準用語一樣，成為我們用語中不可或缺的一部分。日常交流中，它們的作用和普通單字的作用一樣──表達想法和欲望，將意思從一方傳達到另一方。實際上，有的俚語非常實用，它們的使用頻率已經遠遠超過了普通單字的使用頻率，以致於在方言裡留下了一席之地。有時候沒有它們，人們很難去交流。俚語已經在很多領域占領了普通單字的地位，並且在實用程度和影響力方面占絕對優勢。

黑話（cant）和俚語在大眾眼裡經常被混淆。儘管它們很相似，並且都起源於吉卜賽文化，但實際上它們不是同義詞。黑話是特定階層的用語──特定行業、行業、職業的人使用的特定措辭或方言。而且，不是這些行業、行業、職業的人是聽不懂的。它們可能是符合語法規則的正確表達，但並沒有得到普遍使用。黑話僅在一定群體和範圍內使用，只有目標群體能夠理解它們的意思。小偷的行話就屬於黑話，只有小偷能聽懂；同理，專業賭徒發明的用語也是黑話，只有賭徒能聽懂。

另一方面，俚語不單獨屬於任何一個階層，而是適用於全階層。它滲透進了社會的各方面，出現於日常表達中，不同階層的人都能理解它

第十一章
俚語解析：起源與多元用法

的意思。當然，俚語的本質相當程度上取決於它出現的地區，因為俚語與特定地區內常見的口頭用語或片語表達連繫緊密。比如，倫敦地區的俚語和紐約地區的俚語就稍有不同。有的表達在一個城市一聽就懂，但在另一個城市就無人使用。然而，有的俚語則可以說是人人都懂的。to kick the bucket（翹辮子）、to cross the Jordan（跨過約旦河）、to hop the twig（跳過樹枝／死亡）等表達在美國偏遠的森林裡和在澳洲的野外、倫敦或都柏林一樣常見。

簡單來說，俚語就是日常生活中通用，但卻沒有精緻高雅到能夠使用在得體的用語或純文學裡的單字和片語。但正如之前所說的，很多人並沒有意識到自己使用的一些表達是俚語，並且把它們融入了日常交流和談話中。

一些作家有目的地使用俚語，為司空見慣的寫作增添重點、為幽默的文學作品增添樂趣，但這不應該成為新手效仿的對象。像狄更斯那樣的大師這麼寫是可以理解的，但如果新手作家這麼寫的話，那就是不可原諒的。

俚語可以根據職業和社會階層分為幾種，比如大學俚語（college slang）、政治俚語（political slang）、體育俚語（sporting slang）等等。在各個階層自如地流傳是俚語的本質，但有幾類俚語僅在限定的幾個階層裡流傳。俚語中最廣的兩個分類是：未受教育的人使用的俚語和所謂的上層階級，即受到良好教育的富人使用的俚語。貧民區裡調皮的小女孩可不會和閨房裡的淑女使用同樣的俚語，但她們都會說俚語。如果這樣的兩個人進行對話，她們可以互相理解對方的意思。因此，俚語分為兩類——大眾俚語（ignorant slang）和精緻俚語（educated slang）：前者可在街頭巷尾聽到，後者則存在於起居室和客廳裡。

風格的種類

整體而言,人們使用俚語的目的就是透過更加有力、有趣、簡潔的方式,而不是標準、普通的陳述方式來表達自己的觀點。比如:

例 1

女學生讚揚嬰兒的時候會驚呼:

Oh, isn't he awfully cute!(哦,他也太可愛了吧!)

如果只是說他很好的話,就不能有力地突顯出她的讚美之情。

例 2

街上出現一位美女的時候,狂熱的男性崇拜者會用:

She is a peach, a bird, a cuckoo.(她是蜜桃,是小鳥,是杜鵑。)

這句話來表達他的欣賞之情,這些言辭體現了他對這位年輕女性的看法。與下面的表達相比,它要有力得多:

She is a beautiful girl.(她是個漂亮的女孩。)

She is a handsome maiden.(她是個俊俏的少女。)

或者

She is a lovely young woman.(她是個可愛的年輕女性。)

……

例 3

當政客擊敗了他的對手時,他會告訴你:

It was a cinch.(這是小菜一碟。)

他這麼做簡直 walk-over(易如反掌),

以表現他的勝利是一件多麼容易的事情。

第十一章
俚語解析：起源與多元用法

一些俚語表達是暗喻，屬於修辭的範疇，比如：

例 4

to pass in your checks（放棄）

to hold up（稍等）

to pull the wool over your eyes（瞞天過海）

to talk through your hat（胡說八道）

to fire out（開火）

to go back on（重新開始）

to make yourself solid with（和……稱兄道弟）

to be loaded（變富有）

to bark up the wrong tree（追求錯誤的人或事）

don't monkey with the buzz-saw（不要招惹你不了解的東西）

還有 in the soup（在湯裡）

大部分俚語的來源不怎麼好，很多俚語源自於小偷的拉丁語黑話，但隨著時間流逝，它們從罪犯的黑話中脫離出來，逐漸擺脫不光彩的過去，變成現在這種生動的表達。

例 5

Stolen fruits are sweet.（偷來的果實別樣甜美。）

這種表達可以追溯到《聖經》，箴言 ix：17 裡說道：

Stolen waters are sweet.（偷來的水別樣甜美。）

風格的種類

例 6　a bad man（西方的亡命之徒）

和現今該詞表達的意思基本相同，來自史賓賽[57]的《仙后》、馬辛傑[58]的《償還舊債的新方法》，以及莎士比亞的《亨利八世》。

例 7　to blow on（通知）

出自莎士比亞的《皆大歡喜》。

例 8　It's all Greek to me.（我對此一竅不通。）

可追溯至戲劇《裘力斯·凱薩》。

例 9　All cry and no wool.（只聞其聲，不見其人。）

出自巴特勒[59]的《胡迪布拉斯》。

例 10　Pious frauds（偽君子）

同樣出自《胡迪布拉斯》。

例 11　Too thin（藉口）

源於斯摩萊特[60]的《佩雷格林·皮克爾傳》，莎士比亞也用過這種表達。

在現代俚語方面，美國做出了很大的貢獻。

Ways that are dark, and tricks that are vain（黑暗的道路，無用的詭計。）

都來自布雷特·哈特[61]的《誠實的詹姆斯》。

---

[57] 埃德蒙·史賓塞（Edmund Spenser），英國文藝復興時期的偉大詩人。
[58] 菲利普·馬辛傑（Philip Massinger），英國喜劇作家，他是 17 世紀早期英國劇作家中編劇技巧最佳者之一。
[59] 塞繆爾·巴特勒（Samuel Butler），代表作為《眾生之路》。
[60] 托比亞斯·斯摩萊特（Tobias Smollett），被譽為亨利·菲爾丁和塞繆爾·理查遜之後英國 18 世紀最有才能的小說家。
[61] 布雷特·哈特（Bret Harte），美國西部文學的代表作家，代表作《咆哮營的幸運兒》。

第十一章
俚語解析：起源與多元用法

例 12

Not for Joe（不要給喬）

出現於內戰時期，一名士兵拒絕給另一名士兵酒。

例 13　Not if I know myself（如果我了解自己，就不會）

這種表達來自芝加哥。

例 14

What's the matter with ──？He's all right.

（── 怎麼回事？他沒事。）

也來自芝加哥，並且它的前身是：

What's the matter with Hannah?（漢娜是怎麼回事？）

意指一位懶惰的家僕。

例 15

There's millions in it.（裡面有幾百萬。）

by a large majority（絕大多數人）

皆出自馬克‧吐溫的《鍍金時代》。

例 16

pull down your vest（拉下你的背心）

jim-jams（睡衣睡褲）

got 'em bad（好好地整到了他們）

that's what's the matter（就是這麼回事）

take in your sign（記住你的手勢）

風格的種類

dry up（除掉）

it's the man around the corner（轉角處的那個人）

putting up a job（提供工作）

no back talk（不准頂嘴）

staving him off（餓他一頓）

making it warm（保持溫暖）

dropping him gently（溫柔地把他放下來）

dead gone（死了）

busted（被抓到了）

put up or shut up（是忍耐還是閉嘴）

bang up（撞上）

smart Aleck（自作聰明的人）

too much jaw（嘴巴張太大）

chin-music（閒談）

top heavy（頭重腳輕）

champion liar（吹牛大王）

chief cook and bottle washer（主廚和雜役）

bag and baggage（全部財產）

as fine as silk（絲般柔順）

name your poison（你想喝什麼酒？）

died with his boots on（死於非命）

hold your horses（不要急）

第十一章
俚語解析：起源與多元用法

galoot（呆子）

現在人們經常使用的表達都是美式俚語。尤其是加利福尼亞，在這類修辭語言方面最為多產。源自這個州的俚語還有

例 17

go off and die（去死吧）

don't you forget it（你給我記住了）

rough deal（不公平交易）

square deal（公平交易）

flush times（繁榮時期）

pool your issues（把問題集中起來）

a bad egg（壞蛋）

go climb a tree（滾開）

plug hats（高頂禮帽）

Dolly Vardens（花羔紅點鮭）

well fixed（富裕的）

down to bed rock（下至基岩）

hard pan（硬土）

pay dirt（有利可圖的事物）

petered out（逐漸消失）

it won't wash（沒有說服力）

it pans out well（結果很好）

而以下俚語

例 18

soft snap（奉承／不花大力氣的事）

gol durn it（該死的，同 god damn it）

slick（騙子）

short cut（捷徑）

correct thing（正事）

則源自波士頓。

例 19

諸如

innocent（無罪）

bark up the wrong tree（追求錯誤的人或事）

I reckon（我認為）

playing possum（撞死）

dead shot（神槍手）

等表達源自南方各州。

例 20

Doggone it（該死的）

that beats the Dutch（真令人驚奇）

you bet（當然）

you bet your boots（你可以確信）

源自紐約。

第十一章
俚語解析：起源與多元用法

例 21

Step down and out（走出去）

出自比徹爾的審判，正如

brain storm（腦力激盪）

出自索的審判。

在俚語短語中來源於英國的有：

例 22

throw up the sponge（認輸）

draw it mild（不誇張）

dead beat（遊手好閒的人）

on the shelf（束之高閣）

up the spout（處境困難）

stunning（令人震驚的）

gift of the gab（能說會道）

……

很大一部分俚語來自報紙。記者、特約撰稿人，甚至編輯會在被採訪人的話語中加入其他的字句。應該說紐約是俚語的「總部」，尤其是所謂的包厘街。按理說，所有語言中的偏差和訛誤現象都應該出自一個不入流的區域，但實際上，得體的英語在第五大道受到的違背和僭越不比在包厘街的少。當然，外來元素的融入造成的混合英語替包厘街帶來了不好的名聲，但包厘街上的優秀方言演講者和這座偉大城市的其他地區一樣多。然而，每一個經驗不足的新聞記者都把將包厘街放在一個任人嘲笑的位置視為己任。他們坐下來，用自己知識有限的頭腦努力破壞英語語言（而他們一個新詞也造不出來），並將這種破壞歸咎於包厘街。

同樣，報社和作家還極力貶低愛爾蘭人。這些人們從未見過愛爾蘭的青山綠水，卻把愛爾蘭人刻劃成粗魯、莽撞、說話滑稽可笑的人，還使用一些在愛爾蘭境內未曾有人聽過的俚語。眾所周知，古往今來，愛爾蘭是地球上學識豐富的國家之一。幾百年，甚至幾千年以來，教師們都出國去愛爾蘭深造。到目前為止，世上沒有任何一個地方的人能像蘇格蘭西島的城鎮居民一樣把國王的英語說得那麼純粹。

時下熱門、日常生活中的點點滴滴都是俚語產生的來源。在一段時間過後，這些俚語的使用頻率提高，使得它們在日常交流中獲得和普通單字一樣的地位。然後，就如前文所說的，它們的使用者逐漸忘記這些詞的原本身分。比如，愛爾蘭的土地同盟時期產生了 boycott（聯合抵制）這個詞，它是一個非常不受歡迎的地主的名字──Captain Boycott。人們拒絕為他工作，導致他的莊稼腐爛在田地裡。自那以後，任何不受歡迎的、旁人也不願為其提供任何幫助的人都可以說是 to be boycotted（被聯合抵制了）。因此，boycott 的意思是透過拋棄一個人或者剝奪一個人受幫助的權利來懲罰他。最開始，這個詞是一個眾所周知的俚語，但現在它已經成為英語詞典中的標準單字。

國家政治也為俚語添磚加瓦。來源於此的俚語有：

例 23

dark horse（黑馬）

the gray mare is the better horse（牝雞司晨）

barrel of money（一大筆錢）

第十一章
俚語解析：起源與多元用法

buncombe（廢話）

gerrymander（為本黨利益改劃選舉區分，不公正操作）

calawag（無賴漢）

henchman（侍從）

logrolling（政客間互投贊同票以通過對彼此都有利的提案）

pulling the wires（幕後操縱）

machine（核心集團）

slate（候選人名單）

……

例 24

貨幣市場則為俚語界帶來了

bull（牛市）

bear（熊市）

slump（大跌）

以及其他一些表達。

時代習俗和當前表達的需求要求我們按場合使用俚語。我們經常不知道哪些表達是俚語，就像小孩子經常在不知情的情況下說一些褻瀆神靈的話。我們應該盡量避免使用俚語，就算它能以更有力的方式來表達我們的觀點。當一個俚語還沒有在目前的交流環境中獲得穩定的地位時，就不要使用它。記住，幾乎所有的俚語都有粗鄙的來源，它們都帶有扭曲的、粗俗的罪惡。對於來源較好的俚語，也盡量不要使用它。因為這就像墮落的紳士，對誰都沒好處。盡量模仿大師的古典文學作品，

風格的種類

但是一旦碰到俚語，千萬不要學。迪安·史威夫特，著名的愛爾蘭諷刺作家，創造了 phiz 這個詞，意思是臉。不要效仿他。如果你在描述一位美麗的女士的容貌時，無論是口頭語還是書面表達，不要說這是她的 phiz。作為一位文學巨匠，迪安有資格這麼做，但你沒有。莎士比亞用 flush 來指大把的錢。請記住，世上只有一個莎士比亞，只有他能這麼用這個詞。你永遠也不能自稱為莎士比亞，世上也不會再有另一個莎士比亞。大自然在創造出第一個莎士比亞的時候就窮盡了她的心血。布爾沃[62]把 stretch 用作絞死的意思，比如 stretch his neck，不要學他這樣用這個詞。總體來說，避免低階、粗魯、庸俗的俚語，這些詞是街頭的地痞流氓才會使用的。

例 25

如果你談及一個昨晚死去的人，無論是口頭還是書面，都不要說：

He hopped the twig.（他突然離去。）

或者

He kicked the bucket.（他一命嗚呼。）

例 26

如果你不想聽別人誇誇其談一些他自己都不甚了解的東西，不要說：

He is talking through his hat.（他在胡說八道。）

例 27

如果你在講述自己和羅斯福先生握手的經歷，不要說：

He tipped me his flipper.（他拿指尖碰了我。）

---

[62] 愛德華·布爾沃·李頓（Edward Bulwer-Lytton），英國作家。

第十一章
俚語解析：起源與多元用法

例 28

如果你在談論一個富有的人，不要說：

He has plenty of spondulix.（他有很多鈔票。）

或者

He has plenty of the long green.（他有很多綠票子。）所有這些俚語都是低階、粗魯、庸俗的，無論何時何地，使用這些俚語都是不合適的。

如果你要使用俚語的話，用那些高級的俚語，並且要像一個紳士那樣說話，這樣才不會傷害或冒犯他人。紅衣主教紐曼將紳士定義為從不強人所難的人，使用俚語時也要像紳士一樣 —— 不要強人所難。

第十二章
新聞寫作技巧：資格與對象選擇

　　現在這片大陸上的每家每戶都訂閱報紙，曾經華貴的象徵如今成為生活的必需。無論一個人多窮，他都不會吝嗇用這一兩個便士來了解他周邊的新聞，甚至世界各地正在發生的事情。街頭的勞工和辦公室裡的銀行家一樣有可能出現在報紙上。透過報紙，人們可以知悉國家的脈搏，了解國家的活力是在增長還是下降；人們可以閱讀到時代的跡象，搜尋自己感興趣的領域。國外大事一一在我們眼前展開，只需一瞥，我們即可了解地球最偏遠角落裡發生的事情。如果前一天晚上在倫敦發生了一場火災，第二天早上在紐約的人們就能夠知道這個消息，他們獲得的報導甚至可能比倫敦本地人更加具體。如果在巴黎舉行一場決鬥，人們甚至能在決鬥雙方離場前就知曉整個決鬥過程。

　　在美國有高達 3,000 種日報，其中 2,000 多種在城鎮發行，覆蓋不到 10 萬居民。實際上，許多人口不到 1 萬的地方也都發行日報。發行的週報則有 1.5 萬種。一些所謂的鄉村報紙在當地，甚至是外地都頗具影響力。無論是透過新聞傳播還是透過廣告宣傳，它們都為其創辦者和相關機構贏得可觀的利潤。

　　在這個國家，投身於新聞業的人口數量讓人大吃一驚。除了正經的新聞工作者，成千上萬的人們將新聞業當作副業，透過時不時向日報、週報和月刊貢獻文字獲得可觀的「零用錢」，提升收入。這些人中的大部

第十二章
新聞寫作技巧：資格與對象選擇

分都是普通人，只是接受了足夠的教育，能夠透過文字聰明地表達自己的想法。

繼續教育對於新聞工作是必要的，許多人都這麼想，但其實這個想法不一定正確。相反，有的時候，高等教育在這個工作中是障礙，而非助益。一般來說，寫新聞不像專題論文或哲學論文那樣高深。顧名思義，報紙上需要的是見聞，新鮮的見聞、有趣的見聞，可以吸引讀者、引起他們的閱讀興趣並占據他們注意力的見聞。在這個領域，一個男孩寫出的文章可能比大學教授寫的要更出彩。教授筆下使用的，可能大多是超出普通人理解範圍的深奧詞彙；而不知道深奧詞彙的男孩，則會直接地描述他的所見所聞，事故的危害有多大、誰在事故中身亡或受傷，等等，他寫出的文章所有人都能看懂。

當然，在新聞領域確實有一些飽讀詩書的天才學者。但是總體來說，那些著名的撰稿者都是從低起點開始的，他們中的大部分是看國家報紙來學習提高的。現在英國和美國的一些頂尖作家都是從為鄉村報社撰稿開始他們的文學生涯的。他們在撰稿過程中不斷提升、完善自己，直到他們能在通用文學中擁有一席之地。

如果你想為新聞業做貢獻，或者想進軍新聞業、把它當作看家本領的話，不要讓大學教育的缺失阻擋你的腳步。正如本書中提到過的，傑出的英語文學大師中有部分人在讀書學習的過程中極其不占優勢。莎士比亞、班揚、彭斯和其他那些在名人堂裡留下無法磨滅的印記的偉人們，在教育背景這方面沒有值得驕傲的地方，但他們有眾所周知的常識以及對於世界正確的認知。換句話說，他們了解人類的本性，並且將本性發揮到了極致。莎士比亞了解人類因為他自己就是人類的一員，所以他能夠用大師的筆觸描述人類的感受、情緒和激情，將宮殿中國王的形

風格的種類

象刻劃得入木三分，就如同他筆下小屋中的農夫一般。他胸中彷彿有一個觀察員，告訴他萬事萬物的對與錯，就像老蘇格拉底耳邊總有個精靈對他喃喃細語，告訴他無論在什麼情況下都要不懈追求事業。彭斯在犁地的時候孕育出了靈感，並用從來沒有、未來可能也不會被超越的語言包裝它們。這些人聽從了本性的召喚，正是順從本性發展而來的完美為他們戴上了永不消退的名譽桂冠。

如果你試著為報紙撰稿，那麼你要注意遵從本心，用你習慣的方式去表達自己，不要矯揉造作，不要虛飾，也不要模仿花裡胡哨的風格，或沉迷於假、大、空的表達方式，這些都會替作家打上「不僅膚淺、更是愚蠢」的標籤。日報不會替這樣的作品留位置，它們需要的是用平實樸素、未經修飾的語言來傳達事實。確實，你應該盡可能多地讀大家之作，模仿他們的風格，但不要嘗試複製他們。

盡可能地做你自己，而不是其他任何人。

Not like Homer would I write,（我不會像荷馬那樣寫作，）

Not like Dante if I might,（如果讓我選，也不要像但丁，）

Not like Shakespeare at his best,（就算莎士比亞的全盛時期再好，也不要和他一樣，）

Not like Goethe or the rest,（更不用說歌德或其他人，）

Like myself, however small,（要像我自己，無論多麼渺小，）

Like myself, or not at all.（要麼要像自己，要麼就不寫作。）

把自己放在讀者的位置上，寫能夠讓你感興趣的東西，這樣的話你的想法就能夠自然而然地以文字的形式呈現出來。你屬於普通大眾中的一員，因此為新聞撰稿時不要忘記，你是在為大眾寫作，而不是為那些

第十二章
新聞寫作技巧：資格與對象選擇

接受了高等教育且具有良好審美的少數人寫作。

記住你的目標讀者是街上、車裡的人，你的目的是有力地吸引他們的注意力，讓他們閱讀你的文章、了解你的觀點。這些人並不想看到別人賣弄學識，他們想看到的是自己關心的新聞。為此你必須用平實而簡樸的方式告訴他們，就像你在面對面跟他們交流一樣。

你能寫些什麼呢？為什麼不寫一些可以作新聞的內容、當日的熱門事件，或者任何能吸引你的目標讀者閱讀興趣的內容呢？無論你生活在哪裡、無論當地多麼落後，你總能發現可以讓人感興趣的人類事件。如果當地沒有新聞，那就寫一寫你感興趣的話題。人類的構造都是相似的，你感興趣的話題也很有可能引起他人的興趣。一般來說，描寫一場冒險活動是大眾喜聞樂見的，比如獵狐狸、獵獾，或是追蹤野熊。

如果你的住所附近有重要的製造工廠，描述一下它。可能的話，拍一些照片，因為照片在當今的新聞裡扮演了非常重要的角色。如果你身邊住著一位家喻戶曉的「名人」，試著去採訪他，詢問他對於當日大眾提問的看法，描寫一下他的日常生活、家庭環境，以及他的一天。

試著寫一些與當下連繫密切的東西，在剛剛過去的這段時間裡最熱門、最讓你印象深刻的事情。如果一個名人來到英國，無論是男是女，這都是一個記錄他（她）的英國之旅的好時機。比如，在蘇丹的英國之旅中寫一寫蘇祿人和太平洋群島是合適的。如果有人試圖炸掉薩摩亞阿庇亞的美軍戰艦，那麼你就有機會寫一寫薩摩亞和羅伯特·路易斯·史蒂文森[63]的故事。曼努埃爾二世[64]被廢黜的時候正是介紹葡萄牙和葡萄牙國事的完美時機。如果一個國家正在發生大事，比如國王的加冕或君

---

[63] 羅伯特·路易斯·史蒂文森（Robert Louis Stevenson），19世紀後半葉英國偉大的小說家，代表作《金銀島》、《化身博士》、《綁架》、《卡特麗娜》等，1894年逝於薩摩亞。
[64] 曼努埃爾二世，葡萄牙最後一位國王，由於統治混亂被廢黜，後逃亡到英國倫敦。

風格的種類

主的廢黜，此時非常適合寫一寫該國的歷史，介紹引起當前局面的歷史事件。如果附屬國的野生部落發生一場尤為野蠻的暴亂，比如菲律賓的Manobos 的崛起，此時就可以介紹這些部落和他們的周邊地區以及反抗的起因。

時刻尋找對你有益的資訊。讀一讀日報，可能在某個偏僻的角落裡，你會發現一些內容。這些內容能夠為你寫一篇好文章打下基礎，最不濟也能給你一些線索。

謹慎挑選投稿的報紙。先了解目標報紙的論調和主要內容、社會傾向和政治立場，以及宗教態度，還有你能了解到的所有資訊。將一篇寫職業拳擊賽的文章發表到宗教報紙上是不明智的選擇，反過來，教堂集會的新聞出現在體育報社編輯的桌上也是不合適的。

如果你的投稿被拒，不要失望，不要沮喪，堅持不懈在新聞業比在其他任何行業都更加重要。只有堅持不懈，才能到達長跑的終點。你要提升自己的適應能力：被壓下去，要能再次彈起來。無論被拒多少次，都不要氣餒。努力尋找新的動力，再次投稿。是金子總會發光，你的鋒芒總會在新聞業顯露出來。如果你能寫出優秀的稿件，很快，編輯們會來求你撰稿，而不是你求他們刊登你的文章。這群人永遠在尋找能寫出好稿子的人才。

只要堅持到出版階段，你就贏得了這場「戰役」，因為你的每一次堅持不懈和努力提高都有了回報。檢查你的稿件，不斷地修改、刪減，直到不能更完美為止。刪去所有多餘的詞，確認表達與指代不帶歧義。

如果你在為週報撰稿，請記住週報和日報不同。週報不僅僅要吸引街上的男人們的注意力，也要吸引爐火旁的女人們的注意力。他們想知道奇聞趣事、神祕傳說、名人或怪人的逸事、大事件的回顧、無數生活

第十二章
新聞寫作技巧：資格與對象選擇

中的冷門知識合輯。簡而言之，就是任何能夠供普通大眾娛樂、消遣和學習的資訊。你身邊總有事情在發生，其中就會有一些稀奇古怪或令人興奮的事情可以作為撰稿的素材。和日報一樣，你對投稿的週報一定要非常了解，比如基督教先驅報，雖然很明顯它是一個宗教週報，但刊登一些民生新聞能為它吸引更多的讀者。在宗教方面，該報不分教派，囊括了世界各地林林總總的基督教；在社會生活方面，該報以不偏不倚的態度報導所有社會事件。無論處於哪個階層、抱有何種信仰，人們都能對該報的內容產生興趣。

月刊為有文學抱負的人提供了另一個誘人的去處。再說一遍，不要覺得只有大學教授才有資格為月刊撰稿。許多，實際上是大部分最重要的刊物撰稿者都沒有大學文憑，除了在大學前門進後門出。不過整體而言，他們都是經驗豐富的人，對生活有從理論到實踐的全方位了解。

一般來說，月刊很看重熱門問題和事件。重大發現和發明，只要是讓全民關注的事件，比如飛行器、戰艦、摩天大樓、開礦、新大陸的開發、政治問題、黨派領導人的觀點、名人的人物素描等等，總是在當下吸引著全世界的目光。不過，在嘗試為月刊撰稿前，先在日報社當一段時間的寫作學徒是更好的選擇。

在以上所有事情中，請務必記住，毅力是打開成功之門的關鍵，要堅持不懈！如果你遭到拒絕，不要灰心；反過來，要化拒絕為下一次奮鬥的動力。我們時代裡最成功的作家中有很多遭到過無數次拒絕。數日、數月，甚至數年以來，他們來回地為自己的「貨物」叫賣，艱難地尋找著買家。你可能在胚胎裡的時候就是個優秀的作家，但如果你不把天分發揮出來，小小的胚胎永遠也不會發展成胎兒，更不用說完全成熟長大了。給自己一個成長的機會，了解任何能夠擴展視野的知識。睜大雙眼，仔細觀察，一天中總有一些時刻能給予你驚喜，也總有一些時刻能讓你給予他人驚喜。學習閱讀自然之書。萬事萬物，皆有學問——石頭裡、草地上、樹上、潺潺溪流中、鳥聲呢喃裡……在自行學習、理解之後，把學到的知識傳授給他人。永遠要帶著真誠的態度去寫作，帶著堅決的心去寫作。不要膽怯，不要打退堂鼓，要勇敢、勇敢、再勇敢！

On the wide, tented field in the battle of life, With an army of millions before you;

（在廣闊、帳篷遍地的生命戰場裡，你面前有千軍萬馬；）

Like a hero of old gird your soul for the strife And let not the foeman tramp o'er you;

（要像古時的英雄一樣，為戰爭做好準備，不要讓敵軍踐踏你；）

Act, act like a soldier and proudly rush on The most valiant in Bravery's van,

（表現得像個士兵，驕傲地衝向最勇敢的戰車裡最勇敢的人。）

With keen, flashing sword cut your way to the front And show to the world you're a Man.

（用鋒利的、閃閃發光的劍砍向前方，向世界展示你是一個男人。）

如果你是位男士，那麼做一個讓人不吝讚美的人。這是你值得驕傲的最高榮譽，遠遠超過了伯爵、公爵，甚至皇帝和國王。同樣，能讓人不吝讚美對於女士來說也是最光輝的桂冠。當世界不看好你時，一切似乎都在錯誤的軌道上。保有耐心，並懷著美好日子即將到來的希望，因為它會來的。太陽永遠在最黑暗的烏雲後方照耀著。當你一次又一次接到退稿時，不要絕望，也不要控訴編輯的殘酷無情，他也有自己的煩

第十二章
新聞寫作技巧：資格與對象選擇

惱。保持奮鬥的姿態，直到你完成最終的測試，最後一次分析你的才能。如果那時你還是沒能到達最終的出版階段，確認新聞寫作或文學工作不是你的菜之後，就轉戰其他領域吧。如果沒有其他更適合的事情出現，那麼就去試試製鞋、挖溝吧。記住，無論高低貴賤，正當的勞動都是值得尊敬的。如果你是位女士，把筆丟開，找個地方坐下，補一補你兄弟、父親或丈夫的襪子，或者穿上棉圍裙，拿塊肥皂，接一桶水，開始擦地吧。無論你是誰，去做些有意義的事情。「生活虧欠了你」這種鬼話早就沒人聽了。生活不虧欠你任何東西，而是你為生活的付出還不夠。如果你不償還債務的話，你就沒有在服侍全知全能的上帝，也沒有做你生來應該做的事情。你為世界做出奉獻是應該的，因為你生活在這個世界上。你要把它變得更美好、更明亮、更高尚、更神聖、更宏大、更高貴、更富有。無論你身處何種職業，上至總統，下至街頭勞工，你都可以做到這件事。努力奮鬥，贏取勝利。

　　Above all, to thine own self be true,

　　（這比一切都重要：要忠實於你自己！）

　　And 'twill follow as the night the day,

　　（正像有了白晝才有黑夜一樣，）

　　Thou canst not then be false to any man.

　　（對自己忠實，才不會對別人詐欺。）

第十三章
措辭的價值：簡潔與文化影響

　　前文已經提到過，在表意相同的情況下，選擇短詞而非長詞，這一點需要多加強調。深奧的、氣勢過強的詞都應盡量避免。它們體現了使用者的膚淺和虛榮。優秀的語言純粹主義者、措辭大師、風格模範用的都是短小簡單、眾人皆知且沒有歧義的詞。一定要記住，我們是透過文字來傳授知識的，因此，我們有責任使用正確、合適的語言。我們必須注意說話和思考的方式，不能使用含混不清的表達，以致於讓人誤解，或給予人錯誤印象。文字為想法賦予形體和結構。沒有文字，想法就是模糊的，我們無法看出它們哪裡有錯，哪裡有問題。我們要努力使用正確的表達，這樣才能把我們腦海中的想法灌輸到他人的腦海中。這是世界上最偉大的藝術——將我們腦海中的想法用文字表達出來以使他人理解。無論是教師、部長、律師，還是演說家、商人，如果他們想要在各自的領域裡獲得成功，就必須掌握這門藝術。當聽眾對傳達某一想法所使用的語言知之甚少的時候，這個想法就很難令人印象深刻；但如果想法透過不可理解的文字進行表達，那想法的傳達更是不可能實現的。

　　如果我們舉行一場英文演講，但卻使用觀眾無法理解的詞彙，這就像跟他們說科普特語（埃及古語）一樣。因為他們從演講中不能獲得任何好處，運輸我們想法的文字載體對觀眾來說不包含任何有用的資訊。

　　複雜深奧的詞、從其他語言發源而來的詞只能被接受過繼續教育的

第十三章
措辭的價值：簡潔與文化影響

人所理解，而大多數人是沒有這個優勢的。這個偉大而榮耀的國家中的絕大多數人年紀輕輕就要辛勤工作、維持生計。儘管教育是免費的，尤其是義務教育，很多人卻從未在 Three R（reading, writing and arithmetic）的基礎上走得更遠。這些人正是我們在生活中接觸得最多的人。他們有著粗糙的手掌和鋼筋般的肌肉，他們為我們建造房屋、鐵路，他們為我們開汽車、開火車，他們為我們耕種田地、收割莊稼。簡而言之，這些人構成了社會各方面的基柱，這些人讓世界正常運轉。高等教育使用的語言不適用於他們，沒有這些他們也能繼續生活；他們工作的領域對此也並無需求。日常生活中常見的樸實簡單的詞，就是我們面對他們時需要使用的。

這些詞既能被他們理解，也能被教育水準高的人理解。既然如此，為什麼不全面地使用它們呢？為什麼要把語言變成一方的特權，變得只有某一階層的人們，即所謂的教育水準高的人們能夠理解的東西？如果親自去調查的話，我們會發現，在眾人間表現出色的那些人——演說家、律師、傳道者等等——使用的語言都非常簡單。丹尼爾·韋伯斯特[65]是這個國家中眾多的優秀演說家之一，他用自己雄辯的口才觸動了無數參議員和普通大眾。能用簡短的話表達相同意思或相似意思的時候，他堅決不用冗長的話。演講的時候，他總是告訴那些寫新聞稿的人們，去掉所有冗長的表達。研究他的演講，反覆閱讀他說過或寫過的東西，你會發現他的語言永遠簡短、清晰、有力。雖然有時候為了演講聽起來更加順耳、效果更好，他會被迫選擇長一點的表達，但他永遠優先選擇簡短的表達。沒有人能像韋伯斯特那樣說話！他對事物的描述如此清晰，令聽者身臨其境。

---

[65] 丹尼爾·韋伯斯特（Daniel Webster），美國著名政治家、法學家及律師。

風格的種類

亞伯拉罕·林肯則是另一位讓人留下深刻印象的偉人，雖然他既不是演說家，也不是學者。他的名字後面沒有碩士、博士的頭銜，或者任何大學教育能夠給予的頭銜，因為他沒有接受大學教育。他從「困境大學」畢業，在成為美國總統之後，他也沒有忘記母校。他還和當年在桑加蒙縣劈柵欄和開船時一樣那麼樸實、謙遜。他說話不用高深華麗的辭藻，而是人人都能懂的詞句。就算這樣，他也依然能說出感人的話。蓋茨堡演說是英語演講中的經典傑作，名垂青史，聲震寰宇。

一個簡短的單字並不總是意味著它是清晰的，但幾乎所有表意清晰的詞都是簡短的。並且大部分長詞，尤其是那些從其他語言來的外來詞，在相當程度上會被普通大眾所誤解。確實，一些「學者」在使用這些詞的時候能否完全理解它們的文化含義是值得懷疑的。許多的外來詞包含幾層不同的含義，在人們徹底理解一個詞的意義之前必須在交談中大量使用該詞。長詞不僅使語言表達變得模糊、不明確，有時甚至使表達變得混亂，造成誤解等不好的後果。

比如，使用長詞可以掩蓋罪行，因為長詞給了罪行一個不同的外貌。就連最醜陋的罪行都能被長詞掩蓋、包裝成美好的事物。我們把銀行出納員吞掉十萬美元這種罪行禮貌地冠上貪汙的名字，而不是直接用偷竊。不稱之為小偷，我們客氣地稱之為未履行職務者。

例1

在大道上看到有錢人喝醉了跌跌撞撞，在空中胡亂揮舞著手臂、大喊大叫的時候，我們會微笑著說：

Poor gentleman, he is somewhat exhilarated.（可憐的人啊，他太過興奮了。）

第十三章
措辭的價值：簡潔與文化影響

再不濟，我們也會說：

He is slightly inebriated.（他有點醉了。）

但如果我們看到窮人喝醉到不清醒、失態時，我們會用最簡單的語句來表達憤慨：

Look at the wretch; he is dead drunk.（看那個傢伙，他爛醉如泥。）

當我們發現一個人在撒謊時，我們會用搪塞的話語把謊話嚴嚴實實地裹上。莎士比亞說：「玫瑰即使換了名字，也依然芬芳。」同樣，無論你怎麼替謊言換稱呼，它也仍是謊言，應遭到譴責。但為什麼不直呼其名呢？真心說話，說真心話。鏟子就叫鏟子，這是你能給予這個工具最合適的稱呼。

當你嘗試在短時間內用短詞而非長詞進行交談，你會發現你能很輕易地做到這一點。

例2

農夫帶一位城裡人看馬。馬兒被帶進小圍場，圍場裡有隻種豬正在拱土覓食。

What a fine quadruped!（多好的一隻四足動物啊！）

這位城裡人讚嘆道。

「你說的是哪個，豬還是馬？」農夫問道，「因為在我看來，它們都是很好的四足動物。」

當然來訪者說的是馬，如果他用最簡單、普通的名字來稱呼動物會好很多——這樣的話就不會有讓人誤解的因素存在了。不過，他也能從這個小事故中獲益，那就是以後再也不把馬稱為四足動物了。

大部分短小、簡單、美好的詞都來源於英語中的盎格魯撒克遜文化，它們能在有限的範圍內表達盡量多的內容。該文化為許多天體賦予了名字，如太陽、月亮、星星；還包括四元素中的三元素，土、火和水；四季中的三季，春、夏和冬。盎格魯撒克遜文化中的簡單字彙被用於所有關於時間的自然劃分部分（除了一個），白天、夜晚、早上、晚上、黃昏、中午、正午、午夜、日出和日落。光、熱、冷、霜、雨、雪、冰雹、雨夾雪、雷、閃電，以及那些組成大自然中美麗景觀的事物——比如海洋和陸地、山丘和山谷、森林和溪流等等的名字都來源於盎格魯撒克遜文化。我們應感謝這個語言替我們帶來了最古老、最親密的連繫的表達，大自然最強烈、最有力的感受的詞彙，以及那些因此和最深情、最神聖的關係交織在一起的詞彙，這些詞包括父親、母親、丈夫、妻子、兄弟、姐妹、兒子、女兒、孩子、家、家人、朋友、壁爐爐床、屋頂和爐邊。

我們最容易感受到的主要情感也是透過這個語言表達的——愛、希望、恐懼、悲傷、羞愧，以及這些情緒表露出來的行為，比如流淚、微笑、大笑、臉紅、哭泣、嘆氣、呻吟。幾乎我們國家所有的諺語都來自盎格魯撒克遜文化。幾乎所有用來有力地表達憤怒、蔑視和憤慨的術語和片語也來自盎格魯撒克遜文化。

人們所知的時髦人士和所謂的上流社會正在使得很多盎格魯撒克遜文化來源的詞彙蒙塵，這些詞曾經非常適用於他們的祖先。這些自命不凡的措辭權威認為一些盎格魯撒克遜文化來源的詞彙對於他們高級的品味和優雅的雙耳過於粗魯、平庸，於是他們把這些詞從他們的詞庫裡剔除出去，替換成其他語言借來的混血兒和不明來源的混合物。然而對於普通人——街上或田裡的男人們、廚房或工廠裡的女人們——來說，這些詞是可靠真實的。和老朋友一樣，它們應該得到所有人的珍惜和偏愛，無論那些外來詞的來源是哪裡。

第十三章
措辭的價值：簡潔與文化影響

第十四章
英語語言演變：起源與現狀探索

　　英語語言現在不僅是英格蘭人的母語，它已經遍及世界各地，其中也包括美國的大部分。英語是由日爾曼人使用的德語發展而來的，他們在羅馬人征服英國之後來到這個國家。這些日爾曼人包括盎格魯人、撒克遜人、朱特人以及德國北部的幾個其他部落種族的人。他們說不同的方言，但這些方言在新的國家得以交會，複合的語言變成了後來為人所知的盎格魯撒克遜語系，該語系成為現在通用英語的主要基礎，並且仍是主導元素。那些想要使用純粹盎格魯撒克遜語系的人，由於他們的教育水準不足以使他們表達自己的想法，因此他們在破壞英語這個複雜體系中的支柱，這些支柱對英語體系中的重要部分提供了必要的支援。

　　盎格魯撒克遜語係為詞類提供了必不可少的部分，包括冠詞、各類代詞、介詞、助動詞、連詞，以及將單字連成句子、形成語言關節、肌腱和韌帶的小品詞。它為英語詞彙庫提供了最不可或缺的詞彙（見第十三章）。沒有誰能比上帝的禱告者更能欣賞盎格魯撒克遜語系的美了。54個單字是撒克遜詞，其餘的詞可以輕易地被撒克遜詞替換。約翰福音則是另一個幾乎完全使用盎格魯撒克遜詞彙的典範，莎士比亞最佳的作品使用的也是盎格魯撒克遜詞彙。以下是《威尼斯商人》的引文，55個單字中有52個都屬於盎格魯撒克遜語系，其餘3個是法語：

　　All that glitters is not gold —— Often have you heard that told;

第十四章
英語語言演變：起源與現狀探索

Many a man his life hath sold,

But my outside to behold. Guilded tombs do worms infold.

Had you been as wise as bold, Young in limbs, in judgment old, Your answer had not been inscrolled ——

Fare you well, your suit is cold.

發閃光的不全是黃金，

古人的話沒有騙人；

多少人出賣了一生，

不過看到了我的外形，

蛆蟲掘著鍍金的墳。

你要是又大膽又聰明，手腳健壯，

見識卻老成，

就不會得到這樣的回音：

再見，勸你冷卻這片心。[66]

哈姆雷特父親嘴裡說出的憤慨之言，僅次於但丁對地獄大門的描述。這段話中的盎格魯撒克遜詞彙有180個，而拉丁詞彙只有15個。

現代英語的第二個構成成分是拉丁語，它包括直接從羅馬語發展而來的詞彙和間接從法語發展而來的詞彙。前者隨羅馬基督徒而來，它們在6世紀末由奧古斯丁[67]帶入英格蘭。這些詞主要與基督教會事務相關，比如 saint（聖徒）是來自 sanctus，religion（宗教）來自 religio，chalice（聖餐杯）來自 calix，mass（彌撒）來自 missa 等等。其中一部分

---

[66] 威廉·莎士比亞. 威尼斯商人 [M]. 朱生豪，譯. 北京：人民文學出版社，1977：58.
[67] 奧古斯丁（Saint Aurelius Augustinus），古羅馬帝國時期天主教思想家，歐洲中世紀基督教神學、教父哲學的重要代表人物。

風格的種類

詞又來自希臘，比如 priest（祭司）來自 presbyter，presbyter 又是希臘語 presbuteros 的直接衍生詞；還有 deacon（執事）來自希臘語 diakonos。

拉丁語中最龐大的一類來自諾曼法語和羅曼語。諾曼人在基督教的影響下，採用了諾曼化的高盧人和諾曼化的法蘭克人的語言、法律和藝術。在法國生活一個多世紀之後，他們成功地於 1066 年在征服者威廉一世的率領下入侵英格蘭。自此，新的時代開始了。法國的拉丁語可以透過拼寫辨別，因此我們知道 Saviour（救世主）來自法語 Sauveur，後者又來自拉丁語 Salvator；judgement（判決）來自法語 jugement；people（人民）來自法語 peuple，後者又來自拉丁語 populus。

很長一段時間以來，撒克遜語和諾曼語拒絕合併，就像兩股分岔的水流。諾曼語的適用人群是封建城堡、英國議會和法院裡的勳爵和男爵，而撒克遜語的適用人群則是鄉村房屋、田地和工場裡的人們。在 300 多年的歲月中，這兩種語言分道而流，但最終結合在了一起，並且還融入了凱爾特語和丹麥語元素，形成了現代英語這門擁有簡單語法體系和豐富詞彙庫的語言。

雖然威克利夫[68]是公認的英國散文之父，他於1380年翻譯《聖經》，然而世俗詩歌界的桂冠卻落在了喬叟的頭上。

除了日爾曼語和羅曼語這兩個構成英語語言的主要成分，許多其他語言也占到一定份額。其中，凱爾特語可能要算最悠久的。在凱薩入侵英國時，英國人屬於凱爾特家族中的一員。凱爾特語仍在三種方言中使用，威爾士的威爾士語、愛爾蘭蓋爾語以及蘇格蘭高地蓋爾語。英語中的凱爾特詞彙相對而言較少：cart（大車）、dock（碼頭）、wire（電線）、rail（欄杆）、cradle（搖籃）、babe（嬰兒）、grown（生長，過去分詞）、

---

[68] 約翰·威克利夫（John Wycliffe），英國經院神學家、翻譯家，英國散文之父。

第十四章
英語語言演變：起源與現狀探索

griddle（礦篩）、lad（小夥子）、lass（少女）是最常用的一些詞彙。丹麥語的加入可以追溯到9、10世紀的海盜入侵時期。包括 anger（憤怒）、awe（敬畏）、baffle（阻隔）、bang（猛擊）、bark（吠叫）、bawl（大聲叫出）、blunder（大錯）、boulder（巨礫）、box（盒子）、club（俱樂部）、crash（碰撞）、dairy（奶製品）、dazzle（耀眼）、fellow（同胞）、gable（三角牆）、gain（獲得）、ill（生病的）、jam（擁堵）、kidnap（綁架）、kill（殺死）、kidney（腎）、kneel（跪下）、limber（柔軟的）、litter（垃圾）、log（原木）、lull（間歇）、lump（塊）、mast（桅桿）、mistake（錯誤）、nag（嘮叨）、nasty（凶惡的）、niggard（吝嗇的）、horse（馬）、plough（犁）、rump（臀部）、sale（銷售）、scald（燙傷）、shriek（尖叫）、skin（皮膚）、skull（顱骨）、sledge（雪橇）、sleigh（雪橇）、tackle（索具）、tangle（纏結）、tipple（酒精飲料）、trust（相信）、viking（維京人）、window（窗戶）、wing（翅膀）等詞彙。

希伯來語帶來了許多專有名詞（名字），從 Adam（亞當）和 Eve（夏娃）到 John（約翰）和 Mary（瑪麗），還有諸如 Messiah（彌賽亞）、rabbi（拉比，猶太神職人員）、hallelujah（哈利路亞）、cherub（二級天使）、seraph（六翼天使）、hosanna（和撒那）、manna（嗎哪）、satan（撒旦）、Sabbath（安息日）等詞彙。

許多技術名詞和學科名稱來自希臘語。實際上，幾乎所有關於學習和藝術的詞彙——從 alphabet（字母表）到高級的 metaphysics（形而上學）和 theologyic（神學）都是直接來源於希臘語的。包括 philosophy（哲學）、logic（邏輯）、anthropology（人類學）、psychology（心理學）、aesthetics（美學）、grammar（語法）、rhetoric（修辭學）、history（歷史）、philology（語文學）、mathematics（數學）、arithmetic（算術）、astronomy

（天文學）、anatomy（解剖學）、geography（地理學）、stenography（速記）、physiology（生理學）、architecture（建築學）等幾百個相關領域的詞彙；theology（神學）的進一步分類和後果等詞彙包括 exegesis（注釋，尤指對《聖經》的注釋）、hermeneutics（《聖經》註解學）、apologetics（護教學）、polemics（辯論術）、dogmatics（教理學）、ethics（倫理學）、homiletics（講道術）等都來自希臘語。

荷蘭語則為英語帶來了現代航海術語，比如 sloop（單桅帆船）、schooner（縱帆船）、yacht（帆船），以及其他一些諸如 boom（水柵）、bush（襯套）、boor（莽漢）、brandy（白蘭地）、duck（低頭）、reef（礁）、skate（鰩）等詞彙。曼哈頓島的荷蘭人則帶給我們 boss——僱主，或者說監工的名字，還有 coldslaa（切碎的高麗菜加醋）和一些地理術語。

許多發音悅耳的，尤其是音樂領域中的詞彙是直接從義大利語來的。其中包括 piano（鋼琴）、violin（小提琴）、orchestra（管絃樂隊）、canto（詩章）、allegro（快板）、piazza（廣場）、gazette（公報）、umbrella（傘）、gondola（貢朵拉）、bandit（土匪）等。

西班牙語為英語充實了 alligator（鱷魚）、alpaca（羊駝）、bigot（偏執者）、cannibal（食人肉者）、cargo（貨物）、filibuster（阻撓行動）、freebooter（劫掠者）、guano（鳥糞）、hurricane（颶風）、mosquito（蚊子）、negro（黑人）、stampede（驚跑）、potato（馬鈴薯）、tobacco（菸草）、tomato（番茄）、tariff（關稅）等詞彙。

阿拉伯語帶來的則是一些數學、天文學、醫學和化學方面的術語，比如 alcohol（酒精）、alcove（凹處）、alembic（蒸餾器）、algebra（代數）、alkali（鹼）、almanac（曆書）、assassin（暗殺者）、azure（蔚藍色）、cipher（密碼）、elixir（靈丹妙藥）、harem（妻妾）、hegira（逃亡）、sofa

第十四章
英語語言演變：起源與現狀探索

（長沙發）、talisman（護身符）、zenith（天頂）和 zero（零）等。

Bazaar（集市）、dervish（托缽僧）、lilac（丁香花）、pagoda（佛塔）、caravan（大篷車）、scarlet（猩紅色）、shawl（披巾）、tartar（韃靼人）、tiara（冠狀頭飾）和 peach（桃子）來自波斯語。

Turban（包頭巾）、tulip（鬱金香）、divan（無靠背和扶手的長沙發）和 firman（昔日土耳其皇帝等的勒令）是土耳其語。

Drosky（無頂四輪馬車）、knout（皮鞭）、rouble（盧布）、steppe（乾草原）、ukase（諭旨）是俄語。

印第安語對英語幫助很大。它帶來的詞彙發音非常悅耳，包括許多河流和州的名字，比如 Mississippi（密西西比）、Missouri（密蘇里）、Minnehaha（明尼哈哈）、Susquehanna（薩斯奎哈納）、Monongahela（莫農加希拉）、Niagara（尼亞加拉）、Ohio（俄亥俄）、Massachusetts（麻薩諸塞）、Connecticut（康乃狄克）、Iowa（愛荷華）、Nebraska（內布拉斯加）、Dakota（達科塔）等。除了這些專有名詞，還有一些源自印第安語的詞彙，包括 wigwam（圓頂棚屋）、squaw（北美印第安女人）、hammock（吊床）、tomahawk（印第安戰斧）、canoe（獨木舟）、mocassin（莫卡辛鞋）、hominy（碎玉米）等。

英語語言中還有許多「混血兒」，即從兩種或以上的語言中產生的詞彙。實際上，英語一直在不斷地吸收其他語言的內容，擴大自己本就龐大的體系。並且，英語不僅僅壯大自身，還傳播到世界各地。許多人都認為，在不久的將來，英語會成為世界性語言。現在歐洲的優秀大學和學院以及世界各地的商業城市都在教授英語，英語成為高等教育的一個分支。在日本和中國的海港城市，英語得到了大幅度運用，並且這些國家中學習英語的本土人在日漸增加。在南非、賴比瑞亞、獅子山以及

風格的種類

印度洋和南海的眾多島嶼，英語已經奠定了它的地位。它是澳洲、紐西蘭、塔斯馬尼亞的官方語言，基督教的傳教士在努力將它推廣至玻里尼西亞群島。從巴芬灣到墨西哥灣，從大西洋到太平洋，英語可以說是北美大陸的商務語言。南美共和國中很多人也使用英語，英語不受經緯度的限制。英國和美國這兩個說英語的國家在四面八方地向世界各地傳播它。

第十四章
英語語言演變：起源與現狀探索

第十五章
文學巨匠與名作：偉大作家的遺產

　　《聖經》不僅是一部關於上帝的啟示的著作，也是目前為止最完美的文學作品。撇開《聖經》不談，最偉大的三部作品分別來自荷馬、但丁和莎士比亞。緊隨其後的是維吉爾和米爾頓的作品。

必備之書

　　荷馬、但丁、塞凡提斯、莎士比亞和歌德。查普曼（翻譯過《伊里亞德》、《奧德賽》）翻譯的荷馬作品是最好的。諾頓翻譯的但丁的作品和泰勒翻譯的《浮士德》（歌德作品）都值得推薦。

館藏豐富的資源庫

　　除了以上提到的大家之作，所有人還應該拜讀以下作家和作品：普魯塔克的《希臘羅馬名人傳》，馬可・奧理略的《沉思錄》，喬叟、耿稗思的《師主篇》，哲羅米・泰勒的《聖潔的生與死》、《天路歷程》，麥考萊、培根、艾迪生、查爾斯・蘭姆的《伊利亞隨筆選》，雨果的《悲慘世界》，湯瑪斯・卡萊爾的《英雄和英雄崇拜》，帕爾格雷夫的《英詩經典》，華茲

第十五章
文學巨匠與名作：偉大作家的遺產

華斯的《維克斐牧師傳》，喬治‧艾略特的《亞當‧比德》，薩克雷的《名利場》，華特‧史考特爵士的《劫後英雄傳》，奧爾巴赫的《在高地》，巴爾扎克的《歐也妮‧葛朗台》，霍桑的《紅字》，艾默生的文章、包斯威爾的《約翰遜傳》，約翰‧理查‧格林的《英國人民簡史》，達爾文的《物種起源》，以及蒙田、朗費羅、丁尼生、布朗寧、惠蒂爾、拉斯金、赫伯特‧史賓賽的作品。

一本好的百科全書是值得擁有、值得依賴且不可或缺的詞典。

美國文學代表作

《紅字》、《派克曼的歷史》，莫特利的《荷蘭共和國的興起》，格蘭特的《回憶錄》、《富蘭克林自傳》，韋伯斯特的演講，洛威爾的《畢格羅的論文》和他的批判性文章，梭羅的《湖濱散記》，惠特曼的《草葉集》，庫柏的《皮襪子故事集》、《早餐桌上的獨裁者》、《賓虛》、《湯姆叔叔的小屋》。

美國十大詩人

布萊恩特、愛倫‧坡、惠蒂爾、朗費羅、洛威爾、愛默生、惠特曼、拉尼爾、奧爾德里奇和斯托達德。

英國十大詩人

喬叟、史賓賽、莎士比亞、米爾頓、伯恩斯、華茲華斯、濟慈、雪萊、丁尼生和布朗寧。

英國十大散文家

培根、艾迪生、斯梯爾、麥考萊、蘭姆、傑弗瑞、德‧昆西、卡萊爾、薩克雷和馬修‧阿諾德。

莎士比亞的最佳戲劇

按照作品的價值來排序的話應該是：《哈姆雷特》、《李爾王》、《奧賽羅》、《安東尼和克麗奧佩托拉》、《馬克白》、《威尼斯商人》、《亨利四世》、《皆大歡喜》、《冬天的故事》、《羅密歐與茱麗葉》、《仲夏夜之夢》、《第十二夜》、《暴風雨》。

只看精品

如果你沒有條件接觸各大名家的著作，至少保證要看其中一部分。帶著拓展文學視野的心態，仔細閱讀，分析它們。記住，一本好書怎麼讀都是不夠的。而對於不好的作品，我們則應盡力避免接觸它。和其他事物一樣，在文學領域裡，經典永流傳。

第十五章
文學巨匠與名作：偉大作家的遺產

INTRODUCTION

In the preparation of this little work the writer has kept one end in view, viz.: To make it serviceable for those for whom it is intended, that is, for those who have neither the time nor the opportunity, the learning nor the inclination, to peruse elaborate and abstruse treatises on Rhetoric, Grammar, and Composition. To them such works are as gold enclosed in chests of steel and locked beyond power of opening. This book has no pretension about it whatever, —— it is neither a Manual of Rhetoric, expatiating on the dogmas of style, nor a Grammar full of arbitrary rules and exceptions. It is merely an effort to help ordinary, everyday people to express themselves in ordinary, everyday language, in a proper manner. Some broad rules are laid down, the observance of which will enable the reader to keep within the pale of propriety in oral and written language. Many idiomatic words and expressions, peculiar to the language, have been given, besides which a number of the common mistakes and pitfalls have been placed before the reader so that he may know and avoid them.

The writer has to acknowledge his indebtedness to no one in particular, but to all in general who have ever written on the subject.

The little book goes forth —— a finger-post on the road of language pointing in the right direction. It is hoped that they who go according to its index will arrive at the goal of correct speaking and writing.

INTRODUCTION

CHAPTER I
REQUIREMENTS OF SPEECH:
Vocabulary —— Parts of Speech —— Requisites

It is very easy to learn how to speak and write correctly, as for all purposes of ordinary conversation and communication, only about 2,000 different words are required. The mastery of just two hundred words, the knowing where to place them, will make us not masters of the English language, but masters of correct speaking and writing. Small number, you will say, compared with what is in the dictionary! But nobody ever uses all the words in the dictionary or could use them did he live to be the age of Methuselah, and there is no necessity for using them.

There are upwards of 200,000 words in the recent editions of the large dictionaries, but the one- hundredth part of this number will suffice for all your wants. Of course you may think not, and you may not be content to call things by their common names; you may be ambitious to show superiority over others and display your learning or, rather, your pedantry and lack of learning.

CHAPTER I   REQUIREMENTS OF SPEECH:
Vocabulary—Parts of Speech—Requisites

For instance, you may not want to call a spade a spade. You may prefer to call it a patulous device for abrading the surface of the soil. Better, however, to stick to the old familiar, simple name that your grandfather called it. It has stood the test of time, and old friends are always good friends.

To use a big word or a foreign word when a small one and a familiar one will answer the same purpose, is a sign of ignorance. Great scholars and writers and polite speakers use simple words.

To go back to the number necessary for all purposes of conversation correspondence and writing, 2,000, we find that a great many people who pass in society as being polished, refined and educated use less, for they know less. The greatest scholar alive hasn't more than four thousand different words at his 183 command, and he never has occasion to use half the number.

In the works of Shakespeare, the most wonderful genius the world has ever known, there is the enormous number of 15,000 different words, but almost 10,000 of them are obsolete or meaningless today.

Every person of intelligence should be able to use his mother tongue correctly. It only requires a little pains, a little care, a little study to enable one to do so, and the recompense is great. Consider the contrast between the well-bred, polite man who knows how to choose and use his words correctly and the underbred, vulgar boor, whose language grates upon the ear and jars the sensitiveness of the finer feelings. The blunders of the latter, his infringement of all the canons of grammar, his absurdities and monstrosities of language, make his very presence a pain, and one is glad to escape from his company. The proper grammatical formation of the English language, so that one may acquit himself as a correct conversationalist in the best society or be able to write and express his thoughts and ideas upon paper in the right manner, may be acquired in a few lessons.

It is the purpose of this book, as briefly and concisely as possible, to direct the reader along a straight course, pointing out the mistakes he must avoid and giving him such assistance as will enable him to reach the goal of a correct knowledge of the English language. It is not a Grammar in any sense, but a guide, a silent signal post pointing the way in the right direction.

THE ENGLISH LANGUAGE IN A NUTSHELL

All the words in the English language are divided into nine great classes. These classes are called the Parts of Speech. They are Article, Noun, Adjective, Pronoun, Verb, Adverb, Preposition, Conjunction and Interjection. Of these, the Noun is the most important, as all the others are more or less dependent upon it. A Noun signifies the name of person, place or thing, in fact, anything of which we can have either thought or idea. There are two kinds of Nouns, Proper and Common. Common Nouns are names which belong in common to a race or class, as man, city. Proper Nouns distinguish individual members of a race or class as John, Philadelphia. In the former case man is a name which belongs in common to the whole race of mankind, and city is also a name which is common to all large centres of population, but John signifies a particular individual of the race, while *Philadelphia* denotes a particular one

249

CHAPTER I REQUIREMENTS OF SPEECH:
Vocabulary—Parts of Speech—Requisites

of which the cities of the world.

Nouns are varied by Person, Number, Gender, and Case. Person is that relation existing between the speaker, those addressed and the subject under consideration, whether by discourse or correspondence. The Persons are *First, Second* and *Third* and they represent respectively the speaker, the person addressed and the person or thing mentioned or under consideration.

Number is the distinction of one from more than one. There are two numbers, singular and plural; the singular denotes one, the plural two or more. The plural is generally formed from the singular by the addition of *s* or *es*.

Gender has the same relation to nouns that sex has to individuals, but while there are only two sexes, there are four genders, viz., masculine, feminine, neuter and common. The masculine gender denotes all those of the male kind, the feminine gender all those of the female kind, the neuter gender denotes inanimate things or whatever is without life, and common gender is applied to animate beings, the sex of which for the time being is indeterminable, such as fish, mouse, bird, etc. Sometimes things which are without life as we conceive it and which, properly speaking, belong to the neuter gender, are, by a figure of speech called Personification, changed into either the masculine or feminine gender, as, for instance, we say of the sun, *He* is rising; of the moon, *She* is setting.

Case is the relation one noun bears to another or to a verb or to a preposition. There are three cases, the *Nominative*, the *Possessive* and the *Objective*. The nominative is the subject of which we are speaking or the agent which directs the action of the verb; the possessive case denotes possession, while the objective indicates the person or thing which is affected by the action of the verb.

An Article is a word placed before a noun to show whether the latter is used in a particular or general sense. There are but two articles, a or an and the. An Adjective is a word which qualifies a noun, that is, which shows some distinguishing mark or characteristics belonging to the noun.

DEFINITIONS

A *Pronoun* is a word used for or instead of a noun to keep us from repeating the same noun too often. Pronouns, like nouns, have case, number, gender and person. There are three kinds of pronouns, *personal, relative* and *adjective*.

A *verb* is a word which signifies action or the doing of something. A verb is inflected by tense and mood and by number and person, though the latter two belong strictly to the subject of the verb.

An *adverb* is a word which modifies a verb, an adjective and sometimes another adverb.

A *preposition* serves to connect words and to show the relation between the objects which the words express.

A *conjunction* is a word which joins words, phrases, clsuses and sentences together. An *interjection* is a word which express surprise or some sudden emotion of the mind.

CHAPTER I REQUIREMENTS OF SPEECH:
Vocabulary—Parts of Speech—Requisites

THREE ESSENTIALS

The three essentials of the English language are: *Purity, Perspicuity* and *Precision*.

By *Purity* is signified the use of good English. It precludes the use of all slang words, vulgar phrases, obsolete terms, foreign idioms, ambiguous expressions or any ungrammatical language whatsoever. Neither does it sanction the use of any newly coined word until such word is adopted by the best writers and speakers. Perspicuity demands the clearest expression of thought conveyed in unequivocal language, so that there may be no misunderstanding whatever of the thought or idea the speaker or writer wishes to convey. All ambiguous words, words of double meaning and words that might possibly be construed in a sense different from that intended, are strictly forbidden.

Perspicuity requires a style at once clear and comprehensive and entirely free from pomp and pedantry and affectation or any straining after effect.

Precision requires concise and exact expression, free from redundancy and tautology, a style terse and clear and simple enough to enable the hearer or reader to comprehend immediately the meaning of the speaker or writer. It forbids, on the one hand, all long and involved sentences, and, on the other, those that are too short and abrupt. Its object is to strike the golden mean in such a way as to rivet the attention of the hearer or reader on the words uttered or written.

CHAPTER II
ESSENTIALS OF ENGLISH GRAMMAR:
Divisions of Grammar —— Definitions —— Etymology

In order to speak and write the English language correctly, it is imperative that the fundamental principles of the Grammar be mastered, for no matter how much we may read of the best authors, no matter how much we may associate with and imitate the best speakers, if we do not know the underlying principles of the correct formation of sentences and the relation of words to one another, we will be to a great extent like the parrot, that merely repeats what it hears without understanding the import of it is said. Of course the parrot, being a creature without reason, cannot comprehend; it can simply repeat what is said to it, and as it utters phrases and sentences of profanity with as much facility as those of virtue, so by like analogy, when we do not understand the grammar of the language, we may be making egregious blunders while thinking we are speaking with the utmost accuracy.

CHAPTER II ESSENTIALS OF ENGLISH GRAMMAR:
Divisions of Grammar—Definitions—Etymology

DIVISIONS OF GRAMMAR

There are four great divisions of Grammar, viz.:

Orthography, Etymology, Syntax, and *Prosody.*

Orthography treats of letters and the mode of combining them into words.

Etymology treats of the various classes of words and the changes they undergo.

Syntax treats of the connection and arrangement of words in sentences.

Prosody treats of the manner of speaking and reading and the different kinds of verse.

The three first mentioned concern us most.

LETTERS

A letter is a mark or character used to represent an articulate sound. Letters are divided into *vowels* and *consonants*. A vowel is a letter which makes a distinct sound by itself. Consonants cannot be sounded without the aid of vowels. The vowels are *a, e, i, o, u,* and sometimes *w* and *y* when they do not begin a word or syllable.

SYLLABLES AND WORDS

A syllable is a distinct sound produced by a single effort of [Transcriber's note: 1-2 words illegible] shall, pig, dog. In every syllable there must be at least one vowel. A word consists of one syllable or a combination of syllables. Many rules are given for the dividing of words into syllables, but the best is to follow as closely as possible the divisions made by the organs of speech in properly pronouncing them.

THE PARTS OF SPEECH

ARTICLE

An *Article* is a word placed before a noun to show whether the noun is used in a particular or general sense.

There are two articles, a or an and the.

A or *an* is called the indefinite article because it does not point put any particular person or thing but indicates the noun in its widest sense; thus, a man means any man whatever of the species or race.

The is called the definite article because it points out some particular person or thing; thus, *the* man means some particular individual.

NOUN

A *noun* is the name of any person, place or thing as *John, London, book*. Nouns are proper and common.

Proper nouns are names applied to particular persons or places.

Common nouns are names applied to a whole kind or species. Nouns are

CHAPTER II ESSENTIALS OF ENGLISH GRAMMAR:
Divisions of Grammar—Definitions—Etymology

inflected by *number, gender* and *case*.

Number is that inflection of the noun by which we indicate whether it represents one or more than one.

Gender is that inflection by which we signify whether the noun is the name of a male, a female, of an inanimate object or something which has no distinction of sex.

Case is that inflection of the noun which denotes the state of the person, place or thing represented, as the subject of an affirmation or question, the owner or possessor of something mentioned, or the object of an action or of a relation.

Thus in the example, "John tore the leaves of Sarah's book," the distinction between *book* which represents only one object and *leaves* which represent two or more objects of the same kind is called *Number*; the distinction of sex between *John*, a male, and *Sarah*, a female, and *book* and *leaves*, things which are inanimate and neither male nor female, is called Gender; and the distinction of state between *John*, the person who tore the book, and the subject of the affirmation, *Mary*, the owner of the book, leaves the objects torn, and book the object related to *leaves*, as the whole of which they were a part, is called *Case*.

ADJECTIVE

An *adjective* is a word which qualifies a noun, that is, shows or points out some distinguishing mark or feature of the noun; as, A *black* dog.

THE PARTS OF SPEECH

Adjectives have three forms called degrees of comparison, the positive, the comparative and the superlative.

The *positive* is the simple form of the adjective without expressing increase or diminution of the original quality: nice.

The *comparative* is that form of the adjective which expresses increase or diminution of the quality:

nicer.

The *superlative* is that form which expresses the greatest increase or diminution of the quality:

nicest.

Or

An *adjective* is in the positive form when it does not express comparison; as, "A rich man."

An *adjective* is in the comparative form when it expresses comparison between two or between one and a number taken collectively, as, "John is *richer* than James"; "he is richer than all the men in Boston."

An adjective is in the superlative form when it expresses a comparison between one and a number of individuals taken separately; as, "John is the richest man in Boston."

Adjectives expressive of properties or circumstances which cannot be increased have only the positive form; as, A *circular* road; the *chief* end; an *extreme* measure.

Adjectives are compared in two ways, either by adding *er* to the positive

CHAPTER II ESSENTIALS OF ENGLISH GRAMMAR:
Divisions of Grammar—Definitions—Etymology

to form the comparative and *est* to the positive to form the superlative, or by prefixing *more* to the positive for the comparative and *most* to the positive for the superlative; as, *handsome, handsomer, handsomest or handsome, more handsome, most handsome.*

Adjectives of two or more syllables are generally compared by prefixing more and most. Many adjectives are irregular in comparison; as, Bad, worse, worst; Good, better, best.

PRONOUN

A *pronoun* is a word used in place of a noun; as, "John gave his pen to James and *he* lent it to Jane to write her copy with *it.*" Without the pronouns we would have to write this sentence, —— "John gave John's pen to James and James lent the pen to Jane to write Jane's copy with the pen."

There are three kinds of pronouns —— Personal, Relative and Adjective Pronouns.

Personal Pronouns are so called because they are used instead of the names of persons, places and things. The Personal Pronouns are *I, Thou, He, She,* and *It,* with their plurals, *We, Ye* or *You* and *They.*

I is the pronoun of the first person because it represents the person speaking.

Thou is the pronoun of the second person because it represents the person spoken to.

He, She, It are the pronouns of the third person because they represent the persons or things of whom we are speaking.

THE PARTS OF SPEECH

Like nouns, the Personal Pronouns have number, gender and case. The gender of the first and second person is obvious, as they represent the person or persons speaking and those who are addressed. The personal pronouns are thus declined:

First Person.

M. or F.

	Sing.	Plural.
N.	I	We
P.	Mine	Ours
O.	Me	Us

Second Person.

M. or F.

	Sing.	Plural.
N.	Thou	You
P.	Thine	Yours
O.	Thee	You

Third Person,

M.

	Sing.	Plural.
N.	He	They
P.	His	Theirs
O.	Him	Them

CHAPTER II ESSENTIALS OF ENGLISH GRAMMAR:
Divisions of Grammar—Definitions—Etymology

Third Person.

F.

	Sing.	Plural.
N.	She	They
P.	Hers	Theirs
O.	Her	Them

Third Person.

Neuter.

	Sing.	Plural.
N.	It	They
P.	Its	Theirs
O.	It	Them

N.B. —— In colloquial language and ordinary writing Thou, Thine and Thee are seldom used, except by the Society of Friends. The Plural form You is used for both the nominative and objective singular in the second person and Yours is generally used in the possessive in place of Thine.

The *Relative* Pronouns are so called because they relate to some word or phrase going before; as, "The boy who told the truth;" "He has done well, which gives me great pleasure."

Here *who* and *which* are not only used in place of other words, but who refers immediately to boy, and which to the circumstance of his having done well.

The word or clause to which a relative pronoun refers is called the *Antecedent*.

The Relative Pronouns are who, which, *that* and *what*.

Who is applied to persons only; as, "The man who was here."

Which is applied to the lower animals and things without life; as, "The horse *which* I sold." "The hat *which* I bought."

That is applied to both persons and things; as, "The friend that helps." "The bird that sings." "The knife that cuts."

What is a compound relative, including both the antecedent and the relative and is equivalent to *that which*; as, "I did what he desired," i. e. "I did *that which* he desired."

Relative pronouns have the singular and plural alike.

Who is either masculine or feminine; *which* and *that* are masculine, feminine or neuter; what as a relative pronoun is always neuter.

That and what are not inflected.

Who and which are thus declined:

Sing. and Plural		Sing. and Plural	
N.	Who	N.	Which
P.	Whose	P.	Whose
O.	Whom	O.	Which

Who, which and what when used to ask questions are called nterrogative Pronouns.

CHAPTER II ESSENTIALS OF ENGLISH GRAMMAR:
Divisions of Grammar—Definitions—Etymology

Adjective Pronouns partake of the nature of adjectives and pronouns and are subdivided as follows:

Demonstrative Adjective Pronouns which directly point out the person or object. They are this, that with their plurals *these, those,* and *yon, same* and *selfsame.*

Distributive Adjective Pronouns used distributively. They are *each, every, either, neither.*

Indefinite Adjective Pronouns used more or less indefinitely. They are any, *all, few, some, several, one, other, another, none.*

Possessive Adjective Pronouns denoting possession. They are *my, thy, his, her, its, our, your, their.*

N. B. —— (The possessive adjective pronouns differ from the possessive case of the personal pronouns in that the latter can stand alone while the former cannot. "Who owns that book?" "It is *mine.*" You cannot say "it is *my,*" —— the word book must be repeated.)

THE VERB

A verb is a word which implies action or the doing of something, or it may be defined as a word which affirms, commands or asks a question.

Thus, the words John the table, contain no assertion, but when the word strikes is introduced, something is affirmed, hence the word *strikes* is a verb and gives completeness and meaning to the group.

THE PARTS OF SPEECH

The simple form of the verb without inflection is called the *root* of the verb; e. g. *love* is the root of the verb, —— "To Love."

Verbs are regular or irregular, *transitive* or *intransitive*.

A verb is said to be regular when it forms the past tense by adding *ed* to the present or *d* if the verb ends in *e*. When its past tense does not end in *ed* it is said to be irregular.

A *transitive* verb is one the action of which passes over to or affects some object; as "I struck the table." Here the action of striking affected the object table, hence struck is a transitive verb.

An *intransitive* verb is one in which the action remains with the subject; as "*I walk,*" "*I sit,*" "*I run.*"

Many intransitive verbs, however, can be used transitively; thus, "I *walk* the horse;" *walk* is here transitive.

Verbs are inflected by *number, person, tense* and *mood*.

Number and *person* as applied to the verb really belong to the subject; they are used with the verb to denote whether the assertion is made regarding one or more than one and whether it is made in reference to the person speaking, the person spoken to or the person or thing spoken about.

TENSE

In their tenses verbs follow the divisions of time. They have *present tense, past tense* and *future tense* with their variations to express the exact time of action as to an event happening, having happened or yet to happen.

CHAPTER II   ESSENTIALS OF ENGLISH GRAMMAR:
Divisions of Grammar—Definitions—Etymology

MOOD

There are four simple moods, —— the *Infinitive*, the *Indicative*, the *Imperative* and the *Subjunctive*.

The Mood of a verb denotes the mode or manner in which it is used. Thus if it is used in its widest sense without reference to person or number, time or place, it is in the *Infinitive* Mood; as "To run." Here we are not told who does the running, when it is done, where it is done or anything about it.

When a verb is used to indicate or declare or ask a simple question or make any direct statement, it is in the *Indicative* Mood. "The boy loves his book." Here a direct statement is made concerning the boy. "Have you a pin?" Here a simple question is asked which calls for an answer.

When the verb is used to express a command or entreaty it is in the Imperative Mood as, "Go away." "Give me a penny."

When the verb is used to express doubt, supposition or uncertainty or when some future action depends upon a contingency, it is in the subjunctive mood; as, "If I come, he shall remain."

Many grammarians include a fifth mood called the potential to express *power, possibility, liberty, necessity, will* or *duty*. It is formed by means of the auxiliaries may, can, ought and must, but in all cases it can be resolved into the indicative or subjunctive. Thus, in "I may write if I choose," "may write" is by some classified as in the potential mood, but in reality the phrase I may write is an indicative one while the second clause, if I choose, is the expression of a condition upon which, not my liberty to write, depends, but my actual writing.

THE PARTS OF SPEECH

Verbs have two participles, the present or imperfect, sometimes called the active ending in ing and the past or perfect, often called the *passive*, ending in *ed* or *d*.

The *infinitive* expresses the sense of the verb in a substantive form, the participles in an adjective form; as "To rise early is healthful." "An early rising man." "The newly risen sun."

The participle in *ing* is frequently used as a substantive and consequently is equivalent to an infinitive; thus, "To rise early is healthful" and "Rising early is healthful" are the same.

The principal parts of a verb are the Present Indicative, Past Indicative and Past Participle; as:

Love	Loved	Loved

Sometimes one or more of these parts are wanting, and then the verb is said to be defective.

Present	Past	Passive Participle
Can	Could	(Wanting)
May	Might	"
Shal	Should	"
Wil	Would	"
Ought	Ought	"

Verbs may also be divided into principal and *auxiliary*. A *principal* verb is that without which a sentence or clause can contain no assertion or allirma-

CHAPTER II   ESSENTIALS OF ENGLISH GRAMMAR:
Divisions of Grammar—Definitions—Etymology

tion. An *auxiliary* is a verb joined to the root or participles of a principal verb to express time and manner with greater precision than can be done by the tenses and moods in their simple form. Thus, the sentence, "I am writing an exercise; when I shall have finished it I shall read it to the class." has no meaning without the principal verbs *writing, finished read*; but the meaning is rendered more definite, especially with regard to time, by the auxiliary verbs am, *have, shall*. There are nine auxiliary or helping verbs, viz., *Be, have, do, shall, will, may, can, ought,* and *must*. They are called helping verbs, because it is by their aid the compound tenses are formed.

TO BE

The verb To Be is the most important of the auxiliary verbs. It has eleven parts, viz., *am, art, is, are, was, wast, were, wert; be, being* and *been*.

VOICE

The *active voice* is that form of the verb which shows the Subject not being acted upon but acting; as, "The cat catches mice." "Charity *covers* a multitude of sins."

The *passive voice*: When the action signified by a transitive verb is thrown back upon the agent, that is to say, when the subject of the verb denotes the recipient of the action, the verb is said to be in the passive voice. "John was loved by his neighbors." Here John the subject is also the object affected by the loving, the action of the verb is thrown back on him, hence the compound verb *was loved* is said to be in the *passive voice*. The passive voice

THE PARTS OF SPEECH

is formed by putting the perfect participle of any *transitive* verb with any of the eleven parts of the verb *To Be*.

CONJUGATION

The *conjugation* of a verb is its orderly arrangement in voices, moods, tenses, persons and numbers. Here is the complete conjugation of the verb "Love" —— *Active Voice.*

PRINCIPAL PARTS

Present	Past	Past Participle
Love	Loved	Loved

Infinitive Mood

To Love

Indicative Mood

PRESENT TENSE

	Sing.	Plural
1st person	I love	We love
2nd person	You love	You love
3rd person	He loves	They love

PAST TENSE

	Sing.	Plural
1st person	I loved	We loved

267

CHAPTER II   ESSENTIALS OF ENGLISH GRAMMAR:
Divisions of Grammar—Definitions—Etymology

	Sing.	Plural
2nd person	You loved	You loved
3rd person	He loved	They loved

FUTURE TENSE

	Sing.	Plural
1st person	I shall love	They will love
2nd person	You will love	You will love
3rd person	He will love	We shall love

[Transcriber's note: 1st person plural and 3rd person plural reversed in original]

PRESENT PERFECT TENSE

	Sing.	Plural
1st person	I have loved	We have loved
2nd person	You have loved	You have loved
3rd person	He has loved	They have loved

PAST PERFECT TENSE

	Sing.	Plural
1st person	I had loved	We had loved
2nd person	You had loved	You had loved
3rd person	He had loved	They had loved

THE PARTS OF SPEECH

FUTURE PERFECT TENSE

	Sing.	Plural
1st person	I shall have loved	We shall have loved
2nd person	You will have loved	You will have loved
3rd person	He will have loved	They will have loved

Imperative Mood

(PRESENT TENSE ONLY)

	Sing.	Plural
2nd person	Love(you)	Love(you)

Subjunctive Mood

PRESENT TENSE

	Sing.	Plural
1st person	If I love	If we love
2nd person	If you love	If you love
3rd person	If he loves	If they love

PAST TENSE

	Sing.	Plural
1st person	If I loved	If we loved
2nd person	If you loved	If you loved
3rd person	If he loved	If they loved

CHAPTER II   ESSENTIALS OF ENGLISH GRAMMAR:
Divisions of Grammar—Definitions—Etymology

PRESENT PERFECT TENSE

	Sing.	Plural
1st person	If I have loved	If we have loved
2nd person	If you have loved	If you have loved
3rd person	If he has loved	If they have loved

PAST PERFECT TENSE

	Sing.	Plural
1st person	If I had loved	If we had loved
2nd person	If you had loved	If you had loved
3rd person	If he had loved	If they had loved

INFINITIVES

Present	Perfect
To love	To have loved

PARTICIPLES

Present	Past	Perfect
Loving	Loved	Having loved

CONJUGATION OF "To Love"

Passive Voice Indicative Mood Present Tense

	Sing.	Plural
1st person	I am loved	We are loved

THE PARTS OF SPEECH

	Sing.	Plural
2nd person	You are loved	Yourselves
3rd person	He is loved	They are loved

PAST TENSE

	Sing.	Plural
1st person	I was loved	We were loved
2nd person	You were loved	You were loved
3rd person	He was loved	They were loved

FUTURE TENSE

	Sing.	Plural
1st person	I shall be loved	We shall be loved
2nd person	You will be loved	You will be loved
3rd person	He will be loved	They will be loved

PRESENT PERFECT TENSE

	Sing.	Plural
1st person	I have been loved	We have been loved
2nd person	You have been loved	You have been loved
3rd person	He has been loved	They have been loved

PAST PERFECT TENSE

	Sing.	Plural
1st person	I had been loved	We had been loved

CHAPTER II   ESSENTIALS OF ENGLISH GRAMMAR:
Divisions of Grammar—Definitions—Etymology

	Sing.	Plural
2nd person	You had been loved	You had been loved
3rd person	He had been loved	They had been loved

FUTURE PERFECT TENSE

	Sing.	Plural
1st person	I shall have been loved	We shall have been loved
2nd person	You will have been loved	You will have been loved
3rd person	He will have been loved	They will have been loved

Imperative Mood

(PRESENT TENSE ONLY)

	Sing.	Plural
2nd person	Be(you)loved	Be(you)loved

Subjunctive Mood

PRESENT TENSE

	Sing.	Plural
1st person	If I beloved	If we be loved
2nd person	If you be loved	If you beloved
3rd person	If he beloved	If they beloved

PAST TENSE

	Sing.	Plural
1st person	If I were loved	If they were loved

	Sing.	Plural
2nd person	If you were loved	If you were loved
3rd person	If he were loved	If we were loved

PRESENT PERFECT TENSE

	Sing.	Plural
1st person	If I have been loved	If we have been loved
2nd person	If you have been loved	If you have been loved
3rd person	If he has been loved	If they have been loved

PAST PERFECT TENSE

	Sing.	Plural
1st person	If I had been loved	If we had been loved
2nd person	If you had been loved	If you had been loved
3rd person	If he had been loved	If they had been loved

INFINITIVES

Present	Perfect
To be loved	To have been loved

PARTICIPLES

Present	Past	Perfect
Being loved	Been loved	Having been loved

(N. B. —— Note that the plural form of the personal pronoun, you, is used in the second person singular throughout. The old form thou, except in

CHAPTER II ESSENTIALS OF ENGLISH GRAMMAR:
Divisions of Grammar—Definitions—Etymology

the conjugation of the verb "To Be," may be said to be obsolete. In the third person singular he is representative of the three personal pronouns of the third person, *He, She* and *It*.)

ADVERB

An *adverb* is a word which modifies a verb, an adjective or another adverb. Thus, in the example —— "He writes well," the adverb shows the manner in which the writing is performed; in the examples —— "He is remarkably diligent" and "He works very faithfully," the adverbs modify the adjective diligent and the other adverb *faithfully* by expressing the degree of diligence and faithfulness.

Adverbs are chiefly used to express in one word what would otherwise require two or more words; thus, There signifies in that place; whence, from what place; usefully, in a useful manner.

Adverbs, like adjectives, are sometimes varied in their terminations to express comparison and different degrees of quality.

Some adverbs form the comparative and superlative by adding er and est; as, *soon, sooner, soonest.*

Adverbs which end in *ly* are compared by prefixing more and most; as, *nobly, more nobly, most nobly.*

A few adverbs are irregular in the formation of the comparative and superlative; as, *well, better, best.*

THE PARTS OF SPEECH

PREPOSITION

A *preposition* connects words, clauses, and sentences together and shows the relation between them. "My hand is on the table" shows relation between hand and table.

Prepositions are so called because they are generally placed *before* the words whose connection or relation with other words they point out.

CONJUNCTION

A *conjunction* joins words, clauses and sentences; as "John and James." "My father *and* mother have come, *but* I have not seen them."

The conjunctions in most general use are *and, also; either, or; neither, nor; though, yet; but, however; for, that; because, since; therefore, wherefore, then; if, unless, lest.*

INTERJECTION

An *interjection* is a word used to express some sudden emotion of the mind. Thus in the examples, ——

"Ah! there he comes; alas! what shall I do?" *ah*, expresses surprise, and *alas*, distress.

Nouns, adjectives, verbs and adverbs become interjections when they are uttered as exclamations, as, *nonsense! strange! hail! away!* etc.

We have now enumerated the parts of speech and as briefly as possible

CHAPTER II ESSENTIALS OF ENGLISH GRAMMAR:
Divisions of Grammar—Definitions—Etymology

stated the functions of each. As they all belong to the same family they are related to one another but some are in closer affinity than others. To point out the exact relationship and the dependency of one word on another is called parsing and in order that every etymological connection may be distinctly understood a brief resume of the foregoing essentials is here given:

The signification of the noun is limited to one, but to any one of the kind, by the indefinite article, and to some particular one, or some particular number, by the definite article.

Nouns, in one form, represent *one* of a kind, and in another, *any number* more than one; they are the *names of males,* or *females,* or of objects which are neither male nor female; and they represent the *subject* of an affirmation, a command or a question, —— the *owner* or *possessor* of a thing, —— or the *object* of an action, or of a relation expressed by a preposition.

Adjectives express the *qualities* which *distinguish* one person or thing from another; in one form they express quality *without comparison*; in another, they express comparison *between two,* or between one and a number taken collectively, —— and in a third they express comparison between one and a number of others taken separately.

Pronouns are used in place of nouns; one class of them is used merely as the *substitutes* of *names*; the pronouns of another class have a peculiar *reference* to some *preceding words* in the *sentence*, of which they are the substitutes, —— and those of a third class refer adjectively to the persons or things they represent. Some pronouns are used for both the *name* and the *substitute*; and several are frequently employed in *asking questions*.

THE PARTS OF SPEECH

Affirmations and *commands* are expressed by the verb; and different inflections of the verb express *number*, person, *time* and *manner*. With regard to *time*, an affirmation may be present or past or *future*; with regard to manner, an affirmation may be *positive* or *conditional*, it being doubtful whether the condition is fulfilled or not, or it being implied that it is not fulfilled ; —— the verb may express *command* or *entreaty*; or the sense of the verb may be expressed without affirming or commanding. The verb also expresses that an action or state is or was going on, by a form which is also used sometimes as a noun, and sometimes to qualify nouns.

Affirmations are modified by adverbs, some of which can be inflected to express different degrees of modification.

Words are joined together by conjunctions; and the various relations which one thing bears to another are expressed by *'prepositions*. *Sudden emotions* of the mind, and *exclamations* are expressed by *interjections*.

Some words according to meaning belong sometimes to one part of speech, sometimes to another. Thus, in "After a storm comes a *calm*," *calm* is a noun; in "It is a *calm* evening," *calm* is an adjective; and in "*Calm* your fears," *calm* is a verb.

The following sentence containing all the parts of speech is parsed etymologically: "I *now see the old man coming, but, alas, he has walked with much difficulty.*"

I, a personal pronoun, first person singular, masculine or feminine gender, nominative case, subject of the verb *see*.

now, an adverb of time modifying the verb *see*.

CHAPTER II   ESSENTIALS OF ENGLISH GRAMMAR:
Divisions of Grammar—Definitions—Etymology

see, an irregular, transitive verb, indicative mood, present tense, first person singular to agree with its nominative or subject I

the, the definite article particularizing the noun man.

old, an adjective, positive degree, qualifying the noun man.

man, a common noun, 3rd person singular, masculine gender, objective case governed by the transitive verb *see*.

coming, the present or imperfect participle of the verb "to come" referring to the noun man. *but*, a conjunction.

alas, an interjection, expressing pity or sorrow.

he, a personal pronoun, 3rd person singular, masculine gender, nominative case, subject of verb has walked.

has walked, a regular, intransitive verb, indicative mood, perfect tense, 3rd person singular to agree with its nominative or subject *he*.

with, a preposition, governing the noun difficulty

much, an adjective, positive degree, qualifying the noun difficulty.

difficulty, a common noun, 3rd person singular, neuter gender, objective case governed by the preposition *with*.

N.B. —— *Much* is generally an adverb. As an adjective it is thus compared:

Positive	Comparative	Superlative
much	more	most

CHAPTER III
THE SENTENCE:
Different Kinds —— Arrangement of Words —— Paragraph

A sentence is an assemblage of words so arranged as to convey a determinate sense or meaning, in other words, to express a complete thought or idea. No matter how short, it must contain one finite verb and a subject or agent to direct the action of the verb.

"Birds fly ;" "Fish swim ;" "Men walk ;" —— are sentences.

A sentence always contains two parts, something spoken about and something said about it. The word or words indicating what is spoken about form what is called the *subject* and the word or words indicating what is said about it form what is called the *predicate*.

In the sentences given, birds, fish and men are the subjects, while *fly, swim* and *walk* are the predicates.

There are three kinds of sentences, *simple, compound* and *complex.*

The simple sentence expresses a single thought and consists of one subject and one predicate, as, "Man is mortal.

CHAPTER III   THE SENTENCE:
Different Kinds—Arrangement of Words—Paragraph

A *compound sentence* consists of two or more simple sentences of equal importance the parts of which are either expressed or understood, as, "The men work in the fields and the women work in the household," or "The men work in the fields and the women in the household" or "The men and women work in the fields and in the household.

A *complex sentence* consists of two or more simple sentences so combined that one depends on the other to complete its meaning ; as ; "When he returns, I shall go on my vacation." Here the words, "when he returns" are dependent on the rest of the sentence for their meaning.

A *clause* is a separate part of a complex sentence, as "when he returns" in the last example.

A *phrase* consists of two or more words without a finite verb.

Without a finite verb we cannot affirm anything or convey an idea, therefore we can have no sentence.

Infinitives and participles which are the infinite parts of the verb cannot be predicates. "I looking up the street" is not a sentence, for it is not a complete action expressed. When we hear such an expression as "A dog running along the street," we wait for something more to be added, something more affirmed about the dog, whether he bit or barked or fell dead or was run over.

Thus in every sentence there must be a finite verb to limit the subject.

When the verb is transitive, that is, when the action cannot happen without affecting something, the thing affected is called the *object*.

Thus in "Cain killed Abel" the action of the killing affected Abel. In "The cat has caught a mouse," mouse is the object of the catching.

ARRANGEMENT OF WORDS IN A SENTENCE

Of course in simple sentences the natural order of arrangement is subject —— verb —— object. In many cases no other form is possible. Thus in the sentence "The cat has caught a mouse," we cannot reverse it and say "The mouse has caught a cat" without destroying the meaning, and in any other form of arrangement, such as "A mouse, the cat has caught," we feel that while it is intelligible, it is a poor way of expressing the fact and one which jars upon us more or less.

In longer sentences, however, when there are more words than what are barely necessary for subject, verb and object, we have greater freedom of arrangement and can so place the words as to give the best effect. The proper placing of words depends upon perspicuity and precision. These two combined give *style* to the structure.

Most people are familiar with Gray's line in the immortal Elegy —— "The ploughman homeward plods his weary way." This line can be paraphrased to read 18 different ways. Here are a few variations:

Homeward the ploughman plods his weary way.

The ploughman plods his weary way homeward.

Plods homeward the ploughman his weary way.

His weary way the ploughman homeward plods.

Homeward his weary way plods the ploughman.

CHAPTER III   THE SENTENCE:
Different Kinds—Arrangement of Words—Paragraph

Plods the ploughman his weary way homeward.

His weary way the ploughman plods homeward.

His weary way homeward the ploughman plods.

The ploughman plods homeward his weary way.

The ploughman his weary way plods homeward.

and so on. It is doubtful if any of the other forms are superior to the one used by the poet. Of course his arrangement was made to comply with the rhythm and rhyme of the verse. Most of the variations depend upon the emphasis we wish to place upon the different words.

In arranging the words in an ordinary sentence we should not lose sight of the fact that the beginning and end are the important places for catching the attention of the reader. Words in these places have greater emphasis than elsewhere.

In Gray's line the general meaning conveyed is that a weary ploughman is plodding his way homeward, but according to the arrangement a very slight difference is effected in the idea. Some of the variations make us think more of the ploughman, others more of the plodding, and still Most people are familiar with Gray's line in the immortal *Elegy* ——— "The ploughman homeward plods his weary way." This line can be paraphrased to read 18 different ways. Here are a few variations.

others more of the weariness.

As the beginning and end of a sentence are the most important places, it naturally follows that small or insignificant words should be kept from these

ARRANGEMENT OF WORDS IN A SENTENCE

positions. Of the two places the end one is the more important, therefore, it really calls for the most important word in the sentence. Never commence a sentence with And, But, Since, Because, and other similar weak words and never end it with prepositions, small, weak adverbs or pronouns.

The parts of a sentence which are most closely connected with one another in meaning should be closely connected in order also. By ignoring this principle many sentences are made, if not nonsensical, really ridiculous and ludicrous. For instance: "Ten dollars reward is offered for information of any person injuring this property by order of the owner." "This monument was erected to the memory of John Jones, who was shot by his affectionate brother."

In the construction of all sentences the grammatical rules must be inviolably observed. The laws of concord, that is, the agreement of certain words, must be obeyed.

1. The verb agrees with its subject in person and number. "I have," "Thou hast," (the pronoun thou is here used to illustrate the verb form, though it is almost obsolete), "He has," show the variation of the verb to agree with the subject. A singular subject calls for a singular verb, a plural subject demands a verb in the plural; as, "The boy writes," "The boys write."

The agreement of a verb and its subject is often destroyed by confusing (1) collective and common nouns; (2) foreign and English nouns; (3) compound and simple subjects; (4) real and apparent subjects.

(1) A collective noun is a number of individuals or things regarded as a whole; as, *class regiment.* When the individuals or things are prominently

CHAPTER III THE SENTENCE:
Different Kinds—Arrangement of Words—Paragraph

brought forward, use a plural verb; as the class were distinguished for ability. When the idea of the whole as a unit is under consideration employ a singular verb; as The regiment was in camp. (2) It is sometimes hard for the ordinary individual to distinguish the plural from the singular in foreign nouns, therefore, he should be careful in the selection of the verb. He should look up the word and be guided accordingly. "He was an *alumnus* of Harvard." "They were *alumni* of Harvard." (3) When a sentence with one verb has two or more subjects denoting different things, connected by *and*, the verb should be plural; as, "Snow and rain *are* disagreeable." When the subjects denote the same thing and are connected by *or* the verb should be singular; as, "The man or the woman is to blame." (4) When the same verb has more than one subject of different persons or numbers, it agrees with the most prominent in thought; as, "He, and not you, *is* wrong." "Whether he or I am to be blamed.

2. Never use the past participle for the past tense nor *vice versa*. This mistake is a very common one. At every turn we hear "He done it" for "He did it." "The jar was broke" instead of broken. "He would have went" for "He would have gone," etc.

3. The use of the verbs *shall* and *will* is a rock upon which even the best speakers come to wreck. They are interchanged recklessly. Their significance changes according as they are used with the first, second or third person. With the first person shall is used in direct statement to express a simple future action; as, "I shall go to the city tomorrow." With the second and third persons *shall* is used to express a determination; as, "You *shall* go to the city to-morrow," "He *shall* go to the city to-morrow."

ARRANGEMENT OF WORDS IN A SENTENCE

With the first person will is used in direct statement to express determination, as, "I will go to the city to-morrow." With the second and third persons *will* is used to express simple future action; as, "You *will* go to the city to-morrow," "He *will* go to the city to-morrow."

A very old rule regarding the uses of shall and will is thus expressed in rhyme:

In the first person simply *shall* foretells,

In *will* a threat or else a promise dwells.

Shall in the second and third does threat,

Will simply then foretells the future feat.

4. Take special care to distinguish between the nominative and objective case. The pronouns are the only words which retain the ancient distinctive case ending for the objective. Remember that the objective case follows transitive verbs and prepositions. Don't say "The boy who I sent to see you," but "The boy whom I sent to see you." Whom is here the object of the transitive verb sent. Don't say "She bowed to him and I" but "She bowed to him and me" since me is the objective case following the preposition to understood. "Between you and I" is a very common expression. It should be "Between you and me" since *between* is a preposition calling for the objective case.

5. Be careful in the use of the relative pronouns *who, which* and *that*. Who refers only to persons ; which only to things ; as, "The boy who was drowned," "The umbrella which I lost." The relative that may refer to both persons and things; as, "The man *that* I saw." "The hat *that* I bought."

CHAPTER III THE SENTENCE:
Different Kinds—Arrangement of Words—Paragraph

6. Don't use the superlative degree of the adjective for the comparative ; as "He is the richest of the two" for "He is the richer of the two." Other mistakes often made in this connection are (1) Using the double comparative and superlative ; as, "These apples are much more preferable." "The most universal motive to business is gain." (2) Comparing objects which belong to dissimilar classes ; as "There is no nicer *life* than a *teacher*." (3) Including objects in class to which they do not belong; as, "The fairest of her daughters, Eve." (4) Excluding an object from a class to which it does belong; as, "Caesar was braver than any ancient warrior."

7. Don't use an adjective for an adverb or an adverb for an adjective. Don't say, "He acted nice towards me" but "He acted nicely toward me," and instead of saying "She looked beautifully" say "She looked *beautiful*."

8. Place the adverb as near as possible to the word it modifies. Instead of saying, "He walked to the door quickly," say "He walked quickly to the door."

9. Not alone be careful to distinguish between the nominative and objective cases of the pronouns, but try to avoid ambiguity in their use.

The amusing effect of disregarding the reference of pronouns is well illustrated by Burton in the following story of Billy Williams, a comic actor who thus narrates his experience in riding a horse owned by Hamblin, the manager:

"So down I goes to the stable with Tom Flynn, and told the man to put the saddle on him." "On Tom Flynn?"

"No, on the horse. So after talking with Tom Flynn awhile I mounted him." "What! mounted Tom Flynn?"

"No, the horse; and then I shook hands with him and rode off." "Shook hands with the horse, Billy?"

"No, with Tom Flynn; and then I rode off up the Bowery, and who should I meet but Tom Hamblin; so I got off and told the boy to hold him by the head." "What! hold Hamblin by the head?"

"No, the horse; and then we went and had a drink together." "What! you and the horse?"

"No, *me* and Hamblin; and after that I mounted him again and went out of town." "What! mounted Hamblin again?"

"No, the horse; and when I got to Burnham, who should be there but Tom Flynn, —— he'd taken another horse and rode out ahead of me; so I told the hostler to tie him up."

"Tie Tom Flynn up?"

"No, the horse; and we had a drink there." "What! you and the horse?"

"No, me and Tom Flynn."

Finding his auditors by this time in a horse laugh, Billy wound up with: "Now, look here, —— every time I say horse, you say Hamblin, and every time I say Hamblin you say horse: I'll be hanged if I tell you any more about it."

SENTENCE CLASSIFICATION

There are two great classes of sentences according to the general principles upon which they are founded. These are termed the *loose* and the *periodic*.

CHAPTER III   THE SENTENCE:
Different Kinds—Arrangement of Words—Paragraph

In the *loose* sentence the main idea is put first, and then follow several facts in connection with it. Defoe is an author particularly noted for this kind of sentence. He starts out with a leading declaration to which he adds several attendant connections. For instance in the opening of the story of Robinson Crusoe we read: "I was born in the year 1632 in the city of York, of a good family, though not of that country, my father being a foreigner of Bremen, who settled first at Hull; he got a good estate by merchandise, and leaving off his trade lived afterward at York, from whence he had married my mother, whose relations were named Robinson, a very good family in the country and from I was called Robinson Kreutzer; but by the usual corruption of words in England, we are now called, nay, we call ourselves, and write our name Crusoe, and so my companions always called me."

In the periodic sentence the main idea comes last and is preceded by a series of relative introductions. This kind of sentence is often introduced by such words as *that, if, since, because*. The following is an example:

"That through his own folly and lack of circumspection he should have been reduced to such circumstances as to be forced to become a beggar on the streets, soliciting alms from those who had formerly been the recipients of his bounty, was a sore humiliation.

" On account of its name many are liable to think the loose sentence an undesirable form in good composition, but this should not be taken for granted. In many cases it is preferable to the periodic form.

As a general rule in speaking, as opposed to writing, the loose form is to be preferred, inasmuch as when the periodic is employed in discourse the listeners are apt to forget the introductory clauses before the final issue is reached.

Both kinds are freely used in composition, but in speaking, the loose, which makes the direct statement at the beginning, should predominate.

As to the length of sentences much depends on the nature of the composition. However the general rule may be laid down that short sentences are preferable to long ones. The tendency of the best writers of the present day is towards short, snappy, pithy sentences which rivet the attention of the reader. They adopt as their motto multum in parvo (much in little) and endeavor to pack a great deal in small space. Of course the extreme of brevity is to be avoided. Sentences can be too short, too jerky, too brittle to withstand the test of criticism. The long sentence has its place and a very important one. It is indispensable in argument and often is very necessary to description and also in introducing general principles which require elaboration. In employing the long sentence the inexperienced writer should not strain after the heavy, ponderous type. Johnson and Carlyle used such a type, but remember, an ordinary mortal cannot wield the sledge hammer of a giant. Johnson and Carlyle were intellectual giants and few can hope to stand on the same literary pedestal. The tyro in composition should never seek after the heavy style. The best of al authors in the English language for style is Addison. Macaulay says: "If you wish a style learned, but not pedantic, elegant but not ostentatious, simple yet refined, you must give your days and nights to the volumes of Joseph Addison." The simplicity, apart from the beauty of Addison's writings causes us to reiterate the literary command —— "Never use a big word when a little one

CHAPTER III   THE SENTENCE:
Different Kinds—Arrangement of Words—Paragraph

will convey the same or a similar meaning."

Macaulay himself is an elegant stylist to imitate. He is like a clear brook kissed by the noon-day sun in the shining bed of which you can see and count the beautiful white pebbles. Goldsmith is another writer whose simplicity of style charms.

The beginner should study these writers, make their works his vade mecum, they have stood the test of time and there has been no improvement upon them yet, nor is there likely to be, for their writing is as perfect as it is possible to be in the English language.

Apart from their grammatical construction there can be no fixed rules for the 213 formation of sentences. The best plan is to follow the best authors and these masters of language will guide you safely along the way.

THE PARAGRAPH

The paragraph may be defined as a group of sentences that are closely related in thought and which serve one common purpose. Not only do they preserve the sequence of the different parts into which a composition is divided, but they give a certain spice to the matter like raisins in a plum pudding. A solid page of printed matter is distasteful to the reader; it taxes the eye and tends towards the weariness of monotony, but when it is broken up into sections it loses much of its heaviness and the consequent lightness gives it charm, as it were, to capture the reader.

Paragraphs are like stepping-stones on the bed of a shall ow river, which enable the foot passenger to skip with ease from one to the other until he gets across; but if the stones are placed too far apart in attempting to span the distance one is liable to miss the mark and fall in the water and flounder about until he is again able to get a foothold. 'Tis the same with written language, the reader by means of paragraphs can easily pass from one portion of connected thought to another and keep up his interest in the subject until he gets to the end.

"The fire raged with fierce intensity, consuming the greater part of the large building in a short time." "The horse took fright and wildly dashed down the street scattering pedestrians in all directions." These two sentences have no connection and therefore should occupy separate and distinct places. But when we say —— "The f ire raged with fierce intensity consuming the greater part of the large building in a short time and the horse taking fright at the flames dashed wildly down the street scattering pedestrians in all directions," —— there is a natural sequence, viz., the horse taking fright as a consequence of the flames and hence the two expressions are combined in one paragraph.

As in the case of words in sentences, the most important places in a paragraph are the beginning and the end. Accordingly the first sentence and the last should by virtue of their structure and nervous force, compel the reader's attention. It is usually advisable to make the first sentence short; the last sentence may be long or short, but in either case should be forcible. The object of the first sentence is to state a point *clearly*; the last sentence should *enforce* it.

It is a custom of good writers to make the conclusion of the paragraph a restatement or counterpart or application of the opening.

CHAPTER III   THE SENTENCE:
Different Kinds—Arrangement of Words—Paragraph

In most cases a paragraph may be regarded as the elaboration of the principal sentence. The leading thought or idea can be taken as a nucleus and around it constructed the different parts of the paragraph. Anyone can make a context for every simple sentence by asking himself questions in reference to the sentence. Thus —— "The foreman gave the order" —— suggests at once several questions; "What was the order?" "to whom did he give it?" "why did he give it?" "what was the result?" etc. These questions when answered will depend upon the leading one and be an elaboration of it into a complete paragraph.

If we examine any good paragraph we shall find it made up of a number of items, each of which helps to illustrate, confirm or enforce the general thought or purpose of the paragraph. Also the transition from each item to the next is easy, natural and obvious; the items seem to come of themselves. If, on the other hand, we detect in a paragraph one or more items which have no direct bearing, or if we are unable to proceed readily from item to item, especially if we are obliged to rearrange the items before we can perceive their full significance, then we are justified in pronouncing the paragraph construction faulty.

No specific rules can be given as to the construction of paragraphs. The best advice is, —— Study closely the paragraph structure of the best writers, for it is only through imitation, conscious or unconscious of the best models, that one can master the art.

The best paragraphist in the English language for the essay is Macaulay, the best model to follow for the oratorical style is Edmund Burke and for description and narration probably the greatest master of paragraph is the American Goldsmith, Washington Irving.

A paragraph is indicated in print by what is known as the indentation of the line, that is, by commencing it a space from the left margin.

CHAPTER III THE SENTENCE:
Different Kinds—Arrangement of Words—Paragraph

CHAPTER IV
FIGURATIVE LANGUAGE:
Figures of Speech —— Definitions and Examples —— Use of Figures

In *Figurative Language* we employ words in such a way that they differ somewhat from their ordinary signification in commonplace speech and convey our meaning in a more vivid and impressive manner than when we use them in their every-day sense. Figures make speech more effective, they beautify and emphasize it and give to it a relish and piquancy as salt does to food; besides they add energy and force to expression so that it irresistibly compels attention and interest. There are four kinds of figures, viz.: 1. Figures of Orthography which change the spelling of a word; 2. Figures of Etymology which change the form of words; 3. Figures of Syntax which change the construction of sentences; 4. Figures of Rhetoric or the art of speaking and writing effectively which change the mode of thought.

We shall only consider the last mentioned here as they are the most important, really giving to language the construction and style which make it a fitting medium for the intercommunication of ideas.

Figures of Rhetoric have been variously classified, some authorities ex-

CHAPTER IV   FIGURATIVE LANGUAGE:
Figures of Speech—Definitions and Examples—Use of Figures

tending the list to a useless length. The fact is that any form of expression which conveys thought may be classified as a Figure.

The principal figures as well as the most important and those oftenest used are, *Simile, Metaphor, Personification, Allegory, Synecdoche, Metonymy, Exclamation, Hyperbole, Apostrophe, Vision, Antithesis, Climax, Epigram, Interrogation* and *Irony*.

The first four are founded on resemblance, the second six on *contiguity* and the third five, on *contrast*.

A *Simile* (from the Latin similis, like), is the likening of one thing to another, a statement of the resemblance of objects, acts, or relations; as "In his awful anger he was *like* the storm-driven waves dashing against the rock." A simile makes the principal object plainer and impresses it more forcibly on the mind. "His memory is like wax to receive impressions and like marble to retain them." This brings out the leading idea as to the man's memory in a very forceful manner. Contrast it with the simple statement —— "His memory is good." Sometimes Simile is prostituted to a low and degrading use; as "His face was like a danger signal in a fog storm." "Her hair was like a furze-bush in bloom." "He was to his lady love as a poodle to its mistress." Such burlesque is never permissible. Mere likeness, it should be remembered, does not constitute a simile. For instance there is no simile when one city is compared to another. In order that there may be a rhetorical simile, the objects compared must be of different classes. Avoid the old trite similes such as comparing a hero to a lion. Such were played out long ago. And don't hunt for farfetched similes. Don't say —— "Her head was glowing as the glorious god of day when he sets in a flambeau of splendor behind the purple-tinted hills of the West." It is much better to do without such a simile and simply say —— "She had fiery red hair.

A *Metaphor* (from the Greek metapherein, to carry over or transfer), is a word used to imply a resemblance but instead of likening one object to another as in the *simile* we directly substitute the action or operation of one for another. If, of a religious man we say, —— "He is as a great pillar upholding the church," the expression is a *simile*, but if we say —— "He is a great pillar upholding the church" it is a metaphor. The metaphor is a bolder and more lively figure than the simile. It is more like a picture and hence, the graphic use of metaphor is called "word painting." It enables us to give to the most abstract ideas form, color and life. Our language is full of metaphors, and we very often use them quite unconsciously. For instance, when we speak of the bed of a river, the shoulder of a hill, the foot of a mountain, the hands of a clock, the key of a situation, we are using metaphors.

Don't use mixed metaphors, that is, different metaphors in relation to the same subject: "Since it was launched our project has met with much opposition, but while its flight has not reached the heights ambitioned, we are yet sanguine we shall drive it to success." Here our project begins as a *ship*, then becomes a *bird* and finally winds up as a *horse*.

Personification (from the Latin persona, person, and facere, to make) is the treating of an inanimate object as if it were animate and is probably the most beautiful and effective of all the figures.

"The mountains *sing* together, the hills *rejoice* and *clap* their hands."

CHAPTER IV FIGURATIVE LANGUAGE:
Figures of Speech—Definitions and Examples—Use of Figures

"Earth *felt* the wound; and Nature from her seat, *Sighing*, through all her works, gave signs of woe."

Personification depends much on a vivid imagination and is adapted especially to poetical composition. It has two distinguishable forms: (1) when personality is ascribed to the inanimate as in the foregoing examples, and (2) when some quality of life is attributed to the inanimate; as, a *raging* storm; an *angry* sea; a *whistling* wind, etc.

An *Allegory* (from the Greek allos, other, and agoreuein, to speak), is a form of expression in which the words are symbolical of something. It is very closely allied to the metaphor, in fact is a continued metaphor.

Allegory, metaphor and simile have three points in common, —— they are all founded on resemblance. "Ireland is like a thorn in the side of England;" this is simile. "Ireland is a thorn in the side of England;" this is metaphor. "Once a great giant sprang up out of the sea and lived on an island all by himself. On looking around he discovered a little girl on another small island nearby. He thought the little girl could be useful to him in many ways so he determined to make her subservient to his will. He commanded her, but she refused to obey, then he resorted to very harsh measures with the little girl, but she still remained obstinate and obdurate. He continued to oppress her until finally she rebelled and became as a thorn in his side to prick him for his evil attitude towards her;" this is an allegory in which the giant plainly represents England and the little girl, Ireland; the implication is manifest though no mention is made of either country. Strange to say the most perfect allegory in the English language was written by an almost il iterate and ignorant man, and written too, in a dungeon cell. In the "Pilgrim's Progress," Bunyan, the itinerant tinker, has given us by far the best allegory ever penned. Another good one is "The Faerie Queen" by Edmund Spenser.

Synecdoche (from the Greek, sun with, and ekdexesthai, to receive), is a figure of speech which expresses either more or less than it literally denotes. By it we give to an object a name which literally expresses something more or something less than we intend. Thus: we speak of the world when we mean only a very limited number of the people who compose the world: as, "The world treated him badly." Here we use the whole for a part. But the most common form of this figure is that in which a part is used for the whole; as, "I have twenty head of cattle," "One of his *hands* was assassinated," meaning one of his men. "Twenty *sail* came into the harbor," meaning twenty ships. "This is a fine marble," meaning a marble statue.

Metonymy (from the Greek *meta*, change, and *onyma*, a name) is the designation of an object by one of its accompaniments, in other words, it is a figure by which the name of one object is put for another when the two are so related that the mention of one readily suggests the other. Thus when we say of a drunkard —— "He loves the bottle" we do not mean that he loves the glass receptacle, but the liquor that it is supposed to contain. Metonymy, generally speaking, has, three subdivisions: 1. when an effect is put for cause or *vice versa*: as *"Gray hairs* should be respected," meaning old age. "He writes a fine hand," that is, handwriting. 2. when the *sign* is put for the thing *signified*; as, "The pen is mightier than the sword," meaning literary power is superior to military force. 3. When the *container* is put for the thing contained; as "The

CHAPTER IV FIGURATIVE LANGUAGE:
Figures of Speech—Definitions and Examples—Use of Figures

House was called to order," meaning the members in the House.

Exclamation (from the Latin *ex*, out, and *clamare*, to cry), is a figure by which the speaker instead of stating a fact, simply utters an expression of surprise or emotion. For instance when he hears some harrowing tale of woe or misfortune instead of saying, —— "It is a sad story" he exclaims "What a sad story!"

Exclamation may be defined as the vocal expression of feeling, though it is also applied to written forms which are intended to express emotion. Thus in describing a towering mountain we can write "Heavens, what a piece of Nature's handiwork! how majestic! how sublime! how awe-inspiring in its colossal impressiveness!" This figure rather belongs to poetry and animated oratory than to the cold prose of every-day conversation and writing

Hyperbole (from the Greek *hyper*, beyond, and *ballein*, to throw), is an exaggerated form of statement and simply consists in representing things to be either greater or less, better or worse than they really are. Its object is to make the thought more effective by overstating it. Here are some examples: —— "He was so tall his head touched the clouds." "He was as thin as a poker." "He was so light that a breath might have blown him away." Most people are liable to overwork this figure. We are all more or less given to exaggeration and some of us do not stop there, but proceed onward to falsehood and downright lying.

There should be a limit to hyperbole, and in ordinary speech and writing it should be well qualified and kept within reasonable bounds.

An *Apostrophe* (from the Greek *apo*, from, and *strephein*, to turn), is a direct address to the absent as present, to the inanimate as living, or to the abstract as personal. Thus: "O, illustrious Washington! Father of our Country! Could you visit us now!"

"My Country tis of thee —— Sweet land of liberty, Of thee I sing."

"O! Grave, where is thy Victory, O! Death where is thy sting!" This figure is very closely allied to Personification.

Vision (from the Latin videre, to see) consists in treating the past, the future, or the remote as if present in time or place. It is appropriate to animated description, as it produces the effect of an ideal presence. "The old warrior looks down from the canvas and tells us to be men worthy of our sires."

This figure is much exemplified in the Bible. The book of Revelation is a vision of the future. The author who uses the figure most is Carlyle.

An *Antithesis* (from the Greek *anti*, against, and *tithenai*, to set) is founded on contrast; it consists in putting two unlike things in such a position that each will appear more striking by the contrast.

"Ring out the old, ring in the new, Ring out the false, ring in the true."

"Let us be friends in peace, but enemies in war."

Here is a fine antithesis in the description of a steam engine —— "It can engrave a seal and crush masses of obdurate metal before it; draw out, without breaking, a thread as fine as a gossamer; and lift up a ship of war like a bauble in the air; it can embroider muslin and forge anchors; cut steel into ribands, and impel loaded vessels against the fury of winds and waves."

Climax (from the Greek, *klimax*, a ladder), is an arrangement of thoughts

CHAPTER IV   FIGURATIVE LANGUAGE:
Figures of Speech—Definitions and Examples—Use of Figures

and ideas in a series, each part of which gets stronger and more impressive until the last one, which emphasizes the force of all the preceding ones. "He risked truth, he risked honor, he risked fame, he risked all that men hold dear, —— yea, he risked life itself, and for what? —— for a creature who was not worthy to tie his shoe-latchets when he was his better self."

Epigram (from the Greek *epi,* upon, and *graphein,* to write), originally meant an inscription on a monument, hence it came to signify any pointed expression. It now means a statement or any brief saying in prose or poetry in which there is an apparent contradiction; as, "Conspicuous for his absence." "Beauty when unadorned is most adorned." "He was too foolish to commit folly." "He was so wealthy that he could not spare the money."

Interrogation (from the Latin *interrogatio,* a question), is a figure of speech in which an assertion is made by asking a question; as, "Does God not show justice to all?" "Is he not doing right in his course?" "What can a man do under the circumstances?"

Irony (from the Greek *eironcia,* dissimulation) is a form of expression in which the opposite is substituted for what is intended, with the end in view, that the falsity or absurdity may be apparent; as, "Benedict Arnold was an honorable man." "A Judas Iscariot never betrays a friend." "You can always depend upon the word of a liar."

Irony is cousin germain to ridicule, derision, mockery, satire and sarcasm. Ridicule implies laughter mingled with contempt; derision is ridicule from a personal feeling of hostility; mockery is insulting derision; satire is witty mockery; sarcasm is bitter satire and irony is disguised satire.

There are many other figures of speech which give piquancy to language and play upon words in such a way as to convey a meaning different from their ordinary signification in common every-day speech and writing. The golden rule for all is to *keep them in harmony with the character and purpose of speech and composition.*

CHAPTER IV FIGURATIVE LANGUAGE:
Figures of Speech—Definitions and Examples—Use of Figures

CHAPTER V
PUNCTUATION:
Principal Points —— Illustrations —— Capital Letters

Lindley Murray and Goold Brown laid down cast-iron rules for punctuation, but most of them have been broken long since and thrown into the junk-heap of disuse. They were too rigid, too strict, went so much into minutiae, that they were more or less impractical to apply to ordinary composition. The manner of language, of style and of expression has considerably changed since then, the old abstruse complex sentence with its hidden meanings has been relegated to the shade, there is little of prolixity or long- drawn-out phrases, ambiguity of expression is avoided and the aim is toward terseness, brevity and clearness. Therefore, punctuation has been greatly simplified, to such an extent indeed, that it is now as much a matter of good taste and judgment as adherence to any fixed set of rules. Nevertheless there are laws governing it which cannot be abrogated, their principles must be rigidly and inviolably observed.

The chief end of punctuation is to mark the grammatical connection and the dependence of the parts of a composition, but not the actual pauses made

CHAPTER V   PUNCTUATION:
Principal Points—Illustrations—Capital Letters

in speaking. Very often the points used to denote the delivery of a passage differ from those used when the passage is written. Nevertheless, several of the punctuation marks serve to bring out the rhetorical force of expression.

The principal marks of punctuation are:

1. The Comma [,]

2. The Semicolon [;]

3. The Colon [:]

4. The Period [.]

5. The Interrogation [?]

6. The Exclamation [!]

7. The Dash [——]

8. The Parenthesis [()]

9. The Quotation [" "]

There are several other points or marks to indicate various relations, but properly speaking such come under the heading of Printer's Marks, some of which are treated elsewhere.

Of the above, the first four may be styled the grammatical points, and the remaining five, the rhetorical points.

The *Comma*: The office of the Comma is to show the slightest separation which calls for punctuation at all. It should be omitted whenever possible. It is used to mark the least divisions of a sentence.

1. A series of words or phrases has its parts separated by commas: ——
"Lying, trickery, chicanery, perjury, were natural to him." "The brave, daring,

faithful soldier died facing the foe." If the series is in pairs, commas separate the pairs: "Rich and poor, learned and unlearned, black and white, Christian and Jew, Mohammedan and Buddhist must pass through the same gate."

2. A comma is used before a short quotation: "It was Patrick Henry who said, 'Give me liberty or give me death.'"

3. When the subject of the sentence is a clause or a long phrase, a comma is used after such subject: "That he has no reverence for the God I love, proves his insincerity." "Simulated piety, with a black coat and a sanctimonious look, does not proclaim a Christian."

4. An expression used parenthetically should be inclosed by commas: "The old man, as a general rule, takes a morning walk."

5. Words in apposition are set off by commas: "McKinley, the President, was assassinated."

6. Relative clauses, if not restrictive, require commas: "The book, which is the simplest, is often the most profound."

7. In continued sentences each should be followed by a comma: "Electricity lights our dwellings and streets, pulls cars, trains, drives the engines of our mills and factories."

8. When a verb is omitted a comma takes its place: "Lincoln was a great statesman; Grant, a great soldier."

9. The subject of address is followed by a comma: "John, you are a good man."

10. In numeration, commas are used to express periods of three figures:

CHAPTER V PUNCTUATION:
Principal Points—Illustrations—Capital Letters

"Mountains 25,000 feet high; 1,000,000 dollars."

The *Semicolon* marks a slighter connection than the comma. It is generally confined to separating the parts of compound sentences. It is much used in contrasts:

1."Gladstone was great as a statesman; he was sublime as a man."

2.The Semicolon is used between the parts of all compound sentences in which the grammatical subject of the second part is different from that of the first: "The power of England relies upon the wisdom of her statesmen; the power of America upon the strength of her army and navy."

3.The Semicolon is used before words and abbreviations which introduce particulars or specifications following after, such as, namely, as, e.g., vid., i.e., etc.: "He had three defects; namely, carelessness, lack of concentration and obstinacy in his ideas." "An island is a portion of land entirely surrounded by water; as Cuba." "The names of cities should always commence with a capital letter; e.g., New York, Paris." "The boy was proficient in one branch; viz., Mathematics." "No man is perfect; i.e., free from all blemish."

The *Colon* except in conventional uses is practically obsolete.

1.It is generally put at the end of a sentence introducing a long quotation: "The cheers having subsided, Mr. Bryan spoke as follows:"

2.It is placed before an explanation or illustration of the subject under consideration: "This is the meaning of the term:"

3.A direct quotation formally introduced is generally preceded by a colon: "The great orator made this funny remark:"

THE PARAGRAPH

4. The colon is often used in the title of books when the secondary or subtitle is in apposition to the leading one and when the conjunction or is omitted: "Acoustics: the Science of Sound."

5. It is used after the salutation in the beginning of letters: "Sir: My dear Sir: Gentlemen: Dear Mr. Jones:" etc. In this connection a dash very often follows the colon.

6. It is sometimes used to introduce details of a group of things already referred to in the mass: "The boy's excuses for being late were: firstly, he did not know the time, secondly, he was sent on an errand, thirdly, he tripped on a rock and fell by the wayside."

The *Period* is the simplest punctuation mark. It is simply used to mark the end of a complete sentence that is neither interrogative nor exclamatory.

1. After every sentence conveying a complete meaning: "Birds fly." "Plants grow." "Man is mortal."

2. In abbreviations: after every abbreviated word: Rt. Rev. T. C. Alexander, D.D., L.L.D.

3. A period is used on the title pages of books after the name of the book, after the author's name, after the publisher's imprint: American Trails. By Theodore Roosevelt. New York. Scribner Company.

The *Mark of Interrogation* is used to ask or suggest a question.

1. Every question admitting of an answer, even when it is not expected, should be followed by the mark of interrogation: "Who has not heard of Napoleon?"

CHAPTER V PUNCTUATION:
Principal Points—Illustrations—Capital Letters

2.When several questions have a common dependence they should be followed by one mark of interrogation at the end of the series: "Where now are the playthings and friends of my boyhood; the laughing boys; the winsome girls; the fond neighbors whom I loved?"

3.The mark is often used parenthetically to suggest doubt: "In 1893 (?) Gladstone became converted to Home Rule for Ireland."

The *Exclamation* point should be sparingly used, particularly in prose. Its chief use is to denote emotion of some kind.

1.It is generally employed with interjections or clauses used as interjections: "Alas! I am forsaken." "What a lovely landscape!"

2.Expressions of strong emotion call for the exclamation: "Charge, Chester, charge! On, Stanley, on!"

3.When the emotion is very strong double exclamation points may be used: "Assist him!! I would rather assist Satan!!"

The *Dash* is generally confined to cases where there is a sudden break from the general run of the passage. Of all the punctuation marks it is the most misused.

1.It is employed to denote sudden change in the construction or sentiment: "The Heroes of the Civil War, —— how we cherish them." "He was a fine fellow —— in his own opinion."

2.When a word or expression is repeated for oratorical effect, a dash is used to introduce the repetition: "Shakespeare was the greatest of all poets —— Shakespeare, the intellectual ocean whose waves washed the continents of all thought."

3. The Dash is used to indicate a conclusion without expressing it: "He is an excellent man but —— "

4. It is used to indicate what is not expected or what is not the natural outcome of what has gone before: "He delved deep into the bowels of the earth and found instead of the hidden treasure —— a button."

5. It is used to denote the omission of letters or figures: "J —— n J —— s for John Jones; 1908-9 for 1908 and 1909; Matthew VII:5-8 for Matthew VII:5, 6, 7, and 8.

6. When an ellipsis of the words, namely, that is, to wit, etc., takes place, the dash is used to supply them: "He excelled in three branches —— arithmetic, algebra, and geometry."

7. A *dash* is used to denote the omission of part of a word when it is undesirable to write the full word: He is somewhat of a r —— l (rascal). This is especially the case in profane words.

8. Between a citation and the authority for it there is generally a dash: "All the world's a stage." —— *Shakespeare*

9. When questions and answers are put in the same paragraph they should be separated by dashes: "Are you a good boy? Yes, Sir. —— Do you love study? I do."

Marks of Parenthesis are used to separate expressions inserted in the body of a sentence, which are illustrative of the meaning, but have no essential connection with the sentence, and could be done without. They should be used as

CHAPTER V PUNCTUATION:
Principal Points—Illustrations—Capital Letters

little as possible for they show that something is being brought into a sentence that does not belong to it.

1. When the unity of a sentence is broken the words causing the break should be enclosed in parenthesis: "We cannot believe a liar (and Jones is one), even when he speaks the truth."

2. In reports of speeches marks of parenthesis are used to denote interpolations of approval or disapproval by the audience: "The masses must not submit to the tyranny of the classes (hear, hear), we must show the trust magnates (groans), that they cannot ride rough-shod over our dearest rights (cheers);" "If the gentleman from Ohio (Mr. Brown), will not be our spokesman, we must select another. (A voice, —— Get Robinson)."

When a parenthesis is inserted in the sentence where no comma is required, no point should be used before either parenthesis. When inserted at a place requiring a comma, if the parenthetical matter relates to the whole sentence, a comma should be used before each parenthesis; if it relates to a single word, or short clause, no stop should come before it, but a comma should be put after the closing parenthesis.

The *Quotation marks* are used to show that the words enclosed by them are borrowed.

1. A direct quotation should be enclosed within the quotation marks: Abraham Lincoln said, —— "I shall make this land too hot for the feet of slaves."

2. When a quotation is embraced within another, the contained quotation has only single marks: Franklin said, "Most men come to believe 'honesty is

the best policy.'"

3.When a quotation consists of several paragraphs the quotation marks should precede each paragraph.

4.Titles of books, pictures and newspapers when formally given are quoted.

5.Often the names of ships are quoted though there is no occasion for it.

The *Apostrophe* should come under the comma rather than under the quotation marks or double comma. The word is Greek and signifies a turning away from. The letter elided or turned away is generally an e. In poetry and familiar dialogue the apostrophe marks the elision of a syllable, as "I've for I have"; "Thou'rt for thou art"; "you'll for you will," etc. Sometimes it is necessary to abbreviate a word by leaving out several letters. In such case the apostrophe takes the place of the omitted letters as "cont'd for continued." The apostrophe is used to denote the elision of the century in dates, where the century is understood or to save the repetition of a series of figures, as "The Spirit of '76"; "I served in the army during the years 1895, '96, '97, '98 and '99." The principal use of the apostrophe is to denote the possessive case. All nouns in the singular number whether proper names or not, and all nouns in the plural ending with any other letter than s, form the possessive by the addition of the apostrophe and the letter s. The only exceptions to this rule are, that, by poetical license the additional s may be elided in poetry for sake of the metre, and in the scriptural phrases "For goodness' sake." "For conscience' sake," "For Jesus' sake," etc. Custom has done away with the s and these phrases are now idioms of the language. All plural nouns ending in s form the possessive by

CHAPTER V PUNCTUATION:
Principal Points—Illustrations—Capital Letters

the addition of the apostrophe only as boys', horses'. The possessive case of the personal pronouns never take the apostrophe, as ours, yours, hers, theirs.

CAPITAL LETTERS

Capital letters are used to give emphasis to or call attention to certain words to distinguish them from the context. In manuscripts they may be written small or large and are indicated by lines drawn underneath, two lines for SMALL CAPITALS and three lines for CAPITALS.

Some authors, notably Carlyle, make such use of Capitals that it degenerates into an abuse. They should only be used in their proper places as given in the table below.

1. The first word of every sentence, in fact the first word in writing of any kind should begin with a capital; as, "Time flies." "My dear friend."

2. Every direct quotation should begin with a capital; "Dewey said, —— 'Fire, when you're ready, Gridley!'"

3. Every direct question commences with a capital; "Let me ask you; 'How old are you?'"

4. Every line of poetry begins with a capital. "Breathes there a man with soul so dead?"

5. Every numbered clause calls for a capital: "The witness asserts: (1) That he saw the man attacked; (2) That he saw him fall; (3) That he saw his assailant flee."

6. The headings of essays and chapters should be wholly in capitals; as, CHAPTER VIII —— RULES FOR USE OF CAPITALS.

7. In the titles of books, nouns, pronouns, adjectives and adverbs should begin with a capital; as, "Johnson's Lives of the Poets."

8. In the Roman notation numbers are denoted by capitals; as, I II III V X L C D M —— 1, 2, 3, 5, 10, 50, 100, 500, 1,000.

9. Proper names begin with a capital; as, "Jones, Johnson, Caesar, Mark Antony, England, Pacific, Christmas."

Such words as river, sea, mountain, etc., when used generally are common, not proper nouns, and require no capital. But when such are used with an adjective or adjunct to specify a particular object they become proper names, and therefore require a capital; as, "Mississippi River, North Sea, Alleghany Mountains," etc. In like manner the cardinal points north, south, east and west, when they are used to distinguish regions of a country are capitals; as, "The North fought against the South."

When a proper name is compounded with another word, the part which is not a proper name begins with a capital if it precedes, but with a small letter if it follows, the hyphen; as "Post- homeric," "Sunday-school."

10. Words derived from proper names require a Capital; as, "American, Irish, Christian, Americanize, Christianize."

In this connection the names of political parties, religious sects and schools of thought begin with capitals; as, "Republican, Democrat, Whig, Catholic, Presbyterian, Rationalists, Free Thinkers."

CHAPTER V   PUNCTUATION:
Principal Points—Illustrations—Capital Letters

11. The titles of honorable, state and political offices begin with a capital; as, "President, Chairman, Governor, Alderman."

12. The abbreviations of learned titles and college degrees call for capitals; as, "LL.D., M.A., B.S.," etc. Also the seats of learning conferring such degrees as, "Harvard University, Manhattan College," etc.

13. When such relative words as father, mother, brother, sister, uncle, aunt, etc., precede a proper name, they are written and printed with capitals; as, Father Abraham, Mother Eddy, Brother John, Sister Jane, Uncle Jacob, Aunt Eliza. Father, when used to denote the early Christian writer, is begun with a capital; "Augustine was one of the learned Fathers of the Church."

14. The names applied to the Supreme Being begin with capitals: "God, Lord, Creator, Providence, Almighty, The Deity, Heavenly Father, Holy One." In this respect the names applied to the Saviour also require capitals: "Jesus Christ, Son of God, Man of Galilee, The Crucified, The Anointed One." Also the designations of Biblical characters as "Lily of Israel, Rose of Sharon, Comfortress of the Afflicted, Help of Christians, Prince of the Apostles, Star of the Sea," etc. Pronouns referring to God and Christ take capitals; as, "His work, The work of Him, etc."

15. Expressions used to designate the Bible or any particular division of it begin with a capital; as, "Holy Writ, The Sacred Book, Holy Book, God's Word, Old Testament, New Testament, Gospel of St. Matthew, Seven Penitential Psalms."

16. Expressions based upon the Bible or in reference to Biblical characters begin with a capital: "Water of Life, Hope of Men, Help of Christians,

Scourge of Nations."

17. The names applied to the Evil One require capitals: "Beelzebub, Prince of Darkness, Satan, King of Hell, Devil, Incarnate Fiend, Tempter of Men, Father of Lies, Hater of Good."

18. Words of very special importance, especially those which stand out as the names of leading events in history, have capitals; as, "The Revolution, The Civil War, The Middle Ages, The Age of Iron," etc.

19. Terms which refer to great events in the history of the race require capitals; "The Flood, Magna Charta, Declaration of Independence."

20. The names of the days of the week and the months of the year and the seasons are commenced with capitals: "Monday, March, Autumn."

21. The Pronoun I and the interjection *O* always require the use of capitals. In fact all the interjections when uttered as exclamations commence with capitals: "Alas! he is gone." "Ah! I pitied him."

22. All *noms-de-guerre*, assumed names, as well as names given for distinction, call for capitals, as, "The Wizard of the North," "Paul Pry," "The Northern Gael," "Sandy Sanderson," "Poor Robin," etc.

CHAPTER V PUNCTUATION:
Principal Points—Illustrations—Capital Letters

CHAPTER VI
LETTER WRITING:
Principles of Letter-Writing —— Forms —— Notes

Many people seem to regard letter-writing as a very simple and easily acquired branch, but on the contrary it is one of the most difficult forms of composition and requires much patience and labor to master its details. In fact there are very few perfect letter-writers in the language. It constitutes the direct form of speech and may be called conversation at a distance. Its forms are so varied by every conceivable topic written at all times by all kinds of persons in all kinds of moods and tempers and addressed to all kinds of persons of varying degrees in society and of different pursuits in life, that no fixed rules can be laid down to regulate its length, style or subject matter. Only general suggestions can be made in regard to scope and purpose, and the forms of indicting set forth which custom and precedent have sanctioned.

The principles of letter-writing should be understood by everybody who has any knowledge of written language, for almost everybody at some time or other has necessity to address some friend or acquaintance at a distance, whereas comparatively few are called upon to direct their efforts towards any

CHAPTER VI   LETTER WRITING:
Principles of Letter-Writing—Forms—Notes

other kind of composition.

The principles of letter-writing should be understood by everybody who has any knowledge of written language, for almost everybody at some time or other has necessity to address some friend or acquaintance at a distance, whereas comparatively few are called upon to direct their efforts towards any other kind of composition.

Now, that education is abroad in the land, there is seldom any occasion for any person to call upon the service of another to compose and write a personal letter. Very few now-a-days are so grossly illiterate as not to be able to read and write. No matter how crude his effort may be it is better for anyone to write his own letters than trust to another. Even if he should commence, —— "deer fren, i lift up my pen to let ye no that i hove been sik for the past 3 weeks, hopping this will f indye the same," his spelling and construction can be excused in view of the fact that his intention is good, and that he is doing his best to serve his own turn without depending upon others.

Now, that education is abroad in the land, there is seldom any occasion for any person to call upon the service of another to compose and write a personal letter. Very few now-a-days are so grossly illiterate as not to be able to read and 231 write. No matter how crude his effort may be it is better for anyone to write his own letters than trust to another. Even if he should commence, —— "deer fren, i lift up my pen to let ye no that i hove been sik for the past 3 weeks, hopping this will f indye the same," his spelling and construction can be excused in view of the fact that his intention is good, and that he is doing his best to serve his own turn without depending upon others.

CAPITAL LETTERS

In letter writing the first and most important requisites are to be natural and simple; there should be no straining after effect, but simply a spontaneous out pouring of thoughts and ideas as they naturally occur to the writer. We are repelled by a person who is stiff and labored in his conversation and in the same way the stiff and labored letter bores the reader. Whereas if it is light and in a conversational vein it immediately engages his attention.

The letter which is written with the greatest facility is the best kind of letter because it naturally expresses what is in the writer, he has not to search for his words, they flow in a perfect unison with the ideas he desires to communicate. When you write to your friend John Browne to tell him how you spent Sunday you have not to look around for the words, or study set phrases with a view to please or impress Browne, you just tell him the same as if he were present before you, how you spent the day, where you were, with whom you associated and the chief incidents that occurred during the time. Thus, you write natural and it is such writing that is adapted to epistolary correspondence.

There are different kinds of letters, each calling for a different style of address and composition, nevertheless the natural key should be maintained in all, that is to say, the writer should never attempt to convey an impression that he is other than what he is. It would be silly as well as vain for the common street laborer of a limited education to try to put on literary airs and emulate a college professor; he may have as good a brain, but it is not as well developed by education, and he lacks the polish which society confers. When writing a letter the street laborer should bear in mind that only the letter of a street-laborer is expected from him, no matter to whom his communication may be

CHAPTER VI LETTER WRITING:
Principles of Letter-Writing—Forms—Notes

addressed and that neither the grammar nor the diction of a Chesterfield or Gladstone is looked for in his language. Still the writer should keep in mind the person to whom he is writing. If it is to an Archbishop or some other great dignitary of Church or state it certainly should be couched in terms different from those he uses to John Browne, his intimate friend. Just as he cannot say "Dear John" to an Archbishop, no more can he address him in the familiar words he uses to his friend of everyday acquaintance and companionship. Yet there is no great learning required to write to an Archbishop, no more than to an ordinary individual. All the laborer needs to know is the form of address and how to properly utilize his limited vocabulary to the best advantage. Here is the form for such a letter:

17 Second Avenue, New York City.

January 1st, 1910.

Most Rev. P. A. Jordan, Archbishop of New York.

Most Rev. and dear Sir: ——

    While sweeping the crossing at Fifth Avenue and 50th street on last Wednesday morning, I found the enclosed Fifty Dollar Bill, which I am sending to you in the hope that it may be restored to the rightful owner.

    I beg you will acknowledge receipt and should the owner be found I trust you will notify me, so that I may claim some reward for my honesty.

I am, Most Rev. and dear Sir,

Very respectfully yours,

Thomas Jones.

CAPITAL LETTERS

Observe the brevity of the letter. Jones makes no suggestions to the Archbishop how to find the owner, for he knows the course the Archbishop will adopt, of having the finding of the bill announced from the Church pulpits. Could Jones himself find the owner there would be no occasion to apply to the Archbishop.

This letter, it is true, is different from that which he would send to Browne. Nevertheless it is simple without being familiar, is just a plain statement, and is as much to the point for its purpose as if it were garnished with rhetoric and "words of learned length and thundering sound."

Letters may be divided into those of friendship, acquaintanceship, those of business relations, those written in an official capacity by public servants, those designed to teach, and those which give accounts of the daily happenings on the stage of life, in other words, news letters.

Letters of friendship are the most common and their style and form depend upon the degree of relationship and intimacy existing between the writers and those addressed. Between relatives and intimate friends the beginning and end may be in the most familiar form of conversation, either affectionate or playful. They should, however, never overstep the boundaries of decency and propriety, for it is well to remember that, unlike conversation, which only is heard by the ears for which it is intended, written words may come under eyes other than those for whom they were designed. Therefore, it is well never to write anything which the world may not read without detriment to your character or your instincts. You can be joyful, playful, jocose, give vent to your feelings, but never stop to low language and, above all, to language savoring

CHAPTER VI LETTER WRITING:
Principles of Letter-Writing—Forms—Notes

in the slightest degree of moral impropriety.

Business letters are of the utmost importance on account of the interests involved. The business character of a man or of a firm is often judged by the correspondence. On many occasions letters instead of developing trade and business interests and gaining clientele, predispose people unfavorably towards those whom they are designed to benefit. Ambiguous, slip-shod language is a detriment to success.

Business letters should be clear, concise, to the point and, above all, honest, giving no wrong impressions or holding out any inducements that cannot be fulfilled. In business letters, just as in business conduct, honesty is always the best policy.

Official letters are mostly always formal. They should possess clearness, brevity and dignity of tone to impress the receivers with the proper respect for the national laws and institutions.

Letters designed to teach or didactic letters are in a class all by themselves. They are simply literature in the form of letters and are employed by some of the best writers to give their thoughts and ideas a greater emphasis. The most conspicuous example of this kind of composition is the book on Etiquette by Lord Chesterfield, which took the form of a series of letters to his son.

News letters are accounts of world happenings and descriptions of ceremonies and events sent into the newspapers. Some of the best authors of our time are newspaper men who write in an easy flowing style which is most readable, full of humor and fancy and which carries one along with breathless interest from beginning to end.

The principal parts of a letter are 1. the *heading* or introduction; 2. the *body* or substance of the letter; 3. the *subscription* or closing expression and signature; 4. the *address* or direction on the envelope. For the body of a letter no forms or rules can be laid down as it altogether depends on the nature of the letter and the relationship between the writer and the person addressed.

There are certain rules which govern the other three features and which custom has sanctioned. Every one should be acquainted with these rules.

THE HEADING

The *Heading* has three parts, viz., the name of the place, the date of writing and the designation of the person or persons addressed; thus:

73 New Street, Newark, N. J.,
February 1st, 1910.

Messrs Ginn and Co., New York

Gentlemen:

The name of the place should never be omitted; in cities, street and number should always be given, and except when the city is large and very conspicuous, so that there can be no question as to its identity with another of the same or similar name, the abbreviation of the State should be appended, as in the above,

Newark, N. J. There is another Newark in the State of Ohio. Owing to

CHAPTER VI LETTER WRITING:
Principles of Letter-Writing—Forms—Notes

failure to comply with this rule many letters go astray. The date should be on every letter, especially business letters. The date should never be put at the bottom in a business letter, but in friendly letters this may be done. The designation of the person or persons addressed differs according to the relations of the correspondents. Letters of friendship may begin in many ways according to the degrees of friendship or intimacy. Thus:

My dear Wife:

My dear Husband:

My dear Friend:

My darling Mother:

My dearest Love:

Dear Aunt:

Dear Uncle:

Dear George:

etc.

To mark a lesser degree of intimacy such formal designations as the following may be employed:

Dear Sir:

My dear Sir:

Dear Mr. Smith:

Dear Madam:

etc.

For clergymen who have the degree of Doctor of Divinity, the designation is as follows:

Rev. Alban Johnson, D. D.

My dear Sir: or Rev. and dear Sir: or more familiarly Dear Dr. Johnson:

Bishops of the Roman and Anglican Communions are addressed as *Right Reverend*.

The Rt. Rev., the Bishop of Long Island. Or

The Rt. Rev. Frederick Burgess, Bishop of Long Island. Rt. Rev. and dear Sir:

Archbishops of the Roman Church are addressed as Most Reverend and Cardinals as Eminence. Thus:

The Most Rev. Archbishop Katzer.

Most Rev. and dear Sir:

His Eminence, James Cardinal Gibbons, Archbishop of Baltimore.

May it please your Eminence:

The title of the Governor of a State or territory and of the President of the United States is Excellency. However, Honorable is more commonly applied to Governors: ——

His Excellency, William Howard Taft,

President of the United States.

Sir: —— His Excellency, Charles Evans Hughes,

Governor of the State of New York.

CHAPTER VI LETTER WRITING:
Principles of Letter-Writing—Forms—Notes

Sir: —— Honorable Franklin Fort,

    Governor of New Jersey.

Sir: ——

The general salutation for Officers of the Army and Navy is *Sir*. The rank and station should be indicated in full at the head of the letter, thus:

General Joseph Thompson,

    Commanding the Seventh Infantry.

Sir:

Rear Admiral Robert Atkinson,

    Commanding the Atlantic Squadron.

Sir:

The title of officers of the Civil Government is Honorable and they are addressed as *Sir*.

Hon. Nelson Duncan,

    Senator from Ohio.

Sir:

Hon. Norman Wingfield,

    Secretary of the Treasury.

Sir:

Hon. Rupert Gresham,

    Mayor of New York.

Sir:

Presidents and Professors of Colleges and Universities are generally addressed as *Sir* or *Dear Sir.*

Professor Ferguson Jenks,

    President of ...... University.

Sir: or Dear Sir:

Presidents of Societies and Associations are treated as business men and addressed as *Sir* or *Dear Sir.*

Mr. Joseph Banks,

    President of the Night Owls.

Dear Sir: or Sir:

Doctors of Medicine are addressed as *Sir: My dear Sir: Dear Sir:* and more familiarly My dear Dr: or Dear Dr: as

Ryerson Pitkin, M. D.

Sir:

Dear Sir:

My dear Dr:

Ordinary people with no degrees or titles are addressed as Mr. and Mrs. and are designed Dear Sir: Dear Madam: and an unmarried woman of any age is addressed on the envelope as Miss So-and-so, but always designed in the letter as

Dear Madam:

The plural of Mr. as in addressing a firm is Messrs, and the correspond-

CHAPTER VI LETTER WRITING:
Principles of Letter-Writing—Forms—Notes

ing salutation is *Dear Sirs:* or *Gentlemen:*

In England *Esq.* is used for *Mr.* as a mark of slight superiority and in this country it is sometimes used, but it is practically obsolete. Custom is against it and American sentiment as well. If it is used it should be only applied to lawyers and justices of the peace

SUBSCRIPTION

The *Subscription* or ending of a letter consists of the term of respect or affection and the signature. The term depends upon the relation of the person addressed. Letters of friendship can close with such expressions as:

Yours lovingly,

Yours affectionately,

Devotedly yours,

Ever yours, etc.

as between husbands and wives or between lovers. Such gushing terminations as Your Own Darling, Your own Dovey and other pet and silly endings should be avoided, as they denote shallowness. Love can be strongly expressed without dipping into the nonsensical and the farcical.

Formal expressions of Subscription are:

Yours Sincerely,

Yours truly,

Respectfully yours,

and the like, and these may be varied to denote the exact bearing or attitude the writer wishes to assume to the person addressed: as,

Very sincerely yours,

Very respectfully yours,

With deep respect yours,

Yours very truly, etc.

Such elaborate endings as

"In the meantime with the highest respect, I am yours to command,"

"I have the honor to be, Sir, Your humble Servant,"

"With great expression of esteem, I am Sincerely yours,"

"Believe me, my dear Sir, Ever faithfully yours,"

are condemned as savoring too much of affectation.

It is better to finish formal letters without any such qualifying remarks. If you are writing to Mr. Ryan to tell him that you have a house for sale, after describing the house and stating the terms simply sign yourself.

Your obedient Servant

Yours very truly,

Yours with respect,

James Wilson.

Don't say you have the honor to be anything or ask him to believe anything, all you want to tell him is that you have a house for sale and that you are sincere, or hold him in respect as a prospective customer.

CHAPTER VI LETTER WRITING:
Principles of Letter-Writing—Forms—Notes

Don't abbreviate the signature as: *Y'rs Resp'fly* and always make your sex obvious. Write plainly.

Yours truly,

John Field

and not *J. Field*, so that the person to whom you send it may not take you for *Jane Field*.

It is always best to write the first name in full. Married women should prefix *Mrs.* to their names, as

Very sincerely yours,

Mrs. Theodore Watson.

If you are sending a letter acknowledging a compliment or some kindness done you may say, *Yours gratefully*, or *Yours very gratefully*, in proportion to the act of kindness received.

It is not customary to sign letters of degrees or titles after your name, except you are a lord, earl or duke and only known by the title, but as we have no such titles in America it is unnecessary to bring this matter into consideration. Don't sign yourself,

Sincerely yours,

Obadiah Jackson, M.A. or L.L. D.

If you're an M. A. or an L.L. D. people generally know it without your sounding your own trumpet. Many people, and especially clergymen, are fond of flaunting after their names degrees they have received honoris causa, that is, degrees as a mark of honor, without examination. Such degrees should be kept in the background. Many a deadhead has these degrees which he could never have earned by brain work.

Married women whose husbands are alive may sign the husband's name with the prefix *Mrs*: thus,

Yours sincerely,

Mrs. William Southey.

but when the husband is dead the signature should be ——

Yours sincerely,

Mrs. Sarah Southey.

So when we receive a letter from a woman we are enabled to tell whether she has a husband living or is a widow. A woman separated from her husband but not a divorcee should not sign his name.

ADDRESS

The *address* of a letter consists of the name, the title and the residence.

Mr. Hugh Black,

112 Southgate Street,

Altoona,

Pa.

Intimate friends have often familiar names for each other, such as pet names, nicknames, etc., which they use in the freedom of conversation, but such names should never, under any circumstances, appear on the envelope.

CHAPTER VI LETTER WRITING:
Principles of Letter-Writing—Forms—Notes

The subscription on the envelope should be always written with propriety and correctness and as if penned by an entire stranger. The only difficulty in the envelope inscription is the title. Every man is entitled to Mr. and every lady to Mrs. and every unmarried lady to Miss. Even a boy is entitled to Master. When more than one is addressed the title is Messrs. Mesdames is sometimes written of women. If the person addressed has a title it is courteous to use it, but titles never must be duplicated.

Thus, we can write

Robert Stitt, M. D., but never

Dr. Robert Stitt, M. D, or

Mr. Robert Stitt, M. D.

In writing to a medical doctor it is well to indicate his profession by the letters M. D. so as to differentiate him from a D. D. It is better to write Robert Stitt, M. D., than Dr. Robert Stitt.

In the case of clergymen the prefix Rev. is retained even when they have other titles; as

Rev. Tracy Tooke, LL. D.

When a person has more titles than one it is customary to only give him the leading one. Thus instead of writing Rev. Samuel MacComb, B. A., M. A., B. Sc., Ph. D., LL. D., D. D. the form employed is Rev. Samuel MacComb, LL. D. LL. D. is appended in preference to D. D. because in most cases the "Rev." implies a "D. D." while comparatively few with the prefix "Rev." are entitled to "LL. D."

In the case of Honorables such as Governors, Judges, Members of Congress, and others of the Civil Government the prefix "Hon." does away with Mr. and Esq. Thus we write Hon. Josiah Snifkins, not Hon. Mr. Josiah Snifkins or Hon. Josiah Snifkins, Esq. Though this prefix Hon. is also often applied to Governors they should be addressed as Excellency. For instance:

His Excellency,

Charles E. Hughes,

Albany,

N. Y.

In writing to the President the superscription on the envelope should be

To the President,

Executive Mansion,

Washington, D. C.

Professional men such as doctors and lawyers as well as those having legitimately earned College Degrees may be addressed on the envelopes by their titles, as

Jonathan Janeway, M. D.

Hubert Houston, B. L.

Matthew Marks, M. A., etc.

The residence of the person addressed should be plainly written out in full. The street and numbers should be given and the city or town written very legibly. If the abbreviation of the State is liable to be confounded or confused with that of another then the full name of the State should be written. In writ-

CHAPTER VI LETTER WRITING:
Principles of Letter-Writing—Forms—Notes

ing the residence on the envelope, instead of putting it all in one line as is done at the head of a letter, each item of the residence forms a separate line. Thus,

Liberty,

Sullivan County,

New York

215 Minna

St., San Francisco,

California.

There should be left a space for the postage stamp in the upper right hand corner. The name and title should occupy a line that is about central between the top of the envelope and the bottom. The name should neither be too much to right or left but located in the centre, the beginning and end at equal distances from either end.

In writing to large business concerns which are well known or to public or city officials it is sometimes customary to leave out number and street. Thus,

Messrs. Seigel, Cooper Co.,

New York City,

Hon. William J. Gaynor,

New York City.

NOTES

Notes may be regarded as letters in miniature confined chiefly to invitations, acceptances, regrets and introductions, and modern etiquette tends towards informality in their composition. Card etiquette, in fact, has taken the place of ceremonious correspondence and informal notes are now the rule. Invitations to dinner and receptions are now mostly written on cards. "Regrets" are sent back on visiting cards with just the one word "Regrets" plainly written thereon. Often on cards and notes of invitation we find the letters R. S. V. P. at the bottom. These letters stand for the French repondez s'il vous plait, which means "Reply, if you please," but there is no necessity to put this on an invitation card as every well bred person knows that a reply is expected. In writing notes to young ladies of the same family it should be noted that the eldest daughter of the house is entitled to the designation Miss without any Christian name, only the surname appended. Thus if there are three daughters in the Thompson family Martha, the eldest, Susan and Jemina, Martha is addressed as Miss Thompson and the other two as Miss Susan Thompson and Miss Jemina Thompson respectively.

Don't write the word *addressed* on the envelope of a note.

Don't *seal* a note delivered by a friend.

Don't write a note on a postal card. Here are a few common forms: ——

FORMAL INVITATIONS

Mr. and Mrs. Henry Wagstaff request the honor of Mr. McAdoo's presence

CHAPTER VI LETTER WRITING:
Principles of Letter-Writing—Forms—Notes

on Friday evening, June 15th, at 8 o'clock to meet the Governor of the Fort.

19 Woodbine Terrace
June 8th, 1910.

This is an invitation to a formal reception calling for evening dress. Here is Mr. McAdoo's reply in the third person: ——

Mr. McAdoo presents his compliments to Mr. and Mrs. Henry Wagstaff and accepts with great pleasure their invitation to meet the Governor of the Fort on the evening of June fifteenth.

215 Beacon Street,
June 10th, 1910.

Here is how Mr. McAdoo might decline the invitation: ——

Mr. McAdoo regrets that owing to a prior engagement he must forego the honor of paying his respects to Mr. and Mrs. Wagstaff and the Governor of the Fort on the evening of June fifteenth.

215 Beacon St.,
June 10th, 1910.

Here is a note addressed, say to Mr. Jeremiah Reynolds.

Mr. and Mrs. Oldham at home on Wednesday evening October ninth from seven to eleven.

21 Ashland Avenue,
October 5th.

NOTES

Mr. Reynolds makes reply: —— Mr. Reynolds accepts with high appreciation the honor of Mr. and Mrs. Oldham's invitation for Wednesday evening October ninth.

Windsor Hotel

October 7th.

or

Mr. Reynolds regrets that his duties render it impossible for him to accept Mr. and Mrs. Oldham's kind invitation for the evening of October ninth.

Windsor Hotel,

October 7th.

Sometimes less informal invitations are sent on small specially designed note paper in which the first person takes the place of the third. Thus

360 Pine St.,

Dec. 11th, 1910.

Dear Mr. Saintsbury: Mr. Johnson and I should be much pleased to have you dine with us and a few friends next Thursday, the fifteenth, at half past seven.

Yours sincerely,

Emma Burnside.

Mr. Saintsbury's reply:

57 Carlyle Strand

Dec. 13th, 1910.

CHAPTER VI LETTER WRITING:
Principles of Letter-Writing—Forms—Notes

Dear Mrs. Burnside: Yours sincerely, Emma Burnside. 57 Carlyle Strand Dec. 13th, 1910. Let me accept very appreciatively your invitation to dine with Mr. Burnside and you on next Thursday, the fifteenth, at half past seven.

Yours sincerely,
Henry Saintsbury.

NOTES OF INTRODUCTION

Notes of introduction should be very circumspect as the writers are in reality vouching for those whom they introduce. Here is a specimen of such a note.

603 Lexington Ave.,

New York City,

June 15th, 1910.

Rev. Cyrus C. Wiley, D. D.,

Newark, N. J.

My dear Dr. Wiley:

I take the liberty of presenting to you my friend, Stacy Redfern, M.D., a young practitioner, who is anxious to locate in Newark. I have known him many years and can vouch for his integrity and professional standing. Any courtesy and kindness which you may show him will be very much appreciated by me.

Very sincerely yours,
Franklin Jewett.

CHAPTER VII
ERRORS:
Mistakes —— Slips of Authors —— Examples and Corrections —— Errors

In the following examples the word or words in parentheses are uncalled for and should be omitted:

1. Fill the glass (full).

2. They appeared to be talking (together) on private affairs.

3. I saw the boy and his sister (both) in the garden.

4. He went into the country last week and returned (back) yesterday.

5. The subject (matter) of his discourse was excellent.

6 You need not wonder that the (subject) matter of his discourse was excellent; it was taken from the Bible.

7. They followed (after) him, but could not overtake him.

8. The same sentiments may be found throughout (the whole of) the book.

9. I was very ill every day (of my life) last week.

10. That was the (sum and) substance of his discourse.

CHAPTER VII ERRORS:
Mistakes—Slips of Authors—Examples and Corrections—Errors

11. He took wine and water and mixed them (both) together.

12. He descended (down) the steps to the cellar.

13. He fell (down) from the top of the house.

14. I hope you will return (again) soon.

15. The things he took away he restored (again).

16. The thief who stole my watch was compelled to restore it (back again).

17. It is equally (the same) to me whether I have it today or tomorrow.

18. She said, (says she) the report is false; and he replied, (says he) if it be not correct I have been misinformed.

19. I took my place in the cars (for) to go to New York.

20. They need not (to) call upon him.

21. Nothing (else) but that would satisfy him.

22. Whenever I ride in the cars I (always) find it prejudicial to my health.

23. He was the first (of all) at the meeting.

24. He was the tallest of (all) the brothers.

25. You are the tallest of (all) your family.

26. Whenever I pass the house he is (always) at the door.

27. The rain has penetrated (through) the roof.

28. Besides my uncle and aunt there was (also) my grandfather at the church.

29. It should (ever) be your constant endeavor to please your family.

30. If it is true as you have heard (then) his situation is indeed pitiful.

31. Either this (here) man or that (there) woman has (got) it.

32. Where is the fire (at)?

33. Did you sleep in church? Not that I know (of).

34. I never before (in my life) met (with) such a stupid man.

35. (For) why did he postpone it?

36. Because (why) he could not attend.

37. What age is he? (Why) I don't know.

38. He called on me (for) to ask my opinion.

39. I don't know where I am (at).

40. I looked in (at) the window.

41. I passed (by) the house.

42. He (always) came every Sunday.

43. Moreover, (also) we wish to say he was in error.

44. It is not long (ago) since he was here.

45. Two men went into the wood (in order) to cut (down) trees. Further examples of redundancy might be multiplied. It is very common in newspaper writing where not alone single words but entire phrases are sometimes brought in, which are unnecessary to the sense or explanation of what is written.

Further examples of redundancy might be multiplied. It is very common in newspaper writing where not alone single words but entire phrases are sometimes brought in, which are unnecessary to the sense or explanation of what is written.

CHAPTER VII ERRORS:
Mistakes—Slips of Authors—Examples and Corrections—Errors

GRAMMATICAL ERRORS OF STANDARD AUTHORS

Even the best speakers and writers are sometimes caught napping. Many of our standard authors to whom we have been accustomed to look up as infallible have sinned more or less against the fundamental principles of grammar by breaking the rules regarding one or more of the nine parts of speech. In fact some of them have recklessly trespassed against all nine, and still they sit on their pedestals of fame for the admiration of the crowd. Macaulay mistreated the article. He wrote, —— "That a historian should not record trifles is perfectly true." He should have used *an*.

Dickens also used the article incorrectly. He refers to "Robinson Crusoe" as "*an* universally popular book," instead of *a* universally popular book.

The relation between nouns and pronouns has always been a stumbling block to speakers and writers. Hall am in his Literature of Europe writes, "No one as yet had exhibited the structure of the human kidneys, Vesalius having only examined them in dogs." This means that Vesalius examined human kidneys in dogs. The sentence should have been, "No one had as yet exhibited the kidneys in human beings, Vesalius having examined such organs in dogs only."

Sir Arthur Helps in writing of Dickens, states —— "I knew a brother author of his who received such criticisms from him (Dickens) very lately and profited by it." Instead of it the word should be them to agree with criticisms.

Here are a few other pronominal errors from leading authors:

GRAMMATICAL ERRORS OF STANDARD AUTHORS

"Sir Thomas Moore in general so writes it, although not many others so late as *him*." Should be *he*. —— Trench's *English Past and Present*.

"What should we gain by it but that we should speedily become as poor as *them*." Should be *they*. —— Alison's *Essay on Macaulay*.

"If the king gives us leave you or I may as lawfully preach, as *them* that do." Should be *they* or those, the latter having persons understood. —— Hobbes's *History of Civil Wars*.

"The drift of all his sermons was, to prepare the Jews for the reception of a prophet, mightier than *him*, and whose shoes he was not worthy to bear." Should be than *he*. —— Atterbury's *Sermons*.

"Phalaris, who was so much older than *her*." Should be *she*. —— Bentley's *Dissertation on Phalaris*.

"King Charles, and more than *him*, the duke and the Popish faction were at liberty to form new schemes." Should be than *he*. —— Bolingbroke's *Dissertations on Parties*.

"We contributed a third more than the Dutch, who were obliged to the same proportion more than *us*." Should be than *we*. —— Swift's *Conduct of the Allies*.

In all the above examples the objective cases of the pronouns have been used while the construction calls for nominative cases.

"Let *thou* and I the battle try" —— *Anon*.

Here *let* is the governing verb and requires an objective case after it; therefore instead of *thou* and *I*, the words should be *you* (*sing*.) and *me*

CHAPTER VII ERRORS:
Mistakes—Slips of Authors—Examples and Corrections—Errors

"Forever in this humble cell, Let thee and I, my fair one, dwell " —— *Prior*.

Here *thee* and *I* should be the objectives *you* and *me*.

The use of the relative pronoun trips the greatest number of authors.

Even in the Bible we find the relative wrongly translated:

Whom do men say that I am? —— *St. Matthew*.

Whom think ye that I am? —— *Acts of the Apostles*.

Who should be written in both cases because the word is not in the objective governed by say or think, but in the nominative dependent on the verb *am*.

"*Who* should I meet at the coffee house the other night, but my old friend?" —— *Steele*.

"It is another pattern of this answer's fair dealing, to give us hints that the author is dead, and yet lay the suspicion upon somebody, I know not *who*, in the country." —— Swift's *Tale of a Tub*.

"My son is going to be married to I don't know *who*." —— Goldsmith's *Good natured Man*.

The nominative *who* in the above examples should be the objective *whom*.

The plural nominative ye of the pronoun thou is very often used for the objective *you*, as in the following: "His wrath which will one day destroy *ye* both." —— *Milton*.

"The more shame for *ye*; holy men I thought *ye*." —— *Shakespeare*.

"I feel the gales that from *ye* blow." —— *Gray*.

"Tyrants dread *ye*, lest your just decree transfer the power and set the people free." —— *Prior*.

Many of the great writers have played havoc with the adjective in the indiscriminate use of the degrees of comparison.

"Of two forms of the same word, use the fittest." —— *Morell*.

The author here in *trying* to give good advice sets a bad example. He should have used the comparative degree, "Fitter."

Adjectives which have a comparative or superlative signification do not admit the addition of the words *more, most*, or the terminations, *er, est*, hence the following examples break this rule:

"Money is the most universal incitement of human misery." —— Gibbon's *Decline and Fall*.

"The *chiefest* of which was known by the name of Archon among the Grecians." —— Dryden's *Life of Plutarch*.

"The *chiefest* and largest are removed to certain magazines they call libraries." —— Swift's *Battle of the Books*.

The two *chiefest* properties of air, its gravity and elastic force, have been discovered by mechanical experiments. —— *Arbuthno*

"From these various causes, which in greater or lesser degree, affected every individual in the colony, the indignation of the people became general." —— *Robertson's History of America*.

"The extremest parts of the earth were meditating a submission." ——

CHAPTER VII ERRORS:
Mistakes—Slips of Authors—Examples and Corrections—Errors

Atterbury's *Sermons*.

"The last are indeed more preferable because they are founded on some new knowledge or improvement in the mind of man." —— Addison, *Spectator*.

"This was in reality the easiest manner of the two." —— Shaftesbury's Advice to an Author.

"In every well formed mind this second desire seems to be the strongest of the two." —— Smith's *Theory of Moral Sentiments*.

In these examples the superlative is wrongly used for the comparative. When only two objects are compared the comparative form must be used.

Of impossibility there are no degrees of comparison, yet we find the following:

"As it was impossible they should know the words, thoughts and secret actions of all men, so it was more impossible they should pass judgment on them according to these things." —— Whitby's *Necessity of the Christian Religion*.

A great number of authors employ adjectives for adverbs. Thus we find:

"I shall endeavor to live hereafter suitable to a man in my station." —— Addison. "I can never think so very mean of him." —— Bentley's *Dissertation on Phalaris*.

"His expectations run high and the fund to supply them is extreme scanty, —— Lancaster's *Essay on Delicacy*.

The commonest error in the use of the verb is the disregard of the concord between the verb and its subject. This occurs most frequently when the subject and the verb are widely separated, especially if some other noun of a different number immediately precedes the verb. False concords occur very often after *either, or, neither, nor,* and *much, more, many, everyone, each.*

Here are a few authors' slips: ——

"The terms in which the sale of a patent *were* communicated to the public." —— Junius's Letters.

"The richness of her arms and apparel *were* conspicuous." —— Gibbon's *Decline and Fall.*

"Everyone of this grotesque family *were* the creatures of national genius." —— D'Israeli.

"He knows not what spleen, languor or listlessness *are.*" —— Blair's Sermons.

"*Each* of these words *imply,* some pursuit or object relinquished." —— Ibid.

"Magnus, with four thousand of his supposed accomplices *were* put to death." —— Gibbon.

"No nation gives greater encouragements to learning than we do; yet at the same time *none* are so injudicious in the application." —— Goldsmith.

"*There's two* or *three* of us have seen strange sights." —— Shakespeare.

The past participle should not be used for the past tense, yet the learned Byron overlooked this fact. He thus writes in the *Lament of Tasso*: ——

"And with my years my soul *begun* to pant with feelings of strange tumult

CHAPTER VII ERRORS:
Mistakes—Slips of Authors—Examples and Corrections—Errors

and soft pain."

Here is another example from Savage's *Wanderer* in which there is double sinning:

"From liberty each nobler science *sprung*, A Bacon brightened and a Spenser sung."

Other breaches in regard to the participles occur in the following: ——

"Every book ought to be read with the same spirit and in the same manner as it is *writ*" —— Fielding's *Tom Jones*.

"The Court of Augustus had not *wore* off the manners of the republic" —— Hume's *Essays*.

"Moses tells us that the fountains of the earth were *broke* open or clove asunder." —— Burnet.

"A free constitution when it has been *shook* by the iniquity of former administrations." —— *Bolingbroke*.

"In this respect the seeds of future divisions were *sowed* abundantly." —— *Ibid*.

In the following example the present participle is used for the infinitive mood:

"It is easy *distinguishing* the rude fragment of a rock from the splinter of a statue." —— Gilfillan's *Literary Portraits*

Distinguishing here should be replaced by to *distinguish*.

The rules regarding *shall* and *will* are violated in the following:

"If we look within the rough and awkward outside, we *will* be richly rewarded by its perusal." —— Gilfillan's *Literary Portraits*.

"If I *should* declare them and speak of them, they should be more than I am able to express." —— Prayer *Book Revision of Psalms XI*.

"If I *would* declare them and speak of them, they are more than can be numbered." —— *Ibid*.

"Without having attended to this, we *will* be at a loss, in understanding several passages in the classics." —— Blair's *Lectures*.

"We know to what cause our past reverses have been owing and we *will* have ourselves to blame, if they are again incurred." —— Alison's *History of Europe*.

Adverbial mistakes often occur in the best writers. The adverb rather is a word very frequently misplaced. Archbishop Trench in his "English Past and Present" writes, "It rather modified the structure of our sentences than the elements of our vocabulary." This should have been written, —— "It modified the structure of our sentences rather than the elements of our vocabulary."

"So far as his mode of teaching goes he is *rather* a disciple of Socrates than of St. Paul or Wesley.

Thus writes Leslie Stephens of Dr. Johnson. He should have written, —— " So far as his mode of teaching goes he is a disciple of Socrates *rather* than of St. Paul or Wesley."

The preposition is a part of speech which is often wrongly used by some of the best writers. Certain nouns, adjectives and verbs require particular prepositions after them, for instance, the word different always takes the preposi-

CHAPTER VII ERRORS:
Mistakes—Slips of Authors—Examples and Corrections—Errors

tion from after it; *prevail* takes *upon*; *averse* takes *to*; *accord* takes *with*, and so on.

In the following examples the prepositions in parentheses are the ones that should have been used:

"He found the greatest difficulty *of* (in) writing." —— Hume's *History of England*.

"If policy can prevail *upon* (over) force." —— *Addison*.

"He made the discovery and communicated *to* (with) his friends." —— Swift's *Tale of a Tub*.

"Every office of command should be intrusted to persons *on* (in) whom the parliament shall confide." —— *Macaulay*.

Several of the most celebrated writers infringe the canons of style by placing prepositions at the end of sentences. For instance Carlyle, in referring to the Study of Burns, writes: —— "Our own contributions to it, we are aware, can be but scanty and feeble; but we offer them with good will, and trust they may meet with acceptance from those they are intended *for*."

—— "for whom they are intended," he should have written.

"Most writers have some one vein which they peculiarly and obviously excel in." —— *William Minto*.

This sentence should read, —— Most writers have some one vein in which they peculiarly and obviously excel.

Many authors use redundant words which repeat the same thought and idea. This is called tautology. "Notwithstanding which (however) poor Polly embraced them all around." —— *Dickens*.

"I judged that they would (mutualy) find each other." —— *Crockett*.

"as having created a (joint) partnership between the two powers in the Morocco question." —— *The Times*.

"The only sensible position (there seems to be) is to frankly acknowledge our ignorance of what lies beyond." —— *Daily Telegraph*.

"Lord Rosebery has not budged from his position —— splendid, no doubt, —— of (lonely) isolation." —— *The Times*.

"Miss Fox was (often) in the habit of assuring Mrs. Chick." —— *Dickens*.

"The deck (it) was their field of fame." —— *Campbell*.

"He had come up one morning, as was now (frequently) his wont," —— *Trollope*.

The counselors of the Sultan (continue to) remain sceptical —— *The Times*.

Seriously, (and apart from jesting), this is no light matter. —— *Bagehot*.

To go back to your own country with (the consciousness that you go back with) the sense of duty well done. —— *Lord Halsbury*.

The Peresviet lost both her fighting-tops and (in appearance) looked the most damaged of all the ships —— *The Times*.

Counsel admitted that, that was a fair suggestion to make, but he submitted that it was borne out by the (surrounding) circumstances. —— *Ibid*.

Another unnecessary use of words and phrases is that which is termed cir-

CHAPTER VII ERRORS:
Mistakes—Slips of Authors—Examples and Corrections—Errors

cumlocution, a going around the bush when there is no occasion for it, —— save to fill space.

It may be likened to a person walking the distance of two sides of a triangle to reach the objective point. For instance in the quotation: "Pope professed to have learned his poetry from Dryden, whom, whenever an opportunity was presented, he praised through the whole period of his existence with unvaried liberality; and perhaps his character may receive some illustration, of a comparison he instituted between him and the man whose pupil he was" much of the verbiage may be eliminated and the sentence thus condensed:

"Pope professed himself the pupil of Dryden, whom he lost no opportunity of praising; and his character may be illustrated by a comparison with his master."

"His life was brought to a close in 1910 at an age not far from the one fixed by the sacred writer as the term of human existence."

This in brevity can be put, "His life was brought to a close at the age of seventy;" or, better yet, "He died at the age of seventy."

"The day was intensely cold, so cold in fact that the thermometer crept down to the zero mark," can be expressed: "The day was so cold the thermometer registered zero."

Many authors resort to circumlocution for the purpose of "padding," that is, filling space, or when they strike a snag in writing upon subjects of which they know little or nothing. The young writer should steer clear of it and learn to express his thoughts and ideas as briefly as possible commensurate with lucidity of expression.

GRAMMATICAL ERRORS OF STANDARD AUTHORS

Volumes of errors in fact, in grammar, diction and general style, could be selected from the works of the great writers, a fact which eloquently testifies that no one is infallible and that the very best is liable to err at times. However, most of the erring in the case of these writers arises from carelessness or hurry, not from a lack of knowledge.

As a general rule it is in writing that the scholar is liable to slip; in oral speech he seldom makes a blunder. In fact, there are many people who are perfect masters of speech, —— who never make a blunder in conversation, yet who are ignorant of the very principles of grammar and would not know how to write a sentence correctly on paper. Such persons have been accustomed from infancy to hear the language spoken correctly and so the use of the proper words and forms becomes a second nature to them. A child can learn what is right as easy as what is wrong and whatever impressions are made on the mind when it is plastic will remain there. Even a parrot can be taught the proper use of language. Repeat to a parrot. —— "Two and two *make* four" and it never will say "two and two *makes* four."

In writing, however, it is different. Without a knowledge of the fundamentals of grammar we may be able to speak correctly from association with good speakers, but without such a knowledge we cannot hope to write the language correctly. To write even a common letter we must know the principles of construction, the relationship of one word to another. Therefore, it is necessary for everybody to understand at least the essentials of the grammar of his own language.

CHAPTER VII   ERRORS:
Mistakes—Slips of Authors—Examples and Corrections—Errors

CHAPTER VIII
PITFALLS TO AVOID:
Common Stumbling Blocks —— Peculiar Constructions —— Misused Forms

ATTRACTION

Very often the verb is separated from its real nominative or subject by several intervening words and in such cases one is liable to make the verb agree with the subject nearest to it. Here are a few examples showing that the leading writers now and then take a tumble into this pitfall:

1. "The partition which the two ministers made of the powers of government were singularly happy." —— Macaulay. (Should be *was* to agree with its subject, *partition*.)

2. "One at least of the qualities which fit it for training ordinary men unfit it for training an extraordinary man." —— Bagehot. (Should be *unfits* to agree with subject *one*.)

CHAPTER VIII PITFALLS TO AVOID:
Common Stumbling Blocks—Peculiar Constructions—Misused Forms

3. "The Tibetans have engaged to exclude from their country those dangerous influences whose appearance were the chief cause of our action." —— The Times. (Should be *was* to agree with *appearance*.)

4. "An immense amount of confusion and indifference prevail in these days." —— Telegraph. (Should be *prevails* to agree with *amount*.)

ELLIPSIS

Errors in ellipsis occur chiefly with prepositions.

His objection and condoning of the boy's course, seemed to say the least, paradoxical. (The preposition *to* should come after *objection*.)

Many men of brilliant parts are crushed by force of circumstances and their genius forever lost to the world.

(Some maintain that the missing verb after *genius* is *are*, but such is ungrammatical. In such cases the right verb should be always expressed: as —— their genius *is* forever lost to the world.

THE SPLIT INFINITIVE

Even the best speakers and writers are in the habit of placing a modifying word or words between the *to* and the remaining part of the infinitive. It is possible that such will come to be looked upon in time as the proper form but at present the splitting of the infinitive is decidedly wrong. "He was scarcely

THE SPLIT INFINITIVE

able *to* even *talk*" "She commenced *to* rapidly *walk* around the room." "*To have* really *loved* is better than not to *have* at all *loved*." In these constructions it is much better not to split the infinitive. In every-day speech the best speakers sin against this observance.

In New York City there is a certain magistrate, a member of "the 400," who prides himself on his diction in language. He tells this story: A prisoner, a faded, battered specimen of mankind, on whose haggard face, deeply lined with the marks of dissipation, there still lingered faint reminders of better days long past, stood dejected before the judge. "Where are you from?" asked the magistrate. "From Boston," answered the accused. "Indeed," said the judge, "indeed, yours is a sad case, and yet you don't seem to thoroughly realize how low you have sunk." The man stared as if struck. "Your honor does me an injustice," he said bitterly. "The disgrace of arrest for drunkenness, the mortification of being thrust into a noisome dungeon, the publicity and humiliation of trial in a crowded and dingy courtroom I can bear, but to be sentenced by a Police Magistrate who splits his infinitives —— that is indeed the last blow."

ONE

The indefinite adjective pronoun one when put in place of a personal substantive is liable to raise confusion. When a sentence or expression is begun with the impersonal *one* the word must be used throughout in all references to the subject. Thus, "One must mind one's own business if one wishes to succeed" may seem prolix and awkward, nevertheless it is the proper form. You must not say —— "One must mind his business if he wishes to succeed," for

CHAPTER VIII PITFALLS TO AVOID:
Common Stumbling Blocks—Peculiar Constructions—Misused Forms

the subject is impersonal and therefore cannot exclusively take the masculine pronoun. With *anyone* it is different. You may say —— "If anyone sins he should acknowledge it; let him not try to hide it by another sin."

ONLY

This is a word that is a pitfall to the most of us whether learned or unlearned. Probably it is the most indiscriminately used word in the language. From the different positions it is made to occupy in a sentence it can relatively change the meaning. For instance in the sentence —— "I *only* struck him that time," the meaning to be inferred is, that the only thing I did to him was to *strike* him, not kick or otherwise abuse him. But if the *only* is shifted, so as to make the sentence read "I struck him *only* that time" the meaning conveyed is, that only on that occasion and at another time did I strike him. If another shift is made to-"I struck *only* him that time," the meaning is again altered so that it signifies he was the only person I struck.

In speaking we can by emphasis impress our meaning on our hearers, but in writing we have nothing to depend upon but the position of the word in the sentence. The best rule in regard to *only* is to place it *immediately before* the word or phrase it modifies or limits.

ALONE

alone is another word which creates ambiguity and alters meaning. If we substitute it for only in the preceding example the meaning of the sentence will depend upon the arrangement. Thus "I *alone* struck him at that time" signifies that I and no other struck him. When the sentence reads "I struck him *alone* at that time" it must be interpreted that he was the only person that received a blow. Again if it is made to read "I struck him at that time alone" the sense conveyed is that that was the only occasion on which I struck him. The rule which governs the correct use of *only* is also applicable to *alone*.

OTHER AND ANOTHER

These are words which often give to expressions a meaning far from that intended. Thus, "I have nothing to do with that other rascal across the street," certainly means that I am a rascal myself. "I sent the despatch to my friend, but another villain intercepted it," clearly signifies that my friend is a villain.

A good plan is to omit these words when they can be readily done without, as in the above examples, but when it is necessary to use them make your meaning clear. You can do this by making each sentence or phrase in which they occur independent of contextual aid.

AND WITH THE RELATIVE

Never use *and* with the *relative* in this manner: "That is the dog I meant *and which* I know is of pure breed." This is an error quite common. The use of *and* is permissible when there is a parallel relative in the preceding sentence or clause. Thus: "There is the dog which I meant and, which I know is of pure breed" is quite correct.

CHAPTER VIII   PITFALLS TO AVOID:
Common Stumbling Blocks—Peculiar Constructions—Misused Forms

LOOSE PARTICIPLES

A participle or participial phrase is naturally referred to the nearest nominative. If only one nominative is expressed it claims all the participles that are not by the construction of the sentence otherwise fixed. "John, working in the field all day and getting thirsty, drank from the running stream." Here the participles *working* and *getting* clearly refer to John. But in the sentence, —— "Swept along by the mob I could not save him," the participle as it were is lying around loose and may be taken to refer to either the person speaking or to the person spoken about. It may mean that I was swept along by the mob or the individual whom I tried to save was swept along.

"Going into the store the roof fell" can be taken that it was the roof which was going into the store when it fell. Of course the meaning intended is that some person or persons were going into the store just as the roof fell.

In all sentence construction with participles there should be such clearness as to preclude all possibility of ambiguity. The participle should be so placed that there can be no doubt as to the noun to which it refers. Often it is advisable to supply such words as will make the meaning obvious.

BROKEN CONSTRUCTION

Sometimes the beginning of a sentence presents quite a different grammatical construction from its end. This arises from the fact probably, that the beginning is lost sight of before the end is reached. This occurs frequently in long sentences. Thus: "Honesty, integrity and square-dealing will bring anybody much better through life than the absence of either." Here the construction is broken at than. The use of either, only used in referring to one of two, shows that the fact is forgotten that three qualities and not two are under consideration. Any one of the three meanings might be intended in the sentence, viz., absence of any one quality, absence of any two of the qualities or absence of the whole three qualities. Either denotes one or the other of two and should never be applied to any one of more than two. When we fall into the error of constructing such sentences as above, we should take them apart and reconstruct them in a different grammatical form. Thus, —— "Honesty, integrity and square-dealing will bring a man much better through life than a lack of these qualities which are almost essential to success."

DOUBLE NEGATIVE

It must be remembered that two negatives in the English language destroy each other and are equivalent to an affirmative. Thus "I *don't* know *nothing* about it" is intended to convey, that I am ignorant of the matter under consideration, but it defeats its own purpose, inasmuch as the use of nothing implies that I know something about it. The sentence should read —— "I don't know anything about it."

Often we hear such expressions as "He was *not* asked to give *no* opinion," expressing the very opposite of what is intended. This sentence implies that he was asked to give his opinion. The double negative, therefore, should be care-

CHAPTER VIII   PITFALLS TO AVOID:
Common Stumbling Blocks—Peculiar Constructions—Misused Forms

fully avoided, for it is insidious and is liable to slip in and the writer remain unconscious of its presence until the eye of the critic detects it.

FIRST PERSONAL PRONOUN

The use of the first personal pronoun should be avoided as much as possible in composition. Don't introduce it by way of apology and never use such expressions as "In my opinion," "As far as I can see," "It appears to me," "I believe," etc. In what you write, the whole composition is expressive of your views, since you are the author, therefore, there is no necessity for you to accentuate or emphasize yourself at certain portions of it.

Moreover, the big I's savor of egotism! Steer clear of them as far as you can. The only place where the first person is permissible is in passages where you are stating a view that is not generally held and which is likely to meet with opposition.

SEQUENCE OF TENSES

When two verbs depend on each other their tenses must have a definite relation to each other. "I shall have much pleasure in accepting your kind invitation" is wrong, unless you really mean that just now you decline though by-and-by you intend to accept; or unless you mean that you do accept now, though you have no pleasure in doing so, but look forward to be more pleased by-and-by. In fact the sequence of the compound tenses puzzle experienced

SEQUENCE OF TENSES

writers. The best plan is to go back in thought to the time in question and use the tense you would then naturally use. Now in the sentence "I should have liked to have gone to see the circus" the way to find out the proper sequence is to ask yourself the question —— what is it I "should have liked" to do? and the plain answer is "to go to see the circus." I cannot answer —— "To have gone to see the circus" for that would imply that at a certain moment I would have liked to be in the position of having gone to the circus. But I do not mean this; I mean that at the moment at which I am speaking I wish I had gone to see the circus. The verbal phrase I *should have liked* carries me back to the time when there was a chance of seeing the circus and once back at the time, the going to the circus is a thing of the present. This whole explanation resolves itself into the simple question, —— what should I have liked *at that time*, and the answer is "to go to see the circus," therefore this is the proper sequence, and the expression should be "I should have liked to go to see the circus."

If we wish to speak of something relating to a time prior to that indicated in the past tense we must use the perfect tense of the infinitive; as, "He appeared to have seen better days." We should say "I expected to *meet him*," not "I expected to *have met him*." "We intended to *visit* you," not "to *have visited* you." "I hoped they would *arrive*," not "I hoped they *would have arrived*." "I thought I should *catch* the bird," not "I thought I should *have caught* the bird." "I had intended *to go* to the meeting," not "I *had intended* to have gone to the meeting."

CHAPTER VIII PITFALLS TO AVOID:
Common Stumbling Blocks—Peculiar Constructions—Misused Forms

BETWEEN — AMONG

These prepositions are often carelessly interchanged. *Between* has reference to two objects only, among to more than two. "The money was equally divided between them" is right when there are only two, but if there are more than two it should be "the money was equally divided among them."

LESS — FEWER

Less refers is quantity, *fewer* to number. "No man has *less* virtues" should be "No man has fewer *virtues*." "The farmer had some oats and a *fewer* quantity of wheat" should be "the farmer had some oats and a *less* quantity of wheat."

FURTHER — FARTHER

Further is commonly used to denote quantity, *farther* to denote distance. "I have walked *farther* than you," "I need no *further* supply" are correct.

EACH OTHER — ONE ANOTHER

Each other refers to two, *one another* to more than two. "Jones and Smith quarreled; they struck each other" is correct. "Jones, Smith and Brown quarreled; they struck one another" is also correct. Don't say, "The two boys teach one another" nor "The three girls love each other."

EACH, EVERY, EITHER, NEITHER

These words are continually misapplied. *Each* can be applied to two or any higher number of objects to signify *every one* of the number *independently*. *Every* requires *more* than *two* to be spoken of and denotes all the *persons* or *things* taken *separately*. *Either* denotes *one or the other of two,* and should not be used to include both. *Neither* is the negative of either, denoting not the other, and not the one, and relating to *two persons or things* considered separately.

The following examples illustrate the correct usage of these words:

Each man of the crew received a reward.

Every man in the regiment displayed bravery.

We can walk on *either* side of the street.

Neither of the two is to blame.

NEITHER —— NOR

When two singular subjects are connected by *neither, nor* use a singular verb; as, *Neither* John *nor* James was there," not were there.

NONE

Custom has sanctioned the use of this word both with a singular and plural; as —— "None is so blind as he who will not see" and "None *are* so blind as they who will not see." However, as it is a contraction of no one it is better to use the singular verb.

CHAPTER VIII PITFALLS TO AVOID:
Common Stumbling Blocks—Peculiar Constructions—Misused Forms

RISE — RAISE

These verbs are very often confounded. *Rise* is to move or pass upward in any manner; as to "rise from bed;" to increase in value, to improve in position or rank, as "stocks rise;" "politicians rise;" "they have risen to honor."

Raise is to lift up, to exalt, to enhance, as "I raise the table;" "He raised his servant;" "The baker raised the price of bread."

LAY — LIE

The transitive verb *lay*, and *lay*, the past tense of the neuter verb *lie*, are often confounded, though quite different in meaning. The neuter verb to *lie*, meaning to lie down or rest, cannot take the objective after it except with a preposition. We can say "He *lies* on the ground," but we cannot say "He *lies* the ground," since the verb is neuter and intransitive and, as such, cannot have a direct object. With *lay* it is different. *Lay* is a transitive verb, therefore it takes a direct object after it; as "I *lay* a wager," "I laid the carpet," etc.

Of a carpet or any inanimate subject we should say, "It lies on the floor," "A knife lies on the table," not lays. But of a person we say —— "He lays the knife on the table," not "He *lies* —— ." Lay being the past tense of the neuter to lie (down) we should say, "He lay on the bed," and *lain* being its past participle we must also say "He has *lain* on the bed."

We can say "I lay myself down." "He laid himself down" and such expressions.

It is imperative to remember in using these verbs that to *lay* means to do something, and to lie means *to be in a state of rest*.

SAYS I — I SAID

"*Says I*" is a vulgarism; don't use it. "I said" is correct form.

IN — INTO

Be careful to distinguish the meaning of these two little prepositions and don't interchange them. Don't say "He went *in* the room" nor "My brother is *into* the navy." *In* denotes the place where a person or thing, whether at rest or in motion, is present; and *into* denotes *entrance*. "He went *into* the room;" "My brother is *in* the navy" are correct.

EAT — ATE

Don't confound the two. Eat is present, ate is past. "I *eat* the bread" means that I am continuing the eating; "I *ate* the bread" means that the act of eating is past. *Eaten* is the perfect participle, but often eat is used instead, and as it has the same pronunciation (et) of ate, care should be taken to distinguish the past tense, I ate from the perfect I have eaten (eat).

SEQUENCE OF PERSON

Remember that the *first* person takes precedence of the *second* and the *second* takes precedence of the *third*. When Cardinal Wolsey said *Ego et Rex* (I and the King), he showed he was a good grammarian, but a bad courtier.

CHAPTER VIII PITFALLS TO AVOID:
Common Stumbling Blocks—Peculiar Constructions—Misused Forms

AM COME — HAVE COME

"I am come" points to my being here, while "I have come" intimates that I have just arrived. When the subject is not a person, the verb to be should be used in preference to the verb to have; as, "The box is come" instead of "The box has come."

PAST TENSE — PAST PARTICIPLE

The interchange of these two parts of the irregular or so-called strong verbs is, perhaps, the breach often committed by careless speakers and writers. To avoid mistakes it is requisite to know the principal parts of these verbs, and this knowledge is very easy of acquirement, as there are not more than a couple of hundred of such verbs, and of this number but a small part is in daily use. Here are some of the most common blunders: "I seen" for "I saw;" "I done it" for "I did it;" "I drunk" for "I drank;" "I begun" for "I began;" "I rung" for "I rang;" "I run" for "I ran;" "I sung" for "I sang;" "I have chose" for "I have chosen;" "I have drove" for "I have driven;" "I have wore" for "I have worn;" "I have trod" for "I have trodden;" "I have shook" for "I have shaken;" "I have fell" for "I have fallen;" "I have drank" for "I have drunk;" "I have began" for "I have begun;" "I have rang" for "I have rung;" "I have rose" for "I have risen;"

"I have spoke" for "I have spoken;" "I have broke" for "I have broken." "It has froze" for "It has frozen." "It has blowed" for "It has blown." "It has flowed" (of a bird) for "It has flown."

N.B. —— The past tense and past participle of To Hang is hanged or hung. When you are talking about a man meeting death on the gallows, say "He was hanged"; when you are talking about the carcass of an animal say, "It was hung," as "The beef was hung dry." Also say your coat "was hung on a hook."

PREPOSITION SAND THE OBJECTIVE CASE

Don't forget that prepositions always take the objective case. Don't say "Between you and *I*"; say "Between you and *me*"

Two prepositions should not govern one objective unless there is an immediate connection between them. "He was refused admission to and forcibly ejected from the school" should be "He was refused admission to the school and forcibly ejected from it."

SUMMON —— SUMMONS

Don't say "I shall summons him," but "I shall summon him." *Summon* is a verb, *summons*, a noun. It is correct to say "I shall get a *summons* for him," not a *summon*.

UNDENIABLE —— UNEXCEPTIONABLE

"My brother has an undeniable character" is wrong if I wish to convey the idea that he has a good character. The expression should be in that case "My

CHAPTER VIII PITFALLS TO AVOID:
Common Stumbling Blocks—Peculiar Constructions—Misused Forms

brother has an unexceptionable character." An *undeniable* character is a character that cannot be denied, whether bad or good. An unexceptionable character is one to which no one can take exception.

THE PRONOUNS

Very many mistakes occur in the use of the pronouns. "Let you and I go" should be "Let you and *me* go." "Let them and we go" should be "Let them and us go." The verb let is transitive and therefore takes the objective case.

"Give me *them* flowers" should be "Give me *those* flowers"; "I mean *them* three" should be "I mean those three." Them is the objective case of the personal pronoun and cannot be used adjectively like the demonstrative adjective pronoun. "I am as strong as *him*" should be "I am as strong as *he*"; "I am younger than *her*" should be "I am younger than *she*;" "He can write better than *me*" should be "He can write better than I," for in these examples the objective cases *him, her* and *me* are used wrongfully for the nominatives. After each of the misapplied pronouns a verb is understood of which each pronoun is the subject. Thus, "I am as strong as he (is)." "I am younger than she (is)." "He can write better than I (can)."

Don't say "*It is me;*" say "*It is I*" The verb *To Be* of which is is a part takes the same case after it that it has before it. This holds good in all situations as well as with pronouns.

The verb *To Be* also requires the pronouns joined to it to be in the same case as a pronoun asking a question; The nominative *I* requires the nominative *who* and the objectives *me, him, her, its, you, them,* require the objective *whom.*

THAT FOR SO

"The hurt it was that painful it made him cry," say "so painful."

THESE — THOSE

Don't say, *These kind; those sort.* Kind and sort are each singular and require the singular pronouns this and that. In connection with these demonstrative adjective pronouns remember that *this* and *these* refer to what is near at hand, *that* and *those* to what is more distant; as, *this* book (near me), *that* book (over there), *these* boys (near), *those* boys (at a distance).

THIS MUCH — THUS MUCH

"*This much* is certain" should be "*Thus much* or *so* much is certain."

FLEE — FLY

These are two separate verbs and must not be interchanged. The principal parts of *flee* are *flee, fled, fled*; those of *fly* are *fly, flew, flown*. *To flee* is generally used in the meaning of getting out of danger. *To fly* means to soar as a bird. To say of a man "He has *flown* from the place" is wrong; it should be "He has *fled* from the place." We can say with propriety that "A bird has *flown* from the place."

CHAPTER VIII PITFALLS TO AVOID:
Common Stumbling Blocks—Peculiar Constructions—Misused Forms

THROUGH — THROUGHOUT

Don't say "He is well known through the land," but "He is well known throughout the land."

VOCATION AND AVOCATION

Don't mistake these two words so nearly alike. Vocation is the employment, business or profession one follows for a living; avocation is some pursuit or occupation which diverts the person from such employment, business or profession. Thus "His vocation was the law, his avocation, farming."

WAS — WERE

In the subjunctive mood the plural form were should be used with a singular subject; as, "If I *were*," not *was*. Remember the plural form of the personal pronoun you always takes were, though it may denote but one. Thus, "*You were,*" never "*you was.*" "*If I was him*" is a very common expression. Note the two mistakes in it, —— that of the verb implying a condition, and that of the objective case of the pronoun. It should read *If I were he.* This is another illustration of the rule regarding the verb *To Be*, taking the same case after it as before it; were is part of the verb To Be, therefore as the nominative (I) goes before it, the nominative (he) should come after it.

A OR AN

A becomes an before a vowel or before *h* mute for the sake of euphony or agreeable sound to the ear. *An apple, an orange, an heir, an honor*, etc.

CHAPTER VIII PITFALLS TO AVOID:
Common Stumbling Blocks—Peculiar Constructions—Misused Forms

CHAPTER IX
STYLE:
Diction —— Purity —— Propriety —— Precision

It is the object of every writer to put his thoughts into as effective form as possible so as to make a good impression on the reader. A person may have noble thoughts and ideas but be unable to express them in such a way as to appeal to others, consequently he cannot exert the full force of his intellectuality nor leave the imprint of his character upon his time, whereas many a man but indifferently gifted may wield such a facile pen as to attract attention and win for himself an envious place among his contemporaries.

In everyday life one sees illustrations of men of excellent mentality being cast aside and ones of mediocre or in some cases, little, if any, ability chosen to f ill important places. The former are unable to impress their personality; they have great thoughts, great ideas, but these thoughts and ideas are locked up in their brains and are like prisoners behind the bars struggling to get free. The key of language which would open the door is wanting, hence they have to remain locked up.

Many a man has to pass through the world unheard of and of little benefit

CHAPTER IX STYLE:
Diction—Purity—Propriety—Precision

to it or himself, simply because he cannot bring out what is in him and make it subservient to his will. It is the duty of every one to develop his best, not only for the benefit of himself but for the good of his fellow men. It is not at all necessary to have great learning or acquirements, the laborer is as useful in his own place as the philosopher in his; nor is it necessary to have many talents. One talent rightly used is much better than ten wrongly used. Often a man can do more with one than his contemporary can do with ten, often a man can make one dollar go farther than twenty in the hands of his neighbor, often the poor man lives more comfortably than the millionaire. All depends upon the individual himself. If he make right use of what the creator has given him and live according to the laws of God and nature he is fulfilling his all otted place in the universal scheme of creation, in other words, when he does his best, he is living up to the standard of a useful manhood.

Now in order to do his best a man of ordinary intelligence and education should be able to express himself correctly both in speaking and writing, that is, he should be able to convey his thoughts in an intelligent manner which the simplest can understand. The manner in which a speaker or writer conveys his thoughts is known as his style. In other words Style may be defined as the peculiar manner in which a man expresses his conceptions through the medium of language. It depends upon the choice of words and their arrangement to convey a meaning. Scarcely any two writers have exactly the same style, that is to say, express their ideas after the same peculiar form, just as no two mortals are fashioned by nature in the same mould, so that one is an exact counterpart of the other.

Just as men differ in the accent and tones of their voices, so do they differ in the construction of their language.

Two reporters sent out on the same mission, say to report a fire, will verbally differ in their accounts though materially both descriptions will be the same as far as the leading facts are concerned. One will express himself in a style different from the other.

If you are asked to describe the dancing of a red-haired lady at the last charity ball you can either say

—— "The ruby Circe, with the Titian locks glowing like the oriflamme which surrounds the golden god of day as he sinks to rest amid the crimson glory of the burnished West, gave a divine exhibition of the Terpsichorean art which thrilled the souls of the multitude" or, you can simply say —— "The red-haired lady danced very well and pleased the audience."

The former is a specimen of the ultra florid or bombastic style which may be said to depend upon the pomposity of verbosity for its effect, the latter is a specimen of simple natural Style. Needless to say it is to be preferred. The other should be avoided. It stamps the writer as a person of shallowness, ignorance and inexperience. It has been eliminated from the newspapers. Even the most flatulent of yellow sheets no longer tolerate it in their columns. Affectation and pedantry in style are now universally condemned.

It is the duty of every speaker and writer to labor after a pleasing style. It gains him an entrance where he would otherwise be debarred. Often the interest of a subject depends as much on the way it is presented as on the subject itself. One writer will make it attractive, another repulsive. For instance take

CHAPTER IX STYLE:
Diction—Purity—Propriety—Precision

a passage in history. Treated by one historian it is like a desiccated mummy, dry, dull, disgusting, while under the spell of another it is, as it were, galvanized into a virile living thing which not only pleases but captivates the reader.

DICTION

The first requisite of style is choice of words, and this comes under the head of *Diction*, the property of style which has reference to the words and phrases used in speaking and writing. The secret of literary skill from any standpoint consists in putting the right word in the right place. In order to do this it is imperative to know the meaning of the words we use, their exact literal meaning. Many synonymous words are seemingly interchangeable and appear as if the same meaning were applicable to three or four of them at the same time, but when all such words are reduced to a final analysis it is clearly seen that there is a marked difference in their meaning. For instance grief and sorrow seem to be identical, but they are not. Grief is active, sorrow is more or less passive; grief is caused by troubles and misfortunes which come to us from the outside, while sorrow is often the consequence of our own acts. *Grief* is frequently loud and violent, *sorrow* is always quiet and retiring. *Grief* shouts, *Sorrow* remains calm.

If you are not sure of the exact meaning of a word look it up immediately in the dictionary. Sometimes some of our great scholars are puzzled over simple words in regard to meaning, spelling or pronunciation. Whenever you meet a strange word note it down until you discover its meaning and use. Read the best books you can get, books written by men and women who are acknowledged masters of language, and study how they use their words, where they place them in the sentences, and the meanings they convey to the readers.

Mix in good society. Listen attentively to good talkers and try to imitate their manner of expression. If a word is used you do not understand, don't be ashamed to ask its meaning.

True, a small vocabulary will carry you through, but it is an advantage to have a large one. When you live alone a little pot serves just as well as a large one to cook your victuals and it is handy and convenient, but when your friends or neighbors come to dine with you, you will need a much larger pot and it is better to have it in store, so that you will not be put to shame for your scantiness of furnishings.

Get as many words as you possibly can —— if you don't need them now, pack them away in the garrets of your brain so that you can call upon them if you require them.

Keep a notebook, jot down the words you don't understand or clearly understand and consult the dictionary when you get time.

PURITY

Purity of style consists in using words which are reputable, national and present, which means that the words are in current use by the best authorities, that they are used throughout the nation and not confined to one particular part, and that they are words in constant use at the present time.

CHAPTER IX STYLE:
Diction—Purity—Propriety—Precision

There are two guiding principles in the choice of words, —— *good use* and *good taste*. Good use tells us whether a word is right or wrong; good taste, whether it is adapted to our purpose or not.

A word that is obsolete or too new to have gained a place in the language, or that is a provincialism, should not be used.

Here are the Ten Commandments of English style:

1. Do not use foreign words.

2. Do not use a long word when a short one will serve your purpose. *Fire* is much better than *conflagration*.

3. Do not use technical words, or those understood only by specialists in their respective lines, except when you are writing especially for such people.

4. Do not use slang.

5. Do not use provincialisms, as "I guess" for "I think"; "I reckon" for "I know," etc.

6. Do not in writing prose, use poetical or antiquated words: as "lore, e'er, morn, yea, nay, verily, peradventure."

7. Do not use trite and hackneyed words and expressions; as, "on the job," "up and in"; "down and out."

8. Do not use newspaper words which have not established a place in the language as "to bugle"; "to suicide," etc.

9. Do not use ungrammatical words and forms; as, "I ain't;" "he don't."

10. Do not use ambiguous words or phrases; as —— "He showed me all about the house."

PURITY

Trite words, similes and metaphors which have become hackneyed and worn out should be allowed to rest in the oblivion of past usage. Such expressions and phrases as "Sweet sixteen" "the Almighty dollar," "Uncle Sam," "On the fence," "The Glorious Fourth," "Young America," "The lords of creation," "The rising generation," "The weaker sex," "The weaker vessel," "Sweetness long drawn out" and "chief cook and bottle washer," should be put on the shelf as they are utterly worn out from too much usage.

Some of the old similes which have outlived their usefulness and should be pensioned off, are "Sweet as sugar," "Bold as a lion," "Strong as an ox," "Quick as a flash," "Cold as ice," "Stiff as a poker," "White as snow," "Busy as a bee," "Pale as a ghost," "Rich as Croesus," "Cross as a bear" and a great many more far too numerous to mention.

Be as original as possible in the use of expression. Don't follow in the old rut but try and strike out for yourself. This does not mean that you should try to set the style, or do anything outlandish or out of the way, or be an innovator on the prevailing custom. In order to be original there is no necessity for you to introduce something novel or establish a precedent. The probability is you are not f it to do either, by education or talent. While following the style of those who are acknowledged leaders you can be original in your language. Try and clothe an idea different from what it has been clothed and better. If you are speaking or writing of dancing don't talk or write about "tripping the light fantastic toe." It is over two hundred years since Milton expressed it that way in "*L'Allegro.*" You're not a Milton and besides over a million have stolen it from Milton until it is now no longer worth stealing.

CHAPTER IX   STYLE:
Diction—Purity—Propriety—Precision

Don't resurrect obsolete words such as whilom, yclept, wis, etc., and be careful in regard to obsolescent words, that is, words that are at the present time gradually passing from use such as *quoth, trow, betwixt, amongst, froward*, etc.

And beware of new words. Be original in the construction and arrangement of your language, but don't try to originate words. Leave that to the masters of language, and don't be the first to try such words, wait until the chemists of speech have tested them and passed upon their merits.

Quintilian said —— "Prefer the oldest of the new and the newest of the old." Pope put this in rhyme and it still holds good:

In words, as fashions, the same rule will hold, Alike fantastic, if too new or old: Be not the first by whom the new are tried, Nor yet the last to lay the old aside.

PROPRIETY

Propriety of style consists in using words in their proper sense and as in the case of purity, good usage is the principal test. Many words have acquired in actual use a meaning very different from what they once possessed. "Prevent" formerly meant to go before, and that meaning is implied in its Latin derivation.

Now it means to put a stop to, to hinder. To attain propriety of style it is necessary to avoid confounding words derived from the same root; as *respect-*

fully and *respectively*; it is necessary to use words in their accepted sense or the sense which everyday use sanctions.

SIMPLICITY

Simplicity of style has reference to the choice of simple words and their unaffected presentation. Simple words should always be used in preference to compound, and complicated ones when they express the same or almost the same meaning. The Anglo-Saxon element in our language comprises the simple words which express the relations of everyday life, strong, terse, vigorous, the language of the fireside, street, market and farm. It is this style which characterizes the Bible and many of the great English classics such as the "Pilgrim's Progress," "Robinson Crusoe," and "Gulliver's Travels."

CLEARNESS

Clearness of style should be one of the leading considerations with the beginner in composition. He must avoid all obscurity and ambiguous phrases. If he writes a sentence or phrase and see that a meaning might be inferred from it otherwise than intended, he should re-write it in such a way that there can be no possible doubt. Words, phrases or clauses that are closely related should be placed as near to each other as possible that their mutual relation may clearly appear, and no word should be omitted that is necessary to the complete expression of thought.

CHAPTER IX   STYLE:
Diction—Purity—Propriety—Precision

UNITY

Unity is that property of style which keeps all parts of a sentence in connection with the principal thought and logically subordinate to it. A sentence may be constructed as to suggest the idea of oneness to the mind, or it may be so loosely put together as to produce a confused and indefinite impression. Ideas that have but little connection should be expressed in separate sentences, and not crowded into one.

Keep long parentheses out of the middle of your sentences and when you have apparently brought your sentences to a close don't try to continue the thought or idea by adding supplementary clauses.

STRENGTH

Strength is that property of style which gives animation, energy and vivacity to language and sustains the interest of the reader. It is as necessary to language as good food is to the body. Without it the words are weak and feeble and create little or no impression on the mind. In order to have strength the language must be concise, that is, much expressed in little compass, you must hit the nail fairly on the head and drive it in straight. Go critically over what you write and strike out every word, phrase and clause the omission of which impairs neither the clearness nor force of the sentence and so avoid redundancy, tautology and circumlocution. Give the most important words the most prominent places, which, as has been pointed out elsewhere, are the beginning and end of the sentence.

HARMONY

Harmony is that property of style which gives a smoothness to the sentence, so that when the words are sounded their connection becomes pleasing to the ear. It adapts sound to sense. Most people construct their sentences without giving thought to the way they will sound and as a consequence we have many jarring and discordant combinations such as "Thou strengthenedst thy position and actedst arbitrarily and derogatorily to my interests."

Harsh, disagreeable verbs are liable to occur with the Quaker form Thou of the personal pronoun. This form is now nearly obsolete, the plural you being almost universally used. To obtain harmony in the sentence long words that are hard to pronounce and combinations of letters of one kind should be avoided.

EXPRESSIVE OF WRITER

Style is expressive of the writer, as to who he is and what he is. As a matter of structure in composition it is the indication of what a man can do; as a matter of quality it is an indication of what he is.

CHAPTER IX STYLE:
Diction—Purity—Propriety—Precision

KINDS OF STYLE

Style has been classified in different ways, but it admits of so many designations that it is very hard to enumerate a table. In fact there are as many styles as there are writers, for no two authors write *exactly* after the same form. However, we may classify the styles of the various authors in broad divisions as (1) dry, (2) plain, (3) neat, (4) elegant, (5) florid, (6) bombastic.

The *dry* style excludes all ornament and makes no effort to appeal to any sense of beauty. Its object is simply to express the thoughts in a correct manner. This style is exemplified by Berkeley.

The *plain* style does not seek ornamentation either, but aims to make clear and concise statements without any elaboration or embellishment. Locke and Whately illustrate the plain style.

The *neat* style only aspires after ornament sparingly. Its object is to have correct figures, pure diction and clear and harmonious sentences. Goldsmith and Gray are the acknowledged leaders in this kind of style.

The *elegant* style uses every ornament that can beautify and avoids every excess which would degrade. Macaulay and Addison have been enthroned as the kings of this style. To them all writers bend the knee in homage.

The *florid* style goes to excess in superfluous and superficial ornamentation and strains after a highly colored imagery. The poems of Ossian typify this style.

The *bombastic* is characterized by such an excess of words, figures and ornaments as to be ridiculous and disgusting. It is like a circus clown dressed

KINDS OF STYLE

up in gold tinsel Dickens gives a fine example of it in Sergeant Buzfuz' speech in the "Pickwick Papers." Among other varieties of style may be mentioned the colloquial, the laconic, the concise, the diffuse, the abrupt the flowing, the quaint, the epigrammatic, the flowery, the feeble, the nervous, the vehement, and the affected. The manner of these is sufficiently indicated by the adjective used to describe them.

In fact style is as various as character and expresses the individuality of the writer, or in other words, as the French writer Buffon very aptly remarks, "the style is the man himself."

CHAPTER IX STYLE:
Diction—Purity—Propriety—Precision

CHAPTER X
SUGGESTIONS:
How to Write —— What to Write —— Correct Speaking and Speakers

Rules of grammar and rhetoric are good in their own place; their laws must be observed in order to express thoughts and ideas in the right way so that they shall convey a determinate sense and meaning in a pleasing and acceptable manner. Hard and fast rules, however, can never make a writer or author.

That is the business of old Mother Nature and nothing can take her place. If nature has not endowed a man with faculties to put his ideas into proper composition he cannot do so. He may have no ideas worthy the recording. If a person has not a thought to express, it cannot be expressed. Something cannot be manufactured out of nothing. The author must have thoughts and ideas before he can express them on paper. These come to him by nature and environment and are developed and strengthened by studying.

There is an old Latin quotation in regard to the poet which says "Poeta nascitur non fit" the translation of which is —— the poet is born, not made. To a great degree the same applies to the author. Some men are great scholars as

CHAPTER X   SUGGESTIONS:
How to Write—What to Write—Correct Speaking and Speakers

far as book learning is concerned, yet they cannot express themselves in passable composition. Their knowledge is like gold locked up in a chest where it is of no value to themselves or the rest of the world.

The best way to learn to write is to sit down and write, just as the best way how to learn to ride a bicycle is to mount the wheel and pedal away. Write first about common things, subjects that are familiar to you. Try for instance an essay on a cat. Say something original about her. Don't say "she is very playful when young but becomes grave as she grows old." That has been said more than fifty thousand times before.

Tell what you have seen the family cat doing, how she caught a mouse in the garret and what she did after catching it. Familiar themes are always the best for the beginner. Don't attempt to describe a scene in Australia if you have never been there and know nothing of the country. Never hunt for subjects, there are thousands around you. Describe what you saw yesterday —— a fire, a runaway horse, a dog-fight on the street and be original in your description. Imitate the best writers in their style, but not in their exact words. Get out of the beaten path, make a pathway of your own.

Know what you write about, write about what you know; this is a golden rule to which you must adhere. To know you must study. The world is an open book in which all who run may read. Nature is one great volume the pages of which are open to the peasant as well as to the peer. Study Nature's moods and tenses, for they are vastly more important than those of the grammar. Book learning is most desirable, but, after all , it is only theory and not practice. The grandest all egory in the English, in fact, in any language, was written by

KINDS OF STYLE

an ignorant, so-called ignorant, tinker named John Bunyan. Shakespeare was not a scholar in the sense we regard the term to-day, yet no man ever lived or probably ever will live that equalled or will equal him in the expression of thought. He simply read the book of nature and interpreted it from the standpoint of his own magnificent genius.

Don't imagine that a college education is necessary to success as a writer. Far from it. Some of our college men are dead-heads, drones, parasites on the body social, not alone useless to the world but to themselves. A person may be so ornamental that he is valueless from any other standpoint. As a general rule ornamental things serve but little purpose. A man may know so much of everything that he knows little of anything. This may sound paradoxical, but, nevertheless, experience proves its truth.

If you are poor that is not a detriment but an advantage. Poverty is an incentive to endeavor, not a drawback. Better to be born with a good, working brain in your head than with a gold spoon in your mouth. If the world had been depending on the so-called pets of fortune it would have deteriorated long ago.

From the pits of poverty, from the arenas of suffering, from the hovels of neglect, from the backwood cabins of obscurity, from the lanes and by-ways of oppression, from the dingy garrets and basements of unending toil and drudgery have come men and women who have made history, made the world brighter, better, higher, holier for their existence in it, made of it a place good to live in and worthy to die in, —— men and women who have hallowed it by their footsteps and sanctified it with their presence and in many cases conse-

CHAPTER X SUGGESTIONS:
How to Write—What to Write—Correct Speaking and Speakers

crated it with their blood. Poverty is a blessing, not an evil, a benison from the Father's hand if accepted in the right spirit. Instead of retarding, it has elevated literature in allages. Homer was a blind beggarman singing his snatches of song for the dole of charity; grand old Socrates, oracle of wisdom, many a day went without his dinner because he had not the wherewithal to get it, while teaching the youth of Athens. The divine Dante was nothing better than a beggar, houseless, homeless, friendless, wandering through Italy while he composed his immortal cantos. Milton, who in his blindness "looked where angels fear to tread," was steeped in poverty while writing his sublime conception, "Paradise Lost." Shakespeare was glad to hold and water the horses of patrons outside the White Horse Theatre for a few pennies in order to buy bread. Burns burst forth in never-dying song while guiding the ploughshare. Poor Heinrich Heine, neglected and in poverty, from his "mattress grave" of suffering in Paris added literary laurels to the wreath of his German Fatherland. In America Elihu Burritt, while attending the anvil, made himself a master of a score of languages and became the literary lion of his age and country.

In other fields of endeavor poverty has been the spur to action. Napoleon was born in obscurity, the son of a hand-to-mouth scrivener in the backward island of Corsica. Abraham Lincoln, the boast and pride of America, the man who made this land too hot for the feet of slaves, came from a log cabin in the Ohio backwoods. So did James A. Garfield. Ulysses Grant came from a tanyard to become the world's greatest general. Thomas A. Edison commenced as a newsboy on a railway train.

The examples of these men are incentives to action. Poverty thrust them forward instead of keeping them back. Therefore, if you are poor make your circumstances a means to an end. Have ambition, keep a goal in sight and bend every energy to reach that goal. A story is told of Thomas Carlyle the day he attained the highest honor the literary world could confer upon him when he was elected Lord Rector of Edinburgh University. After his installation speech, in going through the halls, he met a student seemingly deep in study. In his own peculiar, abrupt, crusty way the Sage of Chelsea interrogated the young man: "For what profession are you studying?" "I don't know," returned the youth. "You don't know," thundered Carlyle, "young man, you are a fool." Then he went on to qualify his vehement remark, "My boy when I was your age, I was stopped in grinding, gripping poverty in the little village of Ecclefechan, in the wilds of [Transcriber's note: First part of word illegible]-frieshire, where in all the place only the minister and myself could read the Bible, yet poor and obscure as I was, in my mind's eye I saw a chair awaiting for me in the Temple of Fame and day and night and night and day I studied until I sat in that chair today as Lord Rector of Edinburgh University."

Another Scotchman, Robert Buchanan, the famous novelist, set out for London from Glasgow with but half-a-crown in his pocket. "Here goes," said he, "for a grave in Westminster Abbey." He was not much of a scholar, but his ambition carried him on and he became one of the great literary lions of the world's metropolis.

Henry M. Stanley was a poorhouse waif whose real name was John Rowlands. He was brought up in a Welsh workhouse, but he had ambition, so he rose to be a great explorer, a great writer, became a member of Parliament and

CHAPTER X SUGGESTIONS:
How to Write—What to Write—Correct Speaking and Speakers

was knighted by the British Sovereign.

Have ambition to succeed and you will succeed. Cut the word "failure" out of your lexicon. Don't acknowledge it. Remember "In life's earnest battle they only prevail who daily march onward and never say fail."

Let every obstacle you encounter be but a stepping stone in the path of onward progress to the goal of success.

If untoward circumstances surround you, resolve to overcome them. Bunyan wrote the "Pilgrim's Progress" in Bedford jail on scraps of wrapping paper while he was half starved on a diet of bread and water. That unfortunate American genius, Edgar Allan Poe, wrote "The Raven," the most wonderful conception as well as the most highly artistic poem in all English literature, in a little cottage in the Fordham section of New York while he was in the direst straits of want. Throughout all his short and wonderfully brilliant career, poor Poe never had a dollar he could call his own. Such, however, was both his fault and his misfortune and he is a bad exemplar.

Don't think that the knowledge of a library of books is essential to success as a writer. Often a multiplicity of books is confusing. Master a few good books and master them well and you will have all that is necessary. A great authority has said: "Beware of the man of one book," which means that a man of one book is a master of the craft. It is claimed that a thorough knowledge of the Bible alone will make any person a master of literature. Certain it is that the Bible and Shakespeare constitute an epitome of the essentials of knowledge. Shakespeare gathered the fruitage of all who went before him, he has sown the seeds for all who shall ever come after him. He was the great intellectual ocean whose waves touch the continents of all thought.

Books are cheap now-a-days, the greatest works, thanks to the printing press, are within the reach of all, and the more you read, the better, provided they are worth reading. Sometimes a man takes poison into his system unconscious of the fact that it is poison, as in the case of certain foods, and it is very hard to throw off its effects. Therefore, be careful in your choice of reading matter. If you cannot afford a full library, and as has been said, such is not necessary, select a few of the great works of the master minds, assimilate and digest them, so that they will be of advantage to your literary system. Elsewhere in this volume is given a list of some of the world's masterpieces from which you can make a selection.

Your brain is a storehouse, don't put useless furniture into it to crowd it to the exclusion of what is useful. Lay up only the valuable and serviceable kind which you can call into requisition at any moment.

As it is necessary to study the best authors in order to be a writer, so it is necessary to study the best speakers in order to talk with correctness and in good style. To talk rightly you must imitate the masters of oral speech. Listen to the best conversationalists and how they express themselves. Go to hear the leading lectures, speeches and sermons. No need to imitate the gestures of elocution, it is nature, not art, that makes the elocutionist and the orator. It is not how a speaker expresses himself but the language which he uses and the manner of its use which should interest you. Have you heard the present day masters of speech? There have been past time masters but their tongues are stilled in the dust of the grave, and you can only read their eloquence now. You can,

CHAPTER X SUGGESTIONS:
How to Write—What to Write—Correct Speaking and Speakers

however, listen to the charm of the living.

To many of us voices still speak from the grave, voices to which we have listened when fired with the divine essence of speech. Perhaps you have hung with rapture on the words of Beecher and Talmage. Both thrilled the souls of men and won countless thousands over to a living gospel. Both were masters of words, they scattered the flowers of rhetoric on the shrine of eloquence and hurled veritable bouquets at their audiences which were eagerly seized by the latter and treasured in the storehouse of memory. Both were scholars and philosophers, yet they were far surpassed by Spurgeon, a plain man of the people with little or no claim to education in the modern sense of the word. Spurgeon by his speech attracted thousands to his Tabernacle. The Protestant and Catholic, Turk, Jew and Mohammedan rushed to hear him and listened, entranced, to his language. Such another was Dwight L. Moody, the greatest Evangelist the world has ever known. Moody was not a man of learning; he commenced life as a shoe salesman in Chicago, yet no man ever lived who drew such audiences and so fascinated them with the spell of his speech. "Oh, that was personal magnetism," you will say, but it was nothing of the kind. It was the burning words that fell from the lips of these men, and the way, the manner, the force with which they used those words that counted and attracted the crowds to listen unto them. Personal magnetism or personal appearance entered not as factors into their success. Indeed as far as physique were concerned, some of them were handicapped. Spurgeon was a short, podgy, fat little man, Moody was like a country farmer, Talmage in his big cloak was one of the most slovenly of men and only Beecher was passable in the way of refinement and gentlemanly bearing. Physical appearance, as so many think, is not the sesame to the interest of an audience. Daniel O'Connell, the Irish tribune, was a homely, ugly, awkward, ungainly man, yet his words attracted millions to his side and gained for him the hostile ear of the British Parliament, he was a master of verbiage and knew just what to say to captivate his audiences.

It is words and their placing that count on almost all occasions. No matter how refined in other respects the person may be, if he use words wrongly and express himself in language not in accordance with a proper construction, he will repel you, whereas the man who places his words correctly and employs language in harmony with the laws of good speech, let him be ever so humble, will attract and have an influence over you.

The good speaker, the correct speaker, is always able to command attention and doors are thrown open to him which remain closed to others not equipped with a like facility of expression. The man who can talk well and to the point need never fear to go idle. He is required in nearly every walk of life and field of human endeavor, the world wants him at every turn. Employers are constantly on the lookout for good talkers, those who are able to attract the public and convince others by the force of their language. A man may be able, educated, refined, of unblemished character, nevertheless if he lack the power to express himself, put forth his views in good and appropriate speech he has to take a back seat, while someone with much less ability gets the opportunity to come to the front because he can clothe his ideas in ready words and talk effectively.

CHAPTER X SUGGESTIONS:
How to Write—What to Write—Correct Speaking and Speakers

You may again say that nature, not art, makes a man a fluent speaker; to a great degree this is true, but it is art that makes him a correct speaker, and correctness leads to fluency. It is possible for everyone to become a correct speaker if he will but persevere and take a little pains and care.

At the risk of repetition good advice may be here emphasized: Listen to the best speakers and note carefully the words which impress you most. Keep a notebook and jot down words, phrases, sentences that are in any way striking or out of the ordinary run. If you do not understand the exact meaning of a word you have heard, look it up in the dictionary. There are many words, called synonyms, which have almost a like signification, nevertheless, when examined they express different shades of meaning and in some cases, instead of being close related, are widely divergent. Beware of such words, find their exact meaning and learn to use them in their right places.

Be open to criticism, don't resent it but rather invite it and look upon those as friends who point out your defects in order that you may remedy them.

CHAPTER XI
SLANG:
Origin —— American Slang —— Foreign Slang

Slang is more or less common in nearly all ranks of society and in every walk of life at the present day. Slang words and expressions have crept into our everyday language, and so insiduously, that they have not been detected by the great majority of speakers, and so have become part and parcel of their vocabulary on an equal footing with the legitimate words of speech. They are called upon to do similar service as the ordinary words used in everyday conversation —— to express thoughts and desires and convey meaning from one to another. In fact, in some cases, slang has become so useful that it has far outstripped classic speech and made for itself such a position in the vernacular that it would be very hard in some cases to get along without it. Slang words have usurped the place of regular words of language in very many instances and reign supreme in their own strength and influence.

Can't and slang are often confused in the popular mind, yet they are not synonymous, though very closely allied, and proceeding from a common Gypsy origin. Can't is the language of a certain class —— the peculiar phraseology

CHAPTER XI   SLANG:
Origin—American Slang—Foreign Slang

or dialect of a certain craft, trade or profession, and is not readily understood save by the initiated of such craft, trade or profession. It may be correct, according to the rules of grammar, but it is not universal; it is confined to certain parts and localities and is only intelligible to those for whom it is intended. In short, it is an esoteric language which only the initiated can understand. The jargon, or patter, of thieves is can't and it is only understood by thieves who have been let into its significance; the initiated language of professional gamblers is cant, and is only intelligible to gamblers.

On the other hand, slang, as it is nowadays, belongs to no particular class but is scattered all over and gets entre into every kind of society and is understood by all where it passes current in everyday expression. Of course, the nature of the slang, to a great extent, depends upon the locality, as it chiefly is concerned with colloquialisms or words and phrases common to a particular section. For instance, the slang of London is slightly different from that of New York, and some words in the one city may be unintelligible in the other, though well understood in that in which they are current. Nevertheless, slang may be said to be universally understood. "To kick the bucket," "to cross the Jordan," "to hop the twig" are just as expressive of the departing from life in the backwoods of America or the wilds of Australia as they are in London or Dublin.

Slang simply consists of words and phrases which pass current but are not refined, nor elegant enough, to be admitted into polite speech or literature whenever they are recognized as such. But, as has been said, a great many use slang without their knowing it as slang and incorporate it into their everyday

KINDS OF STYLE

speech and conversation.

Some authors purposely use slang to give emphasis and spice in familiar and humorous writing, but they should not be imitated by the tyro. A master, such as Dickens, is forgivable, but in the novice it is unpardonable.

There are several kinds of slang attached to different professions and classes of society. For instance, there is college slang, political slang, sporting slang, etc. It is the nature of slang to circulate freely among all classes, yet there are several kinds of this current form of language corresponding to the several classes of society. The two great divisions of slang are the vulgar of the uneducated and coarse minded, and the high-toned slang of the so-called upper classes —— the educated and the wealthy. The hoyden of the gutter does not use the same slang as my lady in her boudoir, but both use it, and so expressive is it that the one might readily understand the other if brought in contact. Therefore, there are what may be styled an ignorant slang and an educated slang —— the one common to the purlieus and the alleys, the other to the parlor and the drawing-room.

In all cases the object of slang is to express an idea in a more vigorous, piquant and terse manner than standard usage ordinarily admits. A school girl, when she wants to praise a baby, exclaims: "Oh, isn't he awfully cute!" To say that he is very nice would be too weak a way to express her admiration. When a handsome girl appears on the street an enthusiastic masculine admirer, to express his appreciation of her beauty, tells you: "She is a peach, a bird, a cuckoo," any of which accentuates his estimation of the young lady and is much more emphatic than saying: "She is a beautiful girl," "a handsome maiden," or

CHAPTER XI   SLANG:
Origin—American Slang—Foreign Slang

"lovely young woman."

When a politician defeats his rival he will tell you "it was a cinch," he had a "walk-over," to impress you how easy it was to gain the victory.

Some slang expressions are of the nature of metaphors and are highly f igurative. Such are "to pass in your checks," "to hold up," "to pull the wool over your eyes," "to talk through your hat," "to fire out," "to go back on," "to make yourself solid with," "to have a jag on," "to be loaded," "to freeze on to," "to bark up the wrong tree," "don't monkey with the buzz-saw," and "in the soup." Most slang had a bad origin. The greater part originated in the cant of thieves' Latin, but it broke away from this cant of malefactors in time and gradually evolved itself from its unsavory past until it developed into a current form of expressive speech. Some slang, however, can trace its origin back to very respectable sources.

"Stolen fruits are sweet" may be traced to the Bible in sentiment. Proverbs, ix:17 has it: "Stolen waters are sweet." "What are you giving me," supposed to be a thorough Americanism, is based upon Genesis, xxxviii:16. The common slang, "a bad man," in referring to Western desperadoes, in almost the identical sense now used, is found in Spenser's *Faerie Queen,* Massinger's play "*A New Way to Pay Old Debts*," and in Shakespeare's "*King Henry VIII.*" The expression "to blow on," meaning to inform, is in Shakespeare's "*As You Like it.*" "It's all Greek to me" is traceable to the play of "Julius Caesar." "All cry and no wool" is in Butler's "*Hudibras*." "Pious frauds," meaning hypocrites, is from the same source. "Too thin," referring to an excuse, is from Smollett's "*Peregrine Pickle.*" Shakespeare also used it.

KINDS OF STYLE

America has had a large share in contributing to modern slang. "The heathen Chinee," and "Ways that are dark, and tricks that are vain," are from Bret Harte's *Truthful James*. "Not for Joe," arose during the Civil War when one soldier refused to give a drink to another. "Not if I know myself" had its origin in Chicago. "What's the matter with —— ? He's all right," had its beginning in Chicago also and first was "What's the matter with Hannah." referring to a lazy domestic servant. "There's millions in it," and "By a large majority" come from Mark Twain's *Gilded Age*. "Pull down your vest," "jim-jams," "got 'em bad," "that's what's the matter," "go hire a hall," "take in your sign," "dry up," "hump yourself," "it's the man around the corner," "putting up a job," "put a head on him," "no back talk," "bottom dollar," "went off on his ear," "chalk it down," "staving him off," "making it warm," "dropping him gently," "dead gone," "busted," "counter jumper," "put up or shut up," "bang up," "smart Aleck," "too much jaw," "chin-music," "top heavy," "barefooted on the top of the head," "a little too fresh," "champion liar," "chief cook and bottle washer," "bag and baggage," "as fine as silk," "name your poison," "died with his boots on," "old hoss," "hunkey dorey," "hold your horses," "galoot" and many others in use at present are all Americanisms in slang.

California especially has been most fecund in this class of figurative language. To this State we owe "go off and die," "don't you forget it," "rough deal," "square deal," "flush times," "pool your issues," "go bury yourself," "go drown yourself," "give your tongue a vacation," "a bad egg," "go climb a tree," "plug hats," "Dolly Vardens," "well fixed," "down to bed rock," "hard pan," "pay dirt," "petered out," "it won't wash," "slug of whiskey," "it pans out well,"

CHAPTER XI SLANG:
Origin—American Slang—Foreign Slang

and "I should smile." "Small potatoes, and few in the hill," "soft snap," "all fired," "gol durn it," "an up-hill job," "slick," "short cut," "guess not," "correct thing" are Bostonisms. The terms "innocent," "acknowledge the corn," "bark up the wrong tree," "great snakes," "I reckon," "playing 'possum," "dead shot," had their origin in the Southern States. "Doggone it," "that beats the Dutch," "you bet," "you bet your boots," sprang from New York. "Step down and out" originated in the Beecher trial, just as "brain storm" originated in the Thaw trial.

Among the slang phrases that have come directly to us from England may be mentioned "throw up the sponge," "draw it mild," "give us a rest," "dead beat," "on the shelf," "up the spout," "stunning," "gift of the gab," etc.

The newspapers are responsible for a large part of the slang. Reporters, staff writers, and even editors, put words and phrases into the mouths of individuals which they never utter. New York is supposed to be the headquarters of slang, particularly that portion of it known as the Bowery. All transgressions and corruptions of language are supposed to originate in that unclassic section, while the truth is that the laws of polite English are as much violated on Fifth Avenue. Of course, the foreign element mincing their "pidgin" English have given the Bowery an unenviable reputation, but there are just as good speakers of the vernacular on the Bowery as elsewhere in the greater city. Yet every inexperienced newspaper reporter thinks that it is incumbent on him to hold the Bowery up to ridicule and laughter, so he sits down, and out of his circumscribed brain, mutilates the English tongue (he can rarely coin a word), and blames the mutilation on the Bowery.

KINDS OF STYLE

'Tis the same with newspapers and authors, too, detracting the Irish race. Men and women who have never seen the green hills of Ireland, paint Irish characters as boors and blunderers and make them say ludicrous things and use such language as is never heard within the four walls of Ireland. 'Tis very well known that Ireland is the most learned country on the face of the earth —— is, and has been. The schoolmaster has been abroad there for hundreds, almost thousands, of years, and nowhere else in the world to-day is the king's English spoken so purely as in the cities and towns of the little Western Isle.

Current events, happenings of everyday life, often give rise to slang words, and these, after a time, come into such general use that they take their places in everyday speech like ordinary words and, as has been said, their users forget that they once were slang. For instance, the days of the Land League in Ireland originated the word boycott, which was the name of a very unpopular landlord, Captain Boycott. The people refused to work for him, and his crops rotted on the ground. From this time anyone who came into disfavor and whom his neighbors refused to assist in any way was said to be boycotted. Therefore to boycott means to punish by abandoning or depriving a person of the assistance of others. At first it was a notoriously slang word, but now it is standard in the English dictionaries.

Politics add to our slang words and phrases. From this source we get "dark horse," "the gray mare is the better horse," "barrel of money," "buncombe," "gerrymander," "scalawag," "henchman," "logrolling," "pulling the wires," "taking the stump," "machine," "slate," etc.

The money market furnishes us with "corner," "bull," "bear," "lamb,"

CHAPTER XI SLANG:
Origin—American Slang—Foreign Slang

"slump," and several others.

The custom of the times and the requirements of current expression require the best of us to use slang words and phrases on occasions. Often we do not know they are slang, just as a child often uses profane words without consciousness of their being so. We should avoid the use of slang as much as possible, even when it serves to convey our ideas in a forceful manner. And when it has not gained a firm foothold in current speech it should be used not at all. Remember that most all slang is of vulgar origin and bears upon its face the bend sinister of vulgarity. Of the slang that is of good birth, pass it by if you can, for it is like a broken-down gentleman, of little good to anyone. Imitate the great masters as much as you will in classical literature, but when it comes to their slang, draw the line. Dean Swift, the great Irish satirist, coined the word "phiz" for face. Don't imitate him. If you are speaking or writing of the beauty of a lady's face don't call it her "phiz." The Dean, as an intellectual giant, had a license to do so —— you haven't. Shakespeare used the word "flush" to indicate plenty of money. Well, just remember there was only one Shakespeare, and he was the only one that had a right to use that word in that sense. You'll never be a Shakespeare, there will never be such another —— Nature exhausted herself in producing him.

Bulwer used the word "stretch" for hang, as to stretch his neck. Don't follow his example in such use of the word. Above all, avoid the low, coarse, vulgar slang, which is made to pass for wit among the riff-raff of the street. If you are speaking or writing of a person having died last night don't say or write: "He hopped the twig," or "he kicked the bucket." If you are compelled

KINDS OF STYLE

to listen to a person discoursing on a subject of which he knows little or nothing, don't say "He is talking through his hat." If you are telling of having shaken hands with Mr. Roosevelt don't say "He tipped me his flipper." If you are speaking of a wealthy man don't say "He has plenty of spondulix," or "the long green." All such slang is low, coarse and vulgar and is to be frowned upon on any and every occasion.

If you use slang use the refined kind and use it like a gentleman, that it will not hurt or give offense to any one. Cardinal Newman defined a gentleman as he who never inflicts pain. Be a gentleman in your slang —— never inflict pain.

CHAPTER XI SLANG:
Origin—American Slang—Foreign Slang

CHAPTER XII
WRITING FOR NEWSPAPERS:
Qualification —— Appropriate Subjects —— Directions

The newspaper nowadays goes into every home in the land; what was formerly regarded as a luxury is now looked upon as a necessity. No matter how poor the individual, he is not too poor to afford a penny to learn, not alone what is taking place around him in his own immediate vicinity, but also what is happening in every quarter of the globe. The laborer on the street can be as well posted on the news of the day as the banker in his office. Through the newspaper he can feel the pulse of the country and find whether its vitality is increasing or diminishing; he can read the signs of the times and scan the political horizon for what concerns his own interests. The doings of foreign countries are spread before him and he can see at a glance the occurrences in the remotest corners of earth. If a fire occurred in London last night he can read about it at his breakfast table in New York this morning, and probably get a better account than the Londoners themselves. If a duel takes place in Paris

CHAPTER XII WRITING FOR NEWSPAPERS:
Qualification—Appropriate Subjects—Directions

he can read all about it even before the contestants have left the field.

There are upwards of 3,000 daily newspapers in the United States, more than 2,000 of which are published in towns containing less than 100,000 inhabitants. In fact, many places of less than 10,000 population can boast the publishing of a daily newspaper. There are more than 15,000 weeklies published. Some of the so-called country papers wield quite an influence in their localities, and even outside, and are money-making agencies for their owners and those connected with them, both by way of circulation and advertisements.

It is surprising the number of people in this country who make a living in the newspaper field. Apart from the regular toilers there are thousands of men and women who make newspaper work a side issue, who add tidy sums of "pin money" to their incomes by occasional contributions to the daily, weekly and monthly press. Most of these people are only persons of ordinary, everyday ability, having just enough education to express themselves intelligently in writing.

It is a mistake to imagine, as so many do, that an extended education is necessary for newspaper work. Not at all! On the contrary, in some cases, a high class education is a hindrance, not a help in this direction. The general newspaper does not want learned disquisitions nor philosophical theses; as its name implies, it wants news, current news, interesting news, something to appeal to its readers, to arouse them and rivet their attention. In this respect very often a boy can write a better article than a college professor. The professor would be apt to use words beyond the capacity of most of the readers, while the boy, not knowing such words, would probably simply tell what he saw, how great the damage was, who were killed or injured, etc., and use language which all would understand.

Of course, there are some brilliant scholars, deeply-read men and women in the newspaper realm, but, on the whole, those who have made the greatest names commenced ignorant enough and most of them graduated by way of the country paper. Some of the leading writers of England and America at the present time started their literary careers by contributing to the rural press. They perfected and polished themselves as they went along until they were able to make names for themselves in universal literature.

If you want to contribute to newspapers or enter the newspaper field as a means of livelihood, don't let lack of a college or university education stand in your way. As has been said elsewhere in this book, some of the greatest masters of English literature were men who had but little advantage in the way of book learning. Shakespeare, Bunyan, Burns, and scores of others, who have left their names indelibly inscribed on the tablets of fame, had little to boast of in the way of book education, but they had what is popularly known as "horse" sense and a good working knowledge of the world; in other words, they understood human nature, and were natural themselves. Shakespeare understood mankind because he was himself a man; hence he has portrayed the feelings, the emotions, the passions with a master's touch, delineating the king in his palace as true to nature as he has done the peasant in his hut. The monitor within his own breast gave him warning as to what was right and what was wrong, just as the daemon ever by the side of old Socrates whispered in his

CHAPTER XII WRITING FOR NEWSPAPERS:
Qualification—Appropriate Subjects—Directions

ear the course to pursue under any and all circumstances. Burns guiding the plough conceived thoughts and clothed them in a language which has never, nor probably never will be, surpassed by all the learning which art can confer. These men were natural, and it was the perfection of this naturality that wreathed their brows with the never-fading laurels of undying fame.

If you would essay to write for the newspaper you must be natural and express yourself in your accustomed way without putting on airs or frills; you must not ape ornaments and indulge in bombast or rhodomontade which stamp a writer as not only superficial but silly. There is no room for such in the everyday newspaper. It wants facts stated in plain, unvarnished, unadorned language. True, you should read the best authors and, as far as possible, imitate their style, but don't try to literally copy them. Be yourself on every occasion —— no one else.

Not like Homer would I write, Not like Dante if I might,

Not like Shakespeare at his best, Not like Goethe or the rest, Like myself, however small,

Like myself, or not at all.

Put yourself in place of the reader and write what will interest yourself and in such a way that your language will appeal to your own ideas of the fitness of things. You belong to the great commonplace majority, therefore don't forget that in writing for the newspapers you are writing for that majority and not for the learned and aesthetic minority.

Remember you are writing for the man on the street and in the street car, you want to interest him, to compel him to read what you have to say. He does

KINDS OF STYLE

not want a display of learning; he wants news about something which concerns himself, and you must tell it to him in a plain, simple manner just as you would do if you were face to face with him.

What can you write about? Why about anything that will constitute current news, some leading event of the day, anything that will appeal to the readers of the paper to which you wish to submit it. No matter in what locality you may live, however backward it may be, you can always find something of genuine human interest to others. If there is no news happening, write of something that appeals to yourself. We are all constituted alike, and the chances are that what will interest you will interest others. Descriptions of adventure are generally acceptable. Tell of a fox hunt, or a badger hunt, or a bear chase.

If there is any important manufacturing plant in your neighborhood describe it and, if possible, get photographs, for photography plays a very important part in the news items of to-day. If a "great" man lives near you, one whose name is on the tip of every tongue, go and get an interview with him, obtain his views on the public questions of the day, describe his home life and his surroundings and how he spends his time.

Try and strike something germane to the moment, something that stands out prominently in the limelight of the passing show. If a noted personage, some famous man or woman, is visiting the country, it is a good time to write up the place from which he or she comes and the record he or she has made there. For instance, it was opportune to write of Sulu and the little Pacific archipelago during the Sultan's trip through the country. If an attempt is made to blow up an American battleship, say, in the harbor of Appia, in Samoa, it

CHAPTER XII WRITING FOR NEWSPAPERS:
Qualification—Appropriate Subjects—Directions

affords a chance to write about Samoa and Robert Louis Stephenson. When Manuel was hurled from the throne of Portugal it was a ripe time to write of Portugal and Portuguese affairs. If any great occurrence is taking place in a foreign country such as the crowning of a king or the dethronement of a monarch, it is a good time to write up the history of the country and describe the events leading up to the main issue. When a particularly savage outbreak occurs amongst wild tribes in the dependencies, such as a rising of the Manobos in the Philippines, it is opportune to write of such tribes and their surroundings, and the causes leading up to the revolt.

Be constantly on the lookout for something that will suit the passing hour, read the daily papers and probably in some obscure corner you may find something that will serve you as a foundation for a good article —— something, at least, that will give you a clue.

Be circumspect in your selection of a paper to which to submit your copy. Know the tone and general import of the paper, its social leanings and political affiliations, also its religious sentiments, and, in fact, all the particulars you can regarding it. It would be injudicious for you to send an article on a prize fight to a religious paper or, *vice versa*, an account of a church meeting to the editor of a sporting sheet.

If you get your copy back don't be disappointed nor yet disheartened. Perseverance counts more in the newspaper field than anywhere else, and only perseverance wins in the long run. You must become resilient; if you are pressed down, spring up again. No matter how many rebuffs you may receive, be not discouraged but call fresh energy to your assistance and make another stand. If the right stuff is in you it is sure to be discovered; your light will not remain long hidden under a bushel in the newspaper domain. If you can deliver the goods editors will soon be begging you instead of your begging them. Those men are constantly on the lookout for persons who can make good.

Once you get into print the battle is won, for it will be an incentive to you to persevere and improve yourself at every turn. Go over everything you write, cut and slash and prune until you get it into as perfect form as possible. Eliminate every superfluous word and be careful to strike out all ambiguous expressions and references.

If you are writing for a weekly paper remember it differs from a daily one. Weeklies want what will not alone interest the man on the street, but the woman at the fireside; they want out-of-the-way facts, curious scraps of lore, personal notes of famous or eccentric people, reminiscences of exciting experiences, interesting gleanings in life's numberless by-ways, in short, anything that will entertain, amuse, instruct the home circle. There is always something occurring in your immediate surroundings, some curious event or thrilling episode that will furnish you with data for an article. You must know the nature of the weekly to which you submit your copy the same as you must know the daily. For instance, the *Christian Herald,* while avowedly a religious weekly, treats such secular matter as makes the paper appeal to all. On its religious side it is non-sectarian, covering the broad field of Christianity throughout the world; on its secular side it deals with human events in such an impartial way that everyone, no matter to what class they may belong or to what creed they may subscribe, can take a living, personal interest.

CHAPTER XII WRITING FOR NEWSPAPERS:
Qualification—Appropriate Subjects—Directions

The monthlies offer another attractive field for the literary aspirant. Here, again, don't think you must be a university professor to write for a monthly magazine. Many, indeed most, of the foremost magazine contributors are men and women who have never passed through a college except by going in at the front door and emerging from the back one. However, for the most part, they are individuals of wide experience who know the practical side of life as distinguished from the theoretical.

The ordinary monthly magazine treats of the leading questions and issues which are engaging the attention of the world for the moment, great inventions, great discoveries, whatever is engrossing the popular mind for the time being, such as flying machines, battleships, sky-scrapers, the opening of mines, the development of new lands, the political issues, views of party leaders, character sketches of distinguished personages, etc. However, before trying your skill for a monthly magazine it would be well for you to have a good apprenticeship in writing for the daily press.

Above all things, remember that perseverance is the key that opens the door of success. Persevere! If you are turned down don't get disheartened; on the contrary, let the rebuff act as a stimulant to further effort. Many of the most successful writers of our time have been turned down again and again. For days and months, and even years, some of them have hawked their wares from one literary door to another until they found a purchaser. You may be a great writer in embryo, but you will never develop into a fetus, not to speak of full maturity, unless you bring out what is in you. Give yourself a chance to grow and seize upon everything that will enlarge the scope of your horizon. Keep your eyes wide open and there is not a moment of the day in which you will not see something to interest you and in which you may be able to interest others. Learn, too, how to read Nature's book. There's a lesson in everything —— in the stones, the grass, the trees, the babbling brooks and the singing birds. Interpret the lesson for yourself, then teach it to others. Always be in earnest in your writing; go about it in a determined kind of way, don't be faint hearted or backward, be brave, be brave, and evermore be brave.

On the wide, tented field in the battle of life, With an army of millions before you; Like a hero of old gird your soul for the strife and let not the foeman tramp over you; Act, act like a soldier and proudly rush on the most valiant in Bravery's van, With keen, flashing sword cut your way to the front and show to the world you're a *Man*.

If you are of the masculine gender be a man in all things in the highest and best acceptation of the word. That is the noblest title you can boast, higher far than that of earl or duke, emperor or king. In the same way womanhood is the grandest crown the feminine head can wear. When the world frowns on you and everything seems to go wrong, possess your soul in patience and hope for the dawn of a brighter day. It will come. The sun is always shining behind the darkest clouds. When you get your manuscripts back again and again, don't despair, nor think the editor cruel and unkind. He has troubles of his own, too.

Keep up your spirits until you have made the final test and put your talents to a last analysis, then if you find you cannot get into print be sure that newspaper writing or literary work is not your *forte*, and turn to something

CHAPTER XII WRITING FOR NEWSPAPERS:
Qualification—Appropriate Subjects—Directions

else. If nothing better presents itself, try shoemaking or digging ditches. Remember honest labor, no matter how humble, is ever dignified. If you are a woman throw aside the pen, sit down and darn your brother's, your father's, or your husband's socks, or put on a calico apron, take soap and water and scrub the floor. No matter who you are do something useful. That old sophistry about the world owing you a living has been exploded long ago. The world does not owe you a living, but you owe it servitude, and if you do not pay the debt you are not serving the purpose of an all -wise Providence and filling the place for which you were created. It is for you to serve the world, to make it better, brighter, higher, holier, grander, nobler, richer, for your having lived in it. This you can do in no matter what position fortune has cast you, whether it be that of street laborer or president. Fight the good fight and gain the victory.

"Above all, to thine own self be true,

And 'twill follow as the night the day,

Thou canst not then be false to any man."

CHAPTER XIII
CHOICE OF WORDS:
Small Words —— Their Importance —— The Anglo-Saxon Element

In another place in this book advice has been given to never use a long word when a short one will serve the same purpose. This advice is to be emphasized. Words of "learned length and thundering sound" should be avoided on all possible occasions. They proclaim shallowness of intellect and vanity of mind. The great purists, the masters of diction, the exemplars of style, used short, simple words that all could understand; words about which there could be no ambiguity as to meaning. It must be remembered that by our words we teach others; therefore, a very great responsibility rests upon us in regard to the use of a right language. We must take care that we think and speak in a way so clear that there may be no misapprehension or danger of conveying wrong impressions by vague and misty ideas enunciated in terms which are liable to be misunderstood by those whom we address. Words give a body or form to our ideas, without which they are able to be so foggy that we do not

CHAPTER XIII   CHOICE OF WORDS:
Small Words—Their Importance—The Anglo-Saxon Element

see where they are weak or false.

We must make the endeavor to employ such words as will put the idea we have in our own mind into the mind of another. This is the greatest art in the world —— to clothe our ideas in words clear and comprehensive to the intelligence of others. It is the art which the teacher, the minister, the lawyer, the orator, the business man, must master if they would command success in their various fields of endeavor. It is very hard to convey an idea to, and impress it on, another when he has but a faint conception of the language in which the idea is expressed; but it is impossible to convey it at all when the words in which it is clothed are unintelligible to the listener.

If we address an audience of ordinary men and women in the English language, but use such words as they cannot comprehend, we might as well speak to them in Coptic or Chinese, for they will derive no benefit from our address, inasmuch as the ideas we wish to convey are expressed in words which communicate no intelligent meaning to their minds.

Long words, learned words, words directly derived from other languages are only understood by those who have had the advantages of an extended education. All have not had such advantages. The great majority in this grand and glorious country of ours have to hustle for a living from an early age. Though education is free, and compulsory also, very many never get further than the "Three R's." These are the men with whom we have to deal most in the arena of life, the men with the horny palms and the iron muscles, the men who build our houses, construct our railroads, drive our street cars and trains, till our fields, harvest our crops —— in a word, the men who form the foundation of

KINDS OF STYLE

all society, the men on whom the world depends to make its wheels go round. The language of the colleges and universities is not for them and they can get along very well without it; they have no need for it at all in their respective callings. The plain, simple words of everyday life, to which the common people have been used around their own firesides from childhood, are the words we must use in our dealings with them.

Such words are understood by them and understood by the learned as well ; why then not use them universally and all the time? Why make a one-sided affair of language by using words which only one class of the people, the so-called learned class, can understand? Would it not be better to use, on all occasions, language which the both classes can understand? If we take the trouble to investigate we shall find that the men who exerted the greatest sway over the masses and the multitude as orators, lawyers, preachers and in other public capacities, were men who used very simple language. Daniel Webster was among the greatest orators this country has produced. He touched the hearts of senates and assemblages, of men and women with the burning eloquence of his words. He never used a long word when he could convey the same, or nearly the same, meaning with a short one. When he made a speech he always told those who put it in form for the press to strike out every long word. Study his speeches, go over all he ever said or wrote, and you will find that his language was always made up of short, clear, strong terms, although at times, for the sake of sound and oratorical effect, he was compelled to use a rather long word, but it was always against his inclination to do so, and where was the man who could paint, with words, as Webster painted! He could picture things

CHAPTER XIII CHOICE OF WORDS:
Small Words—Their Importance—The Anglo-Saxon Element

in a way so clear that those who heard him felt that they had seen that of which he spoke.

Abraham Lincoln was another who stirred the souls of men, yet he was not an orator, not a scholar; he did not write M.A. or Ph.D. after his name, or any other college degree, for he had none. He graduated from the University of Hard Knocks, and he never forgot this severe Alma Mater when he became President of the United States. He was just as plain, I just as humble, as in the days when he split rails or plied a boat on the Sangamon. He did not use big words, but he used the words of the people, and in such a way as to make them beautiful. His Gettysburg address is an English classic, one of the great masterpieces of the language.

From the mere fact that a word is short it does not follow that it is always clear, but it is true that nearly all clear words are short, and that most of the long words, especially those which we get from other languages, are misunderstood to a great extent by the ordinary rank and file of the people. Indeed, it is to be doubted if some of the "scholars" using them, fully understand their import on occasions. A great many such words admit of several interpretations. A word has to be in use a great deal before people get thoroughly familiar with its meaning. Long words, not alone obscure thought and make the ideas hazy, but at times they tend to mix up things in such a way that positively harmful results follow from their use.

For instance, crime can be so covered with the folds of long words as to give it a different appearance. Even the hideousness of sin can be cloaked with such words until its outlines look like a thing of beauty. When a bank cashier

KINDS OF STYLE

makes off with a hundred thousand dollars we politely term his crime defalcation instead of plain theft, and instead of calling himself a thief we grandiosely allude to him as a defaulter. When we see a wealthy man staggering along a fashionable thoroughfare under the influence of alcohol, waving his arms in the air and shouting boisterously, we smile and say, poor gentleman, he is somewhat exhilarated; or at worst we say, he is slightly inebriated; but when we see a poor man who has fallen from grace by putting an "enemy into his mouth to steal away his brain" we express our indignation in the simple language of the words: "Look at the wretch; he is dead drunk."

When we find a person in downright lying we cover the falsehood with the finely-spun cloak of the word prevarication. Shakespeare says, "a rose by any other name would smell as sweet," and by a similar sequence, a lie, no matter by what name you may call it, is always a lie and should be condemned; then why not simply call it a lie? Mean what you say and say what you mean; call a spade a spade, it is the best term you can apply to the implement.

When you try to use short words and shun long ones in a little while you will find that you can do so with ease. A farmer was showing a horse to a city bred gentleman. The animal was led into a paddock in which an old sow-pig was rooting. "What a fine quadruped!" exclaimed the city man.

"Which of the two do you mean, the pig or the horse?" queried the farmer, "for, in my opinion, both of them are fine quadrupeds."

Of course the visitor meant the horse, so it would have been much better had he called the animal by its simple; ordinary name ——— , there would have

CHAPTER XIII   CHOICE OF WORDS:
Small Words—Their Importance—The Anglo-Saxon Element

been no room for ambiguity in his remark. He profited, however, by the incident, and never called a horse a quadruped again.

Most of the small words, the simple words, the beautiful words which express so much within small bounds belong to the pure Anglo-Saxon element of our language. This element has given names to the heavenly bodies, the sun, moon and stars; to three out of the four elements, earth, fire and water; three out of the four seasons, spring, summer and winter. Its simple words are applied to all the natural divisions of time, except one, as day, night, morning, evening, twilight, noon, mid-day, midnight, sunrise and sunset. The names of light, heat, cold, frost, rain, snow, hail, sleet, thunder, lightning, as well as almost all those objects which form the component parts of the beautiful, as expressed in external scenery, such as sea and land, hill and dale, wood and stream, etc., are Anglo-Saxon. To this same language we are indebted for those words which express the earliest and dearest connections, and the strongest and most powerful feelings of Nature, and which, as a consequence, are interwoven with the fondest and most hall owed associations. Of such words are father, mother, husband, wife, brother, sister, son, daughter, child, home, kindred, friend, hearth, roof and fireside.

The chief emotions of which we are susceptible are expressed in the same language —— love, hope, fear, sorrow, shame, and also the outward signs by which these emotions are indicated, as tear, smile, laugh, blush, weep, sigh, groan. Nearly all our national proverbs are Anglo-Saxon. Almost all the terms and phrases by which we most energetically express anger, contempt and indignation are of the same origin.

What are known as the Smart Set and so-called polite society, are relegating a great many of our old Anglo-Saxon words into the shade, faithful friends who served their ancestors well. These self-appointed arbiters of diction regard some of the Anglo-Saxon words as too coarse, too plebeian for their aesthetic tastes and refined ears, so they are eliminating them from their vocabulary and replacing them with mongrels of foreign birth and hybrids of unknown origin. For the ordinary people, however, the man in the street or in the field, the woman in the kitchen or in the factory, they are still tried and true and, like old friends, should be cherished and preferred to all strangers, no matter from what source the latter may spring.

CHAPTER XIII   CHOICE OF WORDS:
Small Words—Their Importance—The Anglo-Saxon Element

CHAPTER XIV
ENGLISH LANGUAGE:
Beginning —— Different Sources —— The Present

The English language is the tongue now current in England and her colonies throughout the world and also throughout the greater part of the United States of America. It sprang from the German tongue spoken by the Teutons, who came over to Britain after the conquest of that country by the Romans. These Teutons comprised Angles, Saxons, Jutes and several other tribes from the northern part of Germany. They spoke different dialects, but these became blended in the new country, and the composite tongue came to be known as the Anglo-Saxon which has been the main basis for the language as at present constituted and is still the prevailing element. Therefore those who are trying to do away with some of the purely Anglo-Saxon words, on the ground that they are not refined enough to express their aesthetic ideas, are undermining main props which are necessary for the support of some important parts in the edifice of the language.

The Anglo-Saxon element supplies the essential parts of speech, the article, pronoun of all kinds, the preposition, the auxiliary verbs, the con-

CHAPTER XIV ENGLISH LANGUAGE:
Beginning—Different Sources—The Present

junctions, and the little particles which bind words into sentences and form the joints, sinews and ligaments of the language. It furnishes the most indispensable words of the vocabulary. (See Chap. XIII.) Nowhere is the beauty of Anglo-Saxon better illustrated than in the Lord's Prayer. Fifty-four words are pure Saxon and the remaining ones could easily be replaced by Saxon words. The gospel of St. John is another illustration of the almost exclusive use of Anglo-Saxon words. Shakespeare, at his best, is Anglo-Saxon. Here is a quotation from the Merchant of Venice, and of the fifty-five words fifty-two are Anglo-Saxon, the remaining three French:

All that glitters is not gold —— Often have you heard that told;

Many a man his life hath sold, But my outside to behold.

Guilded tombs do worms infold. Had you been as wise as bold, Young in limbs, in judgment old, Your answer had not been inscrolled —— Fare you well, your suit is cold.

The lines put into the mouth of Hamlet's father in fierce intenseness, second only to Dante's inscription on the gate of hell, have one hundred and eight Anglo Saxon and but fifteen Latin words.

The second constituent element of present English is Latin which comprises those words derived directly from the old Roman and those which came indirectly through the French. The former were introduced by the Roman Christians, who came to England at the close of the sixth century under Augustine, and relate chiefly to ecclesiastical affairs, such as saint from sanctus, religion from religio, chalice from calix, mass from missa, etc. Some of them had origin in Greek, as priest from presbyter, which in turn was a direct derivative from the Greek presbuteros, also deacon from the Greek diakonos.

The largest class of Latin words are those which came through the Norman French, or Romance. The Normans had adopted, with the Christian religion, the language, laws and arts of the Romanized Gauls and Romanized Franks, and after a residence of more than a century in France they successfully invaded England in 1066 under William the Conqueror and a new era began. The French Latinisms can be distinguished by the spelling. Thus Saviour comes from the Latin Salvator through the French Sauveur; judgment from the Latin judiclum through the French judgment; people, from the Latin populus, through the French people, etc.

For a long time the Saxon and Norman tongues refused to coalesce and were like two distinct currents flowing in different directions. Norman was spoken by the lords and barons in their feudal castles, in parliament and in the courts of justice. Saxon by the people in their rural homes, fields and workshops. For more than three hundred years the streams flowed apart, but finally they blended, taking in the Celtic and Danish elements, and as a result came the present English language with its simple system of grammatical inflection and its rich vocabulary.

The father of English prose is generally regarded as Wycliffe, who translated the Bible in 1380, while the paternal laurels in the secular poetical field are twined around the brows of Chaucer.

Besides the Germanic and Romanic, which constitute the greater part of the English language, many other tongues have furnished their quota. Of these the Celtic is perhaps the oldest. The Britons at Caesar's invasion, were a part

CHAPTER XIV ENGLISH LANGUAGE:
Beginning—Different Sources—The Present

of the Celtic family. The Celtic idiom is still spoken in two dialects, the Welsh in Wales, and the Gaelic in Ireland and the Highlands of Scotland. The Celtic words in English, are comparatively few; cart, dock, wire, rail, cradle, babe, grown, griddle, lad, lass, are some in most common use.

The Danish element dates from the piratical invasions of the ninth and tenth centuries. It includes anger, awe, baffle, bang, bark, bawl, blunder, boulder, box, club, crash, dairy, dazzle, fellow, gable, gain, ill , jam, kidnap, kill, kidney, kneel, limber, litter, log, lull, lump, mast, mistake, nag, nasty, niggard, horse, plough, rump, sale, scald, shriek, skin, skull, sledge, sleigh, tackle, tangle, tipple, trust, viking, window, wing, etc.

From the Hebrew we have a large number of proper names from Adam and Eve down to John and Mary and such words as Messiah, rabbi, hall elujah, cherub, seraph, hosanna, manna, satan, Sabbath, etc.

Many technical terms and names of branches of learning come from the Greek. In fact, nearly all the terms of learning and art, from the alphabet to the highest peaks of metaphysics and theology, come directly from the Greek —— philosophy, logic, anthropology, psychology, aesthetics, grammar, rhetoric, history, philology, mathematics, arithmetic, astronomy, anatomy, geography, stenography, physiology, architecture, and hundreds more in similar domains; the subdivisions and ramifications of theology as exegesis, hermeneutics, apologetics, polemics, dogmatics, ethics, homiletics, etc., are all Greek.

The Dutch have given us some modern sea terms, as sloop, schooner, yacht and also a number of others as boom, bush, boor, brandy, duck, reef,

KINDS OF STYLE

skate, wagon. The Dutch of Manhattan island gave us boss, the name for employer or overseer, also cold slaa (cut cabbage and vinegar), and a number of geographical terms.

Many of our most pleasing euphonic words, especially in the realm of music, have been given to us directly from the Italian. Of these are piano, violin, orchestra, canto, all egro, piazza, gazette, umbrella, gondola, bandit, etc.

Spanish has furnished us with all igator, alpaca, bigot, cannibal, cargo, f ilibuster, freebooter, guano, hurricane, mosquito, negro, stampede, potato, tobacco, tomato, tarill, etc.

From Arabic we have several mathematical, astronomical, medical and chemical terms as alcohol, alcove, alembic, algebra, alkali, almanac, assassin, azure, cipher, elixir, harem, hegira, sofa, talisman, zenith and zero.

Bazaar, dervish, lilac, pagoda, caravan, scarlet, shawl, tartar, tiara and peach have come to us from the Persian.

Turban, tulip, divan and firman are Turkish. Drosky, knout, rouble, steppe, ukase are Russian.

The Indians have helped us considerably and the words they have given us are extremely euphonic as exemplified in the names of many of our rivers and States, as Mississippi, Missouri, Minnehaha, Susquehanna, Monongahela, Niagara, Ohio, Massachusetts, Connecticut, Iowa, Nebraska, Dakota, etc. In addition to these proper names we have from the Indians wigwam, squaw, hammock, tomahawk, canoe, mocassin, hominy, etc.

There are many hybrid words in English, that is, words, springing from two or more different languages. In fact, English has drawn from all sources,

CHAPTER XIV ENGLISH LANGUAGE:
Beginning—Different Sources—The Present

and it is daily adding to its already large family, and not alone is it adding to itself, but it is spreading all over the world and promises to take in the entire human family beneath its folds are long. It is the opinion of many that English, in a short time, will become the universal language. It is now being taught as a branch of the higher education in the best colleges and universities of Europe and in all commercial cities in every land throughout the world. In Asia it follows the British sway and the highways of commerce through the vast empire of East India with its two hundred and fifty millions of heathen and Mohammedan inhabitants. It is largely used in the seaports of Japan and China, and the number of natives of these countries who are learning it is increasing every day. It is firmly established in South Africa, Liberia, Sierra Leone, and in many of the islands of the Indian and South Seas. It is the language of Australia, New Zealand, Tasmania, and Christian missionaries are introducing it into all the islands of Polynesia. It may be said to be the living commercial language of the North American continent, from Baffin's Bay to the Gulf of Mexico, and from the Atlantic to the Pacific, and it is spoken largely in many of the republics of South America. It is not limited by parallels of latitude, or meridians of longitude. The two great English-speaking countries, England and the United States, are disseminating it north, south, east and west over the entire world.

CHAPTER XV
MASTERS AND MASTERPIECES OF LITERATURE:
Great Authors —— Classification —— The World's Best Books

The Bible is the world's greatest book. Apart from its character as a work of divine revelation, it is the most perfect literature extant.

Leaving out the Bible the three greatest works are those of Homer, Dante and Shakespeare. These are closely followed by the works of Virgil and Milton.

INDISPENSABLE BOOKS

Homer, Dante, Cervantes, Shakespeare and Goethe.

(The best translation of Homer for the ordinary reader is by Chapman. Norton's translation of Dante and Taylor's translation of Goethe's Faust are recommended.)

CHAPTER XV MASTERS AND MASTERPIECES OF LITERATURE:
Great Authors—Classification—The World's Best Books

A GOOD LIBRARY

Besides the works mentioned everyone should endeavor to have the following:

Plutarch's Lives, Meditations of Marcus Aurelius, Chaucer, Imitation of Christ (Thomas a Kempis), *Holy Living and Holy Dying* (Jeremy Taylor), *Pilgrim's Progress, Macaulay's Essays, Bacon's Essays, Addison's Essays, Essays of Elia* (Charles Lamb), *Les Miserables* (Hugo), *Heroes and Hero Worship* (Carlyle), *Palgrave's Golden Treasury, Wordsworth, Vicar of Wakefield, Adam Bede* (George Eliot), *Vanity Fair* (Thackeray), *Ivanhoe* (Scott), *On the Heights* (Auerbach), *Eugenie Grandet* (Balzac), *Scarlet Letter* (Hawthorne), *Emerson's Essays, Boswell's Life of Johnson, History of the English People* (Green), *Outlines of Universal History, Origin of Species, Montaigne's Essays, Longfellow, Tennyson, Browning, Whittier, Ruskin, Herbert Spencer.*

A good encyclopoedia is very desirable and a reliable dictionary indispensable.

MASTERPIECES OF AMERICAN LITERATURE

Scarlet Letter, Parkman's Histories, Motley's Dutch Republic, Grant's Memoirs, Franklin's Autobiography, Webster's Speeches, Lowell's Bigelow Papers, also his *Critical Essays, Thoreau's Walden, Leaves of Grass* (Whitman),

Leather stocking Tales (Cooper), *Autocrat of the Breakfast Table, Ben Hur* and *Uncle Tom's Cabin.*

TEN GREATEST AMERICAN POETS

Bryant, Poe, Whittier, Longfellow, Lowell, Emerson, Whitman, Lanier, Aldrich and Stoddard.

TEN GREATEST ENGLISH POETS

Chaucer, Spenser, Shakespeare, Milton, Burns, Wordsworth, Keats, Shelley, Tennyson, Browning.

TEN GREATEST ENGLISH ESSAYISTS

Bacon, Addison, Steele, Macaulay, Lamb, Jeffrey, De Quincey, Carlyle, Thackeray and Matthew Arnold.

BEST PLAYS OF SHAKESPEARE

In order of merit are: *Hamlet, King Lear, Othello, Antony and Cleopatra, Macbeth, Merchant of Venice, Henry IV, As You Like It, Winter's Tale, Romeo and Juliet, Midsummer Night's Dream, Twelfth Night, Tempest.*

CHAPTER XV MASTERS AND MASTERPIECES OF LITERATURE:
Great Authors—Classification—The World's Best Books

ONLY THE GOOD

If you are not able to procure a library of the great masterpieces, get at least a few. Read them carefully, intelligently and with a view to enlarging your own literary horizon. Remember a good book cannot be read too often, one of a deteriorating influence should not be read at all. In literature, as in all things else, the good alone should prevail.

英語寫作思維重塑！從詞彙到結構，全面提升語言邏輯：

從基礎語法到進階修辭一網打盡，全方位提升表達力

作　　　者：	[愛爾蘭] 約瑟夫・德夫林 (Joseph Devlin)
翻　　　譯：	稅珍珍
責 任 編 輯：	高惠娟
發 　行　 人：	黃振庭
出 　版　 者：	財經錢線文化事業有限公司
發 　行　 者：	崧燁文化事業有限公司
E - m a i l：	sonbookservice@gmail.com
粉 　絲　 頁：	https://www.facebook.com/sonbookss
網　　　址：	https://sonbook.net/
地　　　址：	台北市中正區重慶南路一段 61 號 8 樓

8F., No.61, Sec. 1, Chongqing S. Rd., Zhongzheng Dist., Taipei City 100, Taiwan

電　　　話：	(02)2370-3310
傳　　　真：	(02)2388-1990
印　　　刷：	京峯數位服務有限公司
律 師 顧 問：	廣華律師事務所 張珮琦律師

版權聲明

本書版權為樂律文化所有授權財經錢線文化事業有限公司獨家發行電子書及繁體書繁體字版。若有其他相關權利及授權需求請與本公司連繫。

未經書面許可，不得複製、發行。

定　　　價：580 元
發行日期：2025 年 02 月第一版
◎本書以 POD 印製

國家圖書館出版品預行編目資料

英語寫作思維重塑！從詞彙到結構，全面提升語言邏輯：從基礎語法到進階修辭一網打盡，全方位提升表達力 / [愛爾蘭] 約瑟夫・德夫林 (Joseph Devlin) 著，稅珍珍譯 . -- 第一版 . -- 臺北市：財經錢線文化事業有限公司, 2025.02
面；　公分
POD 版
譯　自:How to speak and write correctly
ISBN 978-626-408-159-7(平裝)
1.CST: 英語 2.CST: 寫作法 3.CST: 學習方法
805.17　　　　　114000811

電子書購買

爽讀 APP　　　臉書